PRIME DECEPTIONS

ALSO BY VALERIE VALDES

Chilling Effect

PRIME
DECEPTIONS

A Novel

Valerie Valdes

HARPER Voyager
An Imprint of HarperCollins*Publishers*

PRIME DECEPTIONS. Copyright © 2020 by Valerie Valdes. All rights reserved. Printed in the United States of America. No part of this book may be used or reproduced in any manner whatsoever without written permission except in the case of brief quotations embodied in critical articles and reviews. For information, address HarperCollins Publishers, 195 Broadway, New York, NY 10007.

HarperCollins books may be purchased for educational, business, or sales promotional use. For information, please email the Special Markets Department at SPsales@harpercollins.com.

Harper Voyager and design are trademarks of HarperCollins Publishers LLC.

FIRST EDITION

Designed by Joy O'Meara

Chapter opener art © happy_fox_art/Shutterstock

Library of Congress Cataloging-in-Publication Data has been applied for.

ISBN 978-0-06-287725-3

20 21 22 23 24 LSC 10 9 8 7 6 5 4 3 2 1

*To all who protect the world from devastation
and extend our reach to the stars above*

ACKNOWLEDGMENTS

As with the first book, attempting to come up with a full accounting of everyone who deserves to be acknowledged for their contributions to this work feels impossible, so here is my best approximation.

Humble and sincere thanks to:

Eric, my husband, for keeping me going in ways big and small every day. If it weren't for you, I would never sleep.

My agent Quressa Robinson, for doing so many things I would never think of, quietly and diligently and without my ever needing to ask.

My editors, Tessa Woodward and David Pomerico, and everyone else at Harper Voyager (Kayleigh! Elle! Lauren! Michelle!), for sending my crew out into space once again, cats and all.

My mother, Nayra, for whom there is not enough wine in the world to convey my gratitude.

Jay Wolf, for an endless outpouring of time and imagination and conversation and emotional fortification, which I can only hope to repay in kind someday.

Matthew, Rick, and Amalia, for the advice and memes and

commiseravens that sustain me when the days are long and the months are short.

My Isle of Write friends, who cheer on my every success and ply me with tea and comfort whenever I need it, and who drive out the brain weasels with fire.

The staff at specialTEA Lounge, who fed me vegan baked goods and made me delicious coffee and tea and cheese wraps for the months that it took to write this book.

My NaNoWriMo folks, new and old, who sprint with me in person and online, for keeping me on track and occasionally yelling with me about nerdy things.

My sister, Laura, for talking to me about things that have absolutely nothing to do with books, but also for sending me pictures of my book in the wild.

My family-in-laws, Aimee and Luis and Vanessa and Ashley and Erik, for childcare and holiday happiness and always being sturdy anchors in stormy seas.

My dad, Keith, and stepmom, Jackie, for believing in me since back when I was hogging the family computer to type up my terrible poems.

My siblings and stepsiblings, Tasha and Kirk and Jennifer and John, and all their excellent spouses, for continuing to support me from near and far.

My many other friends and family, for buying my first book and asking about this one, for showing up to my events and sharing my Facebook posts and Twitter threads, for helping me pack and move my whole damn house when I was losing my mind, and for making sure I remember that I'm a person and not just a name on a book cover.

And finally, all the people who loved the first book and told me how much they're looking forward to this one, thank you for giving me someone to write for besides myself.

PRIME DECEPTIONS

Chapter 1

KICK THE PUPPIES

Captain Eva Innocente ran through the snow, trying to ignore that her pants were on fire.

It wasn't actually snow so much as a highly flammable form of crystalline methane precipitating peacefully from the sky of the aptly named planet Kehma. She also wasn't actually running, more of an aggressive hobble that wanted very badly to be a run, but her left gravboot was randomly malfunctioning and sticking her to the ground, so she kept having to send a deactivation command through her commlink to get moving again.

Her pants were definitely on fire, though, blue and magenta because of the methane. Her spacesuit protected her from burns, or she would have been more worried about it. And while it would have been funny to note that the fire started immediately after she lied to someone, at the moment she was focused on not getting shot by that person and his accomplices, who were chasing her.

Eva darted behind a rock formation as a bolt of plasma seared past her head. She would have loved to get her own pistol out, but she needed both hands to carry the package she'd gone to Kehma to steal. Well, steal back, since it had been stolen in the first place. Regardless, she had no hands with which to defend herself, so she had to rely on others.

((Help,)) she pinged at Vakar, who was supposed to be providing cover fire. Her quennian partner was much faster than she was, given his functioning boots and longer, back-bending legs. She'd lost track of him in the snow, which in her immediate vicinity was now falling in tiny blue flames as the bits stuck to her legs burned higher and brighter. The air around her shimmered with heat, and she was glad her nose was protected by the bubble of her isohelmet, because she was sure it smelled like spicy farts outside.

No answer from Vakar, either because of weather interference or because the Blue Hounder mercenaries behind her had signal scramblers. The doglike bipedal truateg definitely had expensive plasma rifles, no doubt courtesy of their suppliers at The Fridge. Working for an intergalactic crime syndicate had its perks, which Eva was a little salty about. Why did the bad guys always get better stuff than she did?

A shot tore through the air so fast it left a trail of blazing purple-blue, coming from in front of her instead of behind. Either she'd been flanked, or—

A second later, the sonic boom reached her, and Eva grinned. Unless the mercs had added sniper rifles to their arsenal, that was definitely Pink. And if her co-captain had arrived, that meant *La Sirena Negra* couldn't be far behind.

Eva darted from behind her cover toward another rocky pillar, lurching forward and cagando en la mierda every time her gravboot stuck. The methane-fueled fire was up to her chest now, making visibility even more difficult. She shifted the package so most of its weight was on her right side; the damn thing was heavy, and bulky, and she hadn't expected to be carrying it while running and being shot at. Another plasma bolt narrowly avoided her, sizzling against the rock as she ducked behind it. She thanked the Virgin these mercs weren't better shots, though come to think of it, that was a little odd. People who got paid to shoot things to death tended to be pretty good at it, or they didn't get paid for long. Unless they were herding her . . .

The click-whine of a rifle being armed next to her head made her freeze. As much as it was possible to freeze while on fire.

"Give back the cargo," the merc said. His voice came through her translators as whiny despite his broad, jowly features and beady eyes.

"Wasn't yours in the first place, mijo," Eva said. Why hadn't he shot her already?

"Who hired you?" he snarled, a line of drool falling into his collar. "How did you learn about this facility?"

Ah, information. The real currency of the cosmos.

"A little bird told me," Eva said.

He pressed the muzzle of his rifle to the spot where her iso-helmet met her suit. "Do not speak in idioms, human. Answer my questions or die."

"Can't answer questions if I'm dead, mijo," Eva replied. "Nice rifle, by the way, you get that out of a catalogue with your parents' credit line?"

The merc made an angry horking sound. "I earned this, you hairless whelp. I've been a mercenary for longer than you've been alive."

"And you haven't retired yet? Qué lástima, you must not be very good at it."

"Enough!" the truateg shouted. "You and your pack, playing at a profession you barely understand. It makes my testicles itch."

Eva almost snarked at that, but something moved behind the merc: the palest of shadows, silent as snow.

"When I was your age," the merc continued, "we had respect for our elders. For the mercenary code. You don't even have a proper uniform!"

"Times change," Eva said. "Oye, could you hold this for a second?"

She thrust the package at the merc, who grabbed it reflexively. His rifle swung away from her and she activated the present Vakar had gotten her for her last birthdate: a set of sonic knuckles that formed glowing gold rings around her fingers. Her first punch landed in the truateg's gut, the second on his shoulder, and by the third Vakar had stepped up to wrench away the rifle and drop the merc with a blow to the back. Eva deactivated her knuckles and took the stolen package back, giving the half-conscious truateg an extra kick in the junk for good measure.

"Where are the others?" Eva asked.

"Gaining ground." Vakar took the package from her, nearly invisible as his shiny metal armor reflected the whiteness of the not-snow around him. "We should complete our evacuation."

"Did you sabotage their ship like I asked you to?"

"I would have reached you sooner if I had not," he replied. "Their navigation systems will be installing a false software update for the next half cycle at least."

"Dios mío, that's evil," Eva said, grinning. "Vámonos, let's get out of here before I turn into carne asada."

((Location?)) she pinged at Min.

((Look up,)) came the pilot's reply.

La Sirena Negra roared in, its dark hull obscured by the methane snow coating the shields. Min brought the ship to a stop so that it hovered a meter above them, breaking some of the stone spires in the process. Eva and Vakar raced over to the emergency hatch.

"You first," Eva told Vakar. "Get that damn thing inside or we don't get paid."

He shifted the package to one side and began to climb awkwardly with his free claw. Just as Eva started to join him, her gravboot stuck to the ground again. This time, it refused to obey her mental command to deactivate, so she had to release the ladder and crouch down to examine the stubborn thing.

A bolt of plasma streaked past, followed by a gargling howl from the truateg. Coño carajo, Eva thought, staying low and frantically jabbing at the manual release on the outer sole of the boot. Still not responding.

"Worthless feces licker!" shouted one of the mercs. "Taste my vengeance!"

"Tastes like chicken!" Eva shouted back. Not that they knew what chicken was.

A sonic boom overhead told her Pink was providing cover fire, buying her a few plasma-free moments. The methane flames completely coated Eva now, but she still couldn't get her damn gravboot free. With a frustrated groan, she activated her sonic knuckles again and punched the ground around her foot, breaking up the pale rock into gravel-sized pieces. There just needed to be enough left to trick the boots into sticking to them, instead of the solid parts underneath—

A searing pain in her thigh made Eva hiss and bite down hard. Somebody had finally hit her. Unfortunately, that meant her suit was compromised, so she didn't have long before the methane flames worked their way in as well.

Eva punched the ground one last time, and finally her grav-boot shifted. *La Sirena Negra* hovered above her, with Vakar now dangling upside down from the ladder as he reached his free claw out to her.

Grunting, Eva jumped awkwardly with her good leg and grabbed his arm with both hands. Shots sizzled through the snow around her as the ship shifted, her injury making her scream.

Vakar did the galaxy's most insane sit-up and hoisted her into the emergency access, the hatch closing beneath her as soon as she was fully inside. He released her gently and she collapsed onto the floor, breathing heavily.

((Jump,)) Eva pinged at Min. The pilot's response was nearly instant, the whine of the FTL drive preceding the stomach-wrenching sensation of artificial gravity compensating for sudden acceleration. Eva could picture Kehma receding behind them as they flew off into the black, toward the nearest Gate, a few hours away.

They'd made it. And they had the package they'd gone to retrieve, which meant they'd get paid. Despite the pain in her thigh, Eva felt cold with relief.

No, not just relief; also the fire extinguishers coating her in chemicals to stop her from burning up the ship. In moments, she was covered in pale-blue gel, slippery as a dytyrc during mating season but no longer aflame.

Eva deactivated her helmet, which dropped a load of the gel into her black hair. Vakar retracted his helmet as well, releasing mingled smells of incense and licorice; he was worried about her.

"I'll be fine," she muttered to Vakar, tugging off her busted gravboot and throwing it against the hull. "But I'm definitely going to need a new pair of pants."

Eva sat in the med bay, trying not to squirm as Pink's mechanical eye scanned her for injuries beyond the shot to her thigh. Pink had already patched that with a quick-healing compound and numbing agent, and covered it with the usual self-adhesive bandages and a thick mesh designed to restrict movement. Other parts of Eva ached, from muscle to bone, but how many of those complaints were new was debatable.

"You'll live, again," Pink said finally, sliding her eye patch down. "You're lucky they didn't hit an artery."

"I'd be luckier if they had missed entirely," Eva grumbled.

Pink turned around and rummaged through one of the cabinets. "I'm not wasting the good nanites on you, so you have to take it easy for at least a week. Elevate the leg when you can, pain meds every six hours. And of course, you remember your buddy—" She pulled out a cane and handed it to Eva. Its height was adjustable, but they both knew it was already on the lowest setting for the ship's second-shortest crew member.

"How can I forget good old Fuácata?" Eva muttered. "Anything else, Captain Jones?"

"I'm Dr. Jones right now, sass mouth," Pink said. "We still need to have your weekly psych session later. But we should get everyone in the mess to chat, yeah?" She peeled her gloves off and tossed them in the recycler, then gave Eva her arm to help her off the exam chair.

Eva sent a ping to the rest of the crew as she hobbled down the corridor of *La Sirena Negra* to the mess room. The smell of espresso mingled with incense and anise; that meant Vakar was already there, he had made coffee for her, and he was worried but otherwise in a good mood.

"Look at you, smiling like a fool," Pink said, elbowing Eva gently.

Eva scowled, but she couldn't sustain it. Especially not when she saw Vakar waiting, out of his shiny Wraith armor for a change. His pangolin-like scales were freshly scrubbed, and his face palps angled toward her as she entered. The smell of anise shifted to licorice, making Pink groan and roll her eye.

"Are you well?" Vakar asked, his gray-blue eyes staring pointedly at her cane.

"Claro que sí, mi cielo," Eva said. "This is temporary."

"She has to rest," Pink added, pursing her lips and giving Vakar a meaningful look that made him smell grassy, bashful.

There went Eva's plans for later. She sat down at the head of the room's big communal table and let Pink prop her leg up with a stool, then accepted her taza of coffee from Vakar gratefully.

"I'm here, Cap!" Min said cheerfully through the ship's speakers. Eva had assumed so, since Min pretty much was *La Sirena Negra* as long as she was jacked in, which was always. Still, it was good to be sure. The pilot's human body had been in the bridge last time Eva checked, with one of the resident psychic cats asleep in her lap. Probably Mala, the unofficial leader of the pack.

That left one more crew member still unaccounted-for.

((Mess, now,)) Eva pinged at Sue.

((Coming,)) the engineer pinged back. A few moments later Sue ran in, her black hair spiked at odd angles like she'd accidentally run a greasy hand through it. Her pink shirt was smudged and streaked with brown, and two of her tiny yellow robots clung to her tool belt, making shrill noises.

"Sorry, Captain," Sue said breathlessly. "I had to replace a resistor for the aft shields. Min said they were drawing too much power."

"Your bots couldn't handle it?" Pink asked.

Sue's cheeks flushed and she stared at her boots. "I sent Eleven and Nineteen to do it, but they started arguing and I had to separate them."

The bots' shrill noises increased in volume, and Sue grabbed one in each hand and brought them up to her face. "Leaky buckets, knock it off already," she said. "Don't make me put you in time-out!"

Eva didn't know what "time-out" meant for tiny robots, but the bots shut up, so it had to be a serious threat. Sue settled into her chair.

Sometimes it seemed like the last six months had been one firefight after another, between sparse cargo-delivery and passenger transport jobs. Fucking with whatever was left of The Fridge had been her crew's top priority, and thankfully Vakar's bosses were all too happy to subsidize their endeavors. Eva also got to keep or sell portions of any ill-gotten goods they recovered from their raids, or in situations like the one on Kehma, they returned stolen items for a hefty bounty from the original owner.

It wasn't an easy life, but more and more often, Eva was starting to feel like it was a pretty good one. Even the food was better than it used to be. She took a sip of her espresso, savoring the sweet bitterness; Vakar had used the stash of real beans instead of the replicator.

"So we got what we came for, and now we drop it off and get paid," Eva said. Min gave a little cheer of "Jackpot!" while Vakar's smell gained a brief almond spike of delight.

"Also, we pissed off the Blue Hounders and The Fridge," Pink added. "It's like asshole Christmas up in here."

"Feliz Navidad," Eva said. "Min, how long until we reach Atrion?"

"About a quarter cycle," Min replied. "Unless you want to refuel somewhere first."

Eva shrugged. "Anyone have a layover request?"

Sue shook her head, Pink twirled her finger in a circle, and Vakar's palps twitched, but he said nothing.

"If we can make it to Atrion, and their fuel prices aren't ridiculous, let's just get this job done." Eva knocked back the last of her coffee. "Nice work, amigos. Take a break."

Sue wandered back toward the cargo bay, holding one bot in each hand and scolding them quietly. Eva stood and hobbled over to put her taza in the sanitizer, wondering whether she should grab a snack or head straight to her cabin. Vakar appeared at her side, laying a claw gently on her arm.

"Would you like assistance returning to your room?" he asked, smelling like vanilla and lavender under all the licorice.

Eva grinned, raising an eyebrow. "I'm sure Fuácata wouldn't mind the help." The snack could definitely wait.

"I said rest, woman," Pink called from the doorway. "Don't make me confine you to the med bay. I have a bunch of remote patients in my virtual queue, and I don't want to waste my very expensive time patching your sorry ass twice."

Vakar wagged his head in the quennian equivalent of a shrug, while Eva snorted. But as soon as Pink was gone, they shared a look and Eva burst into laughter.

"Come on," she told him. "There's more than one way to rest. I can think of at least three and I'm not even trying."

Eva woke up four hours later with a throbbing pain in her leg, to the sound of Min pretending to be an alarm through the speakers.

"Qué pinga," Eva said sleepily, raising her head off Vakar's chest.

"Sorry to bother you, Cap," Min said, "but you've got a call on the new emergency frequency."

Mierda, Eva thought. That could only be one of three people, and she wasn't in the mood to talk to any of them.

"Should I go?" Vakar rumbled.

"Nah, I don't wanna move," Eva said. "Min, audio only, please."

A holo image projected from Eva's closet door into the dim room. At first it crackled with static, but it quickly resolved into the face and upper body of her sister, Mari. Her brown hair was tied back in a ponytail, and unlike the last time Eva had seen her, she wore a dark-red spacesuit with extra armored plating over the chest. Her expression was neutral, controlled, like she'd done a bunch of deep-breathing exercises before making the call. Which she probably had, given how good Eva was at getting on her nerves.

"Eva?" Mari asked, her neutral expression immediately slipping as a crease appeared between her brows. "Are you there? I can't see you."

"I'm here," Eva replied, slapping Vakar's claw as he ran it up her bare thigh. "It's been a while. What do you need?"

The furrow smoothed out. "What's the passcode?" Mari asked.

Eva sighed and consulted her commlink. The key generator Mari had made her install spat out a long string of letters and numbers, which she dutifully repeated.

"And what's your favorite . . ." Now Mari pursed her lips and narrowed her eyes at Eva. "This doesn't make any sense."

"What?"

"Favorite food."

Eva hmmed wistfully. "Paella. So good."

"You're allergic to shrimp, boba."

Vakar's palps tickled her face and she stifled a giggle. "Pink has been giving me a lot of allergy meds," she said. "Really strong ones."

Mari closed her eyes. Eva could almost hear her silently counting to ten.

"My turn," Eva said. "What's your favorite, uh, Mesozoic species?"

Mari smirked. "Ah, see, someone who didn't know me well might assume it was equisetites, because of the ribbed stems, but actually it's baculites because they—"

"Ya, basta, I know it's you because no one else is this boring." Eva reluctantly sat up and swung her legs over the side of her bed, wincing as her injured thigh protested. "What do you want, Mari?"

Her sister's face grew serious again. "My superiors need to speak with you. In person."

Now Vakar sat up, too, smelling as curious as Eva felt. She knew nothing about Mari's bosses, except that they thought it was totally fine to throw Eva to the proverbial wolves if it meant taking down The Fridge. And now they wanted to talk?

"I thought you didn't want me anywhere near your business?" Eva said, barely concealing the salt in her tone.

"I don't, but I'm not in charge."

Eva's smirk died quickly. "What do they want from me?"

"That's not for me to say," Mari replied, smoothing a stray hair against her head. "But if you'll agree to meet with them and discuss their offer, I'll send you the coordinates."

Secrets, as usual. Great. "I assume I'd get paid for whatever this is?" Eva asked.

"Absolutely. A fair rate, possibly including fuel subsidies."

Eva wrinkled her nose at Vakar, who blinked his inner eyelids pensively. He smelled minty, but otherwise noncommittal. No help there.

"I have to discuss it with my crew," Eva said slowly. "I'm not the only captain anymore, and either we're all in or we're out."

"How egalitarian of you," Mari said. Her features had settled into a mask again, and her gaze flicked up like she was looking at something Eva couldn't see. "I have to go, but please let me know within the next cycle. We're running out of time. And options."

"Right, I'm never the first pick for the spaceball team," Eva muttered. "Call me back in an hour; I'll have an answer for you then."

"Bueno. Cuídate."

The holo image vanished, plunging the room back into darkness except for the dim light from the fish tank above her bed. Vakar's sister, Pollea, had taken care of Eva's fish while Eva was indisposed—okay, no need to be euphemistic, it was while Eva was in cryo after being kidnapped because of shit that was basically Mari's fault. But Eva had gotten her ship back, and her fish, and added a few new creatures to the tank for good measure, including the orange-shelled snail currently stuck to the glass, and the hermit crab digging through the substrate. She hadn't worked up the nerve to add live coral or anemones, but she figured she would get there someday.

That, of course, depended on whether she lived long enough to see "someday" for herself. Her leg throbbed as a reminder that nothing was certain, that every fight she walked into was a roll of the Cubilete dice, and the other side might get a Carabina first.

Eva's stomach grumbled; must be time for a meal. She did a quick visual survey of her injuries, which were recovering as slowly as one might expect without nanites. Her thigh bandages were intact, but definitely in rougher shape than they should have been for someone supposedly resting.

"Pink is gonna be mad at us," she told Vakar.

"It is probable," he agreed, tickling her shoulder with his palps.

"Eh, worth it." She grabbed her nearest article of clothing off the floor. "Help me put on my pants so she doesn't see it yet, and let's get this party started."

Min's human body joined them in the mess this time. She was using the hot plate to make gyeranjjim for herself and Sue, so Eva settled for reconstituting a vague approximation of picadillo along with the last of the instant rice. Pink shoveled her own rice and red-bean concoction into her mouth quickly enough to give Eva a stomachache from watching. Vakar wasn't hungry, and he already knew what the meeting was about, so he sat at the table and waited with a patience Eva found admirable, if baffling.

Eva explained the situation briefly as everyone ate. The first to respond when she finished was Pink, who pushed her empty plate away with a look like she'd bitten a lemon.

"Mari is a liar and an asshole," Pink said coldly. "And her bosses were good with her busted-ass plan that fucked all of us over. That's two strikes already and we don't even know what they want."

"We cannot trust them," Vakar agreed. "However, some of our goals are in alignment overall."

"We all hate The Fridge," Sue said, blowing on her food to cool it. "And it seems like they have, um, you know . . ."

"Money?" Eva supplied. "Resources? Information?"

"Yeah, all of that, pretty much."

"Food?" Min asked, poking what was left of her fluffy egg substitute. She'd gotten way more interested in eating once their options had improved.

Eva gestured at Min with her fork. "That, I don't know."

Pink leaned back in her chair and crossed her arms. "If this were any other client, you'd tell them to go piss up a rope. Is the risk worth what we might get out of it?"

"Mari did say they'd pay us well," Eva said. "Maybe even a fuel allowance."

"Ooh, a fuel allowance, says the liar." Pink nodded sarcastically, her eye wide.

"We do need fuel," Min said. "I mean, I do. The ship me."

Vakar smelled like ozone with a hint of incense—uncertain, concerned—but there was also an undercurrent that reminded Eva of night-blooming jasmine. Thoughtful, which meant he wasn't entirely opposed to the idea. She considered his angle, and what he might stand to gain from it.

"You want to know more about them," Eva told him. "Mari's people, I mean, whoever they are."

Vakar shrugged in the quennian equivalent of a nod. "As a Wraith," he said, "I have been tasked with documenting the activities of the entity known as The Fridge, and disrupting them. Your sister is employed by yet another organization whose identity and motives are unknown, but whose reach appears extensive. Under the right circumstances, they could be a valuable asset."

They certainly seemed to have reached right into The Fridge itself, if Mari was any indication. How many more spies did they have, and how much information might they be willing to trade?

Pink shook her head, her dreads swaying slightly. "So assuming we agree to meet with them, then what?"

"We see what they want." Eva shrugged. "Worst case, we turn them down and walk away."

"Worst case, they blow us up and melt down the scraps," Pink muttered. "I want to believe we're all on the same side, but there's history, and that shit repeats."

Sue spoke up then, in a quiet voice. "Sometimes good people do bad things," she said, staring down at her empty plate. "They think the reasons are good and important, and it will all work out in the end. It's not smart, maybe, but it's . . . it happens."

Sue was thinking of her own past, no doubt. Her brother, Josh, had been kidnapped by The Fridge, after which Sue had robbed a few banks and an asteroid mine in the hopes of paying off his ransom. But Josh was still missing, and none of their Fridge-busting fun had turned up any leads so far. Looking at the dark-haired girl, just out of her teens, Eva would never have believed she was capable of such a thing. Sue could barely curse properly, though Eva was trying to teach her.

Then again, the same things could be said about Eva, or Pink, or anyone else on the ship. Eva most of all, given some of what she'd done back when she worked for her father. She had enough regrets to fill their cargo hold, and more.

Eva didn't seem to be the only one following that plutonium exhaust trail of thought, so she cleared her throat to bring everyone back to the table.

"Vote time?" Eva shifted her butt, wincing at the pain that shot through her leg. "I say we check it out, with another vote to decide whether we take whatever offer they make."

"I also believe we should investigate," Vakar said.

Min brushed her faded blue hair out of her face and smiled. "Fuel sounds good to me."

Sue hesitated, then said, "It can't hurt. Can it?"

"It certainly can," Pink said. She rolled her eyes. "I feel like

I'm having to be paranoid enough for all y'all, but whatever. At least we're being foolish together."

"Look at it this way," Eva said, "if you're right, we can burn them for good."

"If I'm right," Pink said with a scowl, "we're the ones who are gonna be hosed."

Eva really, really hoped Pink wasn't right this time.

Chapter 2

FORGING FATES

The coordinates Mari provided sent them to Suidana, a dying binary star system two cycles from the nearest Gate. Pink insisted on collecting their Fridge bounty first, and Eva was only too happy to do so, since they needed enough credits for the fuel to get to Mari's mystery site. Their client was grateful, if nervous about possible repercussions, but Eva assured them The Fridge would be more pissed at her than they would at him.

"Squirrely little guy," Pink said as they were leaving. "Are we sure he's legit?"

"Min and Vakar both checked him out," Eva said. She smiled as the account-transfer notification pinged into her commlink. "We did our good deed for the week, and now we can sleep like babies all the way to Casa Carajo."

Pink's lip curled. "Sure is a long flight for a big question mark."

Eva had wondered about that as well, but she didn't want to back out now. "Should give you plenty of time for your patients, though," she said.

Pink had joined a pool of remote doctors to handle the massive medical needs of a far-flung universe, the kinds that sophisticated virtual intelligences weren't adept at diagnosing, or that wanted a pseudo-personal touch. It meant more work for her, but as Pink had put it, "My résumé won't pad itself." Besides, she loved helping people, whether by figuring out what ailed them or putting a foot up the right person's ass.

As pressed for time as Mari had said her employers were, Eva wasn't inclined to hurry. She let Min proceed well within safe speed parameters, even dropping to sublight a few times so Sue could repair a particularly fussy ship component. Vakar caught up on reports for his Wraith bosses, Eva caught up on administrative bullshit, and together they caught up on each other as much as her healing leg would allow. Sue fixed Eva's gravboots again and worked on some new mass of metal in the cargo bay, Pink doctored or fiddled with her latest sewing project, Min piloted and played the strategy games she defaulted to when her q-net access was laggy. During the late meal, Min queued up the most recent *Crash Sisters* holovids, so they could all watch former crew member-turned-star Leroy "The King" Cooper stomp around kicking asses and pretending to be a villain. There was even time for Min to help braid Pink's hair, which had to be done in stages because it had gotten so long, and for Min and Sue to hang out, chatting about giant mechanical creations and other girly stuff.

It was as close to a holiday as they had gotten for as long as Eva could remember, and she savored every minute of it, because she wanted to be well rested when the shit hit the air filters.

They arrived at their destination during the third cycle out from the Gate. The station was uncomfortably close to the system's red supergiant, which had already swallowed the planets closest to it. Some of its mass was being stripped by its companion neutron star, but even so, it would collapse into a white dwarf at some point in the near future as cosmic time went, which was at least a few thousand years away.

Eva hated thinking on that scale. It reminded her that the universe was a vast ocean, and she wasn't even a tiny fish: she was an amoeba. One person on one ship drifting through the black between points of light, her life's only purpose and meaning whatever she made of it. It was simultaneously liberating and disheartening to be so relatively insignificant. And it didn't help that people like Mari went around having a huge sense of self-importance about their goals, like every choice they made could wipe out entire galaxies or whatever.

Ending even one life was a big deal, and the farther away from that notion a person got, the more lives became expendable. Numbers in a chart. Collateral damage. Acceptable risks and the cost of doing business, of finishing the mission, of doing what needed to be done according to very particular parameters of need.

Maybe Eva was only one person, but she wasn't keen on being a statistic, or turning anyone else into one.

La Sirena Negra arrived at a station large enough to house thousands of people, drifting serenely along a trajectory that kept the red giant behind it like a huge, watchful eye. Its hull was putty-colored and smooth, broken only by cameras and other instrumentation, and the docking-bay doors that opened to receive their ship. Eva let Min handle all the standard handshakes and code-swaps, because she was busy ogling the thing being towed along by the station like a toy on a string.

It was a Gate. At least, it looked like one, except it was inac-

tive and covered in construction crews. But the idea that someone had stolen a Gate, or more incredibly, was trying to build a
new one? Impossible. Gates were ancient Proarkhe tech, and no
one knew how they worked, only how to use them to open holes
to other parts of the universe.

Then again, The Fridge had managed to make a pair of guns
that created portable Gates, which Eva knew because she'd stolen them and hidden them as well as she could. They didn't
work anymore, but no way did she trust anyone to use tech like
that for good instead of super naughty.

Except apparently Mari's secret club had gotten enough information on their own to do this. And if they could build a
whole damn Gate out here, what else might they be able to do?

They finished docking protocols and Eva disembarked
slowly, still leaning on the mighty Fuácata since her leg wound
wasn't fully healed. Vakar and Pink followed close behind her,
both suited up like they were walking into a fight. The docking bay had enough room for a dozen ships or so, the largest of
which was a Standard Reliance Mk II cruiser. It looked familiar, but Eva had seen a lot of similar ships in her time, especially
in the BOFA fleet. This one was sleek and white with black-and-
red stripes, and Eva coveted it instantly, despite her love for her
own ship.

"Are those antiproton thrusters?" Eva asked Vakar quietly.

"Yes," he murmured back. "And it has kloshian heavy armor
in addition to its kinetic barriers."

Eva gave a soft groan of jealousy.

Mari intercepted them before they made it any farther. She
still wore the same red armored spacesuit Eva had seen during
their call, and her light-brown eyes were wide from whatever
stimulants she was using to stay ahead of fatigue. She hesitated
in front of Eva, her expression guarded.

Eva swallowed her pride and stepped forward, kissing her sister on the cheek. They might not be back up to hugging yet, but they had to start somewhere.

"Welcome to The Forge," Mari said.

"The what?" Eva cocked her head to the side and squinted.

"That's what our group is called, The Forge."

Eva snorted. "You know that sounds a lot like The Fridge, right? Who names this shit?"

"Our group came first," Mari said defensively. "Anyway, thank you for coming."

"Don't thank me yet," Eva replied. "I haven't agreed to anything."

Mari nodded, glancing at Eva's cane. "I think this will be a lot less dangerous than . . . last time."

"We can handle danger," Pink said, putting a hand on her hip. "It's secrets that get us all riled up."

Mari opened her mouth like she was going to launch into a lecture, but stopped herself and held out a hand. "Dr. Jones, it's good to see you again."

"The pleasure is all yours," Pink replied coolly. "Nice suit, it really brings out the bags under your eyes."

Eva choked on a laugh, which she turned into throat-clearing. "You remember Vakar."

"Of course." Mari lowered her hand and offered him a curt bow. "Your work against The Fridge last year was greatly appreciated."

"I did not do it for you," Vakar said. "But you are welcome." His smell and face were hidden by his armor, his voice distorted and gravelly.

They all stood around awkwardly for a few moments, Eva making a fish face and raising her eyebrows, Pink glaring at Mari, Mari almost starting several sentences, and Vakar just looming since he was taller than all of them. Finally, Mari broke the silence.

"Where is Susan?" Mari asked.

"Sue?" Eva blinked. "She's back on the ship with Min. Why?"

Mari took a breath, as if choosing her words carefully. "I was not authorized to bring Dr. Jones and Wraith Memitim to this meeting, but I was specifically asked to bring Susan."

"'Not authorized,'" Pink repeated, drawing out the words for emphasis. "So, what, we wait on the ship?"

"You're welcome to visit our dining hall," Mari replied. "We also have a lovely observation platform. For security reasons I cannot give any of you a full tour of Forge facilities."

((Abort mission?)) Eva pinged at Pink.

((Go on,)) Pink replied. ((Be careful.))

Eva shrugged at her, and Pink sighed and gave her a dismissive gesture. "I'm staying here," Pink said. "I'll send Sue out." She flipped up her eye patch to give Mari one last look, and to Eva's surprise Mari flinched at the scrutiny from the mechanical eye.

"See you around, cupcake," Pink said. Without another word, she turned and left.

Eva rested her hand on Vakar's shoulder. "How about you?"

"I would like to visit the observation platform," Vakar said.

Better than nothing, probably, since he was hoping to get information out of this place. Eva wouldn't be surprised if he was already trying to hack into their systems. Min at least was likely stealing their q-net bandwidth by now.

Sue emerged a few minutes later, a smear of grease on one cheek and a dazed look in her eye. When she saw Mari, her pale skin flushed pink and she stared at her feet.

"Agent Virgo," Sue said. "I'm, I mean, I know I was supposed to stay out of, you know, but—"

"It's fine, Susan," Mari interrupted, her all-business mask sliding firmly into place. "Come along, my superiors are waiting."

Mari let Eva set the pace, leading them out of the docking bay into a sterile white hallway, occasional doors and plants and artwork adding texture and color. A few other people walked past as they went, mostly wearing casual civilian clothes. Some had protective gear Eva associated with laboratories, or spacesuits like Mari's, albeit with less armor. Certainly no one was wearing uniforms with THE FORGE plastered across the chest or back; maybe they all had secret anvil tattoos somewhere. A blue-skinned kloshian conferred with an eac about something that made the eac clack its beak in frustration, while a human and a four-armed buasyr carried boxes marked VOLATILE from one room to another with nervous haste. Everyone looked busy, harried, but also entirely focused on whatever they were doing.

Mari stopped in front of a random door like any other. "The observation platform is here," she said. The door opened to reveal a large room with dark, nonreflective flooring and a wall that was either entirely transparent or a huge viewscreen. It must have been on the side of the station, because the system's red giant wasn't visible, just the blackness of space lit by clusters of stars and galaxies near and far. It was beautiful, awe-inspiring, and not remotely what Vakar probably wanted to see.

"Thank you," Vakar said politely, stepping inside and bending his knees back so he could kneel on the floor. At least he could hack from just about anywhere, depending on their systems.

The door closed and Mari continued to lead Eva and Sue in silence. As full of questions as Eva was, she suspected she wasn't going to get anything out of her sister now, especially with every person they passed glaring at Eva like she'd pissed in their protein powder. Her leg was holding up, no doubt thanks to the painkillers Pink had dosed her with, but Eva was starting to regret that she hadn't asked Mari to get her a hoverchair instead of taking this long walk. At least Sue had fixed her gravboots so they weren't randomly sticking again.

They eventually entered an elevator, which gave Eva an annoyingly anxious flashback to the last time she'd been to Nuvesta and fought off a slew of bounty hunters, but this one was fast and quiet except for the VI announcing "forty-two" when they reached the appropriate floor.

Like the observation platform, this room was large and dark with a floor-to-ceiling view, but it showed the enormous orange-red star, its surface roiling with heat. In the center of the room was a bare metallic desk with two chairs, one behind it and one in front of it, both occupied by people Eva could barely see because of the star's placement. She summoned up her isohelmet and shifted its color to shade her eyes.

"Captain Innocente, Mx. Zafone, thank you for joining us," the figure behind the desk said in a voice that walked the line between smooth and hardass. Her hands were steepled under her chin, the soft glow of an old-fashioned commlink on her arm lighting her face from below. Kloshian, her tentacle-like hair swept back, her skin currently the blue-gray of a Terran marine mammal.

Eva inclined her head politely. "And you are?"

"Agent Elus," she said. "I am the head of operations at this facility. My associate is Agent Miran."

Miran was human, but his eyes had the catlike reflective sheen of implants, and neural tattoos ran down the exposed parts of his dark forearms. Probably heavier upgrades under the surface; expensive, and illegal in some places. He leaned back in his chair, ankle resting on his opposite knee, his posture as relaxed as a lion in its own den.

"Charmed," Agent Miran said gruffly. "Let me be brief."

"I like brief," Eva said. "Cuéntamelo." Sue shifted uneasily beside her, but Eva kept her attention focused on Miran.

"A number of civilian scientists escaped the destruction of the Fridge facility six months ago," he said. "While we recovered a substantial amount of actionable data during our mission, some items were incomplete or indecipherable, so we've been trying to find these missing scientists to obtain their help."

"I assume this relates to the Gate you and your Forge buddies are building out there?" Eva asked. She still wasn't sure it was a Gate, but it was worth a shot. Sue gasped next to her, and Eva hoped that didn't wreck the bluff entirely.

Agent Miran's gaze twitched slightly to one side; he had looked at Mari, behind Eva's left shoulder. Well, if he wanted to think she'd told Eva about it, let him.

"It does," he said. "For security reasons, I can't tell you more."

"You were secure enough to invite us here instead of meeting at a more neutral location."

"Consider it a show of trust," Agent Elus said.

Or a show of their headquarters being a giant space station that would probably disappear to another system before Eva could even think of selling them out. Which she wasn't planning to do anyway. Eva smiled and mimed zipping her lips shut.

With luck, Vakar would have plenty to tell her later anyway.

"We want to hire you to track down one of the Fridge scientists," Miran said, leaning forward with both feet on the floor, resting his forearms on his knees. "You would be compensated appropriately, including a fuel stipend and reimbursement for travel wear and tear on your ship."

Nice. Eva was used to soaking up those expenses herself to stay competitive. But she still didn't trust these people, and a hell of a lot of questions came to mind right away. She settled for the most immediate one.

"Why hire me for this?" Eva asked. "You've had six months to send your own agents after him, with all your resources." She glanced back at her sister standing straight-backed with her arms crossed. "Why do you think I'll do any better?"

"And why am I here?" Sue asked. Eva resisted the urge to pinch Sue's arm, like her mom used to do when she didn't want Eva to talk.

Agent Elus waved her hand over her commlink and a holo image appeared above the desk. A human with wild gray hair, apparently dyed because the roots were dark. His skin was pale, ruddy at the cheeks, and his dark eyes had the hooded, sullen look of someone who hated being interrupted. He wore a white lab coat over a bright-green shirt, black-gloved hand raised as if to stop whoever was taking the picture.

"Holy rusty buckets," Sue said. "Josh?"

"Indeed," Agent Elus said. "Your sibling, Joshua Zafone. He was one of the head engineers on the project whose research we require."

"But he, he was . . ." Sue's mouth opened and closed, and Eva could almost see her thoughts moving at light speed in a hundred different directions. The Fridge had told her Josh was a hostage, that her family had to pay a ransom to free him. "Head engineer" didn't sound very hostage-like, no matter what language you tried it in, no matter how hard his arm had been twisted to do the work.

Eva knew how it felt, to be lied to about something like that. Mari's presence behind her was a stark reminder. She gripped the head of her cane and made a mental note to have Pink talk to Sue about it later, in a private psych session.

"So you think Sue might know something you don't,"

Eva said. "Something that could help us find him where you failed."

Agent Miran nodded, his profile lit by the dying star. "We also suspect that should you locate Mr. Zafone, he will be more cooperative if he's approached by his own sister instead of a stranger."

Eva raised an eyebrow. "He got away from you once, didn't he?"

Miran's gaze flicked in Mari's direction again, and Eva suppressed a smile. It was nice to know her perfect sister could fuck things up occasionally.

"Just to make sure I have this straight," Eva said. "You want me to find Josh and bring him back here, is that it?"

"Correct," Agent Elus said. Her skin color darkened almost imperceptibly.

"Do you have a deadline?"

"Not a fixed one, but time is of the essence." Elus waved a hand over her commlink again and her lips parted briefly, exposing knife-sharp teeth. "We can offer you a bonus if you bring him to us within the next twenty cycles."

That didn't sound like a lot of time, given that Eva had no idea how to even begin looking for the guy, and that it would be two cycles just to get to the nearest Gate. But she wasn't about to tell them that.

"I have to check with the rest of my crew before I agree to anything," Eva said.

"So we were told," Agent Miran said. "I assume you'll have a response soon?"

Eva nodded. Like Mari had told her, this didn't sound dangerous compared to the other stuff they'd been doing for the past six months. But she had no idea where Josh might be, and whether he was in the kind of trouble that called for fists and firearms.

"If we take the job, I'll need half up front and half on delivery," Eva said. "And my ship could use a refuel before we leave here regardless."

"Agent Virgo will see to it," Agent Miran said, gesturing at Mari. "She will also be your contact as the mission proceeds, should you accept our terms. We would expect status updates every three cycles at a minimum."

"Yes, sir," Eva said, flicking two fingers away from her forehead in a mock salute. He certainly seemed confident that she would be on board with this job. She wished he had seen Pink's face earlier; he might not feel so great about his chances. "Anything else I need to know before I go?"

Agent Elus waved the holo image away, returning the room to its reddish darkness, and linked her hands together in front of her. "As Agent Miran indicated, we cannot give you information that might compromise our mission here. I can say this, however: what we are doing is of the utmost importance, and may help us to preserve the lives of every sentient creature in the universe. We cannot, we must not, fail." Her shadowy expression was tense, a nearly perfect mimicry of human somberness on her kloshian features.

Eva blinked hard to keep from rolling her eyes. That was exactly the kind of self-importance she wished she could go after with a flamethrower.

"It was a pleasure to meet you at last, Captain Innocente," Agent Miran said, returning to his relaxed cross-legged position. "And you, Mx. Zafone. Whatever your decision, we appreciate your work against The Fridge."

Even when it fucks you over? Eva wanted to ask, but she offered him a polite smile instead. "It's nice to be appreciated," she said. "It's nicer to get paid. Adiós, hasta luego."

Mari led them out of the room, and Eva prepared for a lecture as soon as the door slid closed behind them. To her surprise,

Mari didn't say a damn thing, leading them back the way they came in the same silence as before, her own face a mask of solemnity with occasional flickers of an emotion Eva couldn't place.

More than Agent Elus and her stirring speech about universe-saving, Mari's silence spoke volumes. She really believed in their cause, didn't she? But could Eva trust these people, after what they'd done? Would they happily throw her out the airlock again if it suited their purpose? And what would it mean for them to have their own private Gate, not to mention the ability to build more of them wherever they wanted? Should anyone have that power, no matter how noble their motives?

Better them than The Fridge, Eva supposed. And if she didn't find Josh first, they might.

Eva leaned on her cane and wondered what exactly these people were getting themselves into, and whether it would be supremely unwise to get involved.

When Eva and the rest of the crew tried to discuss whether they would take the offer, Sue grew so heated that Pink sent her off to cool down. Eva understood: it was Sue's brother on the line, and given his previous disappearance, there were painful questions to be answered. It meant coming to a decision without Sue, though, and it fell to Eva to deliver the news.

Sue sat in the cargo bay, welding gloves and mask in place, tinkering with her latest robotic creation. She had already built a mech she called Gustavo out of scraps, and had upgraded it little by little over the past six months, but she was also working on a present for Min: the kind of battle bot Min used to fight with back when Eva first met her. It took up an unreasonable amount of space, especially when it was in pieces like now, its torso open in the center of the room while its legs were over by the passenger cabin and its arms were dangling by cables from the catwalk like a creepy puppet.

The rest of the cargo bay was the domain of the cats, who ostensibly belonged to Min but actually belonged to themselves, as cats do. These cats more than most, since they were psychic and eerily intelligent. Their climate-controlled shipping container was shoved up against the plating next to the passenger cabin, but the cats themselves were napping or playing or bathing wherever the hell they wanted. Mala, their unofficial leader, stepped out of the enclosed litter box and, with a very dignified air, flopped down and began to lick her butthole profusely.

"Hey," Eva said to Sue, prodding the bot's helmeted head with her cane while Sue turned off the welding torch and flipped her mask back.

"Sorry I yelled," Sue said, her pale cheeks ruddy—from the heat, or from embarrassment, or por qué no los dos?

"It's okay. No one is mad at you."

"Are we—"

"We're going to find your brother, yes."

Sue's eyes filled with tears, which she wiped with her shoulders as soon as they fell. "Thank you," she whispered, her voice hoarse.

"I wish people would stop preemptively thanking me for shit." Eva sighed, swatting idly at one of the dangling arms with her cane. Candy would certainly not fall out if she hit it hard enough. Mala paused in her butt-licking to glare at Eva as if offended by the noise.

"So what now?" Sue asked.

"Now the hard part: figuring out how to track him."

Sue shoved some wiring back into the robot's torso, brushing away one of her little yellow bots as it tried to help. "What did Agent Virgo say?"

Eva collected her thoughts. "His last known whereabouts were Medoral, a big transit hub in a two-Gate system."

"I know that place," Sue said. "My family has shipped stuff through there a bunch."

"Apparently he did a very good job with his identity switch, because he disappeared from there almost immediately."

Sue's expression hardened. "She knew where Josh was the whole time I was here, didn't she? Agent Virgo, I mean."

"I don't know," Eva said. "She never mentioned anything about your brother. She might not have found him until the facility raid."

"I guess." Sue brightened. "Well, now that we know he got away from The Fridge, we can stop looking for him there."

"Right."

"It's strange that he didn't contact me, or my parents." Sue's mask fell over her face, and she shoved it back up, frowning. "Maybe he thought he was protecting us. But we've been making ransom payments this whole time, so I guess The Fridge assumed we didn't know where he was."

"Fair assumption, clearly." One of the cats rubbed against Eva's leg, and she reached down to scratch its head. "So if you were Josh, and you were trying to run away without anyone knowing what you were up to, what would you do?"

"Hmm." Sue tapped the end of her welding torch against the bot's metal torso. "I'm not sure. Steal some credit chits to buy a ticket on a transport?"

"That's a lot of stealing," Eva said. "I'm guessing you've never had to use credit chits, but the people who do, they don't tend to have enough of them for an off-planet shuttle ride."

"Oh, right. He must not have used any of his personal accounts, either, or The Forge would have been able to track those."

Eva nodded, carefully sitting on the floor so she could pet

the cats more easily. "They could probably even find secret accounts. They're pretty good about that stuff." Something Sue had said nudged her brain. "You mentioned your family ships stuff through Medoral. Would Josh have been able to use a company business account, maybe?"

"Oh, maybe!" Sue smiled hopefully, then immediately scowled. "Aw, buckets. No, no, that doesn't work. We have accountants and stuff. Every expense gets shoved into a special category for when they do taxes. If Josh bought a shuttle ticket, someone would have noticed. I remember my parents getting alerts about suspicious activity sometimes."

"Dead end, then." Eva winced as Mala jammed a paw into her leg wound. When had the cat climbed into her lap? So damn sneaky. "Well, I'll get everyone else together and we'll keep thinking. There must be something The Forge missed."

Sue gasped and scrambled to her feet. "I've got it!" Her welding mask fell again, and she pulled it off entirely and tossed it to the ground.

"Got what?" Eva asked.

"The piggy bank!"

"The what?"

"We have a special account, for, um." Sue's cheeks flushed pink again. "Miscellaneous? It may not be, you know, legal. Maybe."

"A lot of things are legal that probably shouldn't be," Eva said. "So this account was what you would use when you wanted to hide purchases, I assume?"

"Sort of. It's for stuff that maybe wouldn't qualify as a business expense, like . . ." Sue stared off into space, half grinning. "Once my parents took us on vacation and charged everything to that account. My dad said it was okay because he talked about business with my mom a few times."

"Sounds like something my dad would have done, too," Eva said. "So this account gets a fair amount of use, and nobody is really tracking it?"

"Pretty much," Sue said. "They charge random things there all the time so it doesn't look too suspicious." Her pale skin flushed pink. "I use it to buy parts for my bots sometimes. Hold on, let me pull it up."

Eva rubbed Mala's head and face while Sue fiddled with her commlink. After a few failed login attempts and fumbling around with the interface, which Sue grumbled was "as intuitive as quantum physics," she was able to pull up a list of transactions from the account. Sue snapped an image and pinged it to Eva, who stared at the lists of numbers and codes for a minute before shaking her head.

"I have no idea what any of this means," Eva said.

"Me either," Sue said gloomily. "And I can't call my parents to ask, assuming they even know. They still think I'm working at a parts depot in Atrion until I 'find myself' and come home."

"Yeah, my mom went through that phase of denial, too." Eva slapped her forehead and groaned. "Of course. I know exactly who can help us."

"Really?" Sue clapped in glee.

"Really. But I need a few minutes to get my story together, because this call is going to suck." Eva lifted a highly offended Mala out of her lap and carefully got to her feet, the sharp pull of her regrowing leg skin and muscle reminding her that it was time for more pain meds. She started to limp out of the cargo bay, avoiding the bits of robot strewn around the floor and the cats who had decided she needed emotional support in the form of aggressive leg rubs.

"Who is it?" Sue called after her. "Who can help?"

Eva took a deep breath and sighed. "My mom."

Chapter 3

MAMITIS

Eva sat on the bed in her cabin and stared at her closet door, from which a holo image would be projected as soon as she summoned up the intestinal fortitude to call her mother. Fuácata rested at the foot of the bed, out of sight so Eva could avoid having to make any bullshit explanations. Her commlink assured her that local time in Libertad was midcycle, so this wouldn't be a rude awakening in the literal sense, just a figurative one. She'd been sitting there for several minutes already, running possible conversation starters through her head, but they all sounded forced and awkward under the circumstances.

She and her mother had stopped speaking to each other thirteen years ago, more or less. A few years after Eva had left home to live with her dad, Pete, she'd gone back to visit her family for her birthday. She'd been a sullen ass the whole time, because instead of celebrating with booze and friends, she sat in the Florida room of her mother's house and watched telenovelas with her abuelos for a week. In retrospect, they'd had plenty of fun, playing dominoes and Cubilete and comiendo mierda while stuffing themselves with albondigas and bistec de pollo and congrí. Her abuelo had even unearthed his ancient deep fryer and made old-fashioned churros, and her abuela had made flan twice because she knew how much Eva loved it. She'd listened to stories about Earth that her abuelos had heard from their bisabuelos, and helped harvest oranges from the big tree outside, and patiently untangled skeins of yarn while her abuela knitted a baby sweater for a pregnant cousin's daughter's niece.

But then Eva had gotten a message about a party she was missing on the other end of the universe, and she'd gotten into a screaming match with her mom about something else entirely so she could feel justified in storming off and going back to Pete. She'd apologized to her abuelos, at least, who then spent the next several years begging her not to be such a cabezona and talk to her mom already.

When she finally got fed up with Pete and left, finally owned up to all the ways she'd been a shitty human for years, Eva also reached out to her mom. But they'd never managed to mend the rift, not with so much hurt between them. They still talked rarely—on birthdates, some holidays—with most of their communication coming in the form of q-mail forwards of things her mother thought were funny. A lot of them were anecdotes about working in an office, which Eva had never done, so she didn't really get the humor.

"Just call her, comemierda," Eva muttered to herself. She opened a line, ran as many security protocols as she could manage to hopefully avoid eavesdroppers, and sent the code through.

The low buzz of the resolving connection was the only sound breaking the silence as Eva held her breath and waited.

The buzzing stopped, and Eva exhaled slowly. No holo image appeared, which was just as well; Eva wouldn't have to control her expressions along with her voice.

"—her to give me one moment. Hello, this is Regina Alvarez?" Her mother's tone was artificially bright, and in the background someone else was speaking in a low, soothing way to a more agitated but equally quiet person.

"Hi, Mami, it's me," Eva said. "It's Eva. Is this a bad time?"

If not for the people arguing on the other end, Eva would have assumed the call had dropped as her mother failed to speak for several long moments.

"Cómo estás, mi vida, is everything okay?" Regina asked.

"Yes, I'm fine, things are fine. How are you?" Eva hated small talk. She stuffed her knuckle in her mouth and tried not to scream from impatience.

"Bueno, you know, poniéndome más vieja cada ciclo," Regina said. "Did Mari tell you I got promoted?"

"No, um, she didn't." Mari hadn't told her a lot of things. But when Eva was in cryo for a whole year after being kidnapped by The Fridge—Mari's fault, technically—at least Mari had the presence of mind to cover for Eva so their mom didn't get suspicious.

The background noise shifted, like her mom had moved. "Ay, you two, que Dios te bendiga. I'll tell you about it later, pero let's just say I used to be catching little fraud fish, and now I'm catching big ones."

As if on cue, Eva's fish tank spat food out of a hidden compartment, and the various fish swarmed to the surface. The hermit crab was unimpressed and continued to dig in the gravel.

Regina sounded so proud of herself. Considering that she'd left Eva's dad because he was a criminal, and Eva herself had spent years doing the conga all over the line between right and wrong, it was hard to share her enthusiasm for law and order. Justice, though, was something Eva could get behind.

"That's great, Mami," Eva said. "How are Abuela and Abuelo?"

"Ay, don't get me started, that's a whole other call." Regina sighed dramatically, and someone in the background shouted something Eva's translators didn't catch. "Mira, I'm working on a big project right now, so I can't really talk for—"

"I need a favor," Eva said, wincing at her own abruptness.

Regina paused. "What kind of favor?"

"I need you to look at some account records and tell me about the transactions," Eva said. "What they were, where they were made, that kind of thing."

"Eva-Benita Caridad Larsen, that is extremely illegal. Where did you get those records?" Regina's voice was quiet but her tone was angry, suspicious, and Eva's own temper rose as her body regressed to being a teenager.

"From the account holder, Mami," Eva said, barely controlling her sarcasm. "What am I going to do with random stolen bank records?"

"Bueno, okay then," Regina said, more calmly. "But why wouldn't the account holder know what they were? And why aren't they just calling the bank to ask?"

The green chromis that Eva associated with her mom bullied the red hawkfish away—her father's, amusingly, which swam back to the bottom of the tank.

"It's complicated," Eva said.

"Uncomplicate it for me," her mother replied.

"Her brother is missing," Eva said, fiddling with her blanket, "and we think he's using the account, so we're trying to see if we can track him that way."

Regina paused again. "Is he in danger? Have you contacted the police?"

"He's fine, it's just . . . a family thing. She doesn't want to make it a big deal. She's afraid he might find out if she calls the bank, and you know how cops can be." Even as she said it, Eva wished she could cram that back into her mouth. She and her mother had always had very different opinions about law-enforcement professionals, with "bastions of order" at one end and "fucking pigs" at the other. Ironic that Eva was basically dating a cop now. . . .

"Oh, I know that very well," Regina said dryly. "Bueno, I really have to get back to work. Send me the information and I'll see what I can do."

Eva's stomach unclenched and her shoulders softened. "Gracias, Mami," she said.

"De nada, mi vida." There was another shout in the background, and Regina sighed. "Cuídate, hija, I'll talk to you later."

"Bye." The call ended, and Eva flopped backward onto her bed, staring up at the ceiling.

That hadn't been so bad. Then again, her mother had a knack for being pleasant in public, when someone whose opinion she valued was nearby, and for sweeping things under the rug when she felt like it. Eva calling out of nowhere to ask for a favor ranked high up there as a shitty thing to do, given their history; she was basically gifting Regina with ammunition to be used against her later.

Eva stuck the copies of the transaction logs Sue had given her in a q-mail and sent it to her mom, with instructions about starting with the items from about six months earlier, especially if any of them occurred on Medoral. She only had twenty cycles to earn that bonus, but with any luck, she'd have something to work with by the time they reached the nearest Gate.

If she didn't hear from Regina beforehand, they might as well see what they could find at Josh's last known location.

Maybe Sue would notice something The Forge's agents hadn't, something only siblings would find significant because they knew each other well.

It was better than nothing, and Eva had worked with less. Plus now, The Forge was paying for her fuel, so she might as well use it.

Two cycles to reach the Gate, then a few hours to Medoral. Eva pinged Vakar with ((Busy?)) and then settled back to wait.

Medoral was a planet, but Medoral Station was where the real action was, orbiting high above the placid chartreuse clouds to make it easier for passenger and large cargo ships to load and unload. Huge, uncomfortable shuttles packed with hundreds of interstellar travelers came and went at regular intervals, dodging the asteroid mine freighters delivering vast quantities of unprocessed ores. Most of the planet was covered in sprawling industrial properties occupied by companies of every size, all storing things and manufacturing things and taking things out of larger containers so they could be repackaged into smaller ones. This was the backbone of commerce, or maybe its entire skeletal structure, supporting the daily lives of a few hundred planets all over the universe.

Eva had once aspired to having clientele with facilities on Medoral. Now she just aspired to having any clients at all.

La Sirena Negra docked at the station, with Min staying aboard to search the local q-net for information on what was happening there around the time Josh would have been passing through. Thanks to Vakar's research while they were in transit, Eva knew about the main corporate and criminal players on the planet, the standard methods for greasing palms and avoiding authorities, and that The Fridge had a presence there, maintaining a variety of shell corporations that helped them quietly move whatever naughty stuff they needed. She wished she had time to fuck with them properly, but her current mission took priority.

Weapons had to stay on the ship due to security regulations, so Eva settled for bringing Fuácata. The week of travel time meant her leg had finished healing enough that she probably didn't need a cane, but it wasn't worth taking the chance. After a leisurely stroll through a sterilizer, she and her crew stood at one of the entrances to the Playa district, which had absolutely nothing to do with beaches and apparently translated to "moderate discount" in the native language.

The place was an unsettling combination of empty and packed, crowds forming and vanishing and re-forming as shuttles came and went, loading and unloading their passengers for appendage-stretching and rapid, impersonal retail transactions. There were restaurants and quick-sleep compartments, and stores that sold the kind of stuff that could probably be printed if you had the right pattern, but that you might prefer to try on first so you didn't waste the mats. There were also places to buy more advanced tech, ship parts and electronic gadgets and such, none of which Eva could afford even with The Forge paying her a pleasantly excellent amount of money for finding Josh.

The commwalls between storefronts were covered in ads for corporate products and services, constantly shifting to attract the attention of whoever was passing by based on the information skimmed from their commlinks. Because there were so many people moving so rapidly, the data was aggregated rather than specific, designed to find majority overlap for maximum appeal rather than targeting specific preferences. Eva had rigged her commlink long ago, so as far as the algorithms were concerned, she was an exceptionally average thirty-four-year-old human. Vakar was the sole quennian in sight, so he'd never show up on a feed even if he hadn't also rigged his commlink, and Pink had turned off the function despite periodic software updates that turned it back on and made it harder to opt out of.

Sue, unfortunately . . .

"Oh, wow, that is so cool!" Sue said, stopping to gawk at yet another ad for holographic mech paint. "And you can program in different designs, like tattoos!"

"Come on," Eva said, grabbing Sue by the arm and towing her back into the crowd, which scrambled up and down the corridor like hyperactive toddlers. "You're supposed to be thinking like Josh. What would he notice? What would he think was important?"

"I'm not really sure," Sue said. Her attention kept wandering back to the walls, bright and flashy and moving. Eva sighed. This whole trip was starting to feel like a waste of fuel, even if she wasn't paying for it.

The crowd thinned suddenly, like someone had punched a hole in the hull and let all the atmo out, leaving them nearly alone except for a pair of kloshians and a chuykrep who was stroking his proboscis nervously. Small service bots zipped out to clean the floors, making tiny agitated beeping noises. On the walls, closer to eye level, there were smaller squares, about thirty to sixty centimeters on a side, advertising jobs and events and professional services. Local stuff, mostly, whatever was able to eke out an existence between the cracks of corporate control like weeds in a sidewalk. Occasionally one of them flickered like it was trying to reboot, sometimes disappearing soon after—hacked, probably, though Eva could never get a good look at what they showed before they were gone.

Eva opened comms to Min. "Find anything yet?" she asked.

"Sorry, Cap," Min replied. "I got distracted. Did you know Leroy was here six months ago?"

"Really?" Interesting. *Crash Sisters* did a lot of touring, but Eva wouldn't have guessed Medoral or its station would be one of their stops.

"Yeah, they did a big show at some stadium on the surface." Min giggled. "I was watching the holovid when you called. They did a Grand Melee, which is—"

"That thing where they get a bunch of locals to fight the regular cast, I remember." Eva rolled her eyes as one of the commwalls started showing an ad for *Crash Sisters*, with prominent corporate sponsorship labeling. "I doubt Josh came here to catch a fake fighting show."

"It's not fake!"

"Sí, claro, totally real. Focus, please."

"Right." Min paused. "The only other thing I'm seeing is a product demonstration. A new robot? I can't tell what it's for."

Eva continued to walk, the thock of her cane hitting the floor echoing in the wide space. "What does it look like?" she asked.

"It's really cute," Min said. "Like a yellowish mouse, with rabbit ears and red cheeks and a long tail. Oh, wait, there's another one, kind of like a tiny todyk without feathers?"

The commwalls shifted again, now showing an ad for what must have been something related to the product. A logo floated into view, a stylized rendering of an ovoid purple-and-white capsule with a button on the front, above words that translated to "Pod Pals" with alternate suggestions of "Shell Sidekicks" and "Ball Buddies"; the latter made Eva bark out a laugh that was uncomfortably loud even to her.

"Ball Buddies," Pink muttered next to Eva, shaking her head. "I swear to god."

Sue, of course, was enraptured. The ad flashed a series of robots that, as Min had said, looked like adorable animals, right down to fake fur and scales and feathers. Children hugged them, adults played with them like they were pets, but then suddenly they were in what looked like a wrestling ring? Two of them faced off, one spitting fire while the other dodged and attacked with a vicious head-butt.

Better than cockfighting, I guess, Eva thought. Much easier to fix a robot, though it could be creepy depending on how sapient they were.

At the end of the ad was a notice that the corporation that made the robots, Sylfe Company, was hiring locals for distribution jobs at their planetside warehouse. Applications available on the q-net, send résumé, minimum two years' experience, etc. That stayed on the wall for a few moments, then the ad was replaced with another one for fancy cooking knives. A current human obsession, probably.

"I want one," Sue said, eyes wide and nearly gleaming.

"A Ball Buddy?" Eva asked. "You could probably build your own if you tried."

Sue's face took on a pensive expression. "Hmm, maybe. I've never worked with synthetic skins or furs before, though."

Vakar had wandered off on his own while they watched the ad, and now came stalking back toward them in a deliberate way that Eva knew was intended to look casual. He had dressed in a civilian spacesuit instead of his Wraith gear so he wouldn't stand out, but he took a smell suppressant before they left so his emotions wouldn't be telegraphed to anyone with scent-translator nanites. He put an arm around Eva's shoulder, leaning closer to butt his head against hers affectionately, but he smelled bothered, like old cigarettes.

"We are being monitored," he said quietly.

Eva smiled up at him. "Who?" she asked, speaking through her teeth.

"The buasyr in the store selling storage containers for travelers. Behind me."

"Humans call it 'luggage,' you know." Eva made a show of smooching the side of Vakar's face while she checked the guy out. Tall, four arms, dark fur, mess of eyes like a spider's. Wearing a tight suit that probably doubled as armor. She might have assumed he was a typical retail employee, killing time by making minute adjustments to the store's displays of suitcases and indestructible boxes and hover straps, but his fingers were twitching like he was furiously sending messages to someone, and he glanced at Eva and looked away repeatedly in the span of a few moments.

"Should we go say hello?" Eva asked.

"It might be more advisable to depart with haste," Vakar replied.

Pink sidled up next to them. "What are you two lovebirds chatting about, hmm?"

"The Fridge agent in the retail establishment behind me," Vakar said.

Eva released him and stepped back, gently whacking his leg with her cane. "You didn't say he was Fridge," she said. "How do you know?"

"His biosignature matches one in Wraith records. Also, he has been joined by two associates."

There were indeed now three employees acting busy in the luggage store: the buasyr, a truateg, and a human. While theoretically none of them were armed, thanks to station security, there were ways of getting around restrictions, especially if they worked here. Hell, if this had been one of her dad's smuggling operations, half the suitcases would already have weapons in them.

"I hate a fair fight," Eva said. "Maybe we should move on. Don't want to attract unwanted attention from any local cops, anyway."

"That's a shame," Pink said. "I always like taking these fools down a peg."

A slow smile spread across Eva's face as she had a wonderful, awful idea.

"Vakar, when is the next shuttle arriving?" she asked.

Vakar's palps moved as he checked his commlink. "In a few moments, actually."

As if on cue, a series of blinking lights and chimes announced the shuttle's arrival. It would still be a couple of minutes before the passengers were able to disembark, especially given decontamination protocols, but a hub like Medoral tended to be quick about that stuff.

Eva walked over to Sue and tapped her on the shoulder. Sue jumped, startled from her rapt viewing of an ad for a particular brand of lubricant.

"Get back to the ship," Eva said. "Stick to the walls in case the crowds get bad. Don't run, but don't stop for anything, and tell Min to prep for a quick takeoff."

Sue nodded, her expression determined. "Okay, I can do that." Off she went, leaving Pink, Eva, and Vakar in the otherwise empty corridor.

"Vakar, can you take care of the security cameras?" Eva asked.

"Take care of . . . yes, I understand." Vakar led Eva over to another storefront, where an extremely bored rani with pink-dyed ears leaned against a wall with the vacant stare of a teenager lost in her commlink. This store was full of sporting equipment, some of which Eva recognized but most of which made little sense to her.

She pointed at a pair of hoverboots. "Maybe I should trade my gravboots for those," she told Vakar. "Being able to run in midair seems pretty great."

"The time limitation renders them less useful, in my opinion," Vakar replied.

((Cameras disengaged,)) he pinged to Eva and Pink.

The trio and the Fridge agents continued studiously ignoring each other while waiting to see who might start something first. Eva left Vakar and casually ambled over to the restaurant adjacent to the luggage store, which had uncomfortable-looking bolted-down seats as well as deactivated floating chairs stacked against one wall. She smiled and waved at the sluglike dytryrc behind the counter, his six spindly robotic arms engaged in a variety of simultaneous food-preparation activities even as his two eyestalks faced in entirely different directions.

"Nice knives," Eva told him.

"I keeps 'em sharp!" the dytryrc said enthusiastically, then returned his attention to his tasks.

After a long minute in which Eva pretended to be very interested in the restaurant's menu, the shuttle passengers rushed in like a gaggle of agitated geese. It was a mixed group: black-suited galactic immigration officials with their trademark optical shades, two sets of tiny pizkees covered head to toe in what looked to be different shades of war paint, a dozen kloshians apparently celebrating the signing of a breeding contract by being extremely inebriated, even a trio of white-robed human nuns whose denomination wasn't entirely clear. They mingled with the usual isolated business travelers and others taking advantage of the relatively low cost of shuttle travel compared to nicer options. The situation between them already seemed tense—long space travel crammed into uncomfortable seats would do that to anyone—and as they got closer to Eva, several strands of argument arose from the various factions.

"—wouldn't have won if the referee hadn't botched that call!" one of the pizkees shouted, her normally blue face painted red and white. For a person who didn't reach the middle of Eva's shin, she was incredibly loud.

"You're just mad your team dropped the fink," another shouted back, his face also painted red, but with a gold symbol near his tiny black eye.

"Peace is the champion of justice," one of the nuns announced to no one in particular, causing several nearby pizkees to hiss and bare their needlelike teeth.

"I love you all," a kloshian said, adjusting his holo-tiara. "Like, really, love you all. So much. Thank you for doing this for me." His friends cooed back at him and he turned a vibrant shade of emerald.

"—keep cutting funding like this, we're going to be walking from one planet to another," the kloshian black suit said to his partner.

"Well, maybe if your hoser hadn't pretended he'd been injured by the scorcher," a pizkee said, "all dropping down on the patch like a sad little—"

"Don't think we're going to find him in Narushe anyway," the other black suit said, adjusting her shades. "Baldessare prefers flashy places, not ruined planets with crazy clown god-emperors."

"In rage, the proud cry out for vengeance," another nun said. "But they shall not be answered."

"I'm not feeling super great," a kloshian said, covering her bright-red eyes.

"Don't disgorge your vapor sac here," her friend told her soothingly, "wait until we can find a waste receptacle."

Eva, who was still loitering near the restaurant, picked up one of the deactivated floating chairs and hefted it experimentally.

((Get ready,)) she pinged at Pink and Vakar.

((For what?)) Pink pinged back.

Eva threw the chair in a perfect arc, right into the center of the agitated crowd. It must have hit someone, because cries of pain followed, yielding to momentary silence.

And then, the silence exploded.

Chapter 4

PULLING MOBS

It wasn't clear who threw the first punch, but the pizkees were definitely ready to go after each other amid battle cries that sounded like references to their respective sports teams. None of them were armed with anything more dangerous than their own bodies, but those were plenty: fists lashed out blindly at anyone in range wearing the wrong colors, which seemed extra challenging because pretty much all of them wore red, but Eva assumed they knew who was who.

The rest of the crowd tried to back away and give the fighters space—difficult given the size of the corridor and the sheer number of people. Then, one of the black suits moved in to break up the fight, at which point a pizkee screamed, "Get boiled, wastehole!" and a half dozen of the face-painted people from both teams scaled pant legs and each other to start attacking.

The other black suit intervened, earning her a separate assault. She yelled as needle teeth sank into her unprotected skin, and a head-butt sent her staggering back into one of the nuns, knocking the white-robed woman to the floor.

Another nun helped her sister to her feet. "Faith is our shield, and we shall endure," she said.

"But do we not also say, 'Our hands are our swords, to defend against chaos'?" the fallen nun asked.

"We do say that," the third nun agreed. "Even so—"

Eva carefully sidled back toward the luggage store, where the Fridge agents were watching the unfolding chaos with some concern. Before they could stop her, she grabbed one of the suitcases and lobbed it at the nearest cluster of combatants, then retreated to the sports-equipment store, where Pink and Vakar waited.

"Welcome to Recreation Supremacy," the bored rani employee intoned, not even glancing at Eva.

As if the fight were a virus, it spread to the luggage store as people grabbed more suitcases and briefcases and boxes and started using them as improvised weapons. Eva peered around the wall at them and snickered as the Fridge agents clustered together and held a rapid discussion, presumably about what to do.

"Oh no, my vapor sac," a kloshian wearing a neho mask said. He released a fine lavender mist from his nostrils, and suddenly the pizkees around him swayed unsteadily, their eyes shifting from black to red. One of the black suits flung off his shades, and his eyes also took on a reddish cast.

The other black suit grabbed her partner's arm. "What is it?" she asked. "What were they taking?"

Her partner's skin started turning bright red as well, and the pizkees began to vibrate.

"It's Blitz," the black suit said through clenched teeth.

Eva, Pink, and Vakar shared a look, then dove behind separate sports displays. Eva chose a large hoverboard, Pink a tall shelving unit covered in plastisteel helmets, while Vakar lucked out and was safe behind a row of jousting shields. Eva winced as her leg pain reignited on impact with the floor, quickly settling to a dull ache. The rani employee gave them all a tilted-head look but didn't move.

If the fight had been bad before, it tripled in intensity now. Blitz did different things to people depending on their physiologies; for most species besides kloshians, it boosted strength and imparted a euphoric sense of invulnerability. The pizkees ran around thrashing whatever they could reach, throwing things at each other and anyone nearby, and even the black suit swung at some of the random passengers caught up in the fray while his partner tried to drag him away.

"Where is station security?" someone shouted in desperation.

((Coming,)) Vakar pinged to Eva.

The nuns, meanwhile, had tied up their robes around their waists and legs, and casually armed themselves with different items from the sporting-goods store. They nodded at each other silently, then set about knocking down one fighter after another with an efficiency Eva admired.

"Hey, get out!" the dytryrc in the restaurant shouted. "I got knives! Sharp ones!" This was followed by a sizzling sound and a pained scream.

Pink threw herself down next to Eva. "This was your plan?" she asked. "Get a bunch of innocent people hurt while we hide in here?"

"No," Eva said. "This was the distraction. Come on."

Eva signaled for Vakar to follow her, giving a jaunty wave to the rani as she hobbled briskly to the back of the store, grateful that she'd brought Fuácata. As expected, there was a door leading to a storeroom, which itself had another door leading to a back corridor that ran straight to the docks. It also led to doors for all the surrounding retail establishments, including a certain luggage store's, which was currently being guarded by a buff human in a tight-fitting shirt.

"Nice muscles," Eva told him.

"Thanks," the human replied, flexing.

"Should you be back here?" Eva asked. "There's a riot going on in there. You should probably help or something."

"Nah, I'm supposed to stay here no matter what," he said. "In case someone tries to sneak in." He narrowed his eyes suspiciously. "Wait a tick, who are—"

Eva swung Fuácata against his knee with a satisfying crack, then thrust the handle up into his throat. He made an uncomfortable choking sound, but still managed to reach for Eva with one of his beefy hands. She ducked and took advantage of his now-exposed back to land a quick punch to his kidney, followed by a knee to his gut and an elbow to the back of his head, at which point either he or his body decided enough was enough and he slid to the ground.

"You are so violent, I swear," Pink said.

"Violence isn't always the answer," Eva said. "I just ask a lot of violent questions." She turned to Vakar, her leg throbbing more after the exertion. "Could you get this unlocked?"

"I have already done so," he replied. "Also I have infiltrated their local network and I am in the process of duplicating its contents."

"Gracias, mi vida." Eva whacked the buff guard once more for good measure and opened the door, strolling into the luggage store's back room.

It was, as expected, full of various kinds of luggage, stacked neatly on shelves.

"Did we seriously just do all this for no damn good reason?" Pink asked.

Eva smirked at her and grabbed a random suitcase, resting it on the floor and tapping the release panel to open it. Inside, a pair of M-7 Centurions rested in a cube of stasis gel, aftermarket heat dispersal units already attached.

"Feliz cumpleaños, amiga," Eva said.

Pink made a shooing motion with one hand. "That ain't for me," she said. "You know I don't do short-range."

Eva gestured at the other cases and boxes surrounding them. "Let's see if we can find something in your size, then."

As quickly and efficiently as they could manage, Eva, Pink, and Vakar pulled down one container after another and examined its contents. They found pistols, rifles, vibroblades, and more esoteric weapons that couldn't be properly operated by humans or quennians. Pink gave an obscene groan at a particular sniper rifle and immediately claimed it, while Eva grabbed a few of her favorites and shoved them into a single suitcase with a built-in antigrav feature to make it easier to carry.

"Security has arrived outside," Vakar said suddenly. "We should retreat before we are located."

"Bueno, let's make like fleas and jump," Eva said.

Pink opened the door and stepped out, nudging the still-prone form of the guard outside. He responded with a groan.

As Eva was about to follow, a random briefcase caught her eye, resting on a shelf just out of her reach, a bright red CAUTION tag wrapped around the handle.

"I'm the most cautious," she muttered to herself. "Hey, Vakar, get that one for me."

He obliged, smelling concerned. "You are aware of what this is?"

"No, but I assume it's awesome."

"It is a Protean Lightweight Omniguard Tactical armor unit."

"Ooh, I've always wanted one of these." Compact, tough, and customizable, but powered by expensive proprietary tech and software, and hell to maintain. Also, if they glitched, they had a habit of turning their users into squishy piles of organ goo.

"Eva, these are dangerous," Vakar said, his concerned smell intensifying.

"Right, I hear you," she said reluctantly. "Someone will definitely pay for that, though. Let's get out of here."

They headed back down the hall and through the sports-equipment store. The rani was still zoned out on her comm-link, idly running a hand over one of her long ears, and made no comment about their sudden acquisitions. "Come again," she said tonelessly as they stepped back into the main station corridor.

The chaos had abated thanks to the arrival of security. The pizkees were lined up along one wall, a few of them still throwing punches at each other when they thought no one was looking. Most of them were injured, some more dazed than others, and the Blitzed ones had been separated from the rest for treatment. The black suits had apparently isolated themselves as well, with the Blitzed one being treated by the other via some medical wand device she was shining into his eyes. The kloshians made low crooning noises at each other in a harmony that made Eva want to barf, their colors shifting between pale green and royal blue and back again, and the breeder's holo-tiara had fallen sideways down the tendrils on his head. The nuns had ungirded their loins but still held their improvised weapons, and appeared to be the least affected of all the groups.

"We have done the work of justice this day, sisters," one of them said.

"Blessed be the victors, who walk among the stars and are unburned," the other two replied.

"Oh, they're Chanters," Eva muttered to Pink. "Madre de dios, those people will fuck you up. I'm glad I wasn't here for that."

Pink shuddered and nodded agreement.

"Did anyone see who threw the chair?" one of the security guards asked, her voice amplified to be heard over the crowd.

Eva picked up her pace and did not look back. She knew what happened to people who looked back, and it wasn't good.

As they zipped away from Medoral, Eva checked her q-mail to find a message from her mom.

"Assuming your missing person wasn't buying new bathroom lighting, he and his companions took a shuttle to Charon and bought three tickets to the gathering there. Hope this helps. Love you."

Charon. Eva groaned. Why would Josh go there? And who was he traveling with? Mari hadn't mentioned anything about him being with other people. At least there was a Gate nearby, so it wouldn't be another few cycles just to reach Pluto.

"Hey, Min," Eva said. "Set a course for Charon."

"Really?" Min asked. "Are we, I mean, do we have time to—"

"Yes," Eva said, rubbing her temple. "We're going to Evercon."

They convened in the mess again to discuss what they'd learned on Medoral and what to expect on Charon. Sue refused to sit, pacing back and forth in front of the table as Eva blew on her instant noodles to cool them. Min watched Sue pace, snacking on a protein bar; it was interesting that she'd ventured out of the bridge yet again, but Eva had more pressing questions on her mind. Mala had deposited herself in the middle of the table, in clear violation of Eva's previous rants about hygiene, and had tucked her paws underneath her so she looked like a loaf of fruity pumpernickel.

"I have confirmed that your sibling did pass through Medoral," Vakar told Sue. "The Fridge agents attempted to apprehend him and were unsuccessful. While they maintained a presence on the station for unrelated purposes, they were tasked with alerting their superiors if Josh were to return." Between statements, he ingested cubes of nutrient paste quickly and methodically, and Eva resisted the urge to tell him to slow down.

"And your mom is sure he went to Evercon?" Pink asked.

"Pretty sure," Eva said. "And with other mystery people, so that's fun."

"I can't believe we're so close to finding him," Sue said, flapping her hands in excitement. "I hope he's okay. I hope they didn't make him do anything too bad."

Pink leaned back in her chair, pursing her lips in a way that told Eva she had opinions. Eva waited, slurping her hot food carefully and burning the roof of her mouth anyway.

"You trust her?" Pink asked finally.

"My mom?" Eva asked, unable to keep the surprise out of her tone. "Yeah, I trust her. She could still be wrong, but I don't think she's lying if that's what you mean."

"I'm just saying, you trusted your sister and look where that got us."

"This isn't like that." Eva put her fork down and sighed. "I know I've probably told you about this before, but my mom left

Pete because he was a lying sack of crehnisk shit who thought laws were blueprints for building better crimes. She was worried about him putting us all in danger, but she hated the lawbreaking and lying more than anything else. She always used to tell me, 'Eva, lie to me and you'll get double punished,' and she meant it."

"You still did it, though," Pink said, smirking.

"Claro que sí," Eva said. "I got away with it enough that it was worth rolling the dice. I didn't even tell her exactly why we were looking for Josh, because what, I'm gonna say we're on retainer for Mari's super-secret intergalactic anti-Fridge club?" She grabbed her fork again, maybe a little too aggressively, and stirred her noodles.

"Agent Virgo said The Forge came first," Sue said, pausing midstride to accept a random ship part from one of her tiny yellow bots.

"Counterpoint: Agent Virgo sucks plutonium exhaust," Eva said, and Min giggled.

"So your mom's not gonna stab us in the back later, then?" Pink asked. "You're sure?"

"I'm sure. She might stop helping us if she thinks something is funky, because she takes the law a little too seriously, but she's not gonna call the cops on us." Sure, Regina worked for BOFA now, but she was auditing files or whatever. Staring at numbers on a holoscreen all cycle didn't translate to calling in strike teams to drag her own daughter to the nearest rehab station.

"If you say so," Pink said, shrugging. Then she smiled, her single eye staring vacantly at the cabinets behind Eva. "My brother was always big on rules, too. We knew he'd make a good lawyer someday, and he is. He can find loopholes a flea would have to squeeze through, and he'll turn an argument right around on you before you can even get a proper grip on it. He's slippery as a greased pig."

"Good thing he uses his powers for awesome and not evil," Eva said, taking another bite of food. "How about you, Vakar, you ever make your parents want to throw a chancleta at you?"

"My parents were not inclined to attack their offspring with improvised projectile weapons," Vakar said, his scent laced with cinnamon as he relaxed. "I encountered some difficulties during my early training modules, primarily because I found them juvenile and uninteresting, but the programming adjusted quickly to compensate."

"Hey, that sounds like me," Min said. "I would get so bored, I would hack into the q-net and play free games instead of working. I totally brought down the whole system with a virus once."

"By accident?" Sue asked, pausing to stare at Min.

"That time, yeah."

Sue finished her circuit, stopping finally to lean against the counter. She flexed her calves so that she went up and down on the balls of her feet. "Josh got in trouble a lot," she said quietly. "He's way older than me, so he was allowed to do big-kid stuff that I wasn't, but he still messed around."

"Are we talking, like, skipping school and tagging buildings?" Eva asked.

Sue grimaced. "More like building prototype rockets and testing them without supervision."

"That's right," Pink said. "Your family makes ships."

"Mostly, yeah," Sue said. "Ships, rockets, mining bots . . . custom stuff, you know? Sometimes we mod, sometimes we build from scratch."

"Did you get in trouble, too?" Eva asked. It was hard to picture the pink-faced girl in front of her acting out, but Sue had robbed banks, so who knew.

"Our parents were less strict with me," Sue replied. "I did a lot of the same stuff, but Josh was usually there to help, and if anyone got in trouble it was him for instigating." Her forehead creased as she frowned. "He got really . . . intense after BOFA made us move."

"Because of the Proarkhe discovery on your home planet," Vakar interjected.

"Yeah. Then he went off to school in a whole other galaxy for a while. He still let me show him my projects, and when he got back he would sometimes hang out with me in the workshop, but mostly he was too busy with paying work." She fell silent, tapping a staccato rhythm against the cabinet with her right hand, and Eva could almost read the thoughts and emotions flashing through her mind, because they weren't far off from how she'd felt about Mari.

"We're going to find him," Eva said.

"Bet your ass we will," Pink agreed.

Sue's eyes welled up with tears. "Thank you," she whispered. "I mean, I know we've been looking this whole time, but it feels like it's really going to happen now."

Min got up, ostensibly to throw her food wrapper into the recycler, but she veered off-course to give Sue a gentle pat on the arm. Sue smiled, her cheeks rosy as she stared at her feet.

Eva finished sipping her noodle broth and wiped her mouth with the back of her hand. "At least our next stop isn't dangerous," she said. "The worst thing we'll have to deal with at Evercon is the clouds of sanitizing spray."

Vakar swallowed the last of his nutrient paste. "Why are there clouds of sanitizing spray?"

Eva shook her head ruefully. "You'll see when we get there. Or smell, I guess."

A few hours later they arrived on Charon, the largest moon of Pluto, in the Kuiper Belt of the Sol system. The local star was distant, but still brighter than any other star in the Milky Way, giving enough light at certain times of the cycle to illuminate the icy gray surface. More impressive was Pluto itself, looming in the sky with its snakeskin landscape mottled by orange and blood-red patches.

"Is it strange?" Vakar asked as Eva stood in the bridge, staring at the viewscreens.

"Strange?" Eva repeated.

"To be in the system where your species originated." He studied her face, his gray-blue eyes hooded slightly by his inner lids.

"A little," she admitted. "My family left Earth a long time ago, and we didn't settle on Mars or Titan like some refugees. We kept going."

"I am given to understand that war had a long reach," he said.

"Long enough," Eva said quietly. "And they knew they were never going back. My family, I mean. Some people, some exiles, figured it was a matter of time and they'd be able to pick up where they left off. Pero no fue tan fácil."

"I never had a home planet," Vakar said, smelling like jasmine with a hint of rust. "Our oldest histories tell us it was rendered uninhabitable by cataclysms, and its location was lost, perhaps deliberately. There is an old saying: 'seeking Thadus,' to mean wasting time on a pointless task."

"We have a saying like that," Eva said, sliding her arm around his waist. "Trying to find the Holy Grail."

"A grail is a vessel of some kind? My translators are unclear."

"A cup, a bowl, who knows." Eva rested her head on the side of his chest. "It was supposed to heal people who drank from it, but only the most holy people could even touch it."

He smelled confused. "What is 'holy' in this context?"

Eva grinned. "Virgins."

"Ah, yes. For a species whose primary stereotypical quality is engaging in sexual intercourse with virtually anything, your various cultural preoccupations with chastity are quite curious."

Eva bumped him with her hip, and he settled an arm around her shoulder. "Plenty of humans have no interest in sex or romance," she said. "Probably about the same number who earn the opposite stereotype, maybe even more."

"How fortunate I am that you are not one of them," he teased, the smell of licorice taking over everything else he'd been sending out.

"Oye, Papi Chulo," Eva said. "Our various cultures have changed a lot over the centuries, mostly for the better. But one thing hasn't changed."

"What is that?"

"Humans still like pretending to be other people for fun." She finalized their Evercon ticket purchases through her commlink, grumbling internally at the cost. "And when it comes to making shit up, humans do not fuck around."

Evercon hadn't always been a convention. The original settlement on Charon was a standard dome habitat, complete with artificial gravity and garden pods, occupied mainly by scientists. Then the local Gate was discovered, BOFA made first contact according to their protocols for sentient species, and suddenly one habitat became a huge way station for newly minted inter-galactic travelers entering and leaving the system. Once humans fully embraced FTL technology, there was less of a need for such a stopover, so the owners of the various hospitality properties rebranded them as a prime location for conferences and corpo-rate retreats and similar functions.

Then one company, Iron Throne Enterprises, bought up the whole damn rock and consolidated.

In retrospect, it seemed obvious that a place with geological features such as Oz Terra, Gallifrey Macula, Mordor Macula, and Vulcan Planum would become host to various fan conven-tions. And indeed, despite best efforts to attract other species—and their money—to the facilities, it remained a uniquely human artifact. But no one anticipated exactly how wildly popular the place would be for pop-culture and nostalgia-seekers alike, and what started as a handful of separate events evolved into a never-ending morass of competing celebrations of humanity's fictional accretions.

As Eva had predicted, Vakar took one smell of the place and backed out, claiming he had work to catch up on. It was just as well: nonhumans were more than welcome, but tended to draw more attention because humans assumed they were celebrities. On the other hand, Min was eager to explore, even if she clung to Sue's hand, unaccustomed to the intensity of the crowds wandering the mazelike halls of the various interconnected buildings. Sue was also excited, mainly because of the dazzling array of technical prowess on display in the various costumes and props. Pink was Pink, and came along mostly to supervise.

Once again, weapons were not allowed, with all props care-fully inspected for potential lethality and confiscated accord-ingly. Eva had left her cane behind this time, opting for a stim and pain meds, so she and her crew were able to make their way to the front more quickly. It still took a solid half hour because the line wound back and forth across the entire length of a room large enough to fit a fleet of short-range starfighters. And this was only one of the dozen possible entrances.

Not everyone wore a costume, but they were common. Eva had been to big parties where dressing up was half the fun, but this was a whole other level. The care and attention to detail, the elaborate layering and stitching and accessorizing, the makeup and prosthetics, the holographic displays and multisensory overlays, even the low-level psychic effects were so impressive that Eva couldn't help but share in a fraction of the exuberance of the people around her who actually knew what the hell was going on.

It was lying, maybe, all this pretend play, but a kind of lying that felt good. It brought people together, made them feel part of something bigger than themselves. Some fans could be shitty, but pa'l carajo with those people.

That wasn't to say it was all happy times, because it quickly became apparent that more was going on under the giddy, squealing surface.

"Run that by me again, please," Eva told Min. "And maybe explain more about, uh, all of it."

They stood against a wall in one of the main corridors in the Dragon wing, clusters of cosplayers drifting past like stately parade floats, pausing occasionally to pose for pictures. Sue could hardly keep her mouth closed, oohing and aahing at everyone, especially the ones with mechanical parts.

"Okay," Min said, tugging on her blue pigtail braid with her free hand. "So even though this place is super huge, it gets full really fast, and some of the rooms are bigger or nicer than others, or have better tech."

"Right," Eva said. "Got it."

An eerily beautiful man with silver hair and one enormous black wing, an absurdly large holo-sword in his hand, stopped in front of Pink. "Your costume is amazing," he said.

"I'm not wearing a costume," Pink replied. Her braids were pulled back in a thick ponytail, and she'd worn a green-and-black jacket over her spacesuit. Perfectly normal clothes for her. The only thing remotely costume-like, to Eva's mind, was Pink's eye patch; she'd worn her nice one, black with a gold crescent moon that almost looked like a simple line drawing of a closed eye.

The man shrugged and moved on. Pink glanced at Eva with a raised eyebrow, and Eva wagged her head noncommittally and returned her attention to Min.

"There are a lot of different groups running events here," Min continued, "and they all have to book space in advance, which is super hard because, like, there's so many of them? And some of them have really famous guests, but some don't, and sometimes there's overlap in the fandoms?"

"I think I'm following so far," Eva said.

Another beautiful man, this one with long white hair and a floor-length fur stole over one shoulder, approached Pink. "I love your costume," he said. "Could I take a picture with you?"

"Sorry, it's not a costume," Pink said.

"Oh, my error," the man replied. "Nice eye patch."

Pink flashed him a close-lipped smile and he moved on.

Min bit her lip pensively. "So, like, the groups form factions, so they can get access to better spaces and hotel block pricing? But they don't always get along with each other. Sometimes it's the people in charge and sometimes it's the fans, but they'll have these alliances that last for a while and then break up because of infighting."

"Qué relajo," Eva said. "It's like diplomacy for geeks."

A pair of teenagers in spacesuits walked past, took one look at Pink, and squealed simultaneously. After some excited but inaudible chatter between them, they ran off, wearing identical expressions of people on a mission. Pink's brow furrowed in confusion.

"So the reason the event listings and panel locations keep changing . . ." Eva said, prompting Min to continue.

"Right," Min said. "So even if it's all negotiated in advance, stuff falls apart at the last minute. Like right now, the fantasy furries are fighting the sci-fi furries, and they're both mad at the equestrian furries, and there was a fantasy medievalist coalition but they split because the reenactors decided they didn't want elves on their costuming panels, and the manga and comic groups are back together so they took over a prime chunk of ballroom space to make their own artists' alley, and the biggest military sci-fi group is having this huge thing over one fandom taking up too much space because their soldiers are, like, literally enormous compared to everyone else—"

"And you lost me," Eva said. "The point is, it's hard to know what the fuck was happening when Josh passed through here."

"Yeah, basically," Min said. "Whatever was on the schedule might have changed at the last minute, and might not have been updated in the official comms channels."

The teenagers in spacesuits returned, their eyes practically sparkling with excitement. They'd brought an entire additional squad of other people in spacesuits, some of them wearing jackets like Pink's but in different colors, some wearing helmets with different symbols on them—flowers, hearts, leaves, coins, and other shapes Eva couldn't identify. One of the teens had apparently been appointed as speaker, because they approached Pink while the others held back, giggling.

"Will you take a picture with us, Lady Masamune?" they

asked, bowing politely. "Please? So we can have the whole group!"

Pink looked at them, then at Eva, who couldn't keep from grinning. With a sigh, Pink nodded.

"Fine," Pink said. "What do you want me to do?"

"You can stand next to Kojuro," they said, pointing at one of the others, who waved excitedly.

The crowds parted around them as they set up their picture, all the people posing in what were presumably ways appropriate to their characters. Pink stood there, hand on her hip, as Kojuro flung a leg dramatically in front of her.

"Say 'samurai'!" the speaker yelled.

"Samurai!" they all answered in unison, except Pink, who maintained her usual amused smirk.

"Everyone give me your comms codes," the speaker said. "I'll send you the holos."

Pink raised a hand as she walked back to Eva. "I'm good, thanks. Enjoy yourselves."

The teenagers loitered a little longer, chattering excitedly amongst themselves. "Look at Masamune," one of them said. "So stoic. She really knows her character."

"I love the eye patch," another said. "So subtle."

Eva laughed. "I can't believe you went along with that."

Pink shrugged. "It made them happy," she said. "Sometimes you gotta do nice shit for no reason."

Eva returned her attention to the task at hand. "Sorry, Sue," she said. "Looks like this might be a dead end. Hopefully my mom will have another lead for us."

Sue's expression fell, even as her gaze kept getting drawn back to the parade of costumes. "At least we got to have a little fun," she said, sounding guilty and sad at once. "Maybe we can go through the dealer's room before we leave. Just for a little while."

"Or we can ask Leroy?" Min said suddenly.

Eva's brow furrowed. "Leroy? Is he here?"

Min nodded. "There's a big *Crash Sisters* thing going on right now. And unless the old event data is totally wrong, he was here six months ago."

A shiver went up Eva's spine. "He was on Medoral, too. That's a hell of a coincidence."

Pink nodded, crossing her arms. "It might be nothing, but it's worth asking. And it would be nice to see him again."

It really would, Eva thought. She hadn't gotten the chance, not after her old boss Tito Santiago had jammed her into that cryostasis pod for The Fridge. By the time she got out a year later, Leroy was well and truly gone, a big holovid star touring the universe to see all his adoring fans. He was housed in a special enclave, a sprawling series of themed sets in which different members of the standard roster would fight depending on the prevailing narrative of the season. Between battles, they were sequestered in a small central bunker, where their interpersonal conflicts and training montages could be captured in High Octane Total Experience Memory Sensation™. Subscriptions were available from several q-net streaming services or individual episodes could be purchased as desired.

They'd chatted a few times, but he was always busy, and his comms code changed all the time to keep some semblance of his privacy intact.

Min tapped Eva on her shoulder. "Uh, Cap, there might be a tiny little problem."

"What's that?" Eva asked.

"You need tickets to see him," Min said, "and they're all sold out."

Chapter 5

THRONE OF GAMES

Eva wasn't one to give up over a simple thing like tickets being unavailable. There had to be other ways to get to Leroy, and she'd find them all and try them until one worked.

"I know he's busy, but there has to be a way he can sneak out for a minute to see us," Eva said. "He sent us his latest comms code, right?"

Pink wrinkled her nose. "Let me check." She stared at the wall for a minute, then shook her head. "The one I have is unassigned. Either it changed recently or he forgot to tell us."

Mierda, mojón y porquería. Of course it couldn't be that easy. "Where is his big event going to be?" Eva asked.

Min checked the program. "Wow, the main ballroom in the Nebula Wing. *Crash Sisters* must be doing really well in a lot of fandoms."

Eva pulled up a map of the massive convention center,

pinpointing the ballroom. "Let's start walking," she said. "It's pretty far away." She took off at a brisk pace, which Pink caught up to easily because her legs were longer and she didn't have a still-healing leg.

"And how are you planning to charm your way into this one?" Pink asked.

"If there are tickets," Eva said, "someone has to be scalping them. Min, check the local q-net." She glanced back to be sure Sue and Min were keeping up, which they weren't, because once again Sue kept stopping to admire costumes and whatnot, and Min was still holding her hand. With a sigh, Eva stopped and waited, ignoring the glares of the people forced to move around her.

"Oh wow," Min said. "These tickets are a lot. Like, a *lot* a lot."

"How much?" Eva asked.

Min told her, and Eva threw her an incredulous look.

"Me cago en diez," Eva said. "What comemierda has that many credits to piss away on a cabrón celebrity?"

"It's a grudge match," Min said, as if that explained it.

Eva shook her head and once again got moving, Pink at her side. "We'll scope out the security situation when we get there," she said. "If it costs that much, there are probably going to be guards."

"No fighting," Pink said. "And no throwing chairs."

That eliminated some possible options. "Fine. We figure out a way to sneak in, maybe disguise ourselves as staff somehow."

"Staff have commlink codes," Sue said, idly swinging Min's hand as they walked. "And special uniforms. I heard a couple of them talking about the codes getting switched again."

"So we get the codes, steal a uniform, and walk in like we own the place," Eva said.

Pink made a sour face. "That's a lot, honey," she said.

"Do you have a better plan?" Eva retorted.

"There's one other thing you could try," Min said. "The Challenge Room."

Eva stopped and turned, earning a face full of sequined bodice, followed by a nasty look from a person in a gorgeous ball gown as they moved past her.

"What," Eva asked, "is the Challenge Room?"

The line of people snaked around and through the low building currently built out as the Challenge Room. They all competed against each other for limited spots for a special meet-and-greet with Leroy himself. Some, like Eva, sat with their backs against the wall and got up only to move forward. Others bounced on the balls of their feet, or did push-ups, or took selfies while flexing. Others stared up at Pluto overhead, and the sun and stars beyond, perhaps imagining themselves as characters in an epic story with destinies written in the glittering canvas of space.

Eva had filled out a number of forms and medical waivers to try the challenge, because as Min had told her repeatedly, the room was "a super hard obstacle course, like, level ten thousand" used as an initial screening tool for contestants who would later compete to be added to the *Crash Sisters* roster. It also changed every time so people couldn't practice for it, had "like, so many traps," and had to be completed in under a minute.

Eva regretted her decision not to buy overpriced food on the way there, or at least coffee, and also questioned whether this was worth the time she was wasting in line when she could be stealing a staff uniform. Well, she could always try that plan if this didn't work. She also wondered idly where the exit was, since no one was leaving the building. Then again, it made sense; wouldn't want anyone giving people in line the heads-up about what to expect.

What felt like hours later, the doors in front of her slid open, revealing a wall with a small corridor that looped around it, obscuring whatever was on the other side. She stepped in and the doors closed behind her, leaving her in darkness.

"Welcome to the Challenge Room," said a voice to her left. Soft, female, like an old human nav computer. "Please listen to the instructions carefully, as they will not be repeated. Your goals are to destroy all visible targets and reach the opposite side of the room, pressing the large green button to open the exit door before time runs out. You will have sixty seconds from the time you hear the starting bell. The room will be illuminated in three, two, one . . ."

Eva threw her arm over her face just in time to avoid being blinded by the massive floodlights that blazed on. A bell jangled so loudly that she almost wished she'd covered her ears instead, but she had more pressing considerations.

Sixty seconds, destroy targets, green button. Go.

The room went deep into the ground, at least three stories down. A number of platforms were arranged in no apparent order, staggered parallel to each other at different heights in a way that created roughly three levels. Each level had walls blocking access at strategic locations, apparently to encourage jumping or dropping to lower platforms. There were a few ladders, spread so far apart as to be almost useless given the time limit.

The green button was on the other side of the room, at the bottom. The targets she had to break were large floating orbs, glowing faintly red, possibly holographic. There were five of them, and she'd already wasted six seconds casing the joint. Time to move.

She shot toward the first target at a run, vaulting a low wall and using her momentum to carry her across a gap between platforms. The target was about as high as her head, and after a moment of hesitation, she threw a punch at it. With a strange musical chime, it popped like a balloon and vanished. Definitely holograms.

It was harder for her to see where all the targets were now, or where the platforms fell away. There was one more target on this level, but another one was closer, one level down with a ladder next to it. She vaulted another wall, a taller one, landing in a roll that took her a few steps from the ladder.

An alarm jangled, and the floor beneath her shimmered and vanished.

As she fell, she managed to grab a corner of the second level's platform, wrenching her left shoulder. Swallowing a yell as pain lanced through her, she grabbed on with her other arm and jackknifed, pulling herself up. The target was just ahead, at waist level, so she kicked it. Poof it went, still with the goofy sound effect. Three more to go: one more on this level, one up top, and the last one at the bottom.

"Thirty seconds remain," said the soft female voice.

Eva ran toward the next target on the same level. She dodged moving walls that slid into and out of her way, stumbling to keep her footing on platforms that did the same.

That teeth-shaking alarm jangled and she rolled forward in time to avoid having the floor disappear under her again. The room wasn't hot, but she was sweating, and the strong smell of ozone gave her a headache. She reached the other target, which she had to wall-jump to hit. The damn things weren't even satisfying to destroy, insubstantial as they were.

Now she had to climb back up, snarling at Past Eva for thinking hitting the lower level targets first was a good idea. One of the moving platforms was going up and down, so she ran over to that, watched it carefully, and leaped onto it as soon as it was within reach. It carried her back up, except at the last moment it made the horrible alarm sound, and she had to jump off before it vanished.

She reached the fourth target just as the voice announced, "Fifteen seconds remain."

The last target was on the bottom floor, near the middle. She wasn't going to make it. Then it occurred to her: the vanishing floors. If she were trying to obstruct someone as much as possible, where would she put those floors?

The elevator floor was gone, so she grabbed the lip of the platform and swung herself to the next one down, rolling into the fall and landing near the edge of a lower platform. Sure enough, the alarm sounded and she was dropped. This time she was ready, turning on her gravboots so her fall went diagonal instead of straight down, which carried her within spitting distance of the target.

"Ten seconds. Nine . . ."

Eva gritted her teeth and ran, leaping into a flying back kick that burst the target apart.

"Seven . . ."

The green button to finish the course was a good six meters away. She grabbed the edge of the nearest platform and vaulted it, turning her gravboots on again, and shot toward the far wall.

"Five, four, three . . ."

Her boots hit the button.

Without warning, all the lights went out, leaving her in darkness that would have been total but for the faint glow coming from the now-open exit door.

She panted, waiting for some sign of what to do next. When none came, she climbed down to the floor and deactivated her gravboots, then walked out the door.

Clinical yellow light greeted Eva in a narrow hallway, along with a buasyr wearing a loose shirt emblazoned with the *Crash Sisters* logo.

"Congratulations, Little Sister," he said, his excitement so artificial it made Eva's teeth ache. "You have passed the Challenge Room and may now proceed to the visitors' room to meet The King. Please enjoy some complimentary light refreshments while you wait."

Eva proceeded. At the end of the hallway, a surprisingly large number of people milled around a bare room trying to conceal their excitement with a veneer of toughness or apathy. A table along one wall contained the promised light refreshments: branded energy drinks and snack foods. Not the kind of stuff she'd normally associate with anyone who took physical fitness seriously.

Eva, however, was too thirsty to care. She made a beeline for the table and grabbed a drink, making sure it was fit for human consumption, which it was. Unfortunately, it was also peach-flavored.

"Nasty," she muttered, holding her nose and chugging it. The rejuvenating power of electrolytes and sugar gave her the energy to control her desire to barf over the peachiness.

Everyone was staring at her, so she burped and waved. As if insulted in unison, they turned their attention back to a holovid along the opposite wall.

It was *Crash Sisters*, of course, probably from the most recent season. Leroy had been the big bad guy for the last few seasons, but word had somehow leaked about his relationship with another one of the fighters, and the writers had decided to go with it. He was still stomping around with his bright-orange hair and yellow costume, but now he got to fawn over his princess girl-friend while they teamed up to fight one of the new people. Min had told her the name, but Eva struggled to retain it. Something like Ultimate Dream?

As she watched Leroy posture and roar in the holovid, a cloud of smoke signaled the dramatic entrance of the villain onto the stage. Eva chuckled to herself at the theatricality of it all; Min and Leroy had always insisted it was real, and certainly the fighting was athletically demanding—as the Challenge Room had proven—but this? This was extra.

The smoke cleared, and Eva's heart would have stopped if it wasn't mechanical.

The villain was a xana.

Bipedal, almost two and a half meters tall, with a long prehensile tail and pinkish fur. His costume was white with a purple stripe down the chest to his crotch, and loose to accommodate the gliding membranes extending between his arms and legs. If he fought the way other xana did, in Eva's experience, he would primarily use his height to his advantage, grabbing and grappling and throwing, occasionally lashing out with the tail for surprise strikes or trips. Then again, Eva had only fought a handful of them, and hadn't seen a xana in years.

Not since Garilia.

Eva stumbled to the nearest wall and sank to the ground, memories cycling through her mind like a bad vid. The wind singing through leaves taller than her. Arms burning with fatigue as she climbed. Barest shifting of shadows above her warning of an imminent attack. Dozens of xana closing in. Her fingers went to the scar on her cheek, the one she got that cycle, when a simple resingado gun-running mission had turned into mass murder. She squeezed her eyes shut against the tears welling up in them, because she didn't deserve to cry, as if she were the victim and not the one who had pulled the trigger.

The Hero of Garilia. The Butcher. Savior. Arsonist. Which one of those would she be to the xana on the holovid?

Why the fuck did it matter?

Breathe, comemierda, she told herself. In and out. Your heart's fake, but your lungs are still meat balloons. They need air.

A door opened at the far end of the room and a buasyr entered, wearing a strangely human-looking beige suit, striped, with two sets of cufflinks. Actual, old-fashioned cufflinks. And a puffy white tie—no, a cravat, that's what it was called. It complemented her dark fur and black spidery eyes, which were only half-focused on the room's occupants, because some people could talk and send messages at the same time. Her whole look screamed "lawyer," so Eva assumed this was Leroy's agent, handler, whatever they were called.

"Congratulations again to you all," she said. "If you would, please form two lines, and we'll begin the session. Autographed copies of your holographs with The King will be available for purchase outside."

Eva snorted and stood, wiping her tears with the back of her hand. She hoped Leroy was getting a big cut of all the credits people were throwing around for this stuff. Good to see he was so popular, though. He deserved it, after everything he'd been through.

She deserved a machete to the back, but she was trying to deserve better.

Swallowing the big lump of emotions gagging her, Eva went to the back of a line. She did a brief dance with a lady who looked like a sumo wrestler with shocking-pink hair, and who apparently wanted to be last for some reason, so Eva let her. She didn't get what the big deal was.

An ear-pounding blast of theme music started up, and an unseen announcer shouted, "Who's ready to meet . . . The King?!"

Everyone but Eva bellowed, so she mustered up as much enthusiasm as she could and joined them. She was happy to see him, truly, after so long; the circumstances were just weird as hell, and now she was feeling extra shaken.

The music managed to get louder somehow, and with a final flourish, Leroy appeared. His suit mimicked his signature costume, yellow with a snakeskin pattern, perfectly tailored to his massive form. His orange-dyed hair was spiked up, and instead of a green mask he wore green shades, but his wrists still sported spiked bands, visible when he raised his fists into the air and roared. Everyone roared back, and he grinned like a fool, and Eva gritted her teeth and sucked in a breath and told herself sternly not to run up and hug him because she'd probably get tackled by his bodyguards.

People at the front of each line prepped the fans for what was apparently a ritual as choreographed as the big fights on the show. Leroy stood off to one side, brightly lit and larger than life, in front of a wall emblazoned with the *Crash Sisters* logo. A handler took one fan at a time up to meet him, at which point he chatted with them briefly, posed for a holograph, then pretended to punch them out of the way so the next person could be brought up. It was efficient, structured, and monitored by a pair of truateg almost as big as Leroy. The agent waited nearby, two of her four arms crossed, half her eyes on Leroy while the other half seemed to be dealing with business over her comms.

He looks so happy, Eva thought. Calm. Collected. Peaceful. He had hunched when he was on her crew, like he was trying to take up less space, avoid calling attention to himself. He'd pulled on his beard all the time from nerves and ground his teeth in his sleep. Now he stood tall, confident, his whole posture relaxed and his fingers slack instead of balled into fists.

Her thoughts sank back into the muck of Garilia, into shame

and regret. Sure, she'd given Leroy a hand when he needed it, but she'd also let him get wrecked by a brain parasite. She'd told herself she was treating him well, but was she? Could she have done better, done more? Every time she talked him down from a fit of rage, or distracted him from a panic attack, was she just keeping him afloat in a pool of shit instead of helping him climb out?

Was it the same for the rest of the crew? Were they holding each other up, or was she holding them back? Especially Vakar, sweet Vakar, who could probably be off somewhere doing real good for the universe, the kind Mari and her Forge amigos thought they were doing. Why was he still with her, after everything? Love? Was that all? Was that enough?

You're in a spiral, she told herself. Focus. You're in a room full of sweaty fans, in the universe's longest continuous convention, and as soon as you get out of here you're going to talk to Pink and take your meds and get your shit together.

Eva thought about Pink posing for that picture with the dozen people in costume, and it made her chuckle just enough to get a hand over the edge of the pit she'd fallen into. If she could get a hand up, she could climb out.

Before she knew it, Eva was coming to the front of the line, and every question she needed to ask Leroy had fucked off to Casa Carajo. She probably looked wild; her nose turned bright red whenever she cried, and her eyes puffed up, and there wasn't a damn thing she could do about it now because time was up. He, meanwhile, continued to look like his best self, and her eyes teared up again with pride.

He froze for a moment when he noticed her, his mouth open, and Eva regretted coming to see him almost more than anything else she'd done to him. It shouldn't have been here, not like this. But then he lowered his shades to show his bright-blue eyes, and grinned so widely that relief flooded her body.

"Captain?" he asked. "Hi! Wow! You're really here?"

Eva nodded mutely, and Leroy pulled her in for a bear hug that took her breath away. His bodyguards took a few steps closer and Leroy waved them off, so they backed up.

"It's just, wow!" Leroy repeated. "It's been so long."

"It has," Eva agreed. "You look great."

"Thanks. You look—" His face screwed up like he was trying to find a nice lie, and Eva laughed.

"I look like shit," she said. "Así es la vida."

"King, the line," Leroy's agent said, raising one of her arms to gesture at the two people still waiting. The woman behind Eva with the pink hair was scowling like Eva had pissed in her protein powder.

Leroy flapped a hand at his agent. "Yeah, it's cool, I'll get to them." He turned back to Eva. "Did you actually do the whole Challenge Room to see me? Is everyone else here? Why didn't you just call?"

"Your comms code changed again," Eva said.

"Oh, right, yeah." His freckled skin turned slightly pink. "Sorry about that, things have been busy, and we're technically on lockdown anyway. Not supposed to make calls, because memvids, and spoilers."

"Hey, no worries. Speaking of busy—"

His agent stalked over, resting two hands on Leroy's expansive back. "King, while it is lovely to see you reconnect with an old friend, we have a schedule, and your real fans are waiting for you."

The pink-haired woman made an affirmative noise, puffing her cheeks up angrily.

Eva's neck went hot and she scowled. "I've been his fan for longer than you've known he existed, mija," she snapped. "Keep your fancy pants on."

The agent raised two fingers, and Leroy's truateg body-guards immediately flanked Eva. They loomed over her, short as she was, and were doused in synthetic hormones meant to trigger reflexive fear in most humans.

Unfortunately for them, Eva wasn't most humans, and she was already on edge. She grinned up at them, silently daring them to lay hands on her so she could give them a taste of a real fight.

"Anji, enough," Leroy said sternly. "I'll finish when I finish." He'd been relaxed before, but now he threw his shoulders back and straightened to his full height, just over two meters of solid muscle. For a moment, Eva worried he was going to lose his temper, fall into a rage the way he used to—the way he pretended to for his adoring fans every time he stepped onto a fighting stage.

Instead, he lowered his shades and glared at his agent, who made a gargling noise and threw him an elaborate series of hand signals that he answered with a smile and a middle finger. The truateg backed away, and Leroy turned his smile to Eva, who was momentarily dazzled.

"Sorry, Captain, you know how it is," he said. His smile faded. "I'm guessing this is something serious, huh?"

"Unfortunately," Eva said. "Not that I don't want to hang out, obviously. We all miss you."

"I know." The corners of his eyes crinkled. "So what is it?"

"You were here six months ago," Eva said, rubbing her neck. "We're looking for a guy named Josh Zafone who was here at the same time."

"I don't know him. Who is he?"

"Sue's brother. The engineer who replaced Vakar, remember?"

Leroy nodded. "Right, she seems nice. But the name isn't familiar, sorry."

Eva shrugged, ignoring the glares Anji was shooting at her

with her spidery eyes. "It's okay, it was a long shot. But it was weird because you were both in Medoral at the same time, too, so we figured we'd ask."

"Oh, yeah, Medoral. That was a wild one!" Leroy laughed. "Ashila was just starting to fight with us. He's a xana, they're a species from this really far-out garden world?"

"Garilia," Eva said. Her stomach clenched at the reminder. "Did anything else happen here or there that you remember? Anything that stood out?"

"Let me think." Leroy's lips pursed and his face twisted, then his eyebrows shot up. "Oh, there were the Pod Pals!"

Eva squinted, then nodded in recognition. "Oh, yeah, the Ball Buddies." She suppressed a snicker.

"Right, those things." Leroy grinned. "They were kind of cool. Little robots, about as big as a cat or a dog. The company that made them was doing a demonstration. They were supposed to be just like the animals from the xana homeworld—what did you say it was called?"

Eva was starting to see a shadow forming on the wall, and she didn't like its shape. "Garilia." Every time she said the word, it tasted more sour.

"King," Anji said, her voice strained. "I apologize for the inconvenience, however our schedule is—"

"I know, I know," Leroy said. He pulled Eva in for another quick hug, then released her. "I don't know if I helped, but it was great to see you again finally. I'm glad you're not, you know. That you didn't . . ."

"Die at some point?" Eva laughed. "You know me. I've got as many lives as all our cats put together."

"I sure hope so. Later, Captain." He gave her one last look over the tops of his shades, his blue eyes misted with emotion, then slid them back into place. Within moments he wasn't merely Leroy Cooper, he was The King again, and Eva was one of his fans who needed to get the hell out of the way so he could take his next holograph.

"Hasta luego, mijo," she told Leroy. "Call me if you need me."

The handler who had led Eva up stepped forward uncertainly and gestured for her to follow them. Eva nodded, waving as she went, and stuck her tongue out at the pink-haired woman as they passed each other. By the time she had left the room, the machinery of fandom was once again running smoothly, as if it had never been disrupted in the first place.

There was nothing smooth about Eva in that moment. She was glad there were no mirrors in the uncomfortably narrow hallway to show her how small and desmondingado she looked. But of course, there was even better.

A chipper woman in a *Crash Sisters* shirt appeared seemingly out of nowhere. "Would you like to purchase the holograph of your meeting with The King?" she asked, smiling broadly and poking her dimpled cheek. "We have versions available with full sensory—"

"No thanks," Eva said. She didn't add that she'd rather wrestle a needle-bear naked while on fire, because the woman was just doing her job; no need to be rude.

The walk down the hallway was longer than any she had taken that day, alone as she was with the minimal information Leroy had given her. No matter how hard she tried to dismiss the Garilia connection, it crept back into her thoughts like a sly cat intent on stealing attention. It could be coincidence. One more random thing, like Leroy's presence in the two places Josh had happened to visit in a row.

With any luck, her mother would have another lead for her. Because the last thing Eva wanted to do, in any of her catlike multiple lives, was go back to Garilia.

Chapter 6

BAD PENNY

Before she even made it back to the main convention area, much less to *La Sirena Negra* and her crew, Eva had sent a half dozen messages—to Pink and Min, to Vakar, even to her mother—with requests or instructions on what to do next. Action meant control, and control was something Eva needed, even if it was an illusion. The other thing she needed was information, because every lead so far had turned up nothing useful, and she was tired of throwing punches and hitting empty air.

Vakar was waiting for her when she walked up the ramp to the cargo bay, smelling minty as he suppressed his own anxiety. She gratefully accepted a hug from him and stood there for as long as her natural antsiness allowed, before stepping back and pinging Min that it was time to go.

"What did you find out about those robots?" Eva asked Vakar once they reached the mess, busying her hands with making coffee. Mala appeared in the doorway and sauntered over, winding her furry body around Eva's legs and purring like a combustion engine.

Vakar stood next to her, leaning against the counter as he spoke. "The Sylfe Company is indeed based in Garilia, as you suspected. It was founded several years ago by—"

"How many?" Eva snapped, then took a deep breath and put down the spoon she was gripping like a weapon. "How many years ago was it founded?" she asked, more calmly.

"Three, by someone called Lashra Damaal." He spoke more slowly than usual, as if he were choosing his words carefully, and his scent carried an undercurrent of concern. "She was not present for the political turmoil that occurred previously, having accepted a BOFA-funded scholarship to pursue educational opportunities off-planet at the time."

Eva picked the spoon back up and finished tamping down the grounds in the filter basket, then filled the reservoir with water. Mala's purring intensified, and she jumped onto the counter, butting her head against Eva's hand as Eva tried to screw the cafetera back together.

"Are bots the only thing the Sylfe Company makes?" Eva asked.

"No. They are a government-contracted entity that also provides necessary items for the residents of the planet, such as food, medications, and durable goods." He reached up and grabbed a cup from the cabinet, handing it to Eva.

"But the robots are what they're pushing now? Off-planet, anyway."

"Correct. Damaal has been traveling to various points in the universe to demonstrate them, and reportedly to secure additional funding for their production on a broader scale."

Eva rubbed Mala's furry head and stared at the cafetera as

the water heated up, as if she could will it to boil faster. "But what does any of that have to do with Josh?" she mused aloud. "He can build robots, sure, but he was locked up by The Fridge the whole time this company was doing their thing." Was he there for the coup? He couldn't have been. Eva's neck went hot and cold all at once, and she shuddered involuntarily.

"A connection is unclear, assuming one exists." Vakar rested a hand on her shoulder, and she turned it into a sideways hug. "I will do additional research, but I . . ." He paused, and his scent shifted to add a nervous tar note.

"What, what happened?" Eva asked, her own nerves already as taut as guitar strings. Mala made an inquisitive noise as Eva stopped petting her.

Vakar hesitated a few moments before proceeding. "My superiors were pleased by our actions on Medoral, as I was able to secure useful intelligence on Fridge activities in the area. However, I am concerned that they will soon request details on my forthcoming intentions, or assign me a specific mission that will run counter to your own."

"Right." Until now, Eva and Pink had been more than happy to tag along with Vakar, since his bosses mostly had him doing work they wanted to do anyway: finding The Fridge and fucking with them. But sometimes he had to run off to do work on his own, especially if Eva had picked up a delivery or transport job that went nowhere near a known Fridge cell.

Eva's arm skin prickled. "What did you tell them about The Forge?"

"I did not."

"You what?" Vakar's inability to lie was nearly legendary. When he became a Wraith, he'd been forced to work past it to maintain appropriate levels of secrecy, but he relied on tech and meds where physical limitations existed. And he hated doing it on principle anyway, unless absolutely necessary. So for him to decide to not just lie, but lie to his bosses, was a lot for Eva to process.

Vakar's gray-blue eyes met hers, then looked toward the far wall. "I did not want to jeopardize your own mission inadvertently. I also did not obtain a substantial amount of actionable data from the Forge facility, and so I determined it was prudent to bide my time."

Prudent. Hah. That sounded like him, at least. Eva flinched as the coffee timer went off, startling her. Reluctantly, she moved away from Vakar, from the comforting licorice smell that nearly always emanated from him. The ritual and rhythm of spooning out sugar, stirring up espumita, and pouring out the rest of the black gold was its own kind of calming, and by the time she took her first sip of scalding sweetness, she was feeling less flustered.

"No sense borrowing trouble," she said finally. "If your bosses get pissy, we'll deal with it. Until then, we keep looking for Josh."

"That was my estimation of the situation as well. But I wanted to be certain you were aware of the potential future difficulties, so you were not taken by surprise." Vakar ran a gloved hand over her hair affectionately, and she smiled up at him. Mala, meanwhile, had wandered off somewhere, perhaps sensing that no further pets were forthcoming.

That cat always did have a mind of her own, Eva thought. Such was the way of cats, more so the psychic ones.

"Hey, Cap," Min said through the speakers. "Sorry to bother you, but your mom just left you a message. Want me to play it in there?"

A message? Weird, considering she could have just talked to Eva.

"Sure, go ahead," Eva said.

The lights dimmed slightly and her mother's image appeared in the center of the table. Regina wore an openmouthed scowl, as if she had just yelled at someone nearby and was returning her attention to the holoscreen.

"Hola, mijita, discúlpame, I'm on my way to another meeting," Regina said. "Qué arroz con mango, estoy agotada. They have me running around like a chicken with my head cut off."

Eva snorted. Her mom, some BOFA big-shot, whatever that meant. Who would have seen it coming?

"Anyway," the message continued, "I checked what you asked and it looks like there were transactions in a place called Tyet-Ruru, on the planet Abelgard. I hope that helps. I'll call you back later. Adiós, love you." The holo image disappeared, and the lights returned to their normal level.

"Abelgard, huh," Eva said. "Why does that sound familiar?" She took another sip of coffee, staring blankly at the now-empty table. Every new bit of information she obtained felt like a single pixel from some giant holovid: totally useless by itself, almost equally useless when put together, and she had no idea how she would ever manage to find a large enough fragment of the big picture to make any sense of it.

In the doorway, someone gasped: Sue, with a crowbar in one hand and a piece of interior hull paneling in the other, paler than usual.

"What?" Eva asked.

"I've always wanted to go to Abelgard!" Min interjected before Sue could answer, her voice shrill with excitement. "Please, you have to let me visit The Sump!"

"Qué coño is a Sump?" Eva asked.

•••••••

"I forbid you from going to The Sump," Mari told Eva, her nose wrinkled like she smelled a fart. She had called for an update on their progress about an hour after *La Sirena Negra* passed through the Gate to the Ashyke System, where Abelgard was located. Eva had to rush her turn in the sonic shower to take the call, so she sat on the edge of her bed wearing nothing but her underwear and a scowl.

Eva stuck her tongue out at her sister's holo image. "You gonna forbid me from other fun stuff, too, like punching people and setting things on fire?"

"Those things are not fun, you anarchist."

"Is anarchy bad now? I'll update my translator nanites." Eva was enjoying teasing her sister too much, maybe because it was so easy and familiar. Like falling off a hoverbike.

Mari closed her eyes and took a visibly deep breath. "Why are you going to Abelgard in the first place? Medoral made sense, but then you went to Charon, and now this?"

Eva had a ready, and interesting, answer for this one. "Josh went to the university there, and my intel suggests it was one of his stops after leaving Medoral." Sue had told her as much once Min finally stopped gushing about The Sump, which was a whole other mess Eva was still making up her mind about, despite what she had told Mari.

"Ay, sí, verdad, he did go to Evident Academy for a few years before returning to Katoru," Mari said. "But how do you know he went there after he escaped The Fridge?"

"I have my ways," Eva said. She wasn't about to explain that she'd called their mom; she could already hear the lecture now, and she wasn't in the mood.

She also didn't mention that Lashra Damaal had gone to

Abelgard as well, because she wasn't ready to admit to herself that the coincidences surrounding the Garilia connection were piling up to an uncomfortable height.

"Fine, be evasive. No me importa." Mari squinted at Eva, as if she could read her sister's mind if she tried, but Eva just smiled back at her.

"Speaking of evasive, you didn't tell me he was traveling with other people," Eva said. "Do you know who they are? Might help me find him faster."

Mari, to Eva's surprise, froze in the way she always did when she was blindsided. "I wasn't aware of that, no. How did you find out?"

Eva wiggled her fingers. "Maaagic!" she replied in a sing-songy voice.

Mari rolled her eyes and sighed. "Whatever. No, I didn't know, so I can't help you there."

"Bueno. Anything else, before I get back to my, uh, very important preparations?" Eva asked.

"I suppose not." Mari sighed again and shook her head slightly. "Send me an update if you find anything."

"Claro que sí," Eva replied. "Hasta luego."

"Adiós." Mari's image vanished, and almost simultaneously there was a polite knock at the door.

Eva sent a mental command to open it, but there was no one waiting. Confused, she stood and walked over, poking her head out to see who it might have been.

"Surprise!" Vakar said, appearing out of nowhere, and Eva shrieked.

"Qué rayo?" Eva asked, holding a hand to her chest. Her heart was fine, being mechanical, but the gesture was a hard habit to break even after so many years.

Vakar smelled mildly confused. "Have I done something un-desirable?"

"You scared the shit out of me, yeah. Why did you . . . ?" Eva gestured dismissively at Pink, who had poked her head out of the med bay and was staring at them with her eyebrows all the way up in her hairline.

"I had inquired of Pink as to ways I might contribute to the ongoing health of our relationship," he replied, now smelling bashful, like fresh-cut grass.

"And she told you what, exactly?" Eva asked, towing Vakar into her room and closing the door with a thought.

"She told me I should surprise you."

Eva stared at him, openmouthed, and then erupted into laughter, unable to contain herself.

"You are," she gasped between giggles, "too sweet to live."

His confusion and embarrassment heightened, so she took pity on him and dragged him over to the bed. They had some time before they got to Abelgard, and she hadn't taken that shower for nothing.

"Let me show you what Pink meant," Eva said, grinning when she was rewarded with the scent of licorice and almonds, among other things.

Abelgard was affectionately termed a garden world by the hu-mans who had settled there, but it was the kind of garden that was overgrown in some places and muddy in others, and had been otherwise trashed by an unfortunate proximity to in-toxicated young people. It featured an exciting mix of densely populated urban nightmares, sprawling city-states, and idyllic country manors maintained by robots for their absent owners.

There was also at least one underwater metropolis periodically resettled and eventually wrecked and abandoned by people whose philosophical leanings prized rational egoism.

Min brought *La Sirena Negra* down in Tyet-Ruru, one of the city-states, which had been built hundreds of years earlier and then rebuilt as buildings sank or were buried by soft sediment from seasonal flooding. It was split in the center by a winding river whose water looked murky and dense enough to stand on, with one side of the city mostly residential and the other more industrial, including the infamous Sump they were supposed to avoid because it was a bot-fighting hot spot. Looming over the shorter structures was the ivory-painted tower of Evident Academy, their first destination, much to Min's disappointment.

"Who builds a skyscraper in the middle of a place like this?" Eva asked, staring at the awkwardly tall building with its holographic time display rotating around the top.

"Rich people," Pink answered, curling her lip up. "Come on, girl, that ain't even a question."

Eva shrugged and checked her weapons. She didn't expect much trouble from students, even assuming some of them were foolish enough to start something, but she had a feeling she and her crew wouldn't be staying in the parent-approved areas of the city. Especially since Min was so keen to see what the bot fights in The Sump were like.

After some targeted q-net searches by Min, local law enforcement and college database hacking by Vakar, and old-fashioned snooping around by Eva and Pink, they learned a few important things.

First, Lashra Damaal had been through the area at the same time as Josh once again. Commwall ads for the Pod Pals were playing all over campus and in local student hangouts, and apparently Sylfe Company had hired a bunch of brand ambassadors to convince their friends how cool the little robots were. Worse, Damaal and Josh had gone to Evident Academy at the same time, and had apparently run in the same circles dealing with engineering and robotics and, to a lesser extent, venture capitalism.

Second, and infinitely more appealing to Eva since it didn't involve Garilia, a mysterious bot-fighting champion in The Sump had been trashing all their opponents with an unreasonably overpowered bot, and they claimed to have connections to The Fridge, having escaped a huge firefight at a secret facility thanks to their own skill and ingenuity.

"That could be Josh!" Sue said, clapping her hands in excitement when she found out.

"It could be," Eva agreed, but she wasn't so sure. If it was, and if he was being so vocal about escaping from The Fridge, how had no one found him already? Surely that would have been easy enough for Mari to track, and she hadn't mentioned it when Abelgard came up in their conversation. So either this person was lying, they had gotten very lucky, or The Fridge had found them already and gave no shits about getting them back.

At the very least, Eva was hoping it might be one of Josh's mystery companions, who could give them more information about what Josh was up to and where he might have gone next.

If Sue was excited about the prospect of exploring The Sump, Min's eyes practically sparkled.

"Jackpot!" she shouted through the speakers of *La Sirena Negra*, so loud Eva's ears rang. "This is gonna be great. I had friends who started fighting here, and they always said it was the most fun, because you had all these rich college kids who thought they were literally the best, and the looks on their faces when you trashed their fancy bots were like, ahhh. So good." She rushed around getting dressed and brushing her wild blue hair and making Pink plait it into a braid while Mala and a handful of other cats watched, their tails lashing back and forth unhappily.

"No fighting," Eva said. "You know that, right?" She stood in the mess munching on one last snack before departure.

Min wagged her finger at Eva. "Come on, Cap, I don't even have a bot. How would I fight without a bot?"

Sue choked on the tea she had been nursing, coughing profusely. Min rubbed her back absently.

"Take it down a level, Number One," Pink teased. She had splurged on a few snacks at Evercon and was happily demolishing a container of something similar to chicharrones.

"I'm not Number One anymore," Min replied. She smiled wistfully and reached up to fiddle with her braid. "I'm sure nobody remembers me. It was so long ago."

Eva witnessed Min's skills back when she first poached the pilot from the bot pits to come fly *La Sirena Negra* instead. "Number One" earned her name along with her reputation by wrecking every opponent who faced her, with whatever bot she could sync her neural implants with. It had been quite the sight: two hulking metal monstrosities facing off in an area the size of a cargo bay, punching and kicking each other before ramping up to more esoteric weapons like flamethrowers and nanoswords and even a last-ditch energy weapon that Min had rendered utterly useless by the simple act of dodging its beam.

And then the loser tried to kill Min, so Eva stomped his arm to jelly with her gravboot. Unfortunately, he had friends—or, rather, like-minded fighters who were tired of not winning. Eva had already planned to offer Min a temporary job, and Min was genuinely delighted to take it.

Ah, the good old days, for loose definitions of good.

Eva suppressed the urge to tousle Min's carefully arranged

hair. "Plenty of people remember you. Especially the ones whose asses you kicked."

"Maybe." Min's expression brightened. "My friend Yeon-ha will be there. They said they could show us around. We used to call ourselves Team Diva, the times we played in doubles matches."

"No fighting," Eva repeated, with substantially less conviction than before. "We don't want to draw too much attention to ourselves. We get in, we find this mystery champion, and we get out."

Sue nodded, but her thoughtful expression remained, and she kept glancing back toward the cargo bay in a way that made Eva's teeth itch.

The Sump was about what Eva expected for a place named after a nasty waste-collecting pit: dirty and overrated. The streets were littered with trash being slowly corralled by ancient sweeper bots, despite the presence of standard waste recyclers at every intersection. The buildings were clustered together without enough room between them for a rat to squeeze through, and their cheap holosigns flickered when they worked at all. It smelled like body-scenting nanites and hormones and the stale ozone tang of single-user transit pods. There were bars and brothels and, of course, places to buy incredibly cheap dorm furniture that would last longer than you would expect, unless someone decided to go on a bender and start throwing chairs.

It reminded Eva of flight school. But instead of jacked-up people with ships for brains, these were the best and brightest minds the universe had to offer, coming together to solve vital, complex problems like how many orifices could intoxicants be pumped into before medical intervention became necessary.

Not everyone was like that. Some of them built robots to beat the shit out of each other for fun.

Their destination was Medsammensvoren, a massive warehouse with a line of wannabe patrons that extended down the street for at least a block. It looked typical enough from the outside, about three stories tall and painted a bland gray covered in layers of graffiti and various unpleasantly smelly bodily fluids. The walls, however, were insulated to absorb all but the slightest whisper of whatever noise was happening inside, and the bouncer was a todyk nearly as tall as the building, her feathers glossy and her teeth each as big as Eva's hand.

Eva knew how these places worked. The line was for appearances, and no one who was ever going to get in would be standing around waiting. She led her crew straight up to the door, ignoring the protests of the people who had probably been there for ages hoping to get noticed.

"Her friend is inside," Eva said, jerking a thumb at Min.

"Naturally," the todyk said, peering down at Eva with her enormous black eyes. "All of these fine personages also have friends inside." Her small arm waved at the line, making the bystanders laugh.

"Their name is Yeon-ha," Min said, clutching Sue's hand and grinning. "They're a fighter. Their bot is Moonbear."

"How absolutely charming that you're still speaking," the todyk replied, then proceeded to ignore them entirely.

Eva rolled her eyes and leaned closer to Min. "Could you just ping your friend, please?" she asked.

A few minutes later, a person about Min's age came zipping around the side of the building in a green hoverchair. Their black hair was chin-length and straight, their eyeliner was fierce, and they wore the kind of red-and-white cat suit that loosened and tightened with a commlink command for ease of removal.

"Min-jung!" they squealed.

"Yeon-ha!" Min shrieked.

They proceeded to do a wild hand-waving dance at each other while making high-pitched noises. Eva grinned at seeing Min so happy, despite the circumstances. Sue looked confused, and maybe a little sad, though Eva wasn't sure why.

"Come on, let's go, I have to show you my bot," Yeon-ha said, spinning their chair around and taking off as quickly as they had appeared. Min raced after them, and after a moment of surprise, Eva followed, making sure the rest of the crew was close behind her.

Where the line was full of rowdy college students, the alleyway they now moved through was peopled with the types who gave The Sump its reputation. A variety of humanoids loitered about, many in privacy bubbles that left the area eerily silent except for the rustling of clothes or shuffling of feet and other mobility-related appendages. Sometimes items exchanged hands, or threatening gestures were made, but none of it was Eva's business so she didn't look too closely except to gauge whether she needed to be worried. It smelled like inhaled stimulants and synthetic lubricants, with an uncomfortably chewy hint of what Eva assumed was the nearby river. There was less graffiti here, and less garbage, and Eva moved a few centimeters closer to Sue just in case.

The back door to Medsammensvoren was the huge roll-up variety, to allow for bots to get in and out, as well as any todyk bouncers. There was also a smaller entrance, and Yeon-ha led them through it, past clusters of people watching holovids of bot fights projected in front of multiple walls, occasionally shouting with joy or anger at the results. Probably because gambling was involved; Min earned plenty of credits betting on herself back in the day, and so did her boss, which made him cranky when she tried to leave.

Not that Eva had cared, since he'd done nothing to keep Min safe in the first place.

Past the remote gambling matches were various other gaming tables, physical and holographic versions of dice and cards and tiles, and all the other exciting methods a whole universe of people addicted to winning had come up with. Lights flashed, wheels clacked, dealers barked orders, and machines played annoying trills and jangled and otherwise made nuisances of themselves. Sue kept pausing to watch, so Eva grabbed her by the arm and dragged her along so they didn't get lost. Vakar, as always, moved through the crowds and machines with easy grace, and Pink brought up the rear like a jaded teacher taking her kids on a field trip. The smell of stims was stronger, coupled with alcohol and cologne and the usual pheromones from whichever species used them to communicate.

Yeon-ha finally came to a halt in front of another small door, clapping their hands in excitement. "Bots are through here!" they said. "Things are getting set up now, but they should be starting soon."

"When are you fighting?" Min asked, her eyes wide.

"Not until later," Yeon-ha replied. "First it's the little bots, you know, and then the students who think they know what they're doing." They giggled, and Min joined them.

Eva stepped up next to Min and put on her friendliest smile. "This is great, definitely," she said. "But do you know where we can find the infamous champion? We need to talk to them as soon as possible."

Yeon-ha nodded, their lips pressed into a serious pout. "Yes, Min-jung told me. He's very, what is the word . . ."

"Secretive?" Eva supplied. "Intimidating?"

"Irritating," Yeon-ha said. "I want to punch him so much, in his face, as many times as I can until my knuckles hurt." They scowled. "But he's the champion, and Rubin Hjerte likes winning, so nobody can bother him."

"Rubin Hjerte is in charge, I presume," Eva said.

Yeon-ha nodded. "She oversees the fights. It's best not to talk to her. She seems very nice, until she pulls someone's teeth out. She has a large chest of teeth on her desk."

"Qué cosa." Eva blinked, suddenly very aware of her own dental situation. "So let's avoid Rubin Hjerte and go straight for the champion, then. Where would he be?"

"He has his own booth in the back, where he sits with his fans and waits for his turn." Yeon-ha shifted their chair to face Eva directly. "Be careful. You cannot harm him, no matter how much you want to, or you will get hurt. Or lose your teeth."

"Thanks for the warning, but we're tougher than we look." Eva smiled in what she hoped was a reassuring way. "And I can be very polite when I want to be. How hard can it be not to hit one guy?"

The door opened, and Yeon-ha led them into the bot-fighting room. It was huge, encompassing about half the total warehouse space, with a fenced-off area in the middle where the actual fights took place. On the far wall was a stage with a small band fronted by a purple-skinned kloshian, flanked by a white-furred kyatto and an annae that looked more like a walking cactus than a Venus flytrap. They blasted out a high-energy song that the assembled audience generally ignored. A second wall featured a bar, where a many-tentacled bartender with a giant eye was serving up whatever unholy combinations their mass of customers requested, as well as multiple levels of tables and booths that would double as prime seating when the fights started. Along the third wall, another massive door allowed bots to come and go, some walking or rolling or hovering under their owners' control, others waiting on floating pallets until it came time to activate them and put them into service. The fourth wall had apparently been broken recently, huge cracks in its surface patched with long strips of Everseal and painted over quickly and inexpertly.

"The champion sits over there," Yeon-ha said, pointing toward the booths. "He's in the back."

"Min, you can stay with your friend," Eva said. "But if I say we have to leave, we leave, okay?"

Min nodded, then swung away from Eva so fast her braid whipped around. "Yay, okay, so tell me about every single bot here," she told Yeon-ha as they began moving through the crowd toward the fighting area.

Eva briefly debated sending Sue with them, then decided against it, since Sue was liable to get lost immediately. Instead she continued to tow the girl along like a wayward escape pod. Short as she was, she couldn't see over the crowds, relying instead on Vakar's steady movements and Pink's constantly scanning eye along with the occasional tiptoed peep to be sure she hadn't been moved off-course by the currents of people.

As she got closer, a single voice stood out from the rest. It wasn't that it was especially loud, compared to the blaring music and the many other conversations going on simultaneously. But it was, as Yeon-ha had said, incredibly irritating, the kind of voice pitched at just the right register to trigger a fight-or-fight response—as opposed to fight-or-flight. Eva's own words, spoken moments earlier, immediately came back to haunt her, and she closed her eyes and prayed that she had heard wrong even as she continued to approach the person speaking.

Her prayers, as they often did, went unanswered.

"Well, actually," the voice said, and the crowd parted in front of Eva, leaving her face to pale, skinny, intensely punchable face with Miles fucking Erck.

Chapter 7

A NEW CHALLENGER APPEARS

For several long moments, Eva became intimately acquainted with how she assumed Mari felt every time Eva was being exasperating in a conversation. She stared at Miles, sitting in his booth surrounded by hangers-on, his arms draped over the back of the seat in a pose of utter relaxation, his limp blond hair hanging over one half-lidded eye.

How had he even survived? When she left him at the Fridge facility, he was unconscious under a table because she'd knocked him out for being a mouthy comemierda. Presumably he'd awakened with enough time to reach an escape vehicle, or his friend—Emily? Emle?—had managed to drag him to safety. And then he had either escaped on his own, or he was one of Josh's two mystery companions on that whirlwind intergalactic tour.

She forced her breaths to come evenly, in and out of her nose, until she mastered herself enough to plaster on a smile and approach the table.

"Hey, Miles," Eva said in the friendliest tone she could manage. "It's been a while."

Miles looked up at Eva, first with his mouth half-open in confusion, then with a sneer that bordered on lewd. "Captain Innocente," he said. "It's been six months, actually."

"It certainly has." Madre de dios, she thought, her hand curling into a fist.

"I'm surprised you're not dead yet," he continued. "Doesn't Gmaargitz Fedorach still have a bounty on you?"

Eva sensed a dozen sets of ears perking up at the word "bounty." One set belonged to a dark-haired man sitting near Miles, wearing a blue exosuit and a scowl that could curdle milk. He stared at Eva as if his eyes were lasers that could zap her into dust, but his only visible weapon was a large cannon that either covered his right arm or had replaced it. Android? Cyborg? She wasn't sure. The weapon looked familiar, though . . .

"No bounty anymore," Eva said, and the attention died. "Turns out even rich, powerful emperors can only waste so much time and money on one lucky human before their subjects start sharpening the guillotines."

"Well, actually," Miles said, "the gmaarg don't use guillotines. They prefer to feed people to giant worms that are basically living oubliettes." He rubbed his hands together gleefully at the thought.

Eva could feel her smile slipping, so she struggled to slide it back into place. "Miles, just to be completely certain before I continue this conversation: you're the current bot-fighting champion here, is that right?"

"Current, and future," he said smugly.

Behind Eva, Pink groaned loud enough to wake the dead. This was going to be a "secret bourbon stash" kind of day.

"I'm looking for someone you were working with at The Fridge," Eva continued. "Josh Zafone. Do you remember him?"

Sue leaned forward eagerly, peering out from behind Eva.

"Well, actually, I do," Miles said. "I saved his life, you know, when everything was blowing up. We were on the same project. I would tell you about it, but it was highly confidential."

"The Proarkhe artifact, yes," Eva said, relishing the frown that flashed across his features before they returned to his normal resting punchface. "Did you and Josh travel together after you escaped, or did you come straight here, and he passed through later?"

Miles crossed his arms and leaned back. "I don't have to tell you anything. I don't even have to keep talking to you losers." He snapped his fingers. "Nara, get rid of them."

"Nara?" Eva blinked, sure she must have heard him wrong.

From the shadows behind the booth, the hulking form of Nara Sumas emerged. Over two meters tall, in her trademark suit of armor with its smooth black helmet and miniature plasma cannon, Nara was normally employed as an extremely expensive bounty hunter. Eva had first met her on Garilia, then again on *La Sirena Negra* when her dad, Pete, had stolen it briefly, and she'd last seen the merc while dropping her ass off somewhere with the rest of Pete's motley crew after the Fridge facility was destroyed.

Vakar, who had stood by quietly up to this point, managed to become somehow more present despite his Wraith armor rendering him scentless. If it made a difference to Nara, she didn't show it.

"Larsen," Nara said, her voice modulated by the helmet.

"It's Innocente," Eva replied coolly. "Is the economy that bad, that you're slumming it here playing bodyguard for this come-mierda?"

"She isn't his bodyguard." The dark-haired guy next to Miles spoke, climbing out of the booth to stand next to Nara. He wore giant boots over his exosuit, and as she watched, a series of yellow status lights on the side of his arm weapon lit up.

"Well, actually," Miles said, "she's on my team right now, which means she does what I say, or she doesn't get what she came here for." He sneered at the man, who glared right back.

"And what did you come here for?" Eva asked.

"Confidential," Nara replied.

"And none of your business," the other man said.

Sue, who had always been a pro at reading a room, stepped forward then. "Please," she said. "I just want to find my brother. Won't you help me?"

Miles leaned forward eagerly, a weird glint in his eye that made Eva want to slap her forehead. "You're Josh's little sister? He talked about you all the time."

"Uh, yeah," Sue said, backing toward Eva again.

"He said you were even better with bots than he was," Miles continued, his expression predatory.

"I . . . Maybe? He's really good." Sue fidgeted nervously.

Nara and the dark-haired man appeared to have a silent argument, given the way he was staring at her and making faces. Eva wondered about that, and whether she should shut Sue up before something else sensitive slipped out. But this felt like a chance to get Miles to slip up, too, so she let it ride.

"I'll tell you what," Miles said, turning his attention back to Eva and steepling his fingers like a caricature of a holovid villain. "Let's have a little bet, you and me. We'll have a fight in the pit, and if you win, then I'll tell you everything I know about Josh."

Eva was going to punch him. She really, really was, one way or another, and it was going to be better than sex.

"And if you win?" Eva asked.

Miles gestured at Sue. "Then she stays here and upgrades my bot. With my supervision and approval, of course."

"What?" Sue squeaked. "No!"

"For how long?" Eva asked, and Pink made a disgusted sound behind her.

"A month," Miles said.

The silent conference between Nara and the other man seemed to intensify. Eva desperately wished she knew what the hell it was all about, but she had more pressing concerns. She couldn't afford to lose Sue for a month, not when they were trying to find her brother well before that. But could she beat Miles? Was she sure enough to bet Sue on it?

Raising a finger at Miles, Eva turned around to Pink and Sue, leaving Vakar to watch her back. "He is, without a doubt, the biggest sinvergüenza I have ever had to deal with," Eva said. "But he knows something, and we need to know it, too."

Pink shook her head. "Min could probably eat him for breakfast, but she's out of practice and it's risky as hell. We should figure out another way."

"Oh, we need a backup plan regardless," Eva said. "This way we get to beat his ass until he cries like a baby with a dirty diaper."

"Not worth it." Pink paused. "Okay, theoretically worth it, but still. Min doesn't even have a bot."

"Um, yeah, she does," Sue said, and both Eva and Pink looked to her simultaneously.

"What are you—oh no," Eva said, shaking her head. "I know you're not talking about that mess of parts I've been graciously ignoring all over the cargo bay."

Sue's pale face flushed pink, but she frowned and jutted her chin out at Eva. "It works fine, I just like tinkering. I can have it ready to fight in under an hour."

"That wouldn't give Min much time to learn how to control it," Pink said. "But she did manage to get qualified for deep-space jaunts faster than a scared rabbit, so I expect she can handle this."

"And in the meantime, we figure out our contingencies," Eva said. "Sue, are you sure you want to do this?"

Sue's face hardened like her features were setting in concrete. "Yes. It's like you said, he knows something."

Eva squeezed the girl's shoulder and leaned in to whisper in her ear. "If he wins, no way are we leaving you here for a month," she said. "We'll bust you out, okay?"

Sue nodded, raising a clenched fist. "We won't lose."

Pink rolled her eyes but nodded acceptance.

Eva turned back to Miles, unable to conceal her grin. "You have a deal, Erck. Better warn your boss that his champion is about to get spanked by a professional."

"Well, actually," Miles said, "I'm going to win, so I don't have to tell her anything, and also you're not a professional bot fighter." He raised his eyebrows and smirked as if he'd just scored a point and leaned back in his seat again.

Before Eva could respond, one of the people in his booth leaned over and said something to him that made him sigh. "I forgot," Miles said. "Tonight is mixed-team fights. So unless you can find two friends to help you out, the bet is off."

Eva rolled her eyes and turned back to Sue and Pink. "Maybe Min's friend would join up?"

Pink shrugged. "We can ask. But we'd still need a third, and a second if they aren't interested."

"I can fight in Gustavo," Sue said. Eva and Pink started to berate her, but she waved them off. "I can do it. You know I can."

She wasn't wrong; Sue had been a help during several Fridge raids in the past six months. Mostly she set things on fire or had her little yellow bots rush out to mob her opponents, but it worked, and she'd only been injured badly once when she slipped on one of her own bots while standing up inside Gustavo to shoot at someone with a pistol.

"Fine." Eva scripted a quick q-mail message to Min, then pinged her to check it in case Min had turned off her notifications.

The response came back quickly: "Yay I will crush him, Yeon-ha won't fight him sorry" with a crying bunny face picture appended.

"Me cago en diez," Eva said. "We need a third."

Miles must have seen her glum expression, because he laughed, and his laughter spread like a farty methane fire to his companions. "Looks like you've already lost." He spread his legs wide under the table and rested his arms on the back of the booth. "It's too bad. If your bots are anything like your terrible spaceship, they'd fall apart before they even made it to the pit. You probably wouldn't have enough useful pieces left to fit in a suitcase."

Eva opened her mouth to reply, then shut it, a slow smile spreading across her face. "Funny you should mention suitcases. I just remembered I have exactly the one I need. See you later, champion." She flipped off Nara and the black-haired man for good measure before turning around and heading toward the exit.

"What in the blue blazes are you talking about?" Pink asked, once they were far enough away that Miles wouldn't hear them.

Eva's smile widened and she sighed happily. "I'm going to get to punch him myself." She whistled a cheerful tune and held on to that thought for their entire trip back to *La Sirena*

Negra, feeling like she'd found a winning lottery ticket and couldn't wait to cash it in.

Eva and her crew returned to Medsammensvoren later. Although bots were presumably a regular sight in The Sump, theirs still earned a lot of curious looks from the people milling about in the streets. Sue sat inside Gustavo with a bunch of her tiny yellow creations climbing all over her making nervous squealing noises, the rest either waiting on the ship or tucked away into their own secret compartments in the mech. Min had immediately christened her new bot Goyangi and was using it to carry her human body in its arms like a baby, occasionally shifting position for comfort. Fully assembled, it was almost three and a half meters tall, humanoid and bulky and built like a tank.

Eva strolled along happily next to Vakar, who carried a certain stolen briefcase with its bright-red CAUTION tag still intact. His smell was an unpleasant mix of tar, incense, and farts, and he had made clear that he wished she wouldn't use the Protean armor because of its inherent dangers, but they agreed it was their only option if they wanted to engage with Miles on his level.

"The odds of it collapsing in the middle of a fight are, what, tiny," Eva had said.

"Thirteen percent," Vakar had replied.

Eva had paused. "I've had worse."

Pink carried her own case, a doctor's bag full of medigel, bandages, splints, quick-casts, a fresh roll of Everseal with its cheerful Grippy the Seal logo, and the disassembled parts of her sniper rifle, Anthia. At Eva's insistence, she had also included a nanoscalpel and a small pistol, though she had insisted on bringing a range extender for it.

Yeon-ha waited for them at the back door, clapping with glee when they saw Min's bot. "I love it!" they said. "It's so different from Daltokki, but still pink."

"Totally 4D," Min agreed. "I can't wait to hit things with it."

Sue ducked her head shyly at the compliments, hiding in Gustavo more than usual.

They headed for the designated waiting area, the crowds parting to allow them through. Fights had already begun, and an assortment of other bots milled around or rested on transport platforms, or in one case were being put together from a stack of boxes. There were remote-controlled models, like Min's, and mechs like Sue's, but no one else seemed daring—or foolish—enough to opt for Eva's approach. The buzz of conversation was almost louder than the clashing of metal on metal and the discordant music from the band, which was still playing off in the background, and between that and the smells of grease and ozone and soldering fumes, Eva was working on a wicked headache.

"So you finally showed up," Miles said, the crowd parting around him.

Eva's headache immediately intensified. "I know you were hoping I wouldn't, since we're going to kick your ass so hard," she said.

"Well, actually, I can't wait to show you what a real fight looks like." He gestured at Nara and the black-haired man from earlier, who flanked him. "Nara and Jei are going to be on my team, as a little test for them."

"Test?" Eva raised her eyebrow at Nara, whose expression was hidden behind her shiny black armor. Jei frowned but said nothing.

"Not your problem." Miles smirked and made a show of examining Eva and her team. "I only see two fighters here. Where's your third?"

Eva gestured at the briefcase Vakar held. "I'm the third."

"Is that Protean armor?" Miles laughed. "This is going to be fun. You've got a shitty mech, a bot that looks like it was built from scraps, and that death trap. I'm not even going to have to tag in."

Eva didn't dignify his taunting with a response. Let him be surprised when Min beats him like an egg, she thought.

Meanwhile, Sue had climbed out of Gustavo and approached Jei with an awkward smile.

"Hi," she said. "I'm Sue. I really like your arm cannon. Is that modular?"

"Why do you want to know?" Jei asked coldly.

Sue blushed and fiddled with a pocket of her jumpsuit. "Sorry, I was just curious. I didn't mean to—"

"Keep your curiosity to yourself," he said.

Sue's expression fell, and the pink of her cheeks darkened. "Rusty buckets, you don't have to be such a jerk about it."

"You don't have to work for a cowardly murderer, and yet you do," he replied. "So which of us is the 'jerk' then?"

"You are," Min said, stepping in front of Sue, eyes wide with an anger Eva had never seen before. "Eat taffy, you little shit."

Eva's neck heated up, and she turned her full attention to Jei even as he shifted away so that he was clearly ignoring Min and Sue. Did she know him? He didn't look familiar, or rather, he looked like plenty of humans she had met over the years. And she had killed enough people that running into someone with a grudge wasn't unbelievable. But what exactly was he referring to?

Does it matter? she thought. He's not wrong, and you know it, and that's part of the shit sandwich you have to eat every day until you die. So stop whining and start chewing.

"Don't worry about him," Eva said. "We're here to deal with Miles, find out what he knows, and get Josh back."

Sue nodded grimly, narrowing her eyes and clenching her jaw even as Min rubbed her arm. She climbed back into her mech, her tiny bots swarming over her like a personal pit crew, and Eva wished for a moment that someone so sweet had never been dragged into a life like this.

That was life, though, always dragging people around who didn't deserve it.

Min shot one more nasty look at Jei, then perked up. "Okay, team," she said, clapping her hands. "We're slotting in for a special time since there was already a championship fight planned for the end of the night. Yeon-ha says this is modified three-on-three rules, so we have to stay alert, keep an eye on the back line, and move quickly during tag-ins. Got it?"

"Not even slightly," Eva said. "What are the rules?"

Min deflated a little, but recovered. "So it's three of us against three of them," she said. She gestured at the pit as she spoke, pointing at the various bots already inside and engaged in their own battles. "One person from each team fights at a time, but you can swap out whenever you want. Like if you need to make quick repairs or something, so you don't get knocked out."

"Knocked out, as in thrown outside the fighting area?" Sue asked, watching the fight nervously.

"Sometimes," Min said. One of the bots in the pit grabbed another one and ripped its arm off, then whacked it into the translucent energy fence. It fell to the floor and didn't move again.

"Oh," Sue said, slipping slightly lower inside Gustavo.

"The match ends when time is up, or when an entire team is knocked out," Min continued. "If everyone on both teams is still able to fight when the timer goes off, there's a sudden-death round."

"Sudden death?" Sue asked, her face pale as bleached protein powder.

"Sue, por favor," Eva said. "This isn't the first time you've fought worse things that were definitely trying to kill you."

"But this is regulated! And people are watching."

"Sudden death means you go until someone is knocked out," Min interjected. "It's not real death." Behind her, a small bot exploded, spraying parts against the fence. The audience roared.

"Bueno, we hit them until they stop moving and we win," Eva said. "Anything else we need to know?"

Min tapped her cheek thoughtfully. "You can pretty much do what you want, as long as your weapons are street legal. It's good to play to the crowd if you can, so if a referee needs to jump in, they're more likely to be on your side."

"You mean like if someone does that?" Eva asked.

One of the back-row bots had snuck forward and landed a punch on the opponent its teammate was fighting, then jumped back into place as if nothing had happened. The bot on the opposing back row made a petulant squealing noise, and its operator shouted at a man wearing a pink uniform that looked like an old-fashioned karate gi—the referee, presumably. They argued briefly, and the fight stalled, until the referee pointed up and the operator followed his finger.

Leaning over the edge of a balcony was a human with long, blond hair wearing an impressively large black hat and a brass-buttoned jacket cut like a corset at the top. Her right eye was covered by a strip of fabric, while her left was dark, and the expression on her olive-skinned face conveyed the kind of disinterest that would at any moment become interest sharp enough to cut bone.

The bot operator immediately stopped arguing and went back to their place, and the match redoubled in intensity.

"Yeah, so," Min said. "Sometimes you can sneak in a hit from the back line, and it's not technically legal, but if you can get away with it . . ." She shrugged. "We maybe shouldn't, since you're both noobs."

A tinny alarm signaled the end of the match, and what was left of the bots inside was collected by their miserable or triumphant operators. The human on the balcony had retreated, but Eva assumed she was the previously mentioned Rubin Hjerte, given the reactions. Running a tongue over her teeth, Eva considered that maybe she would prefer not to rock the boat here.

Aside from absolutely annihilating Miles Erck as much as humanly possible, of course.

"Our turn," Min said, clapping her hands in excitement. "Let's go!"

Pink grabbed Eva's shoulder and they executed their usual handshake, ending in a hip-bump. "Don't lose a limb," Pink cautioned. "I didn't bring any spares."

Eva winked at her, then turned to Vakar, whose expression was hidden behind his shiny Wraith armor. "Keep an eye on things out here for me," she told him.

"I will use both eyes and all my additional senses," he replied, his voice lower and more gravelly from the helmet's modulator. He handed her the briefcase, which was indeed incredibly heavy, and hugged her gently before releasing her and melting into the crowd like a ghost.

Eva proceeded to the staging area, where Min and Sue were already waiting. The crowd had quieted a bit since the end of the previous match, but were muttering about the new team taking on the champion, and wondering what was going on.

Like Min said, we'd better give them a good show, Eva thought. She opened the briefcase and pressed her hand against the control pad that activated the Protean armor.

After the eerie feeling of being subjected to a full-body scan, the pieces of metal polymer in the briefcase began to slide up

Eva's arm and settle into their appropriate locations. The directions had repeatedly warned that she was not to move during this process or risk injury, so she stood rooted to the spot with her hand in the same place.

Her nose, of course, started to itch immediately.

The larger pieces assembled themselves first: helmet, chest plate, braces, greaves, and so on. These were followed by smaller pieces that filled themselves in between the large ones, and extended at the edges to connect to each other with rigid or flexible materials as needed. Once everything was in place, an unpleasant cold filled the suit as a foam-like insulation was pumped in to plug gaps and provide additional protection from concussive damage. Eva was also wearing her spacesuit underneath, which was itself a form of cheap body armor when rigid, but wasn't an extremely useful defense against things like dismemberment.

Also, her spacesuit didn't have all the exciting upgrades this particular Protean suit had been equipped with. Each of her palms sported a propulsion unit that doubled as a weapon, there were miniature explosive devices in shoulder-mounted compartments that could be launched in the direction she was facing, and she even had a single-shot laser cannon that would swivel from her back to her shoulder with a mental command. She'd also heard of ways to override the suit's power unit to fire a blast of energy from where it was housed in the chest plate.

Of course, all these things could only be used once, since she'd never be able to afford repairs or refills, but it would be worth it to wipe Miles's smug face all over the floor, even if only metaphorically.

The briefcase gave a cheerful ding to indicate the suit was finished assembling, but Eva waited an extra ten-count before moving, just in case. The exterior cams flicked on, and she was suddenly overwhelmed by various visualizations provided by the suit interface. With a stern thought, she turned off everything except the suit status, targeting, and peripheral-threat alarm.

Eva took one tentative step, then another, adjusting to the way the armor fit and moved. It was, as advertised, lightweight, with better mobility in the joints than she expected. She was able to make a fist with minimal difficulty, and her gravboots were exposed at the bottom so she'd be able to use them as normal.

"All right," she told Min, her voice slightly distorted by her helmet. "Let's do this. Who's up first?"

Min tapped her cheek. "Sue should be first," she said. "Best to lead with our second strongest, save strongest for last."

Sue nodded, her expression serious, but Eva chuckled.

"So I'm the worst fighter here?" Eva asked. "Ouch."

"No, Cap, you're great! You're just, not a bot fighter, you know?"

"Sin pena, mija, you're in charge here." Eva's nose started to itch again, and she absolutely refused to dignify her urge to pee with a response.

"So cool," Min said. "Okay, team, show time! Let's play to win!"

Min sat in the remote-operator area, slouching down in one of the provided chairs and making herself comfortable. She'd been jacked into her bot the whole time, and now she sent Goyangi over to wait in the pit, near the fence at the back. Eva walked in after, feeling less graceful than the bot triple her size, but growing more used to the suit with every passing moment. Sue came in last, Gustavo stomping around on its wide, round feet, its spherical green body more adorable than intimidating, despite the skull Sue had painted on the front.

Nara and Jei were already waiting inside, the former in her armor as usual. Jei was still in the same blue exosuit with his arm weapon, but had donned a matching blue helmet, and standing behind him was a bright-red robot that looked like a dog.

"He has one of those Pod Pals," Sue said, leaning over the top of Gustavo to talk to Eva. "It's bigger than it looked in the holovids."

Eva squinted at it and frowned. Where had he gotten that? Garilia? Madre de dios, how was he connected to that whole enredo? Bad enough that Josh and Garilia kept coming up in the same places, but with Nara here, and now this . . .

Her thoughts were immediately squashed as Miles guided his bot into the pit. Eva couldn't help herself: she started laughing, as deep a belly laugh as she could manage in a suit of tactical armor.

Miles's bot was even bigger than Min's, at least four meters tall and humanoid, painted shades of red and purple that she assumed were intended to be menacing. Where Min's was more boxy and stiff-looking, this one had meticulously sculpted muscles like a bodybuilder, from its rippling pectorals to its mountainous biceps, washboard abs to bulging thighs. It wore absurdly large spiked armor on its shoulders, along with spiked gauntlets and boots, but Miles had mercifully restrained himself when it came to the crotch.

Gracias a dios, Eva thought, or I would have peed myself for sure.

With a massive effort of will, Eva told herself not to underestimate him. Miles presumably hadn't gotten to be the champion for no reason, so his bot must have some serious tech. How had he managed it, coming here in secret as a former Fridge scientist turned escapee? Had Josh helped him? If so, why, and why had he left Miles behind? And who was their mystery third companion? That other scientist Emle, or someone else entirely?

Questions aside, even if she was positive that Min was the better fighter, Eva had no idea what to expect from Sue's handiwork, and this was going to be a tough match.

They had to win, though. For Sue, and for The Forge, and maybe even for Josh himself.

But mostly so she could beat the shit out of Miles fucking Erck.

One of the referees stepped up to start the fight, another uniformed human with dark skin and a long red braid. "All bets final now," she said, her voice amplified over the still-chatting crowd. "Grudge match, three-on-three. Your challengers are Team Siren, led by the legendary Number One from the bot pits on Tamna, operating Goyangi."

Whatever they'd been chatting about before, the murmurs of the crowd now took on an excited, occasionally nervous timbre. Eva could practically hear a few hundred people searching the q-net for information on Min, assuming they hadn't done so before they placed their bets. Miles himself didn't react, so either he already knew, or he didn't care.

"The challengers will be opposed by Team Conquest," the referee continued, "led by your reigning champion, Pounder!" Miles made his robot flex for the crowd while Nara and Jei stood impassively next to it.

Eva, meanwhile, once again tried not to pee herself with laughter.

"Three minutes on the clock," the referee said. "First fighter, take your position."

Sue moved forward to the middle of the pit, while Jei did the same, his dog-bot trailing after him. Eva sent up a quick prayer to the Virgin for luck and protection, for the others more than herself, though she'd gladly take a little if there were any to spare.

The referee retreated to safety outside the fence and raised an arm. "Ready? Begin!"

Chapter 8

TAKE YOU FOR A RIDE

Jei and Sue stared at each other for a long moment that turned into several, to the point that the crowd started grumbling. Eva glanced up at the balcony where Hjerte had appeared earlier; it was still mercifully empty. They needed to get things moving, or time would run out and it would be sudden death. She didn't like those odds.

"Forfeit now and spare yourself," Jei said suddenly. "This need not devolve into violence."

Sue peeked out of Gustavo. "Why don't you give up, then?" she shouted back. "If you don't want to fight?"

"I must win," he replied, "for the sake of my own mission."

"Yeah, well, me too." Sue stuck her tongue out and pulled her lower eyelid down with her forefinger.

"So be it, then."

Jei was first to attack, leveling his arm cannon at Sue and firing an energy beam that she barely managed to block, with her shield that Eva was pretty sure had once been a trash recycler lid. Jei charged forward, continuing to fire, even leaping into the air with rocket-assisted boots to shoot down at her from above. Sue blocked, and retreated, and Eva wished she could bite her nails through the gauntlets of her armor because the poor girl really was not equipped for such an all-out assault. Jei was fast and nimble, while Gustavo was slow and bulky, but at least now the crowd was getting into it.

Sue was almost to the fence when Jei leaped back, pausing in his attacks as if to assess what damage he had done already. It seemed mostly cosmetic, scorch marks and dents in the mech's exterior plating. Now that she had a chance, though, Sue took it.

With a fierce scream, she launched Gustavo at Jei, throwing a punch boosted by the rockets in the back of its elbow. Jei dodged, only to get a face full of flamethrower that he barely deflected with his raised arms. Before Jei could do more than stumble backward, Gustavo had stretched its arms out and was spinning them like a helicopter, landing a couple of solid hits that knocked Jei to the floor a few meters away.

"Get up, you worthless sack of meat parts!" Miles shouted from the safety of his controller seat. "You're making me look bad!"

If Jei heard him, he didn't react. Instead he got back on his feet just in time to avoid Gustavo's chainsaw, which bit into the floor, sending up sparks. He backed away and whistled, and suddenly his dog robot was next to him, delivering what looked like an alternate arm weapon. Swapping it in quickly, he pointed it at Sue and launched a metallic projectile that proceeded to ricochet all over the pit, hitting Gustavo repeatedly as Sue ducked inside to avoid being struck. This gave Jei the opportunity to once again strike, until finally Sue had enough.

Poking her head over the lip of the mech, Sue fired something at Jei that Eva couldn't track. It hit, but didn't appear to do any damage, and Jei paused to examine himself in confusion.

"Lunch time!" Sue shouted, and every single one of her tiny bots leaped out of the mech and rushed at Jei, washing over him like a yellow tsunami. Some carried miniature blowtorches, some hammers or screwdrivers, and some wielded random things like lengths of pipe or pieces of hull plating. One of them even had a chancleta that Eva had been looking for and assumed a cat had stolen, despite Mala's sullen refusal to admit guilt.

The bots banged away at Jei as he writhed on the floor, trying to get to his feet. Eva cheered along with the crowd, drawn into the spectacle despite herself.

This is real, and dangerous, she thought. Stay focused.

Jei's dog brought him another weapon, which Jei struggled to swap in as the bots continued their assault. Finally he activated it, and it launched a jet of air that blew away half his tiny attackers. They rolled back toward Sue, who collected some of them with Gustavo's giant hands as others climbed back into their respective places on their own.

"Get him out of there," Miles shouted. "This is embarrassing!"

Nara stepped forward to tag Jei out. He retreated reluctantly, and Eva took that moment to check the timer.

Two minutes left. They needed to start knocking people out, or this might come down to sudden death. She really wanted to avoid that if possible.

"You're doing great, Sue!" Min shouted. "Keep going!"

Nara stood still in her black armor, her own arm weapon aimed at Sue but not firing. Sue approached cautiously, her shield raised, and the hairs on Eva's arms stood up despite the foam pressing them down. When Nara still did nothing, Sue lowered her shield and rushed forward, Gustavo's arm swapping from a fist to a drill.

"Sue, no!" Min shrieked, but it was too late.

Nara hadn't been waiting; she'd been charging her plasma cannon. As soon as Sue was close, Nara fired, an enormous ball of energy that knocked Sue across the whole pit and nearly into the fence. With effort, Sue hauled the mech to its feet and swung the shield up to block the homing missiles that Nara had begun to launch as well.

"Cap, tag in!" Min said.

"Against missiles?" Eva asked, gesturing at Nara, who was now darting forward to attack Gustavo directly.

Min's bot made a shooing gesture, and Eva shrugged. With an assisted boost from her suit's hand-propulsion units, she leaped in front of Sue with her leg already out, landing a kick that scooted Nara back and allowed Sue to retreat. Gustavo now sported a giant black scar across its front, and tiny yellow bots squealed and rushed around putting out fires and making other minute repairs. Sue herself seemed shaken but unharmed, thankfully.

"Annihilate her!" Miles shouted at Nara. Eva rolled her eyes; as if the bounty hunter needed tips from Miles fucking Erck, of all people.

"I can't believe you're fighting for that comemierda," Eva said, her voice amplified by her armor.

"I'm fighting on behalf of my employer," Nara replied, also amplified. "A contract is a contract."

They came together in a crash of metallic polymers, trading punches and kicks, blocking and parrying and dodging with tech-assisted speed but their own skills acquired from years of combat experience. Nara was much taller than Eva, and though her suit was bulkier, she'd had years to become acquainted with it while Eva had only worn the Protean armor this once. All the minute adjustments she had to make to compensate began to add up, and Nara pushed her inexorably toward the fence as Eva defended more than she attacked.

She could practically hear her old boss Tito shouting at her, "Stop using your fists and start using your brain, comemierda!"

Or in this case, Eva thought, my bombs.

Eva fired her palm propulsion units to push Nara back just enough for some breathing room, then launched the explosives from her armor's shoulder compartments. Nara dodged sideways, jumping onto the fence and clinging there for a moment before leaping back toward Eva with her arm weapon already blazing. But Eva was ready with her own surprise: she had swiveled the laser cannon forward from her back, and Nara was unable to avoid its intense beam, taking it square in the chest and flying backward toward the still-recovering Jei in a tumble of sparks.

Unfortunately, that was the only time Eva got to use that particular weapon, so now she was back to just her own fists and feet unless she did something drastic. And she had less than a minute left to win this fight before sudden-death overtime.

Before Nara or Jei could go back in, a murmur swept through the previously cheering crowd. On the balcony over the pit, Rubin Hjerte had appeared, a pitiless expression on her face more or less directed at Miles. She didn't raise a hand or say a single word, but Miles was clearly picking up what she was putting down.

"Step aside, you two," he told Nara and Jei. "Let me show you what a real bot fight looks like."

Eva rolled her eyes, causing a minor hiccup in her tracking display that quickly righted itself.

Miles's bot—Pounder, Eva remembered with a snort—stepped

into the main part of the pit, its huge frame towering over Eva by almost two and a half meters. Its spiked armor, while ridiculous, didn't have any clear gaps that Eva could exploit with the minimal weapons at her disposal. If it were an actual human, as its absurd muscles suggested, she would go for the usual vital organs; but it was a bot, and she knew nothing about its features or technical specs.

Well, as Tito had always said: when in doubt, aim for the head.

Eva ran up to the bot and slid between its legs, barely avoiding an energy blast from its massive hands. Scrambling to her feet, she leaped onto its back with the aid of her palm boosters and proceeded to climb. Before she got high enough, a repulsive force threw her off, sending her flying toward Nara and Jei. The former took the opportunity to throw a few punches at Eva for good measure, dividing her attention when she could least afford it.

Thankfully, Sue also decided to help out, and darted forward to distract Miles with her flamethrower. She moved back quickly, before he could return fire, and the crowd roared approval on both counts.

So much for the noobs staying on the back line.

Eva disengaged from Nara and returned her attention to Pounder. Joints were also a common weak point for bots, so she proceeded to attack its knees in the hopes of damaging one enough to hinder its mobility. With a cruel laugh, the bot launched a series of energy pulses along the floor from one hand, knocking her into the air and allowing it to fire a huge laser at her from its mouth. Eva yelped as the Protean armor attempted to redirect and spread the heat and concussive damage, raising the temperature inside to what would have been deeply uncomfortable if she weren't already wearing her spacesuit underneath.

Landing in an awkward roll, Eva struggled to her feet. She must have hurt something in her chest, because while her body wanted to suck in big lungfuls of air from her exertions, her ribs objected with a jagged pain that left her breathless. Her armor was also unhappy, throwing small but insistent status notifications in front of her face that suggested its structural integrity wouldn't survive another hit like that one.

"Feel free to tag in, Number One," Eva shouted.

"Hold him off for a little longer, Cap," Min said. "I'm studying his form." She'd pressed herself up against the fence around the pit, her lips pursed thoughtfully.

"You're going to be studying my dead body in a minute," Eva muttered. She assumed a fighting stance as Miles made Pounder pose for the screaming crowd, flexing as if its muscles were real instead of cables and carbon fiber.

Bueno, keep using your brain, then, Eva thought.

The bot had at least one weapon in each hand, another in its eyes, possibly more it hadn't used yet. It was definitely slower than she was, so if she could keep moving, she might be able to dodge the worst of its attacks. . .

Just as Pounder flexed its biceps yet again, Eva used her palm boosters to give herself extra height and jumped toward the fence. She pushed herself off and flew up toward the bot, latching onto its arm just above the gauntlet that appeared to house one of its weapons. Activating her boosters, she grabbed the arm and triggered the propulsion units, hoping they had enough juice to burn through and do some damage.

Pounder tried to shake her off, but she clung tightly, and her efforts were rewarded by a shower of sparks from the arm she was attacking. The hand was still intact, but hopefully its weapon would no longer be functional.

Eva had to time her next attack carefully or risk losing some limbs. Before the other hand could grab her or knock her off, she swung her legs up and activated her gravboots, which stuck to the bot's helmet. Using the rest of her momentum, she curled her body up, ignoring the pain in her ribs, and grasped the lower part of the helmet's visor, trying to get her palms into position to burn away its eye weapons.

This time, she couldn't make it, and she had to deactivate her boots and push off to avoid being caught by Pounder's other huge hand. She executed an aerial backflip that would have made Tito proud, then landed hard on one foot and stumbled backward, skidding to a stop on her butt. The crowd laughed, and she waved as if she'd meant to do that, eliciting a ragged cheer that did little to ease the pain in her ribs.

"This ends now," Miles said, raising an arm dramatically, and Pounder advanced on Eva with its eyes glowing red as dying suns.

"Min, a little help here!" Eva shouted.

Sue responded instead, tearing a piece of the floor up with her mech's hands and throwing it at Pounder. It hit the bot square in the chest, but did little apparent damage, and Miles gave a gloating chuckle.

"Is that the best you can do?" he asked.

Eva shrugged and settled into a fighting stance once again, gesturing for Miles to come at her. Her suit protested weakly, and she turned the alarm sounds off, ignoring the other flashing indicators that suggested she had indeed done her best and should stage a strategic retreat.

"Showtime," Min said suddenly. Her bot, Goyangi, straightened to its full height, running through a quick series of stretches in which its arms and legs extended past their normal range, then pointed at Pounder. "Game face: on. Number One, ready for combat."

The timer rang out the end of the match. The referee returned, and over the cheers and jeers of the crowd, she coolly announced, "All combatants remain active. Sudden-death round initiated. First team to achieve a total knockout wins."

Eva hadn't even noticed how long the fight had gone on, given how much she was being pummeled. She backed up to the fence around the pit and glared at Min. Not that the pilot could see her expression inside the Protean armor.

"Min, qué coño?" she asked. "We're already beat-up. If you don't take Miles out now, estamos singado."

Min grinned and flashed a victory sign at Eva. "I've got this, Cap." To Miles, she shouted, "Prepare to get owned, noob!"

"Well, actually, if you fight like your captain, you're the one getting owned," Miles said. Pounder posed dramatically again, and Eva stifled a groan.

"Cap's not a bot fighter," Min said, slowly advancing her bot into the center of the pit. "But I am. And Pounder is about to get pounded."

Eva glanced up at the balcony, where Hjerte still stood, arms crossed, her expression flat and distant. A winged todyk, its feathers red as rubies, approached and told her something. The corners of her lips rose in a smile that gave Eva a chill.

They needed to win, and they needed to do it without pissing off the boss. Eva ran her tongue over her teeth and wished her suit had come equipped with stims as well as explosives.

"Ready?" the referee asked. "Begin!"

Min launched Goyangi toward Pounder immediately, her speed boosted by rockets Sue had installed in the bot's shoulder blades and calves. She landed a flurry of punches that drove Pounder back several steps, despite their half-meter size difference. Pounder attempted to retaliate with its hand weapon, but

Eva had apparently damaged it more than Miles realized, and it sparked uselessly instead of firing.

Goyangi leaned on its fists and kicked at Pounder with both legs together, the limbs stretching so that the bot was still just out of reach even as its strikes connected. For the first time, Pounder raised a shield, its shimmering gold energy like a modified version of a spaceship deflector.

That meant Miles was worried. And if he was worried, they had a chance.

As soon as the shield disappeared and Pounder raised its undamaged arm to attack, Goyangi's forearm plating retracted, exposing tiny missiles that Min fired toward her opponent. They exploded harmlessly against the shield, but in the haze of smoke they created, Goyangi once again leaped forward and struck. Step by step, meter by meter, Pounder retreated under the onslaught, and Eva cheered with the crowd, especially reveling in the extremely pissed expression Miles wore on his pale, rage-blotched face.

"Are you even trying?" Min asked, her bot leaping into the air and kicking down at Pounder, its leg stretching just over the upper edge of the shielding to hit the other bot square in the head.

"Well, actually, this isn't even my final form!" Miles snapped, and with a roar, Pounder ripped its own helmet off to show a chrome-colored skull with sharp teeth and pointed fangs descending from its cheekbones. Its eyes shifted from red to a bright magenta-purple that Eva found eerily familiar, just before it fired a pair of eye lasers at Goyangi that burned twin holes through its chest plating.

Mierda, mojón y porquería. Eva's heart would have stopped if it wasn't mechanical.

The crowd roared, bloodthirsty and savage, and the band on the stage played a rousing, boisterous riff as if to punctuate the decisive strike.

Min's bot staggered back, but immediately leaped forward again. This apparently confused Miles, who must have been expecting more of a retreat, so he was entirely unprepared when Goyangi grabbed Pounder and loosed a shock of electricity that lanced through the bot's systems, sending up more sparks from its busted arm.

"Jódete, cabrón!" Eva shouted, even though the fight wasn't over. Min had to win. They couldn't afford to fail.

Pounder shuddered but didn't fall, instead using the same repulsive force it had on Eva to push Goyangi away. But Min's bot had extendable arms and legs, and it landed a flurry of hits even as it was shifted backward.

Eva's sensors alerted her to movement on the back line. Jei, positioning himself to fire at Min, and even Nara angling for a shot from another direction.

"Not a chance, sinvergüenzas," Eva said. "Sue, hit them with your bots!"

Sue noticed what was happening and nodded, firing her strange pistol at both the fighters. With a shrill order, her tiny robots rushed across the pit and leaped onto Jei and Nara both, harrying them in ways that were more annoying than destructive. One bot covered Nara's optical sensors with what looked like a tablecloth—where the hell had it gotten one of those?—while another was waving a frying pan around wildly without actually hitting anything.

This distracted Miles, apparently, because he shouted, "Hey, where's the ref?" and gestured angrily with his bot toward the altercations.

The referee looked up at the balcony where Hjerte stood

impassively. She didn't uncross her arms, didn't move, simply stood like a frozen hologram and waited.

"No penalty," the referee said. The crowd roared, whether in anger or approval, Eva couldn't tell.

Min, certainly, was smiling like a cat who'd gotten a tin of fish. Miles raged, stalking back and forth from his controller position and tugging at his thin blond hair until finally he settled in a wide-legged stance, hands curled into fists.

"This ends now!" he shouted. Pounder's shield sprang up, and the bot charged forward, knocking into Goyangi like a battering ram. Min's bot slid backward, and Pounder's shields dropped as it fired its eye lasers once again.

Except Goyangi wasn't in their path. It had leaped into the air, boosted by its elbow and calf rockets.

Time seemed to slow. Pounder began to raise its arm to strike, but Goyangi was faster. A series of lasers coalesced in a point in front of the bot, forming a force field like a shimmering pink pyramid just in front of its arm. It dove down onto Pounder, the pyramid rotating like a drill, and the force of it drove Pounder into the floor, pieces of its armor peeling away to expose the cables and other anatomy beneath.

Miles screamed, in anger rather than despair. "Worthless thing is lagging!" he shouted. Pounder attempted to stand, but Goyangi gazed down at it in the pitiless way only a robot could manage. Or Hjerte, apparently.

"Aw, you're trying so hard," Min said with a giggle.

Goyangi opened its mouth and fired a blast of energy straight into Pounder's exposed face. It must have hit something vital, because moments later there was a burst of light, then smoke began to pour out of Pounder's eye sockets. The bot hitched once, then lay still, tiny sparks of electricity arcing up from the hole in its formerly fake-buff stomach.

The crowd flipped out like someone had thrown a chair, drowning out the band with their screams and roars and whistles and other assorted sounds. Eva assumed the angrier ones had lost bets and were preparing to take out their feelings in unproductive ways, but the rest of the crowd was living.

"Match complete," the referee said, her voice amplified barely loud enough to be heard. "Your new champion is Number One, piloting Goyangi!"

Sue climbed out of Gustavo and rushed at Eva, hugging her in excitement. "We did it!" she shouted. "We won!"

Goyangi began to dance, waving its arms and spinning in place. Min did her own shimmy in her seat, grinning and shaking her blue-braided head to a music only she could hear. This elicited more cheers from the audience, and a few other people danced as well. The band finally started to become audible once again, and the bar was mobbed so thoroughly that additional bots were deployed to handle orders while the many-tentacled bartender prepared as many drinks as they could manage.

Doors in the fence around the pit opened, allowing the fighters and bots to exit. Miles didn't even bother to check on Pounder; he immediately began shouting at Nara and Jei, jabbing his finger at them accusatorially. Jei frowned, his skin a shade paler than it had been, and Nara stood impassively as usual, her expression hidden by her helmet.

Eva looked up at the balcony where Hjerte had stood. It was empty. A chill ran down her back and she hoped that didn't mean what she thought it did.

((Cover me,)) she pinged at Vakar and Pink. To Sue, she said, "Stay with Min. I'm going to chat with our friend Miles."

Sue began to protest, but Eva silenced her with a gesture and stalked across the pit. Her armor was still sending up grumpy status signals, but at least it wasn't freezing, and she suspected she might need the protection for a few more minutes.

Nara noticed her approach and moved into a defensive position, while Jei simply scowled. Miles was too up his own ass to even see her.

"Hey, Erck," she said, interrupting his foamy-mouthed rant. "Time to settle up. You said you'd tell us about Josh if we won, so start talking."

Miles glared at her as if his own eyes could shoot lasers. "Well, actually," he said, "I don't have to tell you anything."

"Oh, you resingado cabrón hijo de la gran mierda." Eva considered whether she could make it around Nara to punch him in his actual face, but in her suit she would probably end up breaking his jaw. And then he wouldn't be able to talk even if she wanted him to.

"You made an agreement," Jei said, his face slack with shock. Eva pitied him for a moment, but she was too pissed to hold on to any other emotions for long.

"Well, actually, I didn't sign anything," Miles retorted. "And I don't care. She can't make me do it."

"Would you have honored our agreement if we had won?" Jei asked.

Miles shrugged. "You lost, so it doesn't matter. I'm not going anywhere with you two."

So that was their deal. Where had they planned to take Miles? And why? She didn't think they were working for The Fridge; if they were, they would have just grabbed him and left.

"You're as bad as her," Jei said, gesturing at Eva.

"Who the fuck are you, even?" Eva asked, then she raised a hand. "No, you know what, I don't care." To Miles, she said, "I'd threaten to give you a concussion, but you don't have a functioning brain to damage. Talk or I'll kick your ass so hard you'll need a pit crew to help you shit."

Before Miles could choke out more than "Well, actually," a pair of buasyr loomed behind him, carrying multiple stun batons among their four sets of arms.

"Rubin Hjerte wants to speak with you," one of them said. "All of you."

Eva glanced up at the still-empty balcony. "Does she now," Eva replied. She quickly pinged Vakar and Pink with ((Stay close)) before moving to follow the guard.

Miles, to his credit, didn't say anything at all.

Chapter 9

CONTINUE

The two buasyr escorted them up a back elevator to a room with no balcony, and only one visible exit. It was furnished comfortably enough: chairs in various shapes to accommodate multiple physiologies, a gleaming metallic table where light refreshments had been laid out, even a holovid display that currently showed the pit. Pounder was being hauled away by uniformed attendants as the next group of fighters took their places.

Miles stared at the feed sullenly, but then he'd been doing everything sullenly for the past few minutes. Jei's brow was furrowed, but otherwise he wasn't reacting. Nara was Nara; her expression was unreadable inside her armor, which she hadn't taken off.

Min and Sue had been rounded up as well, their smiling faces falling into nervous frowns as they clung to each other's hands.

Min tugged a braid while Sue bit her lip, glancing around like her head was on a swivel.

Eva considered whether she might retract her helmet to sample the food, but decided against it. She did ping her location to Vakar and Pink in case they weren't already tracking her.

No response. The room was probably shielded somehow. That didn't bode well.

After exactly four minutes of stony silence, the door opened and Rubin Hjerte stepped into the room. Her coat reached the tops of her boots, and a hooked weapon hung from a chain on her hip. She stood about a hand taller than Eva, which was middling height for a human, but the sheer force of her personality made her seem like she was looking down on everyone else. It was a trick Eva had never been able to master, and one she envied deeply.

Following after her were the red todyk Eva had seen earlier, and to her surprise, a familiar face.

"Baldessare?" Eva blurted out. "What are you doing here?"

Captain Orlando Baldessare was a kloshian, his face a network of scars that made Eva's look mild by comparison. He wore a long coat, his hairlike tendrils white and kept long as well, and she had last seen him in the brig of a starship several galaxies away when he tried to kidnap an opera singer for his own amusement.

Eva had not been amused. Also, she had gotten kidnapped by The Fridge shortly after, so she wasn't super into the whole kidnapping concept in the first place.

Captain Baldessare stared at her, unblinking. "Do I know you?" he asked.

"I guess not," Eva muttered. She was wearing a helmet that obscured her face, of course, but that didn't mean he'd recognize her without it.

Rubin Hjerte ignored their interaction, turning her attention to Miles. "Miles, my boy," she said, her voice carrying the lilt of an accent Eva couldn't place. "You assured me this would be an entertaining fight, but that you had no possible chance of losing."

"Well, actually, it's not my fault," Miles said bitterly. "These two were worthless, and I was having connection issues with Pounder for some reason."

Jei and Nara didn't dignify his bullshit with a response. Good for them, Eva thought.

Hjerte wandered over to the table, grabbing a grapelike magenta globe and popping it into her mouth. "A good leader takes responsibility for their crew's success or failure," she said.

"Well, actually—"

"Speak again and I'll have your teeth for my chest," Hjerte said, as mildly as if she'd mentioned the weather was cool. Mercifully, Miles obeyed, despite clearly still fuming and outraged at his own perceived victimhood.

"Captain Eva Innocente," Hjerte continued, now directing her piercing gaze at Eva.

"Present," Eva replied, keeping her posture and expression neutral.

"I allowed this grudge match despite, or perhaps because of, your reputations." Hjerte ate another globe, chewing thoughtfully. "Number One has been absent from the pits for several years, but her matches were quite impressive. It was a pleasure to watch her fight."

Min inched closer to Sue, eyes wide.

Eva inclined her head. "The compliment is appreciated, I'm sure. I hope we didn't cause you too much trouble."

"I earned more than I paid out," Hjerte said. "I always do, or I'd be a poor excuse for an entrepreneur. One of the prop bets was particularly lucrative, thanks to you."

"Prop bets?" Eva asked.

"Bets on specific events occurring within the match." Hjerte's lips turned up in the ghost of a smile that vanished quickly. "It was expected that Pounder would knock you out by tossing you over the fence. He's done so before, with smaller bots. And some large ones as well."

Eva thought of the damaged wall outside and winced internally.

"My problem is not financial," Hjerte continued. "My problem is that you've damaged my champion's bot, and his credibility, when he is meant to be fighting the main match of the night in a few hours."

"I see." Eva pursed her lips. "And is there a solution to this problem?"

"That is what we're here to discuss."

Eva traded glances with Min and Sue, who had plastered on stoic expressions despite clearly being scared. They'd been in worse spots, but they were both usually surrounded by a few tons of metal or more, not exposed as they were here. It was usually Eva doing all the physical work of their rough lives, and she felt a pang of regret for dragging them into this in the first place.

((You there?)) she pinged at Pink and Vakar, but still no response.

"Why don't you let the winner fight in place of your former champion tonight?" Captain Baldessare said, gesturing at Min. "She could marshal the rest of his usual team, or all three of these fine ladies could return."

"Insufficient," Hjerte replied. "I need a longer commitment from Number One. She's my new champion by rights, and I'll have her until she's not a champion anymore."

"And the rest of us?" Eva asked.

"That's your own business."

Min's terrified expression told Eva all she needed to know about what the pilot thought of the offer. She moved closer to Min and Sue, standing in front of them protectively.

"Sorry, but no deal," Eva said. "Number One isn't interested, and we've got our own mission to complete. We wouldn't even have fought in the first place if Erck hadn't been such an unreasonable mojón de mierda, so take it up with him if you have a problem."

Hjerte smiled again, so slightly, the smile of someone who was unaccustomed to being spoken to in a particular way and whose preferred reaction was swift and merciless. And involving teeth, according to Min's friend.

"Mr. Erck will be dealt with," Hjerte said. "And I'm afraid you've misunderstood the situation. Your pilot will remain here, and you will be escorted back to your ship, with or without violence, depending."

Eva squinted. "Depending on what?"

"Whether I am inclined to be violent."

The buasyr guards in the room activated their stun batons, which whined to life. Eva had fought similar people and weapons before, but the odds weren't her favorite, especially if she had to protect Min and Sue at the same time. She also had no idea whether other hidden defenses in the room would intervene if she acted. And her injuries still hurt a hell of a lot from her recent pounding, pun intended.

She'd have to leave Min here and figure out how to bust her out later. Assuming Hjerte decided to let them go peacefully after all. Not the best circumstances, but que será, será.

((Play along,)) she pinged at Min.

((Okay,)) Min replied. At least pings were working inside the room.

Eva raised her hands in defeat. "I guess we don't have a choice, then. I'd definitely like to keep my teeth. Sorry, Min."

Min nodded stoically. "I'll do my best, Cap."

"With your permission, we'll return for her when her term is finished?" Eva asked.

Hjerte shrugged. "We'll see what unfolds."

"Wait a tick," Captain Baldessare said. "Innocente. I do remember you." He grinned, exposing pointed teeth as the scars on his face bunched up. "You were in the brig on *Justified Confidence*, with me and Captain Sakai. The legendary smuggler."

Eva rolled her eyes. Of course now his memory would suddenly improve.

"I saw the holovids later, you know," he continued amiably. "Captain Sakai and I met for dinner at a lovely place on Theta Lomi 3. They had something called a lobster, and I had—"

"That's great," Eva said. "I'm glad the two of you hit it off. I hope the holovids were exciting."

He wagged his head. "I was delightfully dashing, as one might expect. You, however . . . no wonder the head of security isolated you and your companion. I had not realized at the time how many truateg mercenaries you personally handled."

Hjerte's smile disappeared again. She pinned Eva with her gaze, and it took every ounce of self-control Eva possessed not to squirm.

"Is that so," Hjerte said. The buasyr guards stepped closer, stun batons humming.

"Whatever happened to your companion?" Captain Baldessare asked. "You two seemed quite attached to each other."

((Take cover,)) Vakar pinged, his timing impeccable as always.

"Ask him yourself," Eva said, and dove under the table, dragging Min and Sue with her.

The side of the building crumpled inward, sending pieces of the walls flying into the room. A ship hovered beyond the newly created hole, brown-hulled and small enough that it was likely a local cruiser with no FTL capability. A door opened near the bottom and a ramp extended out, until it was a few meters away from where Eva crouched. Pink appeared in the doorway, firing her scoped pistol wildly into the cloud of dust.

"That's my podship!" Captain Baldessare shouted, his voice half-choked by debris.

"Gracias, muy amable," Eva said, hustling Sue and Min up the ramp.

Hjerte's chain weapon wrapped around Eva's arm, jerking her away from the ship. Eva immediately shifted to grab the chain, pulling back with the enhanced strength of her Protean armor even as her chest sang with pain.

Hjerte didn't budge. Probably wearing her own enhancements under the coat, Eva thought. They played a silent tug of war briefly, Eva's armor straining to maintain its force.

"I'll have that bot fighter," Hjerte said. "She's wasted on you." A shot from Pink bounced harmlessly away a few centimeters from her face.

"Eat a bag of teeth," Eva said, and activated her palm propulsion units. Within moments the chain melted away, and she threw the hook at Hjerte, who ducked sideways.

A quick glance told her that Miles was gone, along with Nara and Jei. She thought she saw a hint of armored fingers slipping over the edge of the hole in the wall, and cursed inwardly. Now she'd never be able to beat the information about Josh out of that comemierda.

A problem for another time. First, she had to escape. Eva raced up the ramp into the waiting ship as Pink continued to provide cover fire.

As soon as she was inside, the door closed and the ship accelerated away from the warehouse. The interior was absurdly lush, all handcrafted paneling and curves instead of corners, with its own private bar along one wall and a purple sofa-like bed, or bed-like sofa; Eva couldn't decide which, but its purpose was easy to guess. There was even a full-sensory memvid kit tucked into its own alcove, and an array of what Eva was prepared to politely call "toys" arranged in a display case, both within reach of the sofa-bed.

Eva didn't stop to get comfortable, instead barging into the cockpit where Vakar was piloting the pleasure vessel. There was only one seat, so she stood behind him and gripped the back of it while she swayed with the motion of their flight.

"Thanks for the rescue, hero," she said, patting his arm with her still-gauntleted hand.

"I apologize for the delay," he replied.

"You had to hack their commwall, steal a ship, find us, and bust us out. As far as I'm concerned, I'm lucky I still have all my teeth."

"I also retrieved the robot and mech from where they were being sequestered." Vakar paused. "Were your calcified jaw structures in peril?"

Eva grinned. "You have no idea. Let's get the hell out of here."

They flew toward the spaceport, the spire of Evident Academy piercing the sky like a gleaming ivory horn, and Eva wondered what the hell they were going to do next, now that their only lead had fallen through.

Vakar ditched the stolen ship at the spaceport, after which Min reconnected to *La Sirena Negra* and they left Abelgard as quickly as her drives could manage. Sue was overjoyed at seeing her mech again, though she seemed even more pleased that Goyangi more or less belonged to Min now. Still, she immediately set herself up in the cargo bay and began repairing the damage to both units, with help from her squad of tiny yellow bots and with the cats diligently pretending to ignore her. Min hovered around her, chattering excitedly about their victory.

Eva, meanwhile, under Pink's supervision and with Vakar hovering nearby, had grabbed the briefcase for the Protean armor and attempted to follow the instructions for taking it off. After placing her hand in the appropriate position and issuing the mental command, she waited, as unmoving as possible so the suit wouldn't liquefy her organs or whatever.

"Error 13," the suit said, as well as popping up a visual message on the HUD. "Command failure."

"Qué coño?" Eva muttered, repeating the command. The same error message occurred.

"What?" Pink asked. "What happened?"

"It's not working." Eva tried one more time, with the same result. Vakar smelled like tar and incense.

"Hey, Cap," Min asked. "Where are we headed?"

Eva huffed in exasperation. "Stay in the system for now. Pink and I need to talk it over."

Pink peered into the optical cameras of the suit as if she could see inside. "Any news from your mama?"

"Nada." Eva went through her q-mail one more time, but there was nothing waiting from her mom. There also hadn't been a voice message with any more information about Josh's trail. She tried calling again, but all she got was a generic "Please leave your name and briefly describe the reason for your call," at which point she hung up because she didn't feel like talking to another machine.

"Error 13," the suit quietly insisted. "Command failure."

"I heard you the first time," Eva snapped. "Me cago en la mierda."

"You will have to remove the suit manually," Vakar said, his smell intensifying.

"Claro que sí, mi vida," Eva retorted. "Pero no quiero empezarme con esta puñeta—"

"Maybe we should go to Garilia," Sue said.

Sue hadn't spoken loudly, but her words seemed to echo in the cargo bay as if she'd shouted them. Eva stiffened, her shoulders hunching involuntarily as she turned to face the engineer.

"No," Eva said.

Sue flipped the faceplate of her welding helmet open, her brow furrowed. "Why not?"

"Why would we?" Eva asked, but she wasn't a fool. Her mind had already spun the same web of connections that Sue proceeded to tick off, but she distracted herself by opening the file with the manual armor-removal instructions and beginning to scroll through them.

"Well, everywhere we've gone so far, that Pod Pals company was doing stuff at the same time Josh was there," Sue said, gesturing with her soldering gun.

"The same could be said about *Crash Sisters*, and that was a bust," Eva retorted. A pair of cats twined around her ankles and she shooed them away.

"Leroy didn't go to Abelgard," Pink reminded her. Eva scowled, not that anyone could see it under the armor. She continued perusing the instructions, which were apparently in a language that didn't translate fluidly to any of the ones she spoke fluently. She had a feeling "disconnect elbow with wrench" wasn't entirely accurate.

"The person in charge of that company went to Evident Academy with Josh, too," Sue continued. "So they knew each other. I don't think he knew your friend Leroy or anyone else in *Crash Sisters*."

Their new villain for the season was a xana, Eva remembered, to her chagrin. Leroy had said there was talk of product promotion, hadn't he? For the Pod Pals?

Ball Buddies, she thought, chuckling inwardly despite the rising sense of anxiety making her neck hot and spreading to the rest of her body. Another cat rubbed against her boot, its soothing empathy attempting to counter Eva's surge of emotion.

"It's the only lead we have," Pink said quietly. She laid a hand on Eva's shoulder and Eva shrugged it off.

"No," Eva said, more forcefully. "Garilia is cycles from the nearest Gate, and we don't have time to go chasing after another dead end."

Sue's faceplate fell and she propped it back up. "Maybe we could try to contact that president person? What was her name?"

"Lashra Damaal," Vakar said. Eva wished for a moment that his memory wasn't so good.

"If she's president of some big company, we're not going to be able to just send her a q-mail and get a straight answer," Eva said. "She's probably got ten layers of software and underpaid employees sorting through whatever goes to her public account." She scrolled back to the start of the armor instructions and tried to read them again, not that she was retaining a single word.

"I may be able to locate a private address," Vakar said. "Min may also have some methods to—"

"Can we just not!" Eva exclaimed. The silence that fell in the cargo bay was broken only by the low rumble of a dozen cats purring simultaneously.

"Do you have other ideas?" Pink asked, her eyebrows rising

even as she crossed her arms over her chest. Vakar had started to smell a bit minty; Eva hated that he was getting anxious over this.

"We go back to Abelgard and find Miles Erck," Eva said. "We make him tell us what he knows, then we airlock him for the good of the universe and go from there." Her suit's error blinked at her again, and she wished she could rip the whole helmet off at once to be rid of the damn thing. With her luck, it would take her face off with it.

"And if we can't find him?" Pink asked. "Last I saw, he was getting hustled out of there by Nara Sumas and her new friend. What if he isn't even on Abelgard anymore? Or if we do find him and he won't talk? Because we both know he's a slimy piece of rotten egg. Or if he talks and his information doesn't help, then what?"

"We'll figure that out when we get there."

"Eva, stop building your escape pod while the ship is on fire and think ahead." Pink shook her head. "If you want to try going back down to Abelgard, fine. We're already here. But if we come up empty, and you don't get another lead from your mama, we need to work with what we've got."

Eva could feel the walls closing in around her. "I've got to get out of this fucking suit," she said. The Protean armor became twice as oppressive, her breath coming in tense inhalations that didn't seem to fill her lungs, made worse by the injuries she'd already sustained to her rib cage. She leaned forward and rested her hands on her thighs, eyes closed, desperately wishing she could run somewhere, anywhere else in that moment.

"Error 13," the suit repeated. "Command failure."

The purring of the cats intensified, and waves of calm washed over her, but her mental beach was all rocks and broken glass. Instead of being soothed, she was drowning, and it took every scrap of self-control she possessed to stay above water.

"All right," Pink said, suddenly next to her. Eva hadn't even seen her move. "You're going to the med bay now. If you argue, Vakar is carrying your stubborn ass."

Eva didn't argue.

The med bay was always clean, Pink's many tools and gadgets and supplies tucked away into cabinets or other storage containers. A new remote-imaging device had been attached to the ceiling once Pink started her q-net practice, but otherwise it was the same room it had been since they started flying together on *La Sirena Negra* over eight years earlier.

After Garilia.

Eva lay quietly on the examination table as Pink and Vakar determined how to get the Protean armor off. She stayed quiet as they flushed the suit with a solvent to dissolve the protective insulation inside, as they slowly and carefully disassembled the exterior components one at a time in the order described in the manual. Bit by bit, piece by piece, Eva was freed from the confines of the protective layers, but she was also exposed. Unmasked.

By the time the helmet was fully removed, the last of the parts packed away into the briefcase, Eva had more or less calmed down. Except it wasn't so much peace as it was exhaustion, a mere absence of her earlier agitation instead of the presence of positive feelings in its place.

When Pink finally spoke, Eva flinched, then blushed in shame that she'd been distant enough from her surroundings to be so taken by surprise.

"Vakar, would you mind?" Pink asked.

Vakar smelled uncertain for a moment, then shrugged in the quennian equivalent of a nod and left the room, the scent of incense trailing after him. As the door to the med bay closed, Pink turned her attention back to Eva, flipping up her eye patch to let her cybernetic eye do its work.

"You have a few bruised ribs and other minor injuries, and that solvent is gonna leave a rash, but you were lucky as hell." Pink's nose wrinkled. "Bot fights are fine when there's no one inside, but that was reckless."

"When have I ever been reckful?" Eva asked, the corners of her lips turning up when Pink snorted. They both fell into a thoughtful silence as Pink tended to her injuries.

"You wanna talk?" Pink asked quietly.

Eva sighed. "Do I have a choice?"

"You know I'm not gonna twist your arm, hon."

Eva stared into the dark sphere of the holovid projector, its glassy surface reflecting a distorted image of the room, including her own tight-jawed face. Pink waited, applying the appropriate creams and bandages and otherwise letting Eva take the time she needed to get her head together.

"Are you sure Nara took Miles?" Eva asked.

"I watched her do it myself," Pink said. "Dragged him through that hole in the wall like a cat with a naughty kitten."

Eva winced as Pink tagged her with a shot. "I could ask my dad for Nara's contact info. She might—"

"She's a bounty hunter," Pink interrupted, gentle but chiding. "If Miles was her target, she's not going to turn him over to you. She probably won't even take your call, and she'll trash your q-mail faster than we can jump through a Gate."

"We could try."

"We could," Pink said, laying her jet injector on the counter. "Or we could go to Garilia."

Eva closed her eyes, willing them to stop filling up with tears like she was a baby who needed a nap.

"I don't want to go back," she said finally. She aimed at a firm tone, but it sounded strained even to her ears.

"I know," Pink said.

"It's three cycles to get there, and to get back. If it's another dead end, then we've wasted six cycles, which is almost half the time they gave us to find this guy, and it's already been a week."

Pink pulled off her gloves and tossed them into the recycler. "Floating around in the black with no leads isn't any better, is it?"

"We could look for more leads while we floated," Eva said.

"We could do that while we fly to Garilia," Pink countered. "And if we did find something, we could haul ass back, or call Mari and let her do her own damn job while we stuck to our plan."

Eva exhaled, shoulders sagging in defeat. "Yeah. You're right."

"I know, and you knew that before you opened your damn mouth." Pink leaned back against the counter and flipped her eye patch down. "Have you told anyone else about Garilia?"

Eva shook her head, unable to speak.

"Not even Vakar?"

Eva shook her head again. Her fingers moved to her cheek of their own volition, tracing the scar there, the ridges and raised tissue, slowly fading over time as her skin replaced itself but never completely disappearing.

The thing about scars was, they stayed with you. You could almost forget they were there, but then you'd catch a glimpse of them while taking off your pants, or rubbing expired pain gel on a new bruise, or god forbid while looking at your face in the mirror to be sure it wouldn't worry your crew. Sometimes they itched. Sometimes they burned. Sometimes they got stuck like a bad seam of sealant, and they'd stretch the skin around them until you thought you'd tear a new hole in yourself just doing something normal like holstering your gun.

Scars were your body's way of reminding you how you fucked up. And once a thing was well and truly fucked, there was no unfucking it. All you could do was hope the scar would fade over time. That you learned from your mistake so you wouldn't fuck up again.

Eva had a lot of scars. Garilia was the worst of them.

"I think you should," Pink said. "Tell them, I mean. Get it off your chest."

It was all Eva could do to choke out a hoarse "No. I can't."

Pink raised her hands, palms out. "I know. I was there. And I didn't approve of what you did, regardless of what you knew or didn't know, but I'm still here, aren't I?"

Eva hid her face. "I don't deserve you. I never have."

"Hey." A dark finger tucked under Eva's chin and raised her head so that Pink's eye met hers. "I told you before. You don't get to decide that."

That didn't make Eva feel any better. If anything, it made her feel worse, that someone knew the darkest part of her and stayed anyway. Because she probably wouldn't have been so understanding if the situation were reversed. She would be full of righteous indignation like a ship whose fuel was topped off and ready to burn for a month straight.

"You tell the truth," Pink continued, "and you let other people make their own choices, and you live with the consequences. You give them what Pete and Tito didn't give you that day."

She released Eva's chin, and Eva dropped her gaze again, to the scuffed flooring that no longer held a polish, that should probably have been replaced but that didn't seem to bother Pink, either.

"You're right," Eva said again, her voice just above a whisper. Then, louder, "Do you ever get tired of being right?"

Pink smirked. "It's like using a muscle; gets easy the more you do it."

Eva stared at her gravboots, at her hands, at the place inside her mind where she locked away her memories of that day because otherwise she'd never stop shaking. She had always been good at compartmentalizing, at rationalizing her choices, until the day she hadn't. Garilia was where her life had ended, and started, and even though she'd done things she regretted since then—she'd blown up an entire gmaarg fathership, for fuck's sake—she'd never gone back to being the Eva who pulled the trigger that won a revolution. Or lost it, depending on whose side you were on.

"Let's get everyone in the mess," Eva said. "Might as well get this over with."

Pink rested a hand on Eva's arm. "You sure you don't want to take a minute?"

Eva shook her head and stood, swiping at her eyes with the back of her hand. They were surprisingly dry.

"No time to waste," Eva said. "We've got shit to do."

Chapter 10

THE INCIDENT AT GARILIA

So," Eva said, once everyone had settled in the mess. No one had gotten food, or drinks, though Pink handed Eva a cup of water and a pair of pills once she sat down. They all stared at her expectantly, and she took a shaky breath, flattening her palms against the top of the table.

Mala jumped up in front of her, startling her into sitting back in her chair. With a smug rattle of her tail, Mala climbed into Eva's lap and began kneading her thighs.

"Is everything okay?" Sue blurted out. "Are we in trouble? Are we still looking for Josh?"

Eva half smiled at Sue, whose face was blotchy from crying. "We're looking, and we're going to find him. Min has already started flying us toward Garilia."

Sue sat lower in her seat, as if she had deflated slightly from relief.

"Before we get there," Eva said slowly, "I need to tell you all about something that happened . . . Something I did on Garilia. It may make things easier for us there, or harder. I don't know. But you may not like me very much by the end of this story, and if you want us to drop you off somewhere, I'll understand. Even you, Min." She glanced at the pilot, who had moved her human body to the room to join them, possibly under orders from Pink.

"Not likely, Cap," Min replied. Sue, however, had paled, glancing at Pink, who leaned back in her own seat with her arms crossed.

Vakar smelled like someone had crashed into a perfume store. Tar, incense, ozone, vanilla, rosewater, mint, licorice; he was all kinds of worried and unsure of what to expect, but with an underlying anticipation that told Eva he'd never dug into this with all his Wraith tools and skills. He'd respected her privacy this whole time, even as she had respected his when he first joined their crew.

He'd almost left her once because she lied to him. She hoped this wouldn't be a similar situation, even if she didn't deserve him.

Eva's hand began stroking Mala's soft, smooth fur, almost of its own volition. Mala purred, and Eva snorted as she remembered something her father had said once: you were never alone as long as you had a cat.

"So," Eva repeated, gathering her courage. "Once upon a time, there was a mercenary who thought she was hot shit."

Garilia was a BOFA-Defended Emergent Ethno-Zone for Non-contributing Undeveloped Technological Species, which was a fancy way of saying it was a planet discovered by the Benevolent Organization of Federated Astrostates before anyone else.

Standard procedure was to maintain surveillance until particular conditions were met, then make first contact and offer no-strings-attached protected status, then eventually allow the planet to join BOFA as a junior member with economic incentives but no voting privileges, and so on.

By the time Eva got there, they'd been under protected status for almost thirty years, during which time the various cultures and their respective political coalitions had scrambled to put together a unified central government, in order to cohesively negotiate with BOFA and the rest of the suddenly reachable universe.

This had not worked out well.

Back then, Pete Larsen, Eva's father, oversaw a sprawling syndicate of various enterprises of dubious legality with his perfectly lawful spaceship-selling operation as its hub. Smuggling was the least objectionable rung on the ladder of criminal severity, but it could be among the most dangerous; that was where Eva and her fellow mercs came in, under the command of incorrigibly competent asshole Tito Santiago.

As far as Eva had known, their task on Garilia was simple: ensure the cargo of the SS *Yamamoto* reached its destination. Tito had briefed them on the challenges, namely that they were landing in the middle of a rebellion and might have to protect the cargo while fighting their way through to the recipients. The terrain at the drop point was loosely termed forested, with trees the size of skyscrapers whose crowns spread out for hundreds of meters, their branches falling like thick cables halfway to the ground, each leaf the size of an average human. Local buildings were constructed on or between branches, with cable cars or ziplines connecting them to each other. The native sentient species was the xana, who were as susceptible to standard weapons as most people, and whose psychic abilities were intra-species and thus deemed irrelevant.

Tito had a bad habit of deeming things irrelevant when they might have mattered to someone who wasn't him.

When they landed, a pitched battle was already in progress. Later, they would learn that the world government forces had located the main rebel encampment and launched an offensive, which had pushed the rebels to accelerate their plans to complete their total takeover of the planet's capital city, Rilia. When they arrived, the rebels were on the run, more or less, pursued by innumerable soldiers from one branch to the next, their own number dwindling as they struggled to survive.

But Tito's squad were professionals, and they got the job done as long as the pay was good and the danger was surmountable. They located their missing contact, bunkering in a cramped structure in the next tree over from where they had touched down. Between them were clusters of government fighters and the companion animals they called Attuned, some gliding back and forth between branches, others in sniper positions above the rebels, still others setting up complex webs of some sticky substance to restrict movement to particular pathways and airspaces.

All Tito and his people had to do was get through the line, deliver the cargo, and get back to their ship.

Tito informed them that taking out one particular leader of the government fighters would make their job much easier, might even halt the fighting altogether for a while if they were lucky. For the purpose of the mission, she was code named "Mother," and while her location was uncertain, the rebels thought she might be in a section of the tree they'd been unable to reach since they were pinned down.

So Tito's mercs split into three groups. The A Squad was tasked with getting through to the rebels while safeguarding the cargo, while the B Squad was sent to find and eliminate Mother. The C Squad stayed back at the ship in case anyone needed to be extracted quickly.

Tito led the A Squad. Eva led the B Squad. Pink was on the C Squad. None of them were especially worried, as they'd seen worse situations and made it out just fine.

A Squad was hampered by the terrain more than expected; the buildings were translucent and only partially resistant to projectile weaponry, so the squad had to rely on finicky personal shielding rather than structural cover. The government fighters were quick, agile, well camouflaged by the tree, and able to move between branches much more easily than Tito and the others, especially given the restrictive webbing. Their companion Attuned made it even more difficult, striking without warning and retreating into the leaves.

It was like fighting angry psychic ghosts, someone said later.

More like giant flying squirrels, Tito had said, but then he'd always been a little racist.

Meanwhile, Eva and the rest of B Squad followed a circuitous route behind the body of fighters, up and down through the branches to where Mother was expected to be, trying to maintain a low profile so they wouldn't be noticed. There were several buildings where the xana leader could have been stationed, assuming she was even indoors rather than on some open platform behind a giant leaf, or moving between branches along one of the many ziplines, or even traveling up and down in one of the cable cars to get a better view of the conflict.

All their speculation was absurd in retrospect, and could have been avoided if Tito had told them everything he knew.

The things he deemed irrelevant. But he hadn't, and so they proceeded.

B Squad was ambushed by a half dozen xana and their Attuned, working with a cohesion Eva had never seen in her years as a merc. It was like they had rehearsed a carefully choreographed dance for weeks and were simply following the steps, while Eva and her comrades tried in vain to learn it as they went. Their shots met empty air, and in close quarters each of them seemed to find themselves facing multiple foes at a time despite their numbers being even.

One of them managed to knock Eva's helmet off with a weapon like a sharpened spoon, and their Attuned tore her face open with its claws, but she had no time to deal with it in the moment, even as the hot blood ran down into the collar of her armor. There were too many of them, and they were winning, and she hated being a loser.

Eva was as short-tempered as ever back then, but she wasn't a fool. She knew they wouldn't last if they stuck to standard tactics. So she did what she was good at.

She burned it all down.

The fires Eva set were fast, and they were hot, and they sent up clouds of toxic black smoke that obscured the canopy and sky above. The soldiers who had been so focused on her squad shifted to engage in emergency evacuations of that branch and the others around it. Because one of the things Tito hadn't told her, in his infinite wisdom, was that this combat zone was full of civilians.

To her knowledge, they all escaped. The redirection of soldiers and deployment of other local first responders, coupled with appropriate infrastructure, meant the xana weren't entirely unprepared. But they had to cut through the branch to save the tree, and when its massive bulk fell like the tendril of some impossibly huge beast, Eva felt the first stirrings of a sense that this mission was going even more wrong than she realized.

Still, she had a goal: find and eliminate Mother. And while the fires burned, while Tito's crew made their own slow forward progress, Eva returned her squad to their task.

They climbed, and they climbed. The closer they got to the sky, the brighter it became as the layers of leaves decreased. More widespread evacuations had also occurred, because the buildings they passed were all empty, their brightly colored walls and floors translucent and showing only the shapes of furnishings inside. Whether the people had fled or been taken, Eva didn't know, but she pressed on until looking down made her dizzy, and looking up made her angry. Everything smelled green and alive, and she was there to kill, and a seed of doubt that had been planted at some unknown point in her past began to grow faster and faster.

They found Mother on a platform near the top of the canopy. There were no barriers to stop her from falling over the edge, as if she were unconcerned by such things. Eva wasn't entirely sure it was her, except that she was surrounded by other xana who knelt in front of her, pressing their small horns against the edge of her tail one after another. Then they would rise and leave, as if she had issued silent orders and they were eager to follow.

As stealthy as they'd been, B Squad's presence didn't go unnoticed. Soldiers appeared, first in pairs, then in larger groups, until they had no hope of survival, much less success. But Eva had a job to do, and she hadn't come so far to fail now.

She and her comrades huddled in an isosphere as Eva assembled her sniper rifle. There were five rounds in her magazine, but she doubted she would have time to take more than two shots before the xana reached her.

As it turned out, she needed only one.

Eva aimed, letting the scope's targeting systems guide her. The shimmering pearlescent isosphere was deactivated, and she pulled the trigger. The boom came moments later, after the shot had already hit its target, after the recoil had wrenched Eva's shoulder, sore from climbing.

Mother fell over the side of the platform, and as she did, every single xana who had been attacking them fell as well.

Eva had seen meat-puppet soldiers in action, mostly in holovids, but also once on the ground in a far-off war that had not a damn thing to do with her, except she was delivering something to the troops. In the middle of accepting her cargo, the soldier had suddenly frozen, then turned and marched over to the barracks like he'd been possessed. He'd shouted an apology at her as he went, because even though he had to go where he was told, do what he was made to do by his controller, he still retained some basic functions.

As it turned out, one of the things Tito had failed to tell Eva, beyond the civilian presence, was the extent of the psychic abilities the xana possessed. They could mind-link with each other, and by so doing create a neural network that let them share thoughts more quickly than other forms of communication. It meant they could operate as a single unit, a creature with many hands and feet, a tree with many branches.

But if you killed the brain, the rest of the body died with it.

When C Squad arrived to attempt an extraction, Eva was staring down the barrel of a miniature plasma cannon, attached to the arm of a certain Nara Sumas, whom she later learned had been hired by the planetary government to find the rebel leaders and eliminate them. They were surrounded by the corpses of xana soldiers, and Eva was still trying to figure out exactly what had happened, because the scope of it was more than she could handle after being so sure of her own imminent demise.

Nara, in her terse way, explained. Eva didn't believe her. It wasn't until Tito arrived, wearing his smug sinvergüenza face, congratulating her for a successful mission, that she realized he had known all along what would happen.

The rebel leader proclaimed Eva the Hero of Garilia that day, but quietly, in the belly of *Yamamoto* as Pink was tending to her wounds. The revolution had been successful, and a new age of peace and enlightenment would carry his people proudly forth into the wider universe.

Peace. Eva could hardly believe someone like him could use the word without his pants spontaneously combusting.

She had asked him how many people she'd killed, and he had seemed surprised by the question. As if he hadn't expected she might care.

He told her, and she nodded and thanked him. And when he left, Eva screamed and cursed and cried until her voice was gone, until Pink finally sedated her so she would rest.

Within a week, she and Pink were on *Minnow*, newly christened *La Sirena Negra*, and Eva swore she'd never speak to her father or Tito again.

Funny how things worked out.

Eva stared down at the table, unable to look at her crew after she finished her story. She'd told it haltingly, doubling back and repeating details, trailing off and picking back up, because it wasn't a story she had ever told anyone before and the words were slow in coming. No one spoke, though a few times Sue gasped quietly, unable to stop herself. Eva didn't blame her.

The thing she most dreaded now was their reactions. Because no matter what, they would hurt. If her crew were angry, upset, ready to bail out, she would understand, but she would be devastated to see them go. If they were kind, though, it was almost worse. Because she didn't deserve kindness. She didn't deserve sympathy. All she deserved was scorn.

"You don't have to say anything," Eva said. "I'm here if you want to, obviously, but you can talk to Pink instead." If you don't want to talk to me ever again, she thought. If you don't feel safe or comfortable anymore. If you think I'm a fucking monster, because I am.

"Wow," Min said finally. "Wow."

Eva didn't have a response to that, so she stayed quiet. Sue didn't say anything, either, as if her earlier comments about people thinking they were doing good had crashed into an asteroid, and all that was left of her optimism was twisted metal and chunks of rock.

Vakar, though. When his smell hit her, Eva closed her eyes in a vain effort to keep the tears in them from leaking out.

Cigarettes and fire and rust. He was upset, and angry, and in pain, and how could she blame him? What did you do when you found out your partner was not just a killer, but a mass murderer? And one of them would ask, one of them had to ask, because even though Eva hadn't come out and said it—

"How many?" Sue asked, her voice small and hesitant.

Eva swallowed spit, as if it would help the dryness of her throat and mouth.

"Three hundred and nineteen," Eva said.

"Wow," Min said again. "That's a lot."

Is it worse than killing one person? Eva thought. Philosophers tended to focus on questions of life, of whether it was better to save one person or a dozen, a hundred, a million. How many lives would be a reasonable trade for one, and so on. But death? That was the domain of statistics.

In statistics, every person was a number, and numbers didn't kiss their kids before tucking them in, or bring their partners presents on anniversaries, or laugh or sing or dance or do any of the shit that people did. Numbers just added up, and up, and up.

And none of those numbers ever got to see the local star rise above that massive tree again, the light gleaming through the colorful walls of their homes and workplaces and stores, glinting off the leaves, turning the branches and vines a warm, burnished copper. None of them got to fly up into space, explore the universe, touch down on other planets with different stars and different trees.

They were dead, and Eva wasn't, and that would never be good or just, no matter what she might do to atone. And she'd done precious little beyond hiding from her guilt, running away from it, and trying not to be the same kind of person who would turn someone else into a statistic.

Even so, she hadn't left violence behind. She told herself that now she only did it for a good reason, but was there ever a good reason?

"It wasn't your fault, though," Sue said finally. "If you didn't know—"

"That's not how fault works," Eva said. "What matters is the outcome, not the intention."

"Right, but—"

"But nothing." Eva slammed a fist on the table and looked up at Sue, who recoiled like a kicked puppy. "I did it. I can't take it back. I can't undo it. And I . . ." Her lips trembled as she struggled to keep from sobbing. "Even if I'd known, in that moment, I probably would have done it anyway. To save my own life, and my squad. If I had to do it now to save all of you, I'm not sure I'd hesitate."

The room fell silent again, a silence that stretched and grew like a bubble waiting for a sharp edge to pop it. Eva nearly held her breath, for fear that it would be intrusive.

A sound interrupted. Mala, purring like an engine in Eva's lap, her claws digging into the flesh of Eva's thighs.

Another purr joined that one, then another. All of the cats had at some point snuck into the mess, and were clustered around Eva's chair as if it were the most normal thing in the universe. A sea of furry faces looked up at her, their eyes eerily intelligent as always, but none of them seemed to be trying to hypnotize her or manipulate her emotions—not psychically, anyway. They just sat around her and rumbled gently, their tails neatly curled around their bodies and resting on their paws.

Her tears fell, then, finally. She refused to let herself sob, throttled every urge to run back to her room and hide; she simply sat there, like the cats, in the mess of the ship that had helped her start a new life when she probably should have died on Garilia. She sat with the people who had come to mean so much to her that it ached like the sum of every injury she'd ever had all at once. Not for the first time, she considered that maybe they would all be better off without her. That the universe, the grandest statistical experiment of them all, wouldn't register her loss as even a fraction of a percent, but that it would nonetheless shift the average goodness that much higher.

That, in itself, was a kind of egocentricity that had made Pink roll her eyes more than once.

And it was Pink who snorted and spoke first. "Sure, y'all would be sympathetic, you bunch of predators. Get out of here before you start shedding on the food."

They ignored her, as if they were perfectly aware that there was no food to be seen.

Vakar, meanwhile, continued to smell conflicted. Eva didn't dare look at him, because she was afraid of what she would see. This was bigger than anything else they'd ever kept from each other, bigger than him hiding his past as a Wraith to join her crew, bigger than her being a reformed criminal with delusions of morality.

"So, Cap," Min said hesitantly, "are we going to have trouble, you know, landing or whatever when we get there?"

Eva shook her head. "I doubt it. I was Beni Larsen back then, on a whole other ship with a different crew and a doctored bio-signature. As far as they know, Eva Innocente is a completely separate person, and *La Sirena Negra* is just a simple cargo-delivery vessel."

"And they probably won't recognize me," Pink said. "The rebels had their own problems to worry about, and I was busy tending to our people who'd gotten busted up in the fight. I was just a field medic." She squeezed Eva's shoulder for a moment, the briefest of touches.

Still supporting her, as usual. Pink was the backbone of the ship, and Eva was deeply aware of how much work she did, physically and emotionally, for every single person on the crew. Without her, Eva would have burned out almost immediately, like a comet flying straight into the heart of a star. Without her, Leroy would have kept struggling to stay clean and out of trouble. Min would have withdrawn fully into the ship and her virtual worlds—not the worst fate, all told—and Vakar would have kept to himself in the bowels of the ship, quiet and unassuming and secretly hurting in ways he never told anyone.

"You are," Eva said, with an intensity that surprised her, "way more than just a field medic."

Pink chuckled. "I'm also more than a black woman, and a trans woman, and a daughter, and a sister, and a lot of other things. It's nice to hear it from you, though." She raised a hand, as if sensing Eva's shift in position. "Don't hug me. Let's finish this meeting and get back to our own bullshits. My therapy appointment is today, and I definitely don't want to miss it."

"Right." Eva inhaled and exhaled slowly as she gathered her thoughts, still extremely conscious of the fact that Vakar hadn't said anything.

Before she could continue, Min interrupted. "Oh, Cap, you're getting a call. On the emergency frequency. I think it's your mom?"

A brief rush of hope flooded Eva's veins. "Finally," she said. "Maybe she'll have something else we can work with."

"Or something that confirms we should be going to Garilia after all," Pink added.

"Right. Send it to my bunk." She gently placed Mala on the floor and stood, finally looking over at Vakar.

He was staring at the table, now smelling like farts and acrid incense. Eva wanted to say something to him, to reach out and touch him, to beg him to touch her, but fear held her back and she swallowed the feelings threatening to choke her.

"We'll continue this in a few minutes," she said. "Stand by."

This time, the call included visual, and Regina's head and torso floated in front of the closet in Eva's cabin, her face already fixed in a half-frown. Her mother sat in her kitchen, the yellow paint bright and cheerful, and Eva knew if the perspective shifted a bit to the left she would see the same white curtains covered in lemons that had hung there for over twenty years.

For her part, she hoped her mom wouldn't notice she'd been crying.

"I haven't been able to find anything else," Regina said, after the barest of greetings. "Your friend's brother seems to have stopped using their family's account at some point after he reached Abelgard."

Eva's hope vanished like a fart on a breeze. "No te preocupes, Mamita," Eva said. "I appreciate you checking, really. You've helped so much already."

"Bueno, y ahora qué? Maybe you should try contacting the police, por si las moscas."

"Ay, no, por favor." Eva shook her head for emphasis. "We have one other lead we're checking out, and if that doesn't work, we'll try something else."

"And is there anything else I can do?" Regina asked.

Eva shrugged, giving her mom as kind a smile as she could manage after what she'd just been through in the mess.

"Nada, nada, limonada," Eva replied. "I know you've got a new big-deal job, pero there's only so much an auditor can do. Now it's up to me and my crew and a whole lot of flying de aquí a Casa Carajo."

Regina's already-frowning expression grew more pinched, her eyebrows narrowing as her lips thinned. "Oye, Eva-Benita, escúchame bien. I don't know if you think I'm a fool or what, but I looked up your friend. She's a criminal, mija, and something suspicious is going on with everyone in that family."

Mierda, mojón y porquería. Of course her mom wouldn't just do what Eva had asked. She'd always been such a metiche.

Eva could feel her anger rising despite how exhausted she was, or perhaps because of it.

"Sue is my engineer and I trust her," Eva said. "She's a good person, and I—"

"Good people don't rob banks," Regina snapped. "Did she tell you about that?"

"Yes, Mami, she did." Eva resisted the urge to flop backward onto her bed, instead sitting up straighter and staring directly at her mother's eyes. "She had her reasons, and she—"

"Ay, no me diga, reasons," Regina said scornfully. "Your father had all the reasons for doing what he did, y mira lo que pasó. And you, going off to work for him, and ending up doing who knows what." She reached for something, which turned out to be a glass that Eva assumed was a gin and tonic. Her mom was nothing if not consistent, and Eva knew then that any further argument would be pointless.

Not that it would stop Eva, because she was as stubborn as a goat.

"I should never have let you go with that cabrón sinvergüenza," Regina continued, after sipping her drink. "I should have stopped you before you ruined your life."

"My life isn't ruined," Eva said, though after telling the story of Garilia in the mess, part of her wasn't entirely on board with that assessment. "Anyway, this is nothing like that. And I'm a grown woman; I can make my own life choices. No fastidies tanto."

"You're the one who asked me to help!" Regina shouted.

"Fine, coño, gracias y adiós!" Eva shouted back.

"Espérate," Regina said, raising the hand holding the drink to stop Eva before she could disconnect the call. "I don't know where you're going, pero I'm leaving on a business trip. Así que, if you need anything else from me—"

"Don't worry, I won't," Eva snapped.

"Fine. Jódete, malcriada. Que te vaya bien." And with that, the holovid vanished, leaving Eva to stare at her closet and fume in silence.

This was why she and her mother had never gotten along. They always fed into each other's anger, like they were a pair of incendiary devices, both simultaneously starting fires and getting set off by them. And they each knew how to push the other's buttons, knew exactly what to say and how to say it for maximum damage.

And after all that, they still had to go to Garilia. Eva wilted as the rage drained out of her, and she allowed herself to flop back into the bed and stare at the ceiling.

A quiet knock interrupted her thoughts. She opened the door with a mental command, and there stood Vakar, smelling like a cloud of anxiety and remorse.

"We must talk," he said.

Eva suddenly, strongly, wished she had a drink of her own. "Of course. Okay. Come in."

He stepped inside and the door closed behind him. Eva waited quietly, nervously, wondering if he could smell the vinegary sweat she was probably covered in. As usual, she broke down first.

"I'm sorry I didn't—"

"This is not about Garilia," he said. "I have received communications from my superiors. They are reassigning me."

Eva's stomach flipped as if the ship's gravity had stopped working. Her mouth opened and closed like the fish's in the tank behind her. They'd talked about the possibility before, but to have it happen now, of all times . . . She had hoped that, maybe, even knowing what she had done on Garilia, that they could still . . . That nothing would change. But she'd always been good at lying to herself, better even than lying to other people. This was one more example of how lying was a shitty option and created more problems than it solved.

And yet if you had kept lying, maybe he wouldn't be leaving, she thought.

No, that was bullshit. It would have come up eventually, and then what? This, but later, and worse.

His annoyed smell intensified, but with an unexpected undercurrent: licorice. Eva hadn't realized she was staring at the floor, but she looked up at him then, fighting the same feelings of hope that she'd had when her mother called.

"Eva, I did not come in here to inform you that I was leaving," Vakar said. "I wanted to discuss how to convince my superiors to allow me to stay."

"Oh," Eva said, her voice small even to her own ears. The rush of relief she felt was soon dwarfed by guilt, and disgust for feeling relieved when she knew she didn't deserve to keep him to herself. "Are you sure?" she asked.

"Yes," he replied. He hesitated for a moment. "There is more I wish to discuss with you, about your . . . experience on Garilia, but this is urgent."

Eva nodded, her throat tight with a host of emotions she wasn't about to untangle.

Taking that as a cue, Vakar sat next to her on her bed, the smell of his annoyance giving way to relief and pensiveness. "I would like to relay to them that I am trailing a former Fridge agent," Vakar said. "One who escaped from the main facility and may be in possession of data from their experiments. I believe that will more than convince them to allow me to continue on our intended course."

Eva kicked her sluggish brain until it started working again. "Right. Okay. If you tell them about Josh, they would probably make the connection between him and Sue, which could make your case stronger or weaker, depending."

"Indeed. I could omit the specific information regarding the identity of my target, but that may be perceived as suspicious and lead to further questions."

Eva nodded, scratching her head. "The thing is, we need to get Josh out of there and deliver him to my sister. So whatever we tell your people, ideally, won't make them want him for questioning instead."

Vakar's smell gained a dark edge. "They may request that I eliminate him, depending on the nature and extent of the intelligence he provides."

Eva winced. "Definitely can't have that." She flopped backward so she could stare at her fish tank above her bed while she thought. Vakar began to run a claw up and down her leg, until she finally lifted her head to frown at him.

"I can't concentrate with you doing that," she said.

"My apologies, I had not even noticed." He stopped, but his bashful smell sapped any annoyance she'd been feeling right out.

"Thank you," she said. "Not for that, I mean. You know."

"I know."

Eva sat up and hugged him, and he wrapped his arms around her in return, and they sat quietly in her licorice-smelling cabin, sorting things out together for as long as it took.

Chapter 11

CATCHING UP

Garilia was the paradise of islands that Eva remembered from her first approach so many years earlier, several large clusters of green amid vast oceans of teal and darker blue that hearkened back to the Earth she had seen in still pictures and flat movies, the one scientists were working to bring back via careful terraforming. Its cities and towns were spread out, many of them hardly visible because they were constructed among forests of huge trees whose canopies extended like vast umbrellas to hide what lay beneath. Others floated on the top of the water, and still others were cut into the sides of mountains, and one even sat on a series of icebergs that had been lashed together to travel as a group.

Their destination, Spectrum City, was a new offshoot of the capital, Rilia. Several of its buildings rose to the same height as the trees nearby, and mimicked them in other ways as well. They featured the same kinds of canopies and branches, broad tops with falling cables made of some incredibly strong material, the buildings attached to them or stretching between. But instead of solid trunks covered in overlapping layers of colored bark, the core pillars were also buildings, translucent skyscrapers in brilliant geometric patterns of red and green and gold, the interiors almost entirely visible to anyone passing by.

And many people were passing by, because the whole series of structures was connected by various bridges and ziplines and cable cars that moved laterally as well as between levels. The xana wore harnesses with anchors that could quickly attach to a line and allow them to safely traverse short or long distances through the open air. Small vehicles floated between: the local equivalent of hoverbikes and larger transport pods, sometimes stretching out a tendril that attached to an existing line and let the rider coast up or down among the other individual gliders.

There were also the native creatures, though it seemed like fewer of them were interested in climbing or flitting about than Eva remembered from Rilia. They were likely Attuned, the companions of the xana, who had psychic links between them that were different from the ones xana could create with each other. They could communicate, at least in a rudimentary way given the animals weren't fully sapient, and they could share emotions empathically to facilitate this communication.

Anything else they might be able to do wasn't widely known, though Eva was sure of one thing: the Attuned didn't die when their xana did.

She knew that much from experience.

They touched down in the city's spaceport, a vast facility atop the crown of a fake tree, made from the same translucent colored materials as the other buildings but arranged to look like a set of wings catching the wind. It was crowded with small pleasure ships and the shuttles from the cruisers full of tourists that waited in orbit far above, with cargo vessels like *La Sirena Negra* herded into a separate area away from the delicate senses of the leisure class. The planetary customs authorities gave her ship's credentials no trouble whatsoever, to Eva's surprise and relief, and within a few minutes her crew was fully geared up and ready to go.

Eva wasn't ready, emotionally speaking, but she didn't think she ever would be. But she'd taken her meds and done her breathing exercises and was not about to let the worst fucking day of her life keep her from doing what needed to be done.

They were going to find Josh, and find him here, and that was that.

Everyone gathered in the mess before disembarking, for one last review of the plan. Pink also insisted they all eat something, because Min had checked out the local food situation and apparently the tourist economy had led to special tourist pricing.

"So, here's the story," Eva said. "The rebels are still in control—guess I should just call them the government now. It's a communist structure, more or less. Lashra Damaal is technically a government employee, and the company she runs that makes the Ball Buddies—"

"Pod Pals, for heaven's sake," Pink interjected. She was inhaling a plate of beans, greens, and fried things with a speed only mothers and on-call medics could manage. Eva tried to steal a bite but Pink smacked her fork away.

"Fine, the Pod Pals. Sylfe Company is ostensibly owned and operated by the people of Garilia. Damaal also fills some other government roles that I'm not entirely clear on yet, stuff about cultural ambassadorship, for one." Eva scowled. "And I'm hoping it's a translator malfunction, but she's also got a title along the lines of 'Supreme Executive of the Enhanced Community Outreach Program' that sounds like the cabrón comités all over again." She poked at her rice and black beans, which were still slightly too hot to eat.

"The what?" Sue asked, her brow furrowing. "Committees?"

"Snitches," Eva said, curling her lip in a snarl. "Have to make sure your little revolution doesn't start its own counterrebellion. But hey, maybe these folks are just checking to see that every neighborhood is happy and healthy instead of rounding up political prisoners for fun and profit."

"Eva," Pink said, her tone a warning. Eva nodded even as she rolled her eyes.

"Right, so, the plan," Eva said. "Vakar, you're going to—"

"Infiltrate the local networks and attempt to determine whether there is any trace of a Joshua Zafone," Vakar said. He munched on a stack of nutrient cubes, their smell and texture similar to a mild cheese, and washed it down with a plant-based shake.

"Pink?"

"Pop into a medical center and see if they need help," Pink said. "With all these tourists, they could probably use someone with broad cross-species experience, and someone might be willing to talk about recent human patients. As long as it doesn't violate any laws or ethics, mind."

"Sue?" Eva asked, throwing a fake scowl at Pink, who shook her head.

"I'm going with you to, um." Sue stared at her reconstituted potato mash, her pale skin mottled from discomfort. "Talk? To people?"

"Some people will be talked to, yes." Eva took a bite of her own food, talking around it with a hand in front of her mouth. "We're going to scout out the tourist centers to see what kind of human presence there is, and ask around about any particular humans who might have come through in the past six months."

"And I'm coming, too," Min said, slurping up a noodle for emphasis.

Eva paused, fork halfway to her mouth. "No, you're staying on the ship."

Min shook her head, blue hair swaying around her face. "I want to see the Attuned! And the Pod Pals. This place is way too awesome for me to stay in here."

"It's also dangerous," Pink said. "Y'all are soft as a baby kitten."

Min licked sauce off the corner of her mouth. "Oh, right, Mala wants to come, too!"

The calico cat sauntered in as if summoned, her tail straight up, hazel eyes surveying the available food options. With a gentle chirrup, she approached Pink and began to rub against her legs, meowing plaintively.

Eva swallowed. "No me diga," she said. "We're on a mission, not a vacation."

Vakar smelled pensive. "Perhaps you will appear less suspicious or threatening if you are believed to be tourists."

Eva squinted at him, then looked at Pink, who was making a similar face. "What do you think?" Eva asked.

"I don't love it, but he's not wrong," Pink said. "You think you can babysit both of them and still get anything done?"

Min and Sue erupted into complaints about being compared to children, talking over each other almost too fast for Eva to understand. Eva gave a sharp whistle to cut them off, then put her fork down on her plate and shoved her chair back from the table.

"You're not children, but you're also not trained in more than basic self-defense," Eva said. "So the deal is, if I take you, I do any and all fighting while you two run or hide. I do all talking to the locals, all bargaining, everything. You act like you're tethered to my antigrav belt so you don't get lost, and por favor, do not touch anything. Me entiendes?"

"Can we bring our bots?" Sue asked.

"No," Eva and Pink responded in unison.

Sue and Min nodded and murmured assent, continuing to eat their food.

A plaintive meow and gentle pressure drew Eva's attention downward. Mala had rubbed against her leg and was going in for another pass, pausing only to look up at Eva.

"You can't come," Eva said.

"Miau." Mala's pupils dilated briefly.

"No, you're a tiny snack pack, don't be ridiculous."

"Miau."

Eva glared at the cat. "If you come, you're walking. I'm not gonna carry you."

"Miau."

"Fine. If you pee in my backpack, I'm giving you to a local."

Mala purred and rubbed against Eva's leg. Malcriada.

Eva had a bad feeling about all this, but she told herself that was just her own enormous sense of shame talking. With luck, one of them would find something, some hint of a trail that would lead them to Josh quickly, and then it would be smooth sailing back to Mari haloed in the sweet glow of success.

Sure, and maybe they'll elect you the first ever president of space, Eva thought, glaring at the last few bites of beans and rice on her plate.

After a series of cable-car rides—which consisted of the whole crew snuggling in one car that periodically detached from existing cables and floated over to alternate ones—they arrived at the seaside tourist district, itself an arm of Spectrum City that extended directly from the spaceport for the convenience of the many visitors flocking to the pristine white beaches and their accompanying attractions. The water, as Eva's commlink sensors and her newly engaged guide VI informed her, was a di-hydrogen monoxide solution measuring a pleasant thirty-five degrees Celsius, its waves lapping serenely at the accumulation of carbonate minerals that comprised the shoreline. Different species preferred to interact with the natural treasure in different ways, with some taking holovids, some resting on or above the sand, and some swimming or floating languidly in the ocean. Some also appeared to be drinking the water, which struck Eva as highly questionable given her own experience with oceans, but she wasn't there to wreck anyone's good time.

Far enough from the beach to avoid sound pollution, a cluster of standard vacation experiences had been arranged to lure in an array of visiting species. Stores, restaurants, gaming rooms, museums, art galleries, science exhibits, concert halls, parks . . . everything was clean and orderly and had the air of being designed by a committee after extensive research and focus groups. There were also medical facilities and quantumnet cafés, among other modern conveniences, situated on side streets since they had less alluring fabulosity associated with them. All the buildings were constructed from the same translucent materials, their bold colors and geometric shapes forming bright shadows on the ground based on the angle of the blazing-white star overhead.

Eva and her crew passed a trio of xana in pale-gray uniforms wearing antigrav harnesses, all apparently unarmed. They were almost a full meter taller than Eva, their arms and torsos relatively thin but their thighs thick with their species' equivalent of muscle. Soft, short fur covered the exposed parts of their bodies, in different patterns of alternating pale and dark stripes. Their eyes were huge and black, with no visible irises, their ears small and pointed, mouths thin and lipless under a rounded snout. Long prehensile tails were hooked primly into loops extending out from the back of their necks—part of their clothing, not their anatomy.

Each of them also had an Attuned, either nearby or in direct contact with them. One resembled a turtle, but was bipedal and had its own tail that curled into a spiral. Another was like a small featherless todyk, and the third was more or less a walking plant with a face.

None of them spoke, and their facial expressions were neutral, but they emanated a psychic aura of friendliness and power that made Eva's core muscles clench involuntarily. She could almost hear her mother berating her for being so suspicious of authority figures.

Mala, who had nestled herself in the hood of Min's zippered sweater, clambered up to rest her forelegs on Min's shoulders and glare at everyone, her pupils wide and her tail lashing back and forth. The turtle-looking Attuned made a hissing sound like a sudden air leak, and Mala's ears angled back toward her head.

Eva consulted the VI and learned that these xana were called Watchers, and were agents of the aforementioned Community Outreach Program. Apparently, they were tasked with ensuring the city remained peaceful and happy for all its residents and visitors, though how exactly they managed to do that was unclear. Compliance with their requests was strongly recommended; Eva's lip curled up in a snarl that pulled at the scar on her face.

As if that weren't enough, it seemed like every building and statue and decorative element featured at least one form of surveillance equipment. Even Nuvesta, capital of the biggest damn federation of planets in the universe, didn't have the sheer quantity of tech this place did. Whether every centimeter of the city was being recorded, or it was all just used for remote viewing and listening, the sheer density of the devices suggested there must be sophisticated software constantly checking for suspicious activity. That or hundreds of xana somewhere were poring over the feeds; Eva wasn't sure which was creepier.

Eva passed yet another display of "authentic handcrafted local wares" that looked as if they'd been spit out by an authentic local 3-D printer as she continued perusing the guide VI, its helpful overlays almost as distracting as the food smells drifting down the street from somewhere she couldn't see. She came to a section that gave her pause, and she opened it up to examine it more closely.

"Hmm," she said.

"That was a loaded hmm," Pink said. "What are you thinking?"

"I'm thinking we need to adjust our plans," Eva replied. "Get out of this tourist trap and into the kind of place a person might actually disappear into."

Pink's eye narrowed. "Rilia?"

"Sí." Eva passed a clip of what she was reading over to Pink's commlink.

"These tours don't look like they'll take us anywhere useful," Pink said after a few moments.

"Check out the one with the fewest reviews."

"Huh," Pink said. "That's different. 'Explore the true City of Light with an esteemed local historian who is pleased to escort all honored guests along paths not frequented by visitors.' Could work. Vakar, take a look at this." She passed the info to him, and he examined it, waving his palps pensively.

"This listing appears to be relatively new," Vakar said. "Its government licensing key is fraudulent, however. I suspect it will be removed by automated scanning processes in the near future."

Eva grinned like she'd won a prize. "As Min would say, jackpot. I'm setting up a tour now."

Vakar blinked his inner eyelids in confusion. "Why would we hire someone clearly operating illegally and under false pretenses?"

Pink patted his shoulder. "Because he's going to try to hustle us, sweetie."

Eva nodded. "And if he's a hustler, he can get us to where we really need to be."

Their esteemed local historian was named Krachi, and he arrived to pick them up in a cable car that smelled like it had been recently cleaned. His eyes were huge, his face expressionless, but his psychic emanations were overwhelmingly friendly in a way that tipped over the edge into uncomfortable, like he was straining to immediately ingratiate himself to all of them. Instead of hooking his tail onto a neck loop or other body harness strap, he held it in one hand as if it were a hat, occasionally stroking it nervously.

"Welcome, honored guests, welcome," Krachi said, his voice tonally flat as his psychic emanations did the work of adding that layer of meaning. "Please be invited to step into my vehicle for the purpose of transport to the exciting and untraveled paths through the great home-trees of Rilia." He shifted from one leg to the other in a way that, if he were human, would have made him look as if he needed to pee.

"Thanks," Eva said, gesturing for everyone to climb in.

"We're super excited, too. Rilia sounds amazing. Can we get moving?"

A pair of Watchers had apparently noticed what was happening and were conferring silently with each other while staring at Eva. She smiled at them and winked, eliciting a weird horking sound from one of their Attuned, which looked like a huge spiky mouse.

"Are my most excellent and favorite passengers prepared for an experience unlike any other in the entirety of the known and unknown portions of the universe?" Krachi asked, taking up a partially reclined position in a gently swaying hammock-like seat.

"We were born ready," Eva replied, glancing at the Watchers again. "Let's go."

One of the Watchers began to approach the vehicle, but stopped and returned to his companion, and the cable car drifted away as slowly and quietly as a dandelion seed on the wind.

Within a few minutes, the transport had attached itself to a massive cluster of cables that led toward Rilia. They were one of many cars sliding in that direction, though the density was nothing like the traffic Eva had experienced in some places with personal transports. Most of these vehicles held at least a dozen xana, standing or resting in hanging seats like the ones Krachi swung in, exuding cheerfulness as if it were a profusion of sweat. Eva wished he would ease up on the projection, but she wasn't in a position to negotiate yet.

The seaside tourist area was at water level, its small cluster of buildings much lower to the ground than the rest of the city's architecture, so the trip to the capital was by necessity a long, slow rise. Slow enough that Eva got antsy almost immediately.

"Thank you for choosing the services of my excellent and

esteemed self," Krachi said, shifting slightly in his seat. "Is this your first experience in exploring the untold and unique delights of the Rilian culture?"

"Yeah, definitely," Eva replied. She smiled with her mouth closed, not bothering to argue about what the hell "Rilian culture" meant when she was pretty sure a half dozen cultural groups lived in the enormous city. That was tourism for you.

"And what has brought you to our glorious planet, may it forever be embraced by the Light?"

"Sightseeing," Eva replied. "We really like seeing sights."

Pink snorted, but Krachi didn't so much as blink. He did launch into a longer lecture that, despite his lack of verbal tone, had the cadence of something that had been memorized.

The views gradually shifted, from thick building-adorned cables hanging from glassy central towers to a squat sprinkling of what looked like tents arranged haphazardly around vertical farms where xana climbed and glided among their Attuned.

"Much of the sustenance provided to Rilia and Spectrum City is grown in the fields of Verulia," Krachi said as they glided past. "It is also common for Rilians to plant their own gardens in their home-trees for the benefit of the entire branch."

They reached the first rows of saplings that would someday be new home-trees, as Krachi had called them. Despite being young compared to the mature plants, these were hundreds of years old, and already taller than virtually every tree on the planet where Eva had been born. The smells of fresh, slightly salty ocean yielded to the briny soil from which the trees grew, and then as they rose, to a blend of mossy and sappy and floral and even spicy scents from the various plants sprouting from the branches and trunks of the massive home-trees themselves.

As quiet as the vehicles were, the xana who glided along the increasingly ubiquitous ziplines were even more silent, reminding Eva of her former merc buddy comparing them to ghosts. Their Attuned made the most noise, chattering or whining or hooting amongst themselves, and the number of wild creatures grew the deeper into the forest they went. Some flew, others climbed, and still others exclusively clung to their xana the way Mala was latched onto Min's shoulder. Not every critter was Attuned, or the kind that could become that, and the ones who weren't seemed to instinctively avoid the ones who were . . . not special, but different, possessing that extra psychic anatomy that endowed them with the necessary abilities to connect with the xana.

Eventually, Krachi moved them onto a thinner cable, one with far fewer cars. "First, I will take you to a designated Communal Center," he said, his psychic tone suggesting they should all be very excited. "There you will witness many Rilians and their Attuned engaging in typical activities such as socializing; trading or training their Attuned; collecting food rations; and receiving unparalleled medical care."

"That's a lot for one place," Pink said. "What are your medical facilities like?"

Krachi stroked his tail nervously. "They are unparalleled."

You already said that, Eva thought. Maybe they really were, but it certainly sounded more rehearsed than true.

Min took a break from staring slack-jawed out the window to ask, "How do you train your Attuned?"

"It is different for each of them," Krachi replied. "You will have the unrivaled pleasure of observing our traditional practices when we arrive at our destination." His psychic tone remained positive and cheerful, but a quick spike of fear escaped his control, and for a moment everyone in the cable car tensed.

No one seemed inclined to speak after that, and even Krachi's chatter fell away as they entered a deeper, older part of Rilia. The trees were like Eva remembered—massive, the bark consisting of overlapping growths like stained glass, their trunks broad and their leaves big enough to serve as parachutes. Despite the translucence of the buildings clinging to the drooping branches, it was darker in this place, less sunlight making its way through the many layers above to reach a level that, while nauseatingly high off the ground, was toward the lower middle of the hometree. As their guide had suggested, pieces of the plant had been carved out so that small gardens could be grafted on and cultivated inside them, sapping nutrients and fluids from the larger host. A few xana were actively tending these as they passed, but most of the people they saw were resting or preparing food or quietly engaging in other relatively mundane activities. Even the children played in near-silence, occasionally emitting excited trills as they chased each other around a building or from one branch to another.

At some point, Mala left Min's hood and clambered onto Eva's shoulders, settling there like a furry collar. Eva almost grabbed her by the scruff to toss her back at Min, but Mala started purring, so Eva turned the grab into a pet.

Fucking psychic cats, Eva thought, sighing. Knowing Mala, this meant Eva was wound as tight as a spring and needed help.

Their cable car detached from its line and drifted over to a large building: the Communal Center, spread out between multiple branches and at least five stories tall given standard xana heights. Its walls and floors were all varying shades of green, and each level seemed devoted to a different purpose, as Krachi had described earlier.

At the top, a gym-like area took up the entire floor, and Attuned engaged in not only different forms of exercise, but what looked like mock battles with each other. "That is where the Attuned are taught new skills and tested," Krachi explained, his psychic tone one of unfeigned pride. "It is a great honor to prove one's abilities against other xana, for only the strongest trainers may advance to the Tournament in Spectrum City."

"Tournament?" Min asked. "What's that?"

"A great competition among the Attuned, who use their skills and talents to subdue each other until only one remains."

Mala gave a low growl in Eva's ear, so Eva poked her gently to stop her.

"That sounds violent," Min said.

"No Attuned are harmed during our trials," Krachi insisted, his psychic tone soothing. "They are provided with special medications made by our expert physicians, to ensure they are not pained by their injuries, and they are immediately treated to ensure their health is undiminished."

"That doesn't sound like no harm," Pink said, raising an eyebrow. "That sounds like lots of harm that gets fixed in a hurry."

Krachi's tone gained a thorn of irritation that he quickly suppressed. "All Attuned are exceedingly happy and well cared for in every way possible, and only the willing participate in the trials that lead to the Tournament."

Eva knew what Pink was thinking, and why, and frankly she thought it sounded like cockfighting, too. But she wasn't here to get into it with their tour guide over local customs, especially ones she didn't fully understand because she was an outsider.

"What's on the other levels?" Eva asked, to move the conversation along.

Krachi's tone evened out, back to excessively friendly and positive. "The medical facilities are located below the training and testing grounds, so that all may access them with great ease. The physicians treat both xana and their Attuned." He paused, his huge eyes taking in his passengers again. "They are also very capable of treating virtually every other species in the universe, thanks to our excellent educational resources and government-supported extraplanetary experience missions."

Multiple rooms were arranged on the interior of that level, with xana and their Attuned engaging in what Eva assumed were technologically assisted examinations of patients. Pink stared at the operations to the extent that they were clearly visible from their car, through the translucent walls.

"I can't connect to their internal network," Pink muttered. "Probably not set up for non-xana at this location."

"There is a public network available at all Communal Centers," Krachi said, then added quickly, "but you may want to experience the more private local network possibilities for an additional fee, as they are part of the truly immersive experience offered especially by this excellent tour."

A slow smile spread across Eva's face. She'd been wondering when the grift would start. She knew from her research that the government tours were supposed to be free, so she had assumed Krachi would either low-key try to charge them at some point for the trip itself, or start loading on extra costs for random stuff.

"That could be fun," Eva said, earning another raised eyebrow from Pink. Eva winked at her with the eye facing away from Krachi.

Before he could launch into an explanation, Eva pointed at a line of xana circling around the side of the building near the landing platform. "What's that about?"

Krachi psychically winced, but recovered quickly again. "That is the local community members obtaining their allotted nourishment rations from the government distributors. Every Communal Center provides this service to all xana and their Attuned for the well-being of all of Rilia."

Free food sounded plenty good to Eva, even though she

wasn't hungry. She had expected that the government she'd unintentionally helped install by force would be less caring, to be honest. The notion that someone could thank her for murdering hundreds of their people and then turn around and make sure everyone else was always fed . . . There had to be a catch. There was always a catch.

Or was that just her cynical upbringing talking? Could it really be so simple? Just because most planets still hadn't figured out how to offer more than the most basic services to their people, often on a small scale, that didn't mean it was impossible. It meant most of them hadn't tried hard enough to make it work.

Then she thought of the Watchers. She didn't know to what extent they exerted control over the people they ostensibly guarded, but given the VI's assurances about how peaceful Spectrum City and Rilia were, Eva had plenty of suspicions.

"Do we get to go inside?" Min asked. She was already standing, bouncing on the balls of her feet. "I want to see the battles!"

"Of course you do," Pink said, shaking her head.

Krachi stroked his tail, his tone struggling to remain positive and chipper. "There is a particular location to which I would be exceedingly honored to escort you all, once we have safely landed. One of my esteemed compatriots crafts—"

"Sounds awesome, let's do it," Eva said. Once they had landed, he'd probably drag them to some back area where Watchers didn't frequent, at which point she and Vakar could quietly shake him down for information under threat of turning his ass over to the authorities. Worst case, they grabbed another cable car back to Spectrum City and tried again. Best case, they had an in to whatever under-the-table shit went on here.

The cable car touched down on a landing pad near the line for food, one of only two cars present, though there were a number of the smaller open vehicles, and virtually everyone seemed to be wearing their own zipline harness with antigrav for safety. Not every xana had their own Attuned, but many did, clambering over them or flitting around them or merely standing next to them quietly. Krachi led them past the waiting people, whose expressions were flat even as their psychic tones were much more open and varied than anyone's in the tourist area had been.

"My nestmate says it is ahaaki again," one of the waiting xana told another as she broadcast psychically somewhere between irate and grumpy.

"The harvest must have been good this season," the other replied. "Do you have sufficient hirsali to diminish the aroma?"

"No such amount exists," the first xana replied, and they projected amusement at each other even as it was laced with bitterness.

That was its own kind of catch, too, Eva thought as they passed by. It hadn't been very long since her own crew was eating whatever they could afford, cobbling together meals from sacks of protein powder and whatever replicator recipes they'd found on the q-net. Things were better now, but they could get worse again anytime, and even mediocre food was better than nothing.

Around the side of the building was a series of translucent bark overhangs tied together with leaf ropes. Apparently Krachi had informed his people that he was on his way with tourists, because a half dozen xana were already waiting with their wares spread out across a table carved from another piece of bark. Some items seemed meant to be worn like jewelry or as harness accessories, while others were woven packs or garments designed to fit a variety of body types in multiple sizes. Another table held complex carved figures of various Attuned, all of them moving, engaged in what were presumably typical activities for the creatures; those were impressive for their detail and the ingenious way they were put together. A holo projector mounted in the corner showed images of other items or designs available, presumably to be made and delivered later or simply stored elsewhere.

"Behold, honored guests, the magnificent achievements of the finest artisans in Rilia," Krachi said. "Their fees are exceedingly reasonable and they are capable of undertaking custom creations should you desire to describe them." He was unable to hide his nerves, now projecting them psychically in addition to rubbing his tail, and Eva shared a look with Pink that said they were both thinking the same thing.

They were assholes.

This guy wasn't trying to hustle them; he was trying to get a cut of the massive tourist take that Spectrum City was probably hoarding. Or at least, his hustle was so far extremely mild compared to what they had been expecting.

"Ooh, look at these, Sue!" Min exclaimed, examining the Attuned sculptures. They didn't appear to have any electronics making them move, though of course those might be cleverly hidden inside, and their colors had been achieved through the use of thin layers of overlapping bark in different shades.

"They're beautiful," Eva said, and her stomach felt like she'd swallowed rocks. She'd come to this place before to do violence, and had done it to a greater extent than even she had ever dreamed, so of course she'd come back expecting to end up in a fight. She'd believed the worst of this poor xana, for no other reason than he was operating outside official channels—and what the hell had she been doing for years, if not that? She should know better than most that when official channels were restrictive, you went around them. When bureaucracies put up a wall of red tape, you quietly lifted it out of the way and snuck underneath.

Otherwise, all you could do was sit around waiting for other people to decide your life for you. Stand in line. Follow orders. Jump to the instructed height, shoot the target, achieve the mission objectives.

That was no way to live, and these people knew it, too.

"Perhaps you might be interested in these," Krachi said, gesturing slightly at a row of antigrav harnesses decorated in the same kinds of overlapping colors as the figurines. That actually would be pretty useful, depending on how long they stayed in the area, and naturally Eva could think of a few other uses . . . She glanced sideways at Vakar to see what he was up to.

His palps were twitching, and his inner eyelids were closed, which meant he was deep in thought and trying to concentrate on something. Eva's brow furrowed but she didn't interrupt him. Probably still trying to deal with the local networks.

((Information?)) Pink pinged at Eva, whose pensive frown deepened.

Her plan had assumed that she'd have some leverage, partly from being underestimated by their guide. As far as he knew, they were simple tourists, and had he threatened them he would have had a rude surprise. But now?

Well, she could just ask him about Josh, but was that really the wisest option? No, she still had to be careful about this. Trust no one. This was a planet of psychics, for fuck's sake. Just because Krachi wasn't the hardened-criminal type she'd been expecting didn't mean he was a saint.

Unfortunately, before she could so much as formulate how to broach the subject, the xana who was operating a small fruit stand began to radiate hostility. Eva tensed, subtly inspecting the area to figure out what had the woman so riled up.

"I know you," the xana said. Still that calm, neutral inflection, the expressionless black eyes, but waves of psychic rage and sorrow boiled off her. "Prime-killer. Bond-breaker. Extinguisher of Light."

She was staring directly at Eva.

The other xana were unable to contain their surprise, though Krachi valiantly attempted to do so. A quiet conference began among them, wherein they attempted to determine whether the angry one was right, as Krachi clutched his tail so tightly its fur stood up around his hand.

"She burned my branch!" the xana exclaimed, her voice still even but her psychic tone as hot as napalm.

((Shit,)) Eva pinged at Pink.

((Double shit,)) Pink pinged back.

This was Eva's worst nightmare, coming back here. To be recognized. To be remembered. Eva didn't want to start anything, and with innocent people no less. She raised her hands in the universal biped gesture of submission and took a step back.

"We don't want any trouble," Eva said. "We're here to—"

"I do not care," the xana said. From behind her table, her Attuned emerged, a plantlike creature that waddled around on two stubby legs, long leaflike parts sticking up out of its round body like hair. It shook like it was cold, and a cloud of spores drifted out of its leaves.

Eva immediately activated her isohelmet, but enough spores had already been carried by the wind right into her nose, and she sneezed violently. Her suit's filters kicked in, scrubbing the air inside, but she'd already inhaled a bunch of it. She turned to Pink, who was also now bubbled, as was the rest of her crew. Hopefully none of them had been hit.

The question was, what would the spores do to her? And would Pink be able to stop it? Okay, that was two questions, and unfortunately the first one was answered quickly as a jolt of pain shot through her entire body, from feet to fingertip. Her stomach wrenched and she fell to her knees, trying not to vomit.

"Eva!" Pink exclaimed. Within moments she was at Eva's side, and then Vakar was there as well, but Eva struggled to follow what they were doing because she felt like she was having the worst combination of hangover and stomach flu that had ever been suffered by a human.

More Attuned arrived, circling Eva and the rest of her crew, who were now more or less huddled together defensively. A small rat-looking one, a pair of flying creatures, a large green bug-like one with vicious curved arms . . . Here was the threat of violence Eva had been prepared for, but not for the reason she had expected.

This was her fault. Someone had recognized her, someone who had every right to hate her for what she had done. Had Eva killed one of her friends? Her family? One of her children? It was fitting that Eva should be racked with pain and gut-roiling sickness, because she felt almost the same way without being poisoned.

She deserved every moment of this, she knew. But her crew didn't. She needed to get them to safety somehow, before things escalated further.

Except Eva had no idea how she could possibly do that in her present condition.

She struggled to her feet, despite Pink and Vakar protesting beside her, breath coming in fiery gasps as her vision blurred. But as she was preparing to activate her sonic knuckles, something astonishing happened.

"Miau." Mala strolled up to the nearest Attuned and started to purr.

Chapter 12

TE CONOZCO, MASCARITA

Eva blinked at Mala in confusion as the tiny calico cat squared off against hostile creatures, some more than triple her size. The Attuned seemed just as put off, because they paused their advances and appeared to be mutely conferring with their xana, occasionally vocalizing in their own individual ways. The silent standoff continued for several long moments as no one moved a muscle—not wanting to be responsible for the fallout, perhaps.

And then, because why the fuck not, Mala sat down and proceeded to lick her own butthole vigorously.

Alabao, Eva thought. I knew bringing her was a bad idea. The last thing I need is a casual-ass petty anarchist with delusions of superiority bringing her psychic comemierdería out to play.

And yet, for some reason, it worked. The Attuned backed away, and the xana continued to emanate psychic hostility but with an undercurrent of wariness and dismay. Even Krachi had stopped guarding himself so carefully and was nearly trembling with nerves, along with healthy doses of fear and shame.

Eva knew those feelings well. This had all been a mistake. If nothing else, she should have stayed on the ship and let the others handle this, to avoid this exact issue. She had put everyone in danger, when she was the only one who had done anything wrong in the first place.

"What is your companion?" one of the xana asked, their tone cautious. "It is a . . . Miau?"

Eva could hardly breathe without pain, but thankfully Pink stepped in.

"She's a cat," Pink said, lips curled in disdain. "And she's not going to do any damn-fool nonsense, isn't that right, Mala?"

"Miau," Mala said.

"Why do you call her 'cat' when she says Miau?" another xana asked.

Pink didn't have a response to that, so she stared blankly at the xana.

"In my language, it's 고양이," Min said. "And she says 야옹 ."

The xana murmured things to themselves that Eva couldn't hear. The one who had recognized her said, "It is not to be borne!" at a volume that might as well have been a shout for the way her psychic rage and sorrow magnified it.

"Are you okay?" Pink asked Eva quietly.

Eva shook her head, her neck cramping from the minute motion as another wave of nausea and pain wrenched her body. Her muscles were weakening, her vision going spotty. Everything tasted like sour milk. Was she going to die?

"We need to get you in there for treatment," Pink said, pointing her chin at the Communal Center. "But we have to be chill so we don't start shit and get hit."

Mala had stopped licking her butt and moved on to her paws. Eva wondered whether she would accidentally eat some of the Attuned spores, and decided that was Mala's problem, la muy cabrona.

"Watchers are approaching," someone said, and what had been all tense anger directed at Eva was now a flurry of activity as the xana dismantled their displays, packing up their wares so quickly and efficiently that Eva had no doubt they'd done so before. Each table folded into a compact container with straps that easily attached to the xana harnesses, and in what felt like no time at all to Eva's pain-riddled senses, everyone but Krachi had vanished, either into the Communal Center or somewhere else in the home-tree.

((Move,)) Eva pinged the whole crew, unable to speak. Pink and Vakar each slid an arm under her and half walked, half carried her toward the entrance to the building. The xana standing in line for food said nothing, but needles of psychic curiosity and disdain stabbed right into Eva's skull as she struggled to move her aching feet. One step at a time, through the front of the building, past more xana and Attuned. The dim light of the local star was supplemented by long transparent tubes in which luminescent creatures meandered or slept or peered at her with glowing yellow eyes. Eva blinked—

—and found herself floating in an antigrav field. A machine nearby emitted a soft tone, answered by a large pink Attuned that sounded like it said "penis," which Eva assumed was her own mind playing tricks on her.

"She is regaining consciousness, Dr. Jones," an unfamiliar voice said—xana, she was pretty sure. "Captain Innocente, it is my duty to request that you remain unmoving until you are invited to determine the condition of your limbs through carefully monitored diagnostic protocols."

Eva swallowed, her throat weirdly moist. While her vision was slowly resolving, it didn't make any sense for a few moments; everything was moving, colorful wall becoming ceiling becoming floor, until finally she realized she was slowly rotating like a pig on a spit.

Pink's face swam into focus next to Eva. "Hey, you," Pink said softly. "That was a nasty poison, but you're going to be fine, hear?"

Coño, it must have been bad if Pink was being so nice. The last time Eva almost died, Pink had yelled at her to stop making foolish life choices, then sedated her, giving her the middle finger until Eva fell asleep.

Either that, or the overall quiet of the xana was encouraging Pink to tone it down as well. Eva couldn't hear much beyond the distant, muted sounds of Attuned and the gentle footfalls of whoever was walking around and above her. The air smelled like green, like the concept of fresh air her father would pump into used spaceships to make them seem clean and new and appealing.

((Talk okay?)) Eva pinged Pink.

Pink nodded, but pinged back, ((Watchers outside.))

Mierda, mojón y porquería. This kept getting better.

"Everyone else is fine?" Eva asked, trying not to move her head even though the constant slow rotation meant she kept talking to random parts of the room.

"Yeah, even that cat," Pink said disdainfully. "I don't know what she was thinking."

"She's always been a cabezona," Eva said. Where was Vakar?

As if he heard her question, mint and incense smells drifted into the room. She couldn't move to look at him, and he stayed frustratingly outside her field of vision, but it was nice that he'd turned off his scent suppressors for the moment. For her, because certainly he had no other reason to do it.

"I told you she was fine," Pink said, straightening up and turning away so Eva couldn't see her face anymore.

"I did not disbelieve you," Vakar replied.

"But you wanted to see her naked," Pink said, and Eva could picture her lip curling in amusement.

"No, that is not why I . . . You are making a joke." Vakar's smell shifted to a grassy, bashful one that complemented the rest of the room nicely.

Pink snorted. "Lord almighty, you are too easy."

"Thanks for letting me know I'm naked, Dr. Jones," Eva said crossly. As if the whole situation wasn't bad enough, she was now acutely aware that every xana in the entire building could look through the translucent walls and see all her assets on display.

The xana doctor leaned over Eva, projecting professional concern. "The enigmatic grass powder has been cleansed from your physical form, blessed be the Light in which we all may climb."

"Amen," Eva said, not entirely sure how to reply. "Gracias, muy amable," she added awkwardly.

"You may experience some residual effects, including muscular weakness and increased desire for nourishment," the doctor continued. "Your prognosis is positive. You will be discharged soon."

"Awesome." She still hadn't been told to move, so she didn't, but the longer she lay there, the more fidgety she felt. Patience had never been one of her many fine qualities.

Worse, there was a sudden commotion at the door, startling for its loudness in the quiet building.

"Captain Rebecca Jones," a xana said. His voice was surprisingly resonant, but tonally neutral, the translator nanites conveying little difference between the pitches and emphasized syllables. "I am Watcher Rakyra."

"I don't give a single lukewarm shit who you are, you're not going in there," Pink said.

"I have been requested to ensure the safety and security of yourself and Captain Eva Innocente, as well as the other members of your crew," Watcher Rakyra continued. "The Prime was deeply concerned when she learned of the situation here, and hopes you will cooperate fully with an investigation into the matter."

Eva tensed. Who was the Prime? And what would the Watchers do with the xana and their Attuned, the ones who put Eva in the hospital? It probably wouldn't be good, not with how much they apparently prided themselves on all the "safety and security" around Rilia.

Pink clicked her tongue against her teeth. "There's nothing to cooperate with. I told you, Eva poked a critter because she's a fool, and she got a faceful of pollen for it. You would think she'd know better than to lay hands on strange wildlife, but she's not the sharpest tool in the bag."

Gracias a dios, Pink was handling it. While Eva was already coming to terms with the idea of hundreds of strangers seeing her naked through minimal colored barriers, she didn't want to be interrogated like this, especially not before they had their story straight. And she certainly didn't want to cause these poor people any more trouble than she already had.

"We understand," Rakyra said. His psychic emanations were muted, but crisply professional, with a strong layer of authority along with polite respect. "It would be our great pleasure to extend to you an invitation to a private audience with our Supreme Executive, who is eager to make your acquaintance."

Me cago en diez, Eva thought. There was no way everyone who showed up on Garilia got a special trip to the principal's office. They knew who Eva was, probably thanks to the altercation outside, and now the shit was really hitting the air filters.

"Well, when you put it that way," Pink said. "Does the Supreme Executive want my entire crew to come along, or just little ol' me?"

"The invitation is for you and all of your friends," Watcher Rakyra replied, his psychic tone politely deferential. "Especially Captain Innocente."

Mierda. Should they run back to the ship and leave, before something happened? Before it was too late to back out and come up with a safer plan?

Pink and Eva had worn their spacesuits, but Vakar had opted for a more casual jumpsuit instead of his Wraith armor—now scent-suppressing so he wasn't sharing his entire emotional state like an ad on a commwall, but it left him exposed in ways that made Eva uncomfortable now that trouble seemed imminent. And of course Sue was always vulnerable, and with Min and Mala along for this mission as well . . .

That won't get us closer to Josh, she thought. We're here, and we're in this. Might as well see what game this Prime is playing so we can learn the rules and make our own moves.

Also, she told herself, you're naked and rotating in a stasis field, so your options are limited anyway.

((Accept?)) Pink pinged her.

((Accept,)) she told Pink. ((Information.))

((Dangerous,)) Pink replied. ((Sure?))

((Yes,)) Eva said. They'd put themselves in danger just by coming to Garilia. Pink knew that as well as she did.

"We'll be happy to join you as soon as Captain Innocente is discharged," Pink said.

"We await her release with great eagerness and wishes for good health," Watcher Rakyra replied. His psychic tone was now sympathetic, but tiny spikes of anger and relief broke through the overtone of authority he projected continuously.

The pink Attuned entered the room, its mouth open in an approximation of a smile. It was only a bit shorter than Eva, if she were standing, and round as the egg it carried in a harness strapped to its broad chest. "Niss!" it announced, and then disappeared from Eva's view as she continued to revolve.

At least it wasn't saying "penis" like earlier, Eva thought. She began to giggle uncontrollably, her chest shaking in a way that made the Attuned repeat the word in a more chiding voice.

Of course, at precisely that moment she got a call from her dear, lovely sister. Eva switched her commlink to accept subvocalizations and answered. "Qué bola, Mari?"

Mari sounded pissed, as usual, but still her prim and proper self. She ran them through the standard codes and countersigns before finally asking, "Eva-Benita, what exactly are you doing at this precise moment?"

Eva rolled her eyes, hoping that wasn't too much motion for her doctor's orders. "I'm practicing my lechón impression."

Mari paused. "I don't know what that means. Please be serious for a change."

"I'm being serious. Bueno, doesn't matter. Qué quieres?"

The Attuned fiddled with the monitors next to Eva, waving its small hands around and causing the machine to hum weirdly.

"Did you tell Mom something about what you're doing for us?"

Eva froze. Well, more than she already was frozen. And she kept spinning, obviously.

"Why do you ask?" Eva asked.

Mari fell silent. After exactly ten seconds, she took a deep breath and exhaled so loudly that Eva could hear her from across the universe.

"I needed her help with something, but I didn't tell her what it was for," Eva said. "I didn't mention you or anything."

Mari inhaled and exhaled twice more before saying, with a xana-like calm, "Please check your q-mail. Now." Without another word, she ended the call.

Eva had turned off notifications while they were off the ship because she hated being constantly pinged by bullshit gray mail and bill collectors. She opened her logs and waited for them to refresh, closing her eyes so the constantly shifting room wouldn't make her queasy while reading.

Among the exciting offers for lines of credit and unnecessary spaceship upgrades, one item stood out. A message from her mother, which was presumably what had gotten Mari's bloomers in a bunch. Eva opened it.

"Me cago en la hora que yo nací," Eva said.

It was an awkwardly angled selfie of Regina Alvarez, grinning, in front of a very familiar building. One whose translucent, colorful glass walls would have been immediately recognizable even if Eva hadn't passed right in front of them herself only a few hours earlier.

"Niss?" the pink Attuned asked.

"Niss indeed," Eva replied. What the ever-loving fuck was her mother doing in Spectrum City? On Garilia?

• • • • • • • •

Once Eva was finally discharged by her xana physician, after consultation with Pink and not a few assurances that further care would be provided by her personally, the entire crew was escorted out of the Communal Center by Watcher Rakyra and his associates. The food line had not diminished, but the waiting xana must have been actively suppressing or manipulating their psychic emanations, because the only thing Eva got from them as she walked by was deference to the Watcher's authority.

After a long, silent transport ride, they reached their destination. The headquarters of the Enhanced Committee Outreach Program were at the tippy-top of the trunk of a skyscraper in Spectrum City, over a thousand meters up according to Eva's commlink sensors. They rode up in an elevator that was, like virtually every place in the city, surrounded by translucent walls that afforded incredible views of not only the ocean and the neighboring buildings, with their ornament-like hanging structures, but also the city of Rilia in the distance, its organic trees smaller than the constructed ones but no less impressive. But the naturally occurring forest was darker, its leaves and trunks only partially transparent, making Spectrum City seem more glowing and vibrant by comparison.

It was a neat trick, a subtle manipulation of the many species who thrived on light rather than shade. *Come bask in our radiance,* it said. *Shine with us.*

We have nothing to hide.

While virtually every culture in every species across the infinite universe had different definitions of work and play, the xana "offices" appeared entirely leisurely to Eva, who had been raised to believe interrupting dinner to answer q-mail messages or fix a quick account issue was entirely reasonable. Wide woven hammocks hung at intervals in different shapes and configurations, with xana partially or totally reclined inside them, or even curled up in pairs or groups, apparently fast asleep with their tails wrapped around them. They might simply be like Min, resting their bodies while their minds were constantly busy, but Eva still felt like she was stomping through someone's sundrenched bedroom.

"Is the floor moving?" Sue asked in a tense whisper.

"Probably," Eva said. "Must be a lot of wind this high up."

The engineer paled and made a face like she was going to be sick, edging closer to Min, who wasn't as bothered. Eva wasn't a fan of heights, either, but she'd flown enough planetside missions while jacked into a ship that she didn't experience the same vertigo other people did when faced with a long drop to solid ground. Of course, in this case, it didn't help that the floors were made of the same colorful translucent material as the walls. With nearly every step came an awareness of how many levels were below them, each populated by xana engaged in their own daily activities, all capable of looking up or down to see what any other xana was doing at any given time.

Eva hated it. She'd take privacy in a metal box in space over brilliant ocean views any day.

Eventually they reached a door, the first of its kind since they exited the elevator. It was completely clear, as were the walls surrounding it, but the fact that any separation existed in the first place felt like a disturbance, an incongruity that stuck out more than the pack of humans, a quennian, and a cat standing in front of it with no idea what to expect inside.

"The Supreme Executive awaits your esteemed company," Watcher Rakyra said, his psychic tone still courteous and respectful. The door opened, and he made a minute gesture with a three-fingered hand to suggest they enter.

The todyk-looking Attuned behind them emitted a sound like a sigh, intense heat emanating from what Eva assumed was its mouth. Not a threat, per se, but perhaps the creature's version of a suggestion that it was time to move.

At the far end of the room, another xana waited, limned by the warm light of the planet's star. She stood facing away from the door, her tail curled around a loop that hung from her neck, down to the center of her back. Her clothing was loose, layered and diaphanous, granting full mobility to not only her limbs and tail but also to the gliding membranes on either side of her body. She was pale-furred, nearly white, with stripes only a slightly darker shade of gray; soft, beautiful, and when she turned around, Eva had to remind herself to breathe, because the woman was literally exuding a tidal wave of psychic energy designed to inspire awe.

That is a cheap fucking trick, Eva thought. Sinvergüenza.

This time, at least, Mala had the sense to stay tucked away inside Min's jacket. Not the best time to get into a psychic pissing contest.

"Welcome, honored guests. I am Supreme Executive Lashra Damaal." Her voice was as lacking in inflection as the other xana, but somehow mild and warm. "Watchers, please accept my thanks for conveying them to me safely."

"The pleasure is ours, Prime," Watcher Rakyra replied, unblinking but vastly more psychically reverent than he had been to Eva and the others. "Do you require our continued presence or any other service?"

"You may return to your previous assignments unburdened by further obligations at the present time. May the Light embrace you."

The phrasing sounded a little extra to Eva, but she made a note to ramp up her own levels of flowery and polite to keep up with the local customs. After everything else, it would suck to get kicked out for being rude.

Damaal returned her attention to the crew of *La Sirena Negra* as the Watchers and their Attuned left the room, closing that single solitary door behind them. It felt like being in a spotlight, but instead of visual glare it was psychic.

"It is my great privilege to meet the Hero of Garilia, about whom I have heard many tales," Damaal said. "I hope you can forgive my extreme impertinence in requesting your presence so soon after your arrival, when you have not yet been afforded the opportunity to conduct the business that brought you to our bright city."

Eva sensed a few unspoken questions buried in all that bullshit, but despite the psychic pressure to kneel like she was talking to the Virgin herself, she looked straight into Damaal's huge black eyes and smiled.

"I've heard about you as well, Prime," Eva said, figuring the title the Watcher used was her safest bet. "All good things."

Damaal began to walk serenely toward her, so fluidly that she seemed to be hovering. Her psychic tone lost a shade of its intensity, replacing it with gratitude that somehow managed not to suggest any indebtedness whatsoever. "I was not present for the People's Glorious Revolution myself, but your actions will live forever in the hearts and minds of those who soared bravely in the Light that day."

"I appreciate the kind words," Eva said, hoping she didn't sound too sarcastic.

"They are freely given," Damaal replied. "May I impose on you further by extending an invitation to share in an imminent gathering of my fellows, namely a celebratory gathering to be followed by an exciting Tournament?" Her slow drift took her in front of Pink, who regarded the woman coolly, her face impassive, as if Damaal were the kind of troublesome patient who asked if there weren't a more experienced doctor available for a second opinion.

"I think my doctor wanted me to get some more rest," Eva said, pleased that she could be entirely sincere in saying so. Damaal was still fishing for information, trying to get Eva to give her a foothold where she could be more direct in her questioning. Eva wasn't the best at this game, but she could hold her own. Mostly.

But how to find out anything about Josh without giving away their entire mission?

"Perhaps at the time of your next expected hunger interval," Damaal replied, now radiating warmth along with authority. "I would be delighted beyond measure to send transport to retrieve you from your future location."

And I'm not telling you where that is, Eva thought. Climb your own building and take a dive.

"That would be extremely generous of you," Eva said aloud. "I hope it's not rude to assume you can accommodate human and quennian dietary needs?"

"Not at all," Damaal said. She glided past Vakar, whose scents were once again being suppressed. His palps twitched as her psychic emanations targeted him directly. "The expansion of our numerous facilities in Spectrum City has permitted us to obtain the latest in food-replication technology, as well as training and recruiting some of the finest chefs in the universe to extend every possible hospitality to our many honored guests."

She continued her slow walk, but now she stopped in front of Sue, and Eva mentally slapped herself in the forehead. "If there is anything I can do to aid you in your business here, please do not hesitate to ask," Damaal said. The wave of encouragement and goodwill she sent out was subtle but strong, like the scent of baked goods being blown out of a bakery by an industrial fan to lure in passersby.

((Stay quiet,)) Eva pinged at Sue, a moment too late.

"We're trying to find my brother," Sue blurted out, then covered her mouth with her hands and looked at Eva, eyes wide with an unspoken apology.

"Your brother," Damaal said, still warm and encouraging, but Eva caught a hint of something else—surprise? Anger? It was so subtle she wasn't sure it was real. Why had she thought Eva was there?

Sue nodded, but didn't say anything else.

"I understand," Damaal continued. "It must be painful to be separated from your—" Her words translated as "broodmate" and "rest companion" with some minor disagreement as to whether xana placed strong emphasis on either. "Perhaps if you provide more information, I might request that my Watchers assist you in locating him?"

"We wouldn't want to impose," Eva said. "We're not even sure he's here, honestly." That was also true, so she was still in safe territory.

"May I inquire as to the reason you believe he would be on our excellent planet?" Damaal asked. Her tone was politely curious, keen to help, with enough empathy to clog an exhaust port. "We are far from major trade routes, and surely you would not trouble yourself to seek him out so cautiously if you expected him to be merely enjoying the fruits of our many delightful attractions."

Eva weighed how much was worth keeping to herself now that Sue had let the proverbial cat out of the bag. What did Damaal already know, and what did she suspect? *La Sirena Negra* had faked credentials and they were all wearing biometric signature dupers, so she didn't know who Sue was yet, theoretically, but once she did then she'd easily be able to figure out who Josh was. Probably not the Fridge connection, but anything else that was common knowledge on the q-net was fair game.

And all of this assumed that Damaal didn't already know exactly who they all were, and hadn't already been in contact with Josh for reasons of her own. She was certainly acting as if she hadn't, and if she weren't lying, that strongly suggested he really wasn't on Garilia after all.

After everything Eva had been through so far, that would be quite a kick in the teeth. But again: why did she think Eva was there in the first place? Why bring her in for questioning instead of having Watchers follow her and wait to see what she would do?

Unless Damaal had something to hide, and had no intention of letting Eva and her crew leave if she wasn't satisfied that her secrets were safe.

"He was kidnapped," Eva said, choosing her words carefully. "We've been tracking him for some time, and found circumstantial evidence to suggest he might be here."

Damaal continued to broadcast her sympathy and willingness to help toward Sue, whose hands hadn't left her mouth, despite her eyes watering from the effort of containing herself.

"It would bring me great satisfaction to contribute as many resources as I might feasibly manage, to facilitate your success in this endeavor," Damaal said. "If you would provide me with sufficient details to identify your lost brother, I would convey them to my Watchers and see that they were distributed to all Communal Centers for—"

"Thank you for the extremely generous offer," Eva interrupted, wincing as this elicited the psychic equivalent of a frown from Damaal. Must have been impolite, but oh well. "We're concerned that he might be in danger," she continued, "so we're trying to keep our search from becoming public knowledge."

Damaal's psychic tone returned to its prior buffeting of splendor and authority, with a sharp edge that Eva couldn't place. "I am pleased to be able to offer some ease to your mind," she said. "The diligence of our Watchers ensures there is no danger in Spectrum City, or Rilia, or indeed in all of Garilia. Our guests can be assured of complete safety."

The hairs on Eva's arms stood up, and she struggled to keep from showing her disdain on her face. The VI she'd been perusing earlier had suggested much the same thing, but any place that talked the house of shit about cops keeping everything safe was probably anything but. Then something occurred to her, and she smiled politely.

"That's good to hear," Eva said. "In that case, he can't possibly be here, because if he were safe then he certainly would have contacted his beloved sister already. Qué lástima; we came such a long way."

"I share your disappointment as if it were my own," Damaal said, her tone laced with empathy. "I regret that I cannot offer you a more positive outcome, especially when you have done so much for Garilia."

Eva shrugged, maintaining her wistful smile even though her stomach was full of nails. "It happens. We've had other false leads, so this isn't a complete surprise."

Damaal continued her slow walk, now that she apparently had enough information to satisfy her needs. She came to a stop in front of Min, who shrank slightly and wrapped her hands around the cat-shaped lump in her jacket.

"May I inquire as to what you will—" Damaal began, then paused, her tone gaining a surprisingly genuine spike of puzzlement. "What creature are you carrying there?" she asked, staring fixedly at Min, which was unnerving given the enormity of her eyes.

"It's a cat," Min stammered.

Mala emitted a low growl, and a wave of psychic aloofness that nearly made Eva laugh out loud.

"May I bear witness to the specimen?" Damaal said, stepping closer to Min, who retreated while still clutching Mala protectively. "The similarity to our Attuned is fascinating."

"I don't think she wants to come out," Eva said. "But you can find plenty of holovids all over the q-net. Humans are pretty obsessed with them."

Damaal's tail twitched, but she turned away, her tone shifting to benevolence. "The Attuned are also creatures with minds of their own," she said. "To that end, before you depart, perhaps I may offer you a sample of the great bounty of our planet, which we are preparing to share with the rest of the universe?"

She gestured, and another xana entered the room, silent but oozing deference. This new xana carried a translucent box of small capsules, each about the size of a baseball, which she held out for Damaal's perusal. Damaal picked one up and held it out to Min, whose fear was overtaken by curiosity.

"Perhaps you have heard of these," Damaal said. "Our brilliant scientists and engineers have worked tirelessly to re-create our Attuned in artificial form, with some modifications. We hope to shift the paradigm in virtual intelligence to promote synergy in a variety of industries, as well as increasing personal harmony among our users."

"Is that a Pod Pal?" Sue asked, excited. She covered her mouth again and shot Eva an apologetic look. Eva was interested, too, but she wasn't about to fangirl over them.

"That is one of the human terms, yes," Damaal said, her tone gaining shades of pride and amusement. "Please, each of you, accept these as a token of our hospitality. Gromira, if you would?"

Gromira approached each of them, offering the box as if passing out treats. Sue took one immediately, but Pink shook her head politely.

"No, thanks," Pink said, trying to maintain a civil tone. "I don't really play with toys anymore."

"They are far more than instruments of leisure," Damaal said, a sharp edge to her psychic emanation. "They are companions, and partners, intended to fulfill every function of an Attuned with additional features that render them even more useful."

Pink shook her head again, and Vakar also declined by raising his hands and lowering them. Eva had the sense they were being wildly rude, but she also didn't like the idea of accepting random tech from a stranger with questionable motives.

Min took the one Damaal held out, turning it over in her hands with undisguised delight. Sue was also enraptured with hers, letting out a squeak of surprise.

"Oh, it's asking to sync with my commlink," Sue said.

((Don't,)) Eva pinged her, but Sue's blush and guilty expression told her it was too late.

Me cago en la mierda, Eva thought. Some people would let anything past their comms safeguards. She'd have to make sure Min coached Sue on proper safety protocols and did whatever damage control she could.

Damaal's psychic waves turned suddenly apologetic, but still authoritative. "To my intense regret, I must request that you permit my associate to escort you to your next destination," she said. "I have received a summons from my superiors that I am obliged to answer in the affirmative. I hope you can forgive my extreme discourtesy in this and all things that may have occurred within our extremely pleasant visit."

"Sin pena," Eva said, feeling like a rug she hadn't known she was standing on just got yanked. "We're, uh, honored to have met you at all."

"Gromira, my deepest gratitude for your assistance in this matter," Damaal said, but her tone was commanding in a way that Eva found deeply uncomfortable.

Worse, Gromira immediately approached Damaal and knelt in front of her. Damaal extended her tail, which Gromira pressed to her head, just as Eva had seen her target do so many years ago.

Eva fought the urge to gag. They were mind-linked now, the two of them. That meant Damaal had every intention of following their crew herself, whatever bullshit she was spinning about having an important meeting to attend or whatever.

Did she know Eva knew about that? If so, it was pretty bold of her to act this way in front of Eva. Was this a mind game? Her way of deliberately telling Eva she was keeping an eye on them, so they'd better behave?

This place fucking sucks, Eva thought. I hate it and I don't want to be here and fuck everything.

Sue gave another soft gasp of delight, and Eva sighed. There were perfectly good reasons to be there. They had a job to do, for better or worse.

"Farewell, honored guests," Damaal said, interrupting Eva's thoughts as she drifted back to the other end of the room. "May you walk in the Light."

Pretty hard not to with all the windows, Eva thought, but she plastered on a smile and inclined her head politely. Her crew followed suit, each in their own way, and without another word they followed Gromira back out into the common area with all the resting xana.

It wasn't until they reached the elevator that Gromira turned her enormous black eyes to Eva and projected polite helpfulness at her. "To what destination may I convey you and your companions?" Gromira asked.

"It's getting late," Eva said, looking to Pink for confirmation. "Would we be able to stay overnight somewhere? Rest up, start fresh in the morning, kind of thing?"

Gromira paused as if conferring with someone silently. "As honored guests, we would be delighted to extend to you the hospitality of local accommodations," Gromira said slowly. "I will have Watcher Rakyra deliver you to an appropriate location."

"Perfecto." Eva snuggled up to Vakar as they began their descent. His scents were still suppressed, but he wrapped an arm around her shoulders, his palps twitching as if in surprise.

Or concern, maybe. If the xana knew they were a couple, it could be dangerous for both of them. But different species treated the various stages of mating and relationships in different ways, so she had no way of knowing whether they'd realize it was a potential piece of leverage in their case.

Also, she didn't give a shit; she really needed a damn hug. Because once they got to the hotel or whatever it was, she was going to call her mother, and that was going to be a bigger pain than any poison spores.

Chapter 13

LOCA COMO UNA CHIVA

The local accommodations were astonishingly beautiful, housed as they were in one of the skyscraper-trees. The lobby, for lack of a better word, was a wide-open space whose ceiling was four stories up, decorated in the same vivid reds and greens and golds that proliferated elsewhere. They were arranged into shapes like leaf patterns, light and shadows playing on each other like in the home-trees of Rilia, somehow both geometric and organic in a way that blended seamlessly. There were also representations of different Attuned etched into the gold lines that served as boundaries between colors, visible when the light hit them from different angles.

As a concession to the tourists, while the walls and ceilings and floors were translucent, technology had been added to render them blurry, frosted, so light would pass through but the guests could retain some semblance of privacy. It was unnerving to look up and see so many shadows milling around, dark spots against the bright colors, like a mold or contagion spreading across what should have been pure and unmarked.

A few lights were also present, some similar to the ones they'd had at the Communal Center in Rilia: tubes or large clear vessels filled with creatures that glowed softly, including a massive central pillar with so many of them that it lit most of the room. But apparently that wasn't enough, because mechanical lights had been added in other places—subtle, hidden, so as not to disrupt the effect created by the natural ones.

Eva was reminded of her fish, swimming around in their tank back on *La Sirena Negra*. At least these bioluminescent critters were useful for more than looking pretty. Maybe she could invest in a glowing fish or two . . .

Watcher Rakyra conferred briefly with a xana who was apparently in charge, and who then escorted them, amid constant waves of psychic deference and friendliness, to a private room on a floor high enough to make Eva's ears pop more than once on the way up. Multiple hammocks hung from the ceiling, presumably serving double duty as beds and chairs, though there was also a small piece of furniture like a couch. A holovid station was set up discreetly in one corner, while the bathing and toilet facilities were in another corner behind clear partitions that Eva hoped could be made opaque for privacy. Enough people had seen her bare ass today, and she was very interested in the oblong thing that might be a tub. She couldn't remember the last time she'd had a real bath instead of a sonic shower.

Probably the last time you visited your mom, her sullen head-voice supplied.

Thanks for reminding me to call her, Eva thought back, but she was just arguing with herself and frankly it was tiring. She groaned loud enough to cause someone in the next room over to startle.

"You said it," Pink said. "You sure you want to do this here instead of back on the ship?"

"We can't be sure we'd ever get back off the ship," Eva said. "Let's go to comms." She allowed herself a deeply satisfying scowl after maintaining a pleasant expression for so long, then summoned her isohelmet and set it to private mode, darkening it to avoid lip-reading software. Pink and Vakar followed suit.

Vakar spoke first. "I have already penetrated some of their security systems," he said, "but their networking methods are highly dependent on their own innate physiologies, which complicates the situation."

"And I tried to volunteer for doctor duties back in Rilia," Pink said. "They assured me they didn't need any help. I can try again at another center, but the way things are locked down here, it'll probably be more of the same."

"I doubt I'll be able to chat anyone up now, with Watchers up my ass everywhere we go." Eva sighed again. No plan survived contact with the enemy, as the saying went. And speaking of enemies . . .

"My mom is here," Eva added without further preamble.

"She's what?" Pink asked.

"Why?" Vakar asked simultaneously.

"Did you mention anything about this to her?" Pink asked.

Eva racked her brain, pacing in a tight circle. "I don't think so," she said finally. "And we didn't get the info from her that led us here, not really. That came from poking around at all the random places Josh went before he disappeared."

"I would also note that we have only arrived earlier this cycle," Vakar said. "She would have had to depart at roughly the same time we did in order to arrive concurrently."

None of it made sense. Her mother was a lot of things, including overbearing, but somehow sniffing out what Eva was up to enough to track her here was some next-level shit. She was a fucking bank auditor, not a Wraith.

Except she was working for BOFA now, she'd said. Doing what, exactly?

"I wonder if she's here for work," Eva said slowly. "She was going on a business trip . . . Maybe it actually is a coincidence?"

"God works in mysterious ways," Pink said. "But that's a hell of a coincidence."

"I'm going to call her," Eva said. "See if I can't get an answer without blowing our mission."

Vakar rested a hand on Eva's shoulder. "That seems prudent," he said. "But be cautious."

Eva almost snapped that she was always cautious, but that would be a lie, so she took his hand and squeezed it instead.

"Well, as long as we're here, I'm taking a bath," Pink said, stretching her arms all the way up.

"Me next," Eva said.

They all deactivated their helmets, Eva plopping down on the couch with a sigh after Pink got up. Vakar joined her, and she leaned her head against his shoulder.

Sue and Min had taken their Pod Pals out of their storage containers, which was itself a physics-defying feat since the capsules were way too small to fit what had come out of them. Each robot was about the same size as Mala, and moved with a fluidity that suggested they were extremely high quality.

Min's Pal resembled a large caterpillar or other insect larva, a buttery yellow with multiple segments and small legs, its sides adorned with circular markings that looked like eyes. It inched along the floor, raising itself up occasionally as if to get a better look around, its tiny forehead stalks wiggling like it was sniffing the air or using some other sense beyond human perception.

Sue's Pal, on the other hand, looked like a sphere with a giant eye in the middle, with two metallic arms and a thick antenna on the top. It floated around her like a combat drone, rotating its arms and making buzzing noises that Eva expected would get very old, very quickly.

Both Min and Sue were completely enamored with their strange new toys. Min crouched next to hers, watching it scoot back and forth and occasionally petting it on the back, eliciting a wriggle that suggested the bot was pleased by the contact. Sue giggled over and over, turning in place to track the Pal's airborne trajectory, even though it seemed to be orbiting her.

Something about them made Eva uneasy. Hell, everything about them did. Hopefully Sue and Min hadn't been foolish enough to give unrestricted commlink access to the bots, or they could be rummaging through confidential information easier than they were currently meandering around the room.

And speaking of that, no sense in further delaying the inevitable.

"I'd better make that call," Eva told Vakar. She stood and summoned her isohelmet in full privacy mode again, running a few scrubbers and relays before the harsh buzz of the line connecting began to make her teeth ache. It took so long for her mother to answer that she had already started composing a message she probably wouldn't leave, because she hated voicemail.

"Hello?" Regina said. "Eva, qué se cuenta, mija?"

"Mami," Eva replied. "I, uh, got your picture. You're on Garilia? Looks like you're having fun."

Regina paused, the sounds around her shifting as she apparently moved. "Sí, bueno. The ocean is beautiful, and everyone has been very nice. So much personal attention, more than any other resort I've visited, and I've been to a few."

"Good, good. Are you on vacation, or was this the big work trip you were telling me about?" Eva paced around the room, avoiding Sue, who had grounded her Ball Buddy and was examining it while a pair of her own yellow bots watched.

Regina paused again, and this time all the background noise vanished. "I'm flattered you're so interested. You usually ignore my q-mails."

Mierda. That was true. Hell, Eva had already spoken to her mom more in the last week than she had for years, and they hadn't ended their last call on good terms. Then again, it was also a dodge.

"Just curious," Eva replied. "Garilia is pretty far out there, and not super well known."

"Sí, cierto," Regina said. "I'm surprised you've heard of it. Y además, I'm wondering how you know where I am. I never mentioned it in the q-mail."

Mierda again. Eva had punctured her hull and everything she said made the hole bigger.

"The building behind you was pretty unique," Eva said casually. "I had one of my people look it up. Are you sure things are safe there?" Not that she expected any Attuned to randomly attack her mother, of all people, but she didn't know what the xana were up to. The vibe she got from Damaal wasn't good, and while that wasn't a lot to go on, it was enough that she didn't want anyone else she cared about to get involved.

Worse, since Damaal knew who Eva was, it might not be a huge leap to connect her to Regina . . .

"It seems perfectly safe to me," Regina said. "The coup was years ago, and things have been mostly peaceful since then."

"Mostly peaceful," Eva repeated. "Cuídate, vieja, 'Mostly peaceful' can turn into 'arroz con mango' in a second." Madre de dios, she sounded like Mari. It made her want to scream.

"I'm sure you would know, Eva-Benita," Regina said, her

voice growing colder. "The last time I talked to you, you were still trying to find that missing engineer for his criminal sister. Y ahora qué?"

Eva exhaled in a huff, weaving around Min, whose caterpillar-like bot regarded her curiously, its antennae waving at her. "How long are you planning to stay?" The last thing she needed was to run into her mom while she was trying to find Josh.

"Why, do you need me to help you again?"

"I was just curious."

"You already said that. Are you writing a book, mija? Ya tu sabes what you can do with this chapter."

"Shove it up my ass and make it a mystery?" Still not a straight answer. Eva made a disgusted noise. "Bueno, ya, whatever. Enjoy your trip." Watch your back, she almost said, but instead she hung up before her mother could respond. Then she immediately felt guilty for doing something so immature, so she stalked over to the corner of the room and screamed into her isohelmet before resuming her pacing.

So that conversation had gone nowhere. But she was fairly certain of one thing: this was the business trip, not a vacation. If it had just been a vacation, her mom wouldn't have evaded her questions the way she did. Regina hated lying, but she was loyal to her work, the same way Mari was, so it made sense that she would duck and weave instead of saying something outright untrue. Which meant that not only was this a work trip, it was probably confidential.

What was BOFA up to on Garilia, and why was her mom involved?

She stopped her agitated pacing just in front of Sue, recoiling with a shouted "Ave Maria!" when she saw what the engineer was doing.

Sue was systematically disassembling her Pod Pal, which stared sightlessly, serenely up at the ceiling. She'd started by taking apart the larger sections, which meant it was already in three main segments, and she was now sitting cross-legged on the floor with one of the segments in her lap, surrounded by tiny glittering pieces of robot.

Eva deactivated her helmet and glared down at Sue. "What are you doing?" When Sue didn't answer, Eva nudged her with the toe of her gravboot.

"Ah!" Sue shouted, startled. She dropped the piece she was working on, and tiny shards flew off like a spray of glitter, clattering against the hard floor.

"This is a giant mess," Eva said. "How are you going to put it back together?"

"Don't worry, I've been tagging every piece as I remove it." Sue tapped her head. "Got a working schematic open, you know?"

Eva nodded. "Find anything interesting yet?"

Sue frowned, her lips pursed in an exaggerated way that made Eva think of a cartoon fish. "A lot of this is weirdly familiar, but there are things that don't make sense. I'm trying to figure out how it grows and shrinks without, you know."

"Violating all the known laws of physics?" Pink asked. She'd emerged from the bath and was dressed in her newly laundered spacesuit.

"What does a doctor know about physics?" Eva asked, eyebrow raised.

"Enough to know nobody's invented a shrink ray yet."

Min, also still fiddling with her Pod Pal, perked up. "I saw a holovid about that! It was pretty funny. This guy made himself super small, and he found this whole species that like, rode tardigrades and he had to save them from an evil scientist."

"I remember this holovid," Vakar said, smelling like jasmine.

"You and Leroy were very concerned about whether a particular tardigrade would survive the hostilities."

Min laughed, her robot buddy climbing her leg. "You were so confused. You kept telling us it wasn't real and that we probably ate tardigrades every day by accident."

Eva crouched next to Sue and picked up a random piece of Pod Pal. It felt like metal—smooth, oblong, with no sharp edges and no dangerous points. Almost like one of Vakar's scales, but much smaller and a dull gray.

"Does this use nanotech of some kind?" Eva asked Sue. "I've seen . . . things that can take apart a living creature and replicate its form. Would something like that be able to shrink and grow?"

"Nanotech is by definition incredibly small," Sue said, brushing away one of her yellow bots as she spoke. "Like, we don't bother using it in our custom ships mostly because it can't do much." She pursed her lips again, as if thinking, then continued. "Like, imagine a tardigrade trying to move an orange. It can't. Even bazillions of them are still too tiny. Nanotech is best for dealing with things on the, you know, molecular or atomic level."

"So even if there was nanotech, it would need bigger stuff to work with, and that stuff shouldn't be able to shrink and grow?" Eva asked.

Sue nodded, her attention drifting back to her lap. Eva wandered into her own thoughts as she paced the full length of the room, and her thoughts were shaped like a particular Proarkhe artifact that had once transformed in front of her, from a large rectangular object to a much, much larger humanoid robot. And Josh had been at that facility, working on something, for which Mari and her Forge friends now needed him . . .

Eva didn't like the picture she was forming with those available materials. Especially given that his trail had led them here, to the place where these Pod Pals had been invented. But no, the timeline made no sense. Lashra Damaal and the Sylfe Company had been shilling these things all over the universe before Josh ever made it out of the Fridge facility. Whatever Josh was up to, whatever had happened to him, couldn't be related to these robot Attuned knockoffs.

Probably. Maybe. Eva couldn't shake the thought, but she tucked it away into the back of her mind because it wasn't helping anything.

"I need some fresh air," she announced, heading for the door. "Anyone want to join me?"

Min and Sue barely acknowledged the question, as distracted as they were. Pink and Vakar, meanwhile, shared a look as if they were playing a mental rock-paper-scissors to decide who was going to offer. Eva wasn't sure whether it would be the winner or the loser, and she squinted at them with her lip curled into a half-snarl.

"Are you sure you're up to walking around?" Pink asked, crossing her legs. "That was a hell of a poison you got hit with, and there may be more of those things out there. Or other ones that can do worse."

You may be recognized again, was the warning, the threat she very carefully did not say out loud.

Eva nodded. "Lo siento, pero I can't stay in here if we're going to have a chance of finding Josh."

"And you're going to, what, start interrogating random strangers?" Pink asked, leaning forward to rest an elbow on her knee.

"I'm going to keep gathering intel about the situation here," Eva said. "This whole place reeks of rotten fish, and not just because we're near the ocean."

Now Pink's expression softened slightly. "You know you can't fix this, right?"

"Fix what?"

"Garilia. What's done is done."

Eva did know that. It was her fault the revolution, or coup, or whatever it should be called, had succeeded in the first place. And were things worse for it? Maybe, maybe not. She hadn't seen much of Garilia when Tito brought her here, had only known about her mission and its parameters and what she had to do to make sure it succeeded. Afterward, she'd alternated between refusing to think about it entirely and bingeing research to learn more about the place, its people, its political situation—and, of course, searching for any mention of her name, any image that might show her, any scrap of a whisper of something to connect her to the awful thing she had done.

That was how she knew she'd acquired names beyond the Hero of Garilia. It was rare that she'd turn up anything, because the new planetary government was thorough in its control and scrubbing of any unofficial versions of the events of that cycle. But every so often, she'd find a post on some random message board, an amateur q-net site with an eyewitness testimony, even a passing mention on a documentary holovid whose other topics were conspiracy theories in line with the extreme trash Leroy had always been obsessed with.

But apart from her actions, there was the question of outcomes. Had she made life better for the people here? Some of them certainly believed that. Some of them didn't. They were probably both right, and wrong, because nothing was that simple and clear-cut. So why did she care about finding out what Damaal was up to? Why did it matter to her, to know the situation on the ground, to see for herself the full trajectory of the shot she had fired almost nine years earlier? Especially when she had other shit to worry about?

Échale tierra y dale pisón, she told herself. Don't be such a metiche. Focus on finding Josh and getting him back to Mari.

"It's all for the mission," Eva told Pink, who smirked skeptically. "Really. And now that we're back in Big Brother territory, I'm sure I'll be fine."

Vakar stepped forward, smelling like ozone, like the air before a heavy rain. "I will go with you. My superiors expect a report on our progress, and my findings so far are minimally useful to satisfy my established mission parameters."

That was its own shitty problem. If Vakar didn't turn up something, his Wraith bosses would yank on his leash and he'd be gone. With everything else happening, Vakar leaving was the last thing Eva wanted. Sure, they'd spent plenty of time apart in the last six months, off and on, but right now, in the middle of Garilia . . .

"We'll find something," Eva said, with more certainty than she felt.

Pink stood as if weary and they exchanged their usual hand slaps, snaps, and hip-bump. "Stay safe," she said. "I'll keep these two from burning down the place."

Eva winced as claws sunk into her shoulder. "Seriously?" she asked Mala, who had once again settled across her neck as if she belonged there.

"Miau." Mala's hazel eyes were half-lidded, and she purred as she sent out a wave of contentment.

"Whatever. Probably need to shit somewhere at this point." Eva sighed. After the way Mala had deescalated that situation with the Attuned, maybe having her along wasn't such a bad idea. But hopefully, whatever she and Vakar found on this particular reconnaissance foray would be less dangerous.

Shouldn't have even thought that, Eva told herself. Now you're definitely going to end up punching someone before the cycle is over.

Chapter 14

CURIOSITY KILLS

If the xana in the lobby was surprised to see Eva, he didn't say anything, and his psychic emanations were as deferential and eager to please as they had been when she arrived. He tried to assure her that there were many excellent food options in the building when she asked, but she insisted right back that she wanted to take a walk outside, and eventually he directed her to a few potential restaurant equivalents nearby. She felt the barest sour twinge from him when she was far enough away that she probably didn't think she would notice.

Eva had a feeling there would be Watchers dogging her every step, and she wasn't wrong. They weren't especially subtle, so she assumed there were more of them she couldn't see loitering elsewhere, or monitoring the surveillance devices stationed regularly throughout the streets.

She thought of all the apparently sleeping people in Damaal's office and her skin flashed hot and cold.

Speaking of cold, the weather was almost absurdly pleasant to her human perceptions. Not too warm, not too chill, a light breeze drifting in from the nearby ocean that brought with it smells both salty and oddly sweet. The local star slowly sank into the water, turning the sky a brilliant shade of teal darkening to velvety blue, and leaving a coppery orange shimmer on the tip of every wave like tongues of flame. The surface was occasionally breached, whether by wildlife or tourists she couldn't tell from so far away, and keening songs echoed softly over the broad swath of sand separating nature from civilization.

Other tourists were enjoying the scenery as well, meandering from place to place with no apparent destination in mind, some of them with Pod Pals of their own. She and Vakar mimicked them, walking slowly, leisurely, as if they had nowhere to be, which wasn't entirely untrue. But they were also both surveying their surroundings, assessing threat levels, all the little habits picked up from years of training and being thrown into the deep end of space to see if they could swim. He'd just been an engineer when she met him, and she'd been the captain of a small ship whose business was composed entirely of side hustles, but they both had secrets in their pasts that lurked below the surface like whatever was out there in the ocean.

His secrets, at least, were nobler. A Wraith was basically a glorified cop, but unlike the petty stungun-wielding assholes Eva was used to dealing with, Vakar had been using his skills and resources to harass The Fridge. He was a tool of the quennian government, yes, but over and over again he had proven that his ethics and loyalties were more complex than any simple tool. While he had been on her crew, he had followed orders as long as she never gave bad ones, and heaven knew she had tried to honor that. Now, he mostly did the same, but with a different set of bosses.

Eva, for all her rebelliousness, for all her sarcasm and aversion to authority, had followed plenty of bad orders before she left her dad's business behind. She'd always been good at justifying them to herself, at rationalizing, at ignoring the parts that now made her want to scream at her past self. She'd wanted to please people, to impress people: her father, Tito, her crewmates, even whomever she happened to be punching or shooting or screwing, as if life were one of Min's games and she was trying to level up, look cool, feel powerful.

Okay, she still wanted those things, but at least now she wasn't an asshole about them.

((Find anything?)) Eva asked, giving Mala a brief neck scratch. She assumed Vakar was passively scanning local networks or the q-net for information even as he observed their surroundings.

He smelled briefly of grass, maybe bashful at being called out? She wasn't sure why; it didn't bother her.

((Local graynet,)) he pinged back.

((Anything interesting?))

((Possibly,)) he replied. He reached for her hand and she let him take it, guiding her toward one of the side streets that branched off the main pedestrian corridor. They still moved slowly, casually, but Vakar was now following some internal map she couldn't see. He doubled back a few times, had them pause to examine some building or other. Finally, he pulled her into an embrace behind a random tree—ignoring Mala's chirp of protest—holding her quietly as if they were sharing a tender moment, smelling of licorice underneath the stronger aromas of anticipation. She half expected Watchers to pop up at any time to stop them, ask them what they were doing, but no one did.

"The density of surveillance equipment has diminished in this area," Vakar said. "I have created multiple feedback loops that should give us some time to move freely."

Eva kissed his face, relishing the moment even if it was meant as a distraction. "So what did you find?"

"The graynet credentials have shifted more than once, leading me to believe that access is obtained through direct interaction."

"How do you interact directly with quantum?"

"I mean that login capabilities are conveyed between individuals, in order to limit the ability of the authorities to locate and infiltrate them."

"Ah, gotcha." She grinned up at him. "So where are we headed?"

He touched his forehead to hers. "An event where locals will congregate, if I have understood the translations correctly."

Mala yawned and dug her claws into Eva's clavicle, making Eva hiss in surprise and pain.

"Knock it off," Eva said, "or I'm leaving you here."

The claws retracted slightly, and Mala exuded calm that made Eva roll her eyes.

Vakar led them toward the outskirts of the city, among small prefab buildings and smaller trees in which hammocks had been strung up. Lights hung in front of open doorways, the people inside clearly visible through the translucent walls, moving about their evening routines or resting or appearing to rest while engaging in stationary activities. But many buildings were empty, their interiors dark aside from the last sliver of a glow from the swiftly vanishing local star, their occupants perhaps not yet arrived from wherever they spent the daylight portion of their cycles, or off to do whatever they did at night.

As it turned out, that was precisely where Vakar was taking them. At the end of a path whose surface suggested it was newly laid down, they reached a construction site, where preparations were under way for what would likely be another enormous skyscraper-tree. Eva wasn't a building engineer, but given the depth and width of the pit being dug, whatever was going in would be huge, and various fabrication devices were neatly lined up next to barrels of the raw materials used to print out girders and trusses and whatnot. Some parts had already been put together and were stacked nearby, waiting for their turn to be assembled into whatever they were meant to be.

And the whole place was teeming with xana. Many of them carried lights, artificial ones or their glowing creature-globes, gently illuminating the otherwise entirely dark site. A few seemed to be in charge, directing others on where to go, gradually forming small groups of a dozen or so spread out around the pit. Some had Attuned lingering near them, and some carried children in pouches attached to the fronts of their harnesses, or hugged them from behind, presumably to keep them from wandering off as children did. They were nearly silent, though murmurs passed between the groups and occasionally louder instructions were conveyed from one leader to another for some unknown purpose.

Their psychic emanations were thick with anticipation, excitement, and some nervousness. They were waiting for something, that much was obvious. But what?

"The surveillance equipment monitoring this site has been circumvented," Vakar murmured in her ear. "It is broadcasting a false impression that the area is deserted."

"Is that so?" Eva's eyes narrowed. "What is this supposed to be, anyway?"

"I am not certain. The information on the graynet called it a Hatching, but also a Storm. I believe the translation is not precise."

While Vakar had led them closer slowly and cautiously, he had not taken pains to hide their presence. The xana noticed them but for a while no one bothered them, until finally someone approached, emanating politeness with a hostile edge.

"You are tourists?" the xana asked.

"Yes," Eva replied. "Is it okay that we're here, or should we leave?" She didn't want to go, because this might be a chance to start digging for intel about Josh among locals, but she also didn't want to piss anyone off or disrupt some important ceremony.

Or, god forbid, be recognized again.

"You may observe safely from a distance," the xana replied cautiously. Her enormous eyes fixed on Mala, still draped over Eva's neck and shoulders. "Is that creature Attuned to you?"

"She's Attuned to herself mostly," Eva said, reaching up to scratch Mala's chin. The cat purred.

"She will not interfere unbidden?" the xana asked. "It would be unfortunate for her to injure herself in the Storm."

Eva shrugged. "She does what she wants. If she gets hurt, that's her fault. But she doesn't usually go running into trouble." Usually. Aside from facing down a bunch of Attuned like it was nothing and almost getting poisoned.

"May the Light embrace you then," the xana said, and left without another word.

"What's a Storm, anyway?" Eva called after her. "Is it going to rain?" There wasn't a cloud in the sky, but weather was its own wild force, different on every planet.

"There may be moisture" was the reply, but nothing else.

She turned to Vakar. "I don't suppose you've dug up anything on the q-net about what to expect?"

Vakar smelled like jasmine and roses and vanilla. Thoughtful, but with some anticipation. "I think this will be . . . interesting."

Even though he wouldn't tell her more, he didn't seem worried, so she settled in to wait.

Eventually, there was movement at the bottom of the pit. Eva pulled up her isohelmet so she could use its distance-vision enhancement tech to get a closer look.

Oblong objects like large eggs were spread around the ground, each several meters away from the other. There were maybe ten of them, ranging in color from a delicate pink to a pale yellow to a deep bluish-gray, almost silvery. The pink ones were the smallest, while the silvery one must have been at least two meters tall if Eva's sensors were accurate. Each of them was moving, some more frequently or violently than others, and now it was clear why this was called a Hatching.

But why a Storm?

That became clear as soon as one of the eggs finally burst open, a yellow one. The creature inside, far from being a fragile chick or wobbly legged lizard, was fully formed and apparently aggressive. It was a quadruped, with sea-green skin or fur or scales—hard to tell from a distance—and a long, forked tail. Its ears resembled the fins of a fish, with a matching fin on the top of its head, and a pale ruff around its neck like a collar. Black eyes peered at the xana, who quickly surrounded it, and with a high-pitched cry it began to swing its tail around defensively.

It was one of the Attuned. Except it wasn't bonded to anyone yet, was it?

The xana didn't move, didn't make a sound, not even the children. They stood in a loose circle around the creature, which continued to posture, lowering its head and raising its tail, then reversing that position, almost like it was making a wave with its body. It crouched low to the ground, staring down a xana who couldn't have been more than a fist taller than it was, and

Eva's breath caught in her throat as she waited for the animal to pounce.

Only it didn't. Instead, the xana released a wave of concentrated psychic energy, all aimed directly at the creature. It was like what Mala did to calm Eva down, but on a whole other level, a pure emanation of empathy and understanding and acceptance. And beneath that, it was an invitation, an offer, a hand extended in friendship. There was nothing controlling about it, no sense of coercion or mandate, only a gentle coaxing, like when Min tried to get the cats to come over to her when she wanted to pet them.

Nothing like what Damaal had leveled at them in her office, which had been about as gentle as a brick to the face.

Slowly, maintaining the psychic effects, some of the xana produced small offerings of food from their pockets or harness pouches. They held these out without waving them around or otherwise trying to attract additional attention, but the creature was clearly interested in the people with food more than the others. Nonetheless, no one reduced their contribution to the communal activity—what would one call it? Storm seemed more aggressive than what was happening, but then again, Eva hadn't seen a storm on Garilia yet. Maybe their weather was calmer, more soothing.

Finally, the Attuned did one last slow rotation at the center of the circle, then stopped and ambled toward one of the xana. The others remained where they stood, but withdrew psychically, emanating continued support without that underlying coaxing. The chosen xana was young, the equivalent of a teenager if Eva had to guess, and he was unable to contain his excitement as the Attuned nudged him with its short snout. The xana offered his tail to the creature and it rested its head on it, and they shared a long moment of psychic communion that ended with a burst of sheer joy. The circle slowly dissolved then, and other xana approached the newly bonded one and its Attuned to press against him like a gentle, armless hug.

"Wow," Eva said.

"Indeed," Vakar said.

They stood together quietly, continuing to watch as this scene repeated for each of the eggs that hatched. Once the groups finished, they left the dig site, moving carefully around the construction equipment and materials and assisting those who had difficulty navigating by themselves. Some xana chatted quietly, all in good spirits if the emotions they were broadcasting were genuine, and a few mentioned other Storms they hoped to attend since they still had no Attuned of their own.

The local star had set completely, leaving the area dark except for the lights each xana carried with them. There were two moons, Eva knew, but at this time in the planet's rotation they weren't visible, so the sky was an uninterrupted stretch of velvety blue-black bright with stars. This planet was far enough from the center of its spiraling galaxy to give a good view of the most distant arms, less like the wide scar of the Milky Way and more like a gentle wave, glittering and vast, slowly cresting for eons.

Eva had a sudden sense of being watched, the hairs on the back of her neck standing up. "We should probably go," she said. They would be alone soon anyway; there was only one egg left.

"Please stay a moment, if you would be so gracious," someone said behind them. A xana, her dark-brown fur striped black, huge eyes contemplating Eva and Vakar as she stood next to, of all people, Nara Sumas. It took a moment for Eva to realize it was her because Nara wasn't wearing her armor, which made her marginally less tall and broad, but she was still imposing as hell. Her long, green hair was pulled back into a ponytail tight enough to give Eva a headache, and her spacesuit was the same color as the sky.

The scuff of a footstep to her left alerted her to another arrival: Jei, the cyborg-guy from Abelgard. His arm weapon wasn't raised, but if the lights on the side were any indication, it was primed to fire.

"We're unarmed, you know," Eva said, taking a small step away from Vakar.

Nara snorted derisively. "So am I," she said, her voice a deep contralto.

Yeah, okay, they both knew that didn't mean shit. "What can I do for you?" Eva asked the xana.

"First, may I inquire as to whether you are carrying prototypes of the synthetic Attuned?" the xana asked.

"We're not packing any Ball Buddies, no," Eva replied. "Should we be?"

"They serve as ever-vigilant sentinels for the Watchers," the xana said. "Through them, the government monitors multiple sensory outputs within a radius of several meters."

Eva suppressed an eye roll. She knew those things were trouble. "Robot spies. Awesome." She'd have to be sure Min and Sue got rid of theirs when she went back to the room.

"I'm not getting any readings from her," Nara said. "She's clean."

Eva raised an eyebrow. "Why bother asking if you were—you wanted to see if I would lie about it?"

Nara smiled, close-lipped, but didn't say anything.

"We are here to extend a request for you to have a discussion with certain interested parties," the xana said. "A discussion regarding the current Garilian regime and securing potential aid for its . . . detractors." Her hands were clasped together in front of her, the gesture almost absurdly human, perhaps meant to put Eva at ease.

Detractors. A nice way of saying "rebels" if she ever heard

one. Her stomach twisted; go figure that she would help one revolution the first time she came to Garilia, only to get tagged by the other side as soon as she came back.

"I'm assuming you want to have this discussion somewhere else?" Eva asked. A glance toward the pit told her the remaining xana were almost gone, which would leave her and Vakar alone with their new companions.

"We have more secure facilities for that purpose, yes," the xana replied. "If you are willing."

"And if we are not?" Vakar asked. His posture had barely shifted, but Eva knew he was ready to throw elbows.

"We depart to our separate destinations," the xana said. "Coercion is not intended, nor useful to our cause."

Eva looked to Nara for confirmation, but Nara's expression didn't change. A sideways glance at Jei said his weapon was still charged, but he hadn't moved, either.

She had to admit, she was curious. Seeing Nara and Jei here was confirmation that whatever they had been doing on Abelgard was related to Garilia somehow. Who had hired them, and for what purpose? And why did they want to drag Eva into it now?

More importantly, could they help her find Josh?

((Go?)) Eva pinged at Vakar.

((Tell Pink,)) he pinged back.

Legit. Eva couldn't very well raise her on comms, but she shot off a message quickly explaining the situation.

"Bueno," Eva said. "Party at your house. Sorry we're coming empty-handed."

"Honored guests need not bring offerings to a gathering," the xana said, radiating calm.

And it's not really a party, Eva thought. But so long as it wasn't a trap, hopefully something useful would come of it.

The xana walked toward a vehicle, tail demurely wrapped around her own neck, as Nara and Jei flanked Eva and Vakar. If something went down, Eva was pretty sure she could take them. Probably.

Pink sent her a terse message that conveyed a whole host of concerns in a few words, but also cautious approval, and Eva closed it down with a sigh, leaving behind the gaping hole in the ground that had been filled with friendship and support only a few minutes earlier. It felt like a metaphor for something, but Eva was no good at metaphors, so she settled for taking a seat in the transport and calculating how many ways she might be able to overpower Nara if the shit hit the air filters.

Their secret meeting place was a nondescript building on the outskirts of Rilia, among the vertical farms, which were much taller now that Eva was right up close to them. Then again, most things were taller than her.

The building's walls were as translucent as any in the area, until she stepped inside and realized the interior didn't match the exterior. She backed up and looked again, and sure enough, some kind of tech was projecting an alternate image, of a group of xana cooking and resting. There was even a child playing with an Attuned, one of the yellow mouse-looking ones. Even more impressive, she could feel psychic emanations from all the people shown on the walls, as if they were actually present rather than complete fabrications.

"For every action, an equal and opposite reaction," Eva murmured. She'd had a conversation with Vakar once, about quennian scents and evolution, and how different groups changed in light of their own physiological and cultural expectations. It wasn't a linear process, and outside influences could take root and grow like an invasive plant or be viciously rejected by the indigenous life. Either way, it was interesting to see the process firsthand.

Two people waited for her and Vakar: a human and a xana, along with an Attuned. The xana was tinkering with a small box, his psychic emanations suggesting intense concentration as well as frustration and bitterness, even anger. Strange that he was so easily read, given how hard other xana worked to control their expressions. Maybe he had a condition like Vakar with his smells, or maybe he just wore his heart on his sleeve or whatever the xana equivalent was. His fur was on the lighter side, though not as pale as Damaal's had been, and his stripes were an amber color that blended into his harness.

The other person was human, dark-skinned and about Vakar's height, his head shaved close to the skin, a full beard and mustache making him look older than his barely lined forehead suggested. Then again, as Pink was fond of saying, black don't crack; he could have been anywhere from late thirties to fifties and Eva wouldn't have been surprised. The bags under his narrow eyes pointed to either lack of sleep or the upper end of that range, or maybe both.

He stopped what he was doing when Eva and Vakar entered, which was apparently working on Jei's dog robot from the fight on Abelgard. Scientist, then, or engineer. How had he fallen in with these rebels, and what exactly were they up to?

"We have brought Eva Larsen and her companion," the xana announced to the room.

"Innocente," Eva corrected. "Captain."

"My apologies for the misnaming," the xana said, projecting a brief wave of contrition. "I am called Felsira."

"Real name or code name?" Eva asked. The xana didn't respond, and Eva shrugged.

"I am Sapri," the other xana said. "And this is Dr. Lucien."

The doctor stood and offered his hand to Eva, who shook it, then was surprised when he leaned in to trade cheek kisses. It had been years since she'd been around someone for whom that was typical, and it brought back a wave of nostalgia for her own childhood. Mala seemed unsurprised by the gesture, or at least she didn't move from her position around Eva's neck.

"A pleasure to meet you, Captain Innocente," Dr. Lucien said. His voice was lilting, with an accent she couldn't place, familiar as it was.

"Mucho gusto," Eva said. "This is my partner, Vakar."

Vakar smelled like hot cooking oil and incense, but said nothing. He still wasn't a fan of this expedition, but she was glad he'd come. She was less glad for Mala, who was once again digging claws into her skin.

Before Eva could ask what was up, Sapri spoke. "I continue to believe this option is undesirable," he said, his huge eyes boring into Eva's. That explained his psychic hostility.

"We agreed that she has contacts and access that we lack," Felsira said, still calm and collected. "We must approach the problem from multiple lines if we are to ensure success."

"She is the Butcher," Sapri said.

"She is the Hero," Felsira replied.

Eva stared at her boots, hands clenched into fists. "I know who the fuck I am," she said. "I know what I did. What is it you want from me now?"

Dr. Lucien raised a hand as if to forestall a response from the two xana. "The situation here is not as it was when you . . ." He paused, a furrow developing in his forehead. "I will explain who I am, and how I came to be involved. Perhaps this will serve as an answer to your question."

"I'm listening," Eva said.

Jei's face was about as sour and surly as Sapri's psychic projection, even as he moved to stand next to Dr. Lucien and his robo-dog, still watching Eva like she was going to lash out at any moment. Nara stood near the door, staring out through the translucent walls at the quiet night scenery outside, but Eva had no doubt she was completely aware of what was going on behind her.

"I was approached by Lashra Damaal at my laboratory on my home planet," Dr. Lucien continued. "She desired to experiment with the Attuned here, to better serve her people, she claimed. My experience with cybernetic technology led her to believe I would be an asset to her existing team."

"She was messing with the Attuned?" Eva asked. The people here seemed to almost revere them; she was surprised anyone would go along with something that might cause them harm.

"Initially, yes," Dr. Lucien replied. He began to tinker with the robot dog again, as if his hands didn't want to stay idle. "She had even compelled a change in certain laws—quite unpopular, as I understand it—to allow the work to occur. There was resistance among the local scientists, which led her to seek outside assistance."

"And you agreed to help?" Eva's estimation of him dropped as she reached a hand up to rub Mala's face.

"I did not," Dr. Lucien replied, eyes narrowing. "My cybernetic work is intended to aid disabled people and creatures, with rare exceptions. I would never operate on healthy species who cannot consent to the procedure."

Eva glanced at Jei, noting his arm cannon, and wondered whether he was one of the rare exceptions. She'd certainly known a few humans who embraced what they called "upgrades" with all the gross baggage that entailed, as well as ones like Pink who'd lost her eye and opted for a new one that would help her a little more at work—not that she needed it, since there was plenty of other tech that did the same stuff, but she liked it and felt like having it.

"I told the Prime this, and she agreed that a change in her project's goals would be welcome," Dr. Lucien continued. "So I was brought here to help develop an alternative to the Attuned. An entirely robotic version that would not rely on breeding and harvesting the creatures of this planet, and would instead make use of other local resources and facilities." He removed a component from the robot dog and peered into the cavity it left, squinting and frowning thoughtfully.

"It was all a ruse," Sapri interjected, his psychic tone growing angrier. "An excuse for the government to develop new ways to spy on its people, as if it had not already done enough."

Dr. Lucien nodded. "Truly. I was collaborating with multiple colleagues on this, so I did not realize the extent of the Prime's intentions until recently."

Vakar still smelled suspicious, but a fiery anger was starting to encroach. Eva resisted the urge to reach out and squeeze his arm for reassurance.

"Once I learned of the surveillance components, I immediately resigned," Dr. Lucien said. "A member of the resistance contacted me and asked me to work for them instead. At first I was concerned about meddling in local affairs, but . . ." He shrugged, pinning Eva with a look. "It is important to do what is right, is it not?"

Eva forced her face to remain neutral, despite her squirming guts. "And who gets to decide what's right or wrong?" she asked. "You? Me? Them?" She gestured at the two xana, whose huge eyes didn't blink.

"I decide for myself and no one else," Dr. Lucien said quietly. "But I will tell you this: freedom is important to me, and I have seen what the government here does with its people when they do not obey. It is not to be borne."

"What does the government do?" Vakar asked.

Sapri spoke up this time. "They force Bonding. Their minds no longer belong to themselves alone, and they become yet another set of senses for the Watchers."

Bonding. The mind-linking thing the xana did. To make them do it involuntarily, coño carajo . . . For the second time in as many hours, Eva thought of the xana in Damaal's office. Maybe they were engaged in a different kind of surveillance entirely.

Eva could understand why Dr. Lucien might feel compelled to help. She was halfway there herself. Mala began to purr, as if to calm her, and Eva reached up absently to rub her ears.

"What about you?" Eva asked Felsira. "What's your angle?"

"It is much the same," Felsira replied, her psychic emanation still calm but with an undercurrent of resolve. "I lost many things to the rebellion, but the loss of my freedom has been a constant cry, as if it were my Attuned and it had been taken from me."

Fancy talk, Eva thought. Especially since Felsira didn't seem to have an Attuned in the first place. Given what Eva had just seen at the Storm, that probably didn't mean a lot. The process was unpredictable at best.

She did notice that the xana called it a rebellion. Interesting.

"And you?" she asked Sapri.

"I was part of the revolution," he said, his own emanations rippling with hurt and anger. "Many things were promised, many changes to help the people of Rilia and beyond. The previous planetary government was a rotten home-tree that had to be cut to spare the forest, but the new tree is a false one, filled with shadows."

More fancy talk. Eva wondered if most revolutionaries were

naturally poets or if she had just ended up with two of them at once.

"What about you, Nara?" Eva asked. "You're here because you're getting paid, I assume?"

"Claro," Nara said, not bothering to turn around. Portuguese, but the word was the same in Spanish.

"Mx. Sumas was hired because she had prior experience here," Dr. Lucien said, his expression suggesting he wasn't entirely happy with the notion.

"And your amigo over there?" Eva asked, gesturing at Jei.

"I go where the doctor goes," Jei said stiffly. His tone suggested he wasn't interested in further questions, and frankly, that was good enough for Eva. Maybe she'd get his story later—assuming there was a later.

"All right, good talk," Eva said, clapping and rubbing her hands together. "So now you get to explain what exactly it is you want from me. Something about contacts and access?"

There was a quiet shared conference between the xana and Dr. Lucien, mostly in psychic emanations and glances. After a few moments, Dr. Lucien returned his attention to the robot dog he was working on, Sapri fiddled with his strange box, and Felsira radiated determination.

"We are aware that you were invited to speak with the Prime as an honored guest," Felsira said, clasping her hands in front of her again. "Our contacts within the Watchers suggest they are extremely concerned with your whereabouts and actions, and are diligently attempting to accommodate you despite some who believe it would be more prudent to require that you leave the planet."

Eva had wondered about that; if they were spending so much time chasing after her, why not just kick her out? Certainly she wouldn't be able to refuse, and it would be a huge pain in the ass to figure out how to sneak back onto the planet. Assuming it was even necessary; they still hadn't been able to establish that Josh was there at all.

"You have any thoughts on that?" Eva asked, staring directly into Felsira's large, dark eyes.

Felsira turned slightly, so that she was gazing out through the wall at the starlit farmland. "We are uncertain, but we believe there may be a way to utilize your . . . relationship with the Prime to aid the resistance."

"How, exactly?" Eva asked. "And what's in it for me?" Vakar still smelled mostly like cigarettes and suspicion, but there was the smallest hint of jasmine in there, so he wasn't entirely put off these people.

"You are searching for someone," Dr. Lucien said, pausing in his work. "Joshua Zafone."

And there was the sound of the other shoe dropping, heavy as a gravboot. "How did you hear about that?" Eva asked. She hadn't even told Damaal, though Sue had let enough slip that presumably the xana might have figured it out, if she got past the layers of identity fluff Eva tried to maintain between her crew and shady places like Garilia.

"I told them," Nara said, and Eva mentally cursed herself for being a comemierda. Of course the bounty hunter knew; they'd more or less told Miles fucking Erck the whole story to get him to give up his intel, that sinvergüenza.

"Did you tell them I wiped the floor with your sorry ass in that bot fight?" Eva said.

"No, because you're the one who stepped on the ball there, anus," Nara replied coolly. She still hadn't turned around.

Eva rolled her eyes. "So yes, great, looking for Josh," she said. "And you can help with that?"

"Joshua is currently employed by the Sylfe Company in the

development of their robotic Attuned," Felsira said quietly. "Dr. Lucien worked with him briefly before leaving the project."

Me cago en diez, Eva thought. He had been here the whole time. And if he was working on the Ball Buddies, that meant Damaal knew exactly who he was, any nebulous ideas of being old college friends aside. But that raised a whole new set of questions.

"He's not being held here against his will?" Eva asked the doctor.

"He did not appear to be," Dr. Lucien replied. "In fact, he was quite eager to join our team. I was only acquainted with him for a few cycles, but in that time he toured the facilities and took extensive notes, occasionally conferring with the Prime about changes he hoped to make in the design and production of the robots."

Right, he and Sue were two peas in a pod that way. A chill ran up Eva's back; could Josh have stolen some of the Proarkhe tech he'd been working on with The Fridge? That would explain why Sue thought some of the mechanisms of the bots were strange, and why they seemed to be able to defy the laws of physics. Those mysterious ancients were worse than humans the way they popped up in random places to turn a normal planet into an arroz con mango.

Eva pursed her lips. "So I help you do whatever, and you help me get to Josh, is that right?"

"Correct," Felsira replied.

"And if I don't want to help you?" Eva asked.

Sapri burst with psychic revulsion. "I warned you that the Butcher could not be trusted. We should end her now, while she is—"

"Easy there, Papito," Eva said, readying the command to activate her sonic knuckles. "You haven't told me what you want me to do, and for all I know, it's a big pile of mierda that I don't feel like touching." Vakar hadn't moved, but he smelled just as on edge as she was, and Mala's purring had stopped.

"Do you intend to betray us?" Dr. Lucien asked, his tone mild, his expression carefully neutral. His dark eyes studied Eva like she was a robot whose guts he could dig into, given the right tools.

"No," Eva said. "I'm not here to start problems for anyone. I have enough of my own."

Now it was Jei who spoke up, almost as hostile as Sapri. "This was a waste of time. Anyone who would do what she did isn't worth dealing with." To Dr. Lucien, he said, "Why would you take the word of that bounty hunter anyway? She's no better."

Eva raised an eyebrow and glanced at Nara. "Qué rayo, Sumas?" she asked. What had Nara said to them?

"I vouched for you," Nara said. She looked sideways at Eva, her green hair touched with red from the wall behind her. "Me, I'm loyal to my bank account, and whoever feeds it. You saved those hostages on Pupillae and you didn't get paid for it. You didn't even take the credit." She turned away again. "I think you're a fool, but you're the same kind of fool as these people."

Nara had been here when Eva killed all those xana, had held her at gunpoint until it was clear that her employers would no longer be able to afford Nara's services. They'd crossed paths here and there since then, but mostly they ran in different circles; Eva's hustle was delivering shit, while Nara's was capturing or protecting people.

And as far as Eva knew, Nara would take any job she was offered, for the right price. Hell, she'd worked for Eva's father, Pete, when he'd stolen *La Sirena Negra* out from under Eva's crew, which Eva had never understood, given that Pete had nothing to pay with at the time. Ethics didn't enter into it; odds, maybe, though Nara had a reputation for beating bad ones, hence her outrageous prices. If stories were to be believed, she'd single-handedly cleared an entire planet of space pirates once.

Eva didn't believe that, but then again, she had trouble believing some of the shit she herself had done.

"Joshua is kept with the other scientists working on the project," Dr. Lucien said quietly. "We all but lived in the laboratories in order to meet the requested production schedule. To stop the Prime's plan, we must infiltrate those facilities and destroy them. If you aided us, you would be able to reach Joshua and do whatever you must."

Which will be a lot harder if he isn't interested in leaving, Eva thought. Hopefully Sue would be able to convince him, or he'd take the bait that Mari and The Forge were dangling in terms of working with their own Proarkhe tech and secret project. Maybe their "save the universe" talk would resonate with him; Eva certainly felt the allure of being a big damn hero, even if it was never as simple as people made it sound.

She had to admit, the thought of undoing some of the damage she had done on Garilia was tempting. The Watchers were shady as hell, Damaal was worse, and the whole new government reeked of an oppression that Eva felt in her bones needed fighting. Maybe the resistance was the wrong way to do it, but maybe not. It was worth finding out.

"I have to consult with the rest of my crew," Eva said. "But this is the best chance we've had yet to do what we came here for. So . . ." She looked at Vakar, who shrugged in the quennian equivalent of a nod.

"We work together for now," Eva said. "Let's do this."

Dr. Lucien nodded approval, then hesitated. "One question," he said.

"Yeah?" Eva asked.

"Why do you have a cat with you?"

Chapter 15

DON'T BLOW IT

Eva and Vakar were quiet on the way back to the construction site, escorted by a sullen Jei and Nara, with Mala still draped across her neck. The giant pit was empty now, dark, a strange wound on the landscape that would someday be another building stretching up into the sky. Funny how holes could be filled that way, could go from void to life-containing with the work of many hands.

Eva could relate. Maybe her life wasn't quite as grand as one of the home-trees or their fabricated counterparts, but it had been empty and now it was so full that sometimes it threatened to overflow. She had others to thank for that, a whole crew—a family—who had given her a hand up out of the pit she'd dug for herself and now they'd built something worth inhabiting. She hoped they all felt that way, at least.

Certainly they'd been through enough together already—

dangerous jobs, raids on Fridge facilities, space fights and bot fights and everything in between, all for the enormous goal of bringing down an organization that was a starwhale when they were tardigrades. And now she was going to explain to them why they should help yet another group of people who were facing impossible odds to do something that felt right but might be very, very wrong. She wasn't looking forward to that conversation, but it needed to be had, and if her crew decided not to help the resistance, she would abide by that. They'd find another way to reach Josh, even if it meant crawling back to Damaal and begging.

Eva didn't think that would be so easy, either, but she had to consider their options.

As she was about to climb out of the vehicle, she stopped. "Random question," she said.

Nara put a hand on her hip in a way that suggested she'd been reaching for a weapon that wasn't there. "What," she said.

"Why were you on Abelgard?" Eva asked. "You never told us."

"It was none of your business," Jei replied. He sat on the floor of the transport, his arm weapon still charged; she wondered whether he had to maintain that with concentration or whether it was automatic.

"You can tell me now that we're such good amigos," Eva said, smiling at him with her mouth closed.

"Erck," Nara said. "Same as you."

Eva hadn't gone to Abelgard for Erck in the first place, but she wasn't about to contradict the woman. "What did the resistance want Erck for?"

"What do you want Josh for?" Jei asked, frowning.

"His sister has been looking for him," Eva replied coolly. "She's my crew, so I'm helping her."

Nara looked her up and down, a slow gaze that ended with meeting Eva's eyes. "Right." Her tone bristled with sarcasm.

"If that were so, you would have no reason to be sneaking around here the way you are," Jei said. "And you would not have a reason to extract him. Simply knowing he is here and well would suffice. You might even be able to go straight to the Prime and ask that she let you visit him, and she would likely allow it."

"Maybe I never trusted Damaal," Eva said. "She certainly didn't give me a reason to, and I still don't have one."

Jei didn't look convinced, and Nara . . .

"Don't make a liar out of me, Larsen," Nara said.

"Innocente," Eva corrected. "And don't pretend you don't lie all the time."

"I lie for money," Nara said. "I lie when a job requires it. I don't lie for myself." Her eyes were deep blue, like the sky darkening to night, like the places underwater where light barely reached and everything was cold and crushing.

"I'm not going to screw you over," Eva said. "Don't worry." As if telling anyone not to worry had ever worked.

Nara didn't even bother rolling her eyes, just gestured dismissively at Eva. Jei glared at her like she'd insulted his parents, which hey, maybe she had. She still wasn't sure what his beef with her was.

Eva and Vakar climbed out of the transport and watched it take off, zipping away faster than virtually anything seemed to happen on the whole damn planet.

"I guess we go back to the room now," Eva said.

"Yes," Vakar replied. Mala yowled agreement as well.

They began to walk, with Vakar leading the way as he had before, though they hadn't coordinated it. Some things didn't need to be discussed.

Then again, some things did.

"Is this a bad idea?" Eva asked.

Vakar smelled like incense, like the air before rain, like ozone and jasmine and a shade of mint. All anxiety and worry and a pit of thoughts as deep as the one they were leaving behind them.

"There is a story I learned when I was young," Vakar said finally.

"Story time," Eva said, grinning. "My favorite."

Vakar's smell gained a bashful spike of green, which faded quickly. "When the quennians first began to explore space, we encountered a sapient species called the ibbyhn. This was before translator nanites were fully developed, and before we had joined any interspecies coalitions, but with time and patience we made ourselves understood."

"What were your first-contact protocols?" Eva asked. She'd learned the basics in school, like most other humans, and had to review them when she was getting her pilot's license, but that had been a long time ago.

"We approached cautiously, peacefully," Vakar replied. The smell of jasmine overpowered the others as he delved into his thoughts. "Ours were among the protocols eventually adopted by other species, who had often been more aggressive, even if unintentionally. We offered knowledge and asked nothing in return."

Eva chuckled. "Knowledge is plenty dangerous. There's more than one way to be a colonizer."

"Of course." A brief fart smell of dismay. "We were more naïve then, and optimistic."

The stars continued their slow progress above as they walked. Eva leaned closer to Vakar, even though it wasn't remotely chilly. He reached out and took her hand absently, instinctively. It was a human gesture, not a quennian one; she smiled to think he'd internalized it over their short time together.

"So what happened to the ibbyhn?" Eva asked. "Typical first-contact problems?"

"Indeed. They had been a kind species, a communal one as the xana appear to be, their technology devoted to granting themselves easy lives where all were cared for as needed."

"Sounds too good to be true," Eva said. "Are you sure the quennians didn't make this up? Bedtime story sort of shit?"

Vakar wagged his head, palps twitching. "It is possible. We are not as dedicated to storytelling as your species, but certainly we have cultures who value emotional manipulation for lesson-teaching purposes."

"Such terrible liars," Eva teased.

He smelled amused for a moment, then introspective again. "The ibbyhn split into factions. Some took up weapons, dissatisfied with their lives and believing that force was the tool best suited to the problem. Others defended themselves, hoping to return to the circumstances under which they had lived peacefully for so long."

"Civil war is a fun plot twist," Eva muttered. "Why does life always get violent? Can't people just be nice to each other without someone throwing a chancleta?" She glanced sideways at Vakar. "And yes, I know it's rich for me to be the one saying that, after—" Her words stuck in her throat.

After everything she had done, not just on Garilia, but all over the universe. Hell, she'd loved being aggressive when she was younger. It made her feel powerful. Strong. Proud of herself in ways nothing else seemed to accomplish, because she was good at it.

Qué mierda. Her neck flushed hot with shame, and Vakar's grip on her hand tightened. Mala began to purr again, a little furry engine of tension reduction.

"One of the factions did not resort to violence," Vakar said quietly. "Or so we are told. They spoke words of peace to any who would listen, and attempted to halt conflicts where they could, often by placing their own bodies in the way of harm."

"Sounds like an easy way to die," Eva murmured.

"Many of them did." Vakar smelled pained, like rust and copper. "But they attempted to break the cycle of violence. Their example served to lessen the conflicts, and encouraged others to find alternate methods of engagement."

"And everyone lived happily ever after?" Eva frowned at her own sarcasm. Vakar didn't deserve it.

"They did not," he replied. "The story claims that some of them went into hiding while the rest committed genocide. No ibbyhn has been seen since."

"So they're either all gone, or the ones who hid are still out there somewhere?" Eva asked.

Vakar hesitated, smelling sad. "It is likely that the notion of their hiding was added to the account in order to provide a sense of optimism rather than complete failure. As noted, quennians are not known for being good liars, but we have our methods."

Eva nudged him with her hip. "If this story was supposed to make me feel better somehow, it's not doing the best job."

"You questioned whether intervening in the politics on this planet was a good idea," Vakar said. "When the ibbyhn began their civil wars, the quennians did nothing. They did not believe it was their place to interfere."

"That's more or less BOFA policy, too," Eva said. "That everyone has to deal with their own problems, and they'll be around to help whoever comes out on top."

"It is the only way to ensure each species is allowed full autonomy." Vakar smelled like rust, and fire, and copper. "It is supposedly the height of arrogance to assume one might know better from the outside than those within. Perhaps it is arrogant, but I cannot help but think, if only someone had done something more, perhaps the ibbyhn would not be extinct."

"And maybe they would have blown themselves up even faster. Maybe they would have screwed themselves up in a hundred other ways no one could predict."

"Perhaps," Vakar said. "Ultimately, we each must make our own choices. Whether to fight with words or weapons. Whether to fight at all."

Eva fell silent. Around them, the trappings of civilization grew more dense, the lights within buildings casting red and green and gold squares on the ground, while the stars continued their slow rotation overhead. In the distance, waves lapped against a pristine white shore, and the smell of salt and night-blooming plants drifted along a breeze so faint it hardly stirred Eva's hair.

Nothing was easy. No answers seemed like the right ones. For years Eva had regretted what she had done here, regretted all the lives she had taken in a single moment. But she'd taken other lives before that, and others after; the only difference was the size of the body count. Coming back to Garilia felt like a chance to atone, or to undo what she'd done, but she couldn't undo death. No amount of apology or effort would change the past, so all she could do was consider how her actions would affect the future. And for all she knew, the resistance would be just as bad as the current regime—or worse.

But she still needed to find Josh and get him to Mari. She and her crew needed to get paid, and this job would keep the ship fueled and repaired for a long time if she was prudent. Initially, she had expected she might be riding to Josh's rescue, but it certainly seemed like that wasn't the case. That said, if he was here voluntarily, the rest of the universe might be safer if she convinced him to do what Mari wanted instead.

Eva had seen the ads herself; Sylfe Company was planning to distribute the Pod Pals all over the universe. BOFA would inspect them, but if Proarkhe tech was being used, and the BOFA folks didn't figure that out and flag it, or if regulations weren't tight enough, it was possible the little bots could end up spying on millions of people, maybe billions. If the rebels were trying to disrupt what Damaal and her people were up to with their surveillance bots, that alone might be worth an alliance.

Tech like that could cause violence, or it could end it, depending on who controlled it. Knowledge was power, and power could be bought and sold, traded and taken.

There were fewer tourists around, but the number of Watchers seemed undiminished. Every pair of eyes followed Eva and Vakar as they walked back to the skyscraper where they would be staying for the rest of the cycle. Waves of psychic calm emanated from them, of authority, of the certainty that came from being the government's eyes and ears and fists. Any of them could approach Eva, detain her, whisk her away somewhere, and bury her like The Fridge had. If she stepped out of line. If she acted up. If she said something they deemed unacceptable.

The urge was strong, but she suppressed it, gripping Vakar's hand tighter. They had work to do.

Pink was practically climbing the walls when they got back, despite Eva already messaging her that they were on their way and pinging her from the elevator. The room's door opened and Eva was all but dragged inside, Mala leaping off her shoulders with a hiss.

Min lay in one of the hammocks, eyes closed, limbs twitching—probably playing one of her games. Sue was still on the floor with her Ball Buddy, which was now in even more pieces than it had been when Eva left. And Pink, well.

"Welcome back from your walk," Pink said, her eye wide with emotions Eva couldn't read yet. "I hope you two had a good time out there, enjoying the fresh night air and all that."

"It was very nice," Eva replied. "Relaxing. I can't remember the last time I got to unwind like that."

"Yeah, we work hard," Pink agreed. "Did you eat?"

"No, and I could definitely use a bite if you've got something."

"Right over here." Pink guided Eva to the corner under the holovid unit, where a table had been set up with stuff on it.

Except it hadn't. It wasn't there at all. The corner was completely empty.

Pink pressed a finger to Eva's lips and activated her isohelmet. Eva did the same.

"I had Sue and Min work on a loop of us eating so we could talk," Pink said.

"How did they—"

"Min had some old recordings from *La Sirena Negra* and Sue rigged up other stuff."

"But why can't we just—"

"Talk in privacy mode like we did before?" Pink folded her arms and leaned against the wall. "Do you know how many times people came up here to check on us since you left?"

"How many?"

"Six. In less than three hours."

Eva whistled. "Coño. That's some devotion to hospitality."

"Hospitality my sweet ass. This whole place is bugged to hell and back." Pink sighed and rubbed her forehead. "Where did you go and what happened?"

Eva explained as quickly as she could, because she didn't think the eating ruse would last forever, and if the building's staff were checking in all the time, they'd be arriving any minute. Pink listened intently, interrupting for questions once or twice, then settled into a pensive stance with her arms loosely crossed, fingers drumming on her bicep.

"So do we help them or not?" Eva asked.

"You think we should," Pink said, even though Eva had tried to present the whole situation as neutrally as possible.

"I think we could use their help to get to Josh without dealing with Damaal." Eva wrinkled her nose at Sue, who had made an excited noise and flipped her visor up to sniff something, for whatever reason. "Our other option is to keep poking around on our own. We might be able to find someone willing to talk about Josh, or the lab where they work on the Ball Buddies—"

"Do we really need to keep calling them that?" Pink asked.

"Fuck yes, it's hilarious."

"Fine, so we can try to find our own way to Josh, or we can go straight back to Lashra Damaal and give her the business, or we can help these folks and maybe start another pussy riot in this club."

Eva nodded, then snarled. "We can also leave. That's always an option, but then we don't get paid."

"And Sue doesn't get to see her brother." Pink shook her head. "Nah, that's not on the table. Just the other shit."

"You think Damaal will bite?" Eva asked.

"Nope," Pink said. "I'm surprised she hasn't shipped our asses off-planet yet."

"Me too. So we keep busting ass alone or we take the deal."

Pink shrugged, uncrossing her arms. "Let's see where these resistance folks want to take us. If it's ugly, we can back out and let them do their own dirty work."

Eva raised her eyebrows. "You think we can trust them?"

"Girl, I don't trust anyone, you know that. We find out what they're up to and we watch our own backs."

"All right." Eva pensively eyed the rest of the crew. "Vakar is in, too. Let's make sure Min and Sue are on board and go from there."

A delicate sound like a combination wind chime and whistle echoed through the room, accompanied by a psychic projection outside that was like if courteousness were a knuckle gently rapping on the door.

"There's our chaperone checking in," Pink said sourly. "Careful getting out of the holo."

"Yeah, don't want to walk out of a table," Eva said. They deactivated their isohelmets and Eva took her sweet time strolling over to the door.

A cream-furred xana with dark stripes awaited her. "Greetings, honored guest," he said. "May I inquire as to whether our accommodations continue to meet your standards?"

"You just did, mijo," Eva replied with a smile. "And yes, they're fine, thanks."

"We are pleased to know this. We humbly request that you do not hesitate to reach out to us should you require anything whatsoever."

"Sí, bueno, gracias, muy amable," Eva said, sliding the door closed manually. The xana leaned slightly to the side to continue looking into the room until his view was completely obstructed, the translucent material clouded to mask the interior for privacy.

As if that made a difference, given that the room was bugged. Eva flopped down on the couch-like chair and sighed. Mala leaped up and began to knead Eva's thighs, purring softly.

"Like you haven't been all over me all day," Eva muttered.

Mala paused and looked in Sue's direction, growling low in her throat at the disassembled Ball Buddy.

"Yeah, she's made quite a mess," Eva said, but what she wanted to say was: *That thing is bad news, for sure, if even a cat knows enough to hate it.*

Not much they could do about it now, though. Stay vigilant, trust nothing, and hope they didn't get marched out by Watchers at some point. At best, they'd get escorted back to their ship, but at worst . . .

Eva slouched lower in the seat and closed her eyes. Might as well rest while she had the chance.

Her stomach growled louder than Mala, eliciting a grumpy chirrup from the cat.

"Fine, that first," she muttered to herself. She had a bad feeling this was going to be a long night.

Eva was awakened from her moderately comfortable nap in one of the hammocks, by the weight of a furry body on her chest and a paw gently patting her nose. Mala stared directly into her face, whiskers trembling, the hazel of her eyes nearly eclipsed by wide, black pupils.

"Qué bola?" Eva murmured.

"Miau," Mala replied, leaping to the ground. She turned in a circle, tail lashing back and forth, as if asking Eva to follow her.

The room was dark, lit only by the distant glow coming from other rooms around theirs, ones likely occupied by people less inclined to sleep at night. Everyone else was asleep, except Vakar, who didn't sleep so much as quietly meditate while his body rested. With some awkwardness, Eva climbed out of the hammock and trailed after the cat, who stopped in front of Min's backpack. Eva squinted, crouching and leaning closer. Mala growled and pawed at the bag, then made a figure eight in front of it and shook her tail angrily.

Eva hesitated. She didn't want to go through Min's things, but she also didn't want to wake the pilot up over a cat being weird.

Mala patted the bag once, twice, in what seemed to be a specific place. "Miau," she repeated.

I guess I'll apologize later, Eva thought. She carefully opened the bag where Mala indicated, a small outer pocket that contained only one item.

The Pod Pal. Ball Buddy. Whatever.

Eva removed the container and examined it. Seemed easy enough to operate: simple button press and out popped the robot. She still couldn't believe something the size of a cat could fit into a ball that she could grasp with one hand, but the proof was right there.

And so was Mala, growling and lashing her tail back and forth, her ears nearly flat against her head. This was definitely what was bothering her, but why? It was just a robot; weird, maybe, but Mala had never been this aggressive toward Sue's little yellow bots.

Eva turned it over carefully and rubbed it with her thumb. She brought it to her face and sniffed it, as if that would yield some clue. It smelled like Min's backpack, for one thing—apparently she'd stashed a half-eaten container of spicy rice cakes somewhere—but underneath was a standard metallic polymer scent. Something else, too, something familiar that Eva couldn't place . . .

The barest hint of a psychic emanation touched Eva, like the stray brush of fingertips against skin, except in her mind. Mala hissed, as if she felt it, too. Was it coming from the robot?

Psychic spying, on top of everything else? Eva didn't want the damn thing anywhere near her for another minute.

The room didn't have windows, so she couldn't very well throw the ball out that way. If she tried to leave it somewhere in the building, she had a feeling the extremely helpful staff would bring it right back to her. And if she told them she didn't want it anymore, they'd probably want to know why, and that might be the cue for the Watchers to swoop in and escort them away.

But if there were an accident . . .

Eva mentally apologized to Min for what she was about to do. Quietly, avoiding the leg-twining Mala, she crept over to the garbage recycler and slid the cover open. It was a standard model, theoretically capable of handling items of varying kinds and compositions, and a very popular plot device in many crime holovids. It was also just large enough for her to cram the Ball Buddy inside.

With a sigh, she tapped the activation button on the device's panel. It chimed softly, whirred to life—

And exploded.

Eva was thrown back against the couch, where Vakar had been sitting peacefully, and was now squirming underneath her in surprise. Her ears rang, the skin on her face and neck shrieked with pain, and her chest felt like she'd been kicked by a todyk. Everything smelled like lechón, which probably meant she'd been badly burned.

Things went fuzzy after that. She was mostly extremely aware of the amount of discomfort she was experiencing, then of something cold being sprayed on her injuries, and then the sting of quick-heal nanites being delivered via injection. The pain gradually receded, though there was a nagging sense that someone nearby was very upset with her, and someone else was worried, and at least one other person was radiating waves of psychic distress that suggested they were afraid of being punished.

Also, there was purring. Eva assumed that was Mala, but who knew.

Eventually the haze receded, and Eva found herself stretched out on the couch with her legs hanging over the side. She blinked at the ceiling above her, whose colors seemed to shift and shimmer as the lights on upper floors moved around, lit up or were extinguished. But she could see, which was good, since it meant her eyes had survived whatever had happened.

Someone shifted on the floor next to her—hearing, check, also good—and Eva turned her head to stare directly into Vakar's gray-blue eyes. Some part of her said she should be startled, but the rest was on some excellent medications that assured her everything was perfectly fine and she had no need to move.

"Oye," she said. It felt like she was talking through a mouthful of soggy beans. "Qué pasó, mi vida?"

Vakar's palps twitched, his gaze holding hers steadily. "Someone appears to have unintentionally placed something volatile in the recycler. Due to an unknown triggering mechanism, this caused the disintegrator to detonate, damaging our room as well as several adjacent rooms." He paused. "Also, you sustained injuries to multiple portions of your anatomy in the explosion."

"Gwao," Eva said, blinking slowly. "Y ahora qué?"

"Watchers have been stationed at various points outside our room and near available exits," Vakar said. "We have been assured that a new room is being prepared for us and we will be relocated presently. Pink has been arguing with Watcher Rakyra regarding whether you require transport to a Communal Center for more advanced treatment. Sue and Min are with her."

Eva shook her head, which left unpleasant trails of motion blur wherever she looked. "I should go. I . . . should go? I should . . . go." She giggled, then frowned. "I need to tell you things. Privately."

Vakar activated his isohelmet, and after a few failed attempts, Eva managed to activate hers as well.

"The Ball Buddies," she said.

"Yes?" Vakar replied.

"It's a terrible name for a product," Eva said. "I think the human who helped translate it was not very professional. De pinga, bro."

Vakar paused. "Is that all you wanted to tell me?"

"No, no, espérate." Eva's mental fog thinned and she scrambled to gather the thoughts milling around aimlessly like grazing sheep. "I put a Ball Buddy in the disintegrator. That's what exploded. But it shouldn't have."

"Unless one of its components was something that would react explosively to the molecular destabilization technology." Vakar's face was hidden by his darkened helmet, but he smelled all kinds of worried and mad. "That would suggest there is the equivalent of a bomb within every one of the robotic Attuned."

They both turned to look at the pieces of Sue's robot, still spread out across the floor. One central part was still intact, and Eva was suddenly very grateful that Sue hadn't managed to take that apart yet.

"I'm also pretty sure there's psychic tech in those things," Eva said. "Like, what the xana can do, the neural networking thing, but in a robot. Maybe more."

"That would explain why Mala was so averse to them," Vakar

said. "New technology may be able to circumvent existing hardware or software safeguards. If these robots were able to create a universe-wide neural network among any sapient species, that would be—"

"You're cute," Eva said.

"I . . . what?"

"Sorry." Eva gathered a few more sheep. "Okay, I need to make a call, and then we're getting out of here. Make everyone get ready to leave."

Vakar smelled confused and concerned. Eva wished he would knock it off, because the room already had enough smoky aromas going on from the explosion.

"Where will we go?" Vakar asked.

"One second." Eva held up a finger as she activated her comms and opened a line. The dull buzz of the call attempting to connect made her teeth ache more than usual.

The person on the other end answered, their voice bleary with sleep. "Hello?"

"Hey, Mami?" Eva asked. "Where are you? I need to crash with you tonight."

Chapter 16

GIRLS JUST WANNA HAVE

Regina Alvarez was staying in one of the low buildings closer to the ocean, its walls like thick, cloudy stained glass thanks to the opacity controls. A winding pebbled path led down to the water, partially obscured by waist-high bushes dotted with small berrylike growths that reminded Eva of pitangas. The gentle rush of the waves and the accompanying breeze toyed with her still-skewed senses, because everything smelled like sulfur instead of salt.

Eva leaned on Vakar as she walked, and was flanked by Pink, while Sue and Min trailed after. Mala was back in Min's backpack, apparently content to be there now that the Pod Pal was gone.

Behind them a half dozen meters away, Watcher Rakyra and several other Watchers, well, watched them go, standing outside a transport and emanating authority and a concern that Eva had initially taken as politeness related to her health. Now she wasn't so sure.

They reached the panel that functioned as a door, but before Eva could knock or figure out some other presence-announcing system, it slid open and a glossy black hoverchair glided through.

"Eva-Benita, mija, ven acá, entra!" Regina Alvarez said, gesturing excitedly at Eva. Her magenta-dyed hair had been chopped short and styled to fall in careless-looking layers, and her light-brown eyes were lined with makeup, as if she hadn't been awakened only a few minutes earlier. She turned the chair away slightly, then back, studying Eva critically.

"What happened to your face?" Regina asked. "You look completamente desmondingado."

"Thanks," Eva replied, leaning down to plant a kiss on her mother's cheek. "Why are you wearing high heels at this hour?"

Regina pursed her lips. "Bueno, just because it's late doesn't mean I can't look nice. Especially when I'm about to meet your friends for the first time." Her tone shifted to excessive friendliness at the end of her statement. "Hello, mucho gusto, I'm Regina Alvarez. Por favor, come in, make yourselves at home."

With an imperious wave, Regina floated back inside, and Eva reluctantly followed. Yes, this had all been her idea, and she was still fairly sure it was the right call, but part of her wanted to run screaming into the nearby ocean and swim until she reached another island. Maybe another planet.

The interior of the building was surprisingly large and well furnished, apparently with humans in mind. Kitchen with typical food-synthesizing equipment, living area with plush-looking couches and seats, dining room with a table and chairs made from colorful carved bark pieces. One of the chairs had been relocated to allow access to her mom's hoverchair, but everything else was already arranged so as not to impede her movement or be frustratingly unreachable. A hallway led to more rooms, the translucent walls obscured by the privacy fogging mechanism.

"Bueno, so," Regina said, shifting in her chair to lean on the right arm, laying a red-nailed finger on her cheek. "Evita, dale, introduce me to everyone, please."

Eva refrained from rolling her eyes and instead started with Pink, who was closest. "This is my co-captain, Dr. Rebecca Jones," Eva said.

"Pleasure to meet you, ma'am," Pink said, offering a hand to Regina, who shook it delicately.

"A doctor and a captain?" Regina asked. "Very impressive. My abuelo was a doctor, you know. He and a few colleagues opened a hospital together near a university, and he was the chief resident for several years. Did you attend university?"

"No, I trained remotely," Pink said, the temperature of her voice dropping slightly.

"Ah, okay," Regina said, eyes wide even as her smile remained plastered on her face. Eva could almost see the drive core in her mind firing desperately as she tried to reroute. "Well, remote training must be difficult, since your facilities are limited. You have to work harder, sí?"

Pink flashed a brief, sardonic grin. "There are certainly fewer options for getting laid, but we manage."

Eva snorted a laugh and bumped Pink with her hip. Regina laughed as well, hearty and not entirely genuine or comfortable.

"This is Park Min-jung, our pilot," Eva continued, gesturing at Min, who had removed her shoes and was examining an elaborate-looking VR setup pushed against the far wall.

"Happy to meet you!" Min replied, rushing over and giving a polite bow, Mala on her heels. "Thank you for looking after us."

"Ay, no, sin pena," Regina said. "I'm always happy to help my daughter and her friends. And their cats?" She eyed Mala curiously, and Mala purred, twining in a figure eight.

Eva cringed internally. Her memories of growing up didn't exactly support the idea that her mother was happy to help—more like she was happy to be involved, the metiche—but Eva wasn't about to be contrary. Not when she'd called out of nowhere in the middle of the night to ask for yet another favor.

"Aren't you a little young to be a pilot?" Regina asked Min.

"Mami, por favor, she's an excellent pilot," Eva said. "No empiezas."

"Qué, ya, I'm not starting anything," Regina replied. "It was just a question." She gestured at Sue. "She seems very young, too, mija. I hope you're not running any unpaid internships."

"Her name is Susan." Eva shook her head. "And no, that's illegal."

"Bueno," Regina said, drawing the word out and raising her hands defensively. They both knew what she meant: that hadn't stopped Eva before.

And yes, in fairness, Min and Sue had been in a lot of dangerous situations that Eva would never, ever tell her mother about in a million years. But she did pay them well for it, and more importantly, they did it because they wanted to.

"So you're Susan Zafone," Regina said, staring at Sue, who blushed and scooted closer to Min. Eva tensed, preparing to sidestep a lecture about criminal activity.

Vakar entered the room then, smelling like menthol-flavored tobacco. "The Watchers have departed," he said. "I also searched the perimeter and interior for surveillance equipment and did not detect any active devices."

Eva froze like she'd been stuffed into a cryo locker. Vakar. Coño carajo, she had never told her mom about Vakar. Hadn't even mentioned she was in a relationship at all because she didn't want to answer the inevitable prying questions, which would lead to some story about her mom's latest unpleasant date with Fulano de Tal and how Eva really needed to be careful out there.

Why hadn't she stuffed herself into the recycler instead? And why hadn't she spent the entire cabrón ride over here figuring out how to deal with this unbearably awkward moment?

Before Eva could say anything, her mother dove in headfirst. "Dios mío, is this your security guard?" Regina asked, moving her chair closer to the door. Her tone was laced with suspicion and dismay, her lips pressing together as she scrutinized the now grassy-smelling Vakar.

"This is Vakar Tremonis san Jaigodaris," Eva said, her mouth dry. "He's not security, he's my partner."

Regina raised an eyebrow. "You have a partner and a co-captain? Un poco extraño, pero bueno, allá tú."

Eva closed her eyes and inhaled. "No, Mami, not that kind of partner." She stared down at her mother, who stared up at her with raised eyebrows. Behind Eva, Pink snorted a laugh.

Finally, Regina lifted her head in a slow nod. "Oh," she said. "Mija, you didn't tell me you—"

"I forgot," Eva said. "Anyway. It's late, everyone is tired, I'm sure you're tired, so we should—"

But Regina had already slid up next to Vakar, whose bashful grassy smell was intensifying and gaining layers of tar and ozone. Her mother was a lot at the best of times, but new-significant-other meetings were a whole other level.

"Regina Alvarez," Regina said, holding her hand out to Vakar. He took it gravely, carefully, shaking it once with his own gloved claw.

"It is a pleasure to make your acquaintance," Vakar replied solemnly.

"Are you nervous, mijo?" Regina said, smiling, patting his hand. "Ay, don't be. It's not your fault Eva-Benita is so secretive. I'm glad we were able to finally meet! You can tell me all about yourself. How long have you known each other?"

Alabao, it was like a searchlight being pointed directly at Vakar's face. Eva took his hand away from her mother's and flashed a pained and very forced grin. "Mami, por favor, can this wait?"

They stared at each other for several long moments, various expressions flashing across both their faces. Finally, Regina pursed her lips and wagged her head.

"Bueno, qué suerte, this place has plenty of beds and those hammocks the xana prefer," Regina said, waving in the direction of the hallway. "I had been using one of the spare rooms as an office, but I put my things in the master bedroom so you don't have to worry about it."

Eva narrowed her eyes. "So what does BOFA have you doing all the way out here?" she asked.

Regina smiled with her mouth closed. "I thought we were all very sleepy, mija," she replied.

Touché. Eva nodded and yawned, lacing her fingers together and stretching her arms out in front of her.

"Gracias, Mami," Eva said. "We'll talk more in the morning."

"Cierto," Regina agreed, and Eva wondered briefly whether they could somehow wake up extra early and sneak out before her mother noticed.

The smell of coffee, proper Cuban coffee, greeted Eva when she startled awake from a nightmare. She'd been back at her childhood home, lying in her mom's bed, and the xana they'd called Mother had stood in the doorway staring down at her.

Had drifted closer while Eva clutched her blanket and tried to scream, tried to leave, but her muscles wouldn't respond, her voice was a whisper, no one could hear her and no one would come to save her, and then a tiny perfect circle bloomed on Mother's forehead as purple blood trailed down between her enormous, dark eyes . . .

Eva sucked in a lungful of air and wiped her face with the back of her hand. That had been milder than usual, and no less than she deserved, but it wasn't the best way to start a cycle that promised to be its own special brand of unpleasant.

She'd opted to sleep on the couch, with Vakar sitting across from her, close to the door in case someone tried to get in—or leave, though where her mother went was less of a worry at the moment than whether they were about to be rounded up by agents of the Prime.

Part of her was still wondering why they hadn't been, why the Watchers had agreed to bring them all here when asked. Lashra Damaal was playing a hell of a game of dominoes, laying down one tile after another with no clear strategy. And Eva had a bad feeling she'd be the one locked out and left knocking on the table.

"Good morning, good morning, good morning to you!" Regina sang, hovering over with a tacita of coffee for Eva, complete with espumita. "I know you prefer a cortadito, but I forgot to bring any milk, and I can't figure out how to get this cabrón máquina to work." She gestured at the synthesizer in the kitchen behind her.

"It's fine, gracias, Mami," Eva said, and took the tiny cup. "I'm surprised they even have tazas de café here."

"Ay, no, I brought my own," Regina said. "And my cafetera. When you travel as much as I do, you realize very quickly that no one has what you need, so . . ." She shrugged and returned to the kitchen, retrieving her own cafecito and sipping it delicately.

Eva inhaled the dark, bittersweet scent and sighed happily. For all the other reasons this whole trip had been shit, a cup of good coffee almost made it worthwhile. Almost.

Regina returned, inching toward Eva, but with her eyes on Vakar. He was resting, his eyes closed and his palps still, scales gently shifting as he breathed.

Regina leaned in close to Eva's ear. "Is he asleep?" she whispered.

"He doesn't sleep," Eva whispered back. "Also he can hear you, he's just being polite." You sang a whole song a minute ago, Eva thought, shaking her head in disbelief.

"Ah, bueno, good morning then," Regina said. "Do any of your . . . friends drink coffee, too?"

"Not Cuban coffee, no," Eva replied. "Pink prefers iced sweet tea, Min likes hot green tea, and Sue drinks some weird thing she calls 'root beer' that's like if licorice and malta had a baby."

"I hope they can get the synthesizer to work, because I didn't bring any of that." Regina studied Eva critically, continuing to sip her coffee, lips perfectly lined and colored the same dark red she'd worn for years. Eva waited, wondering which of them would break the silence first, and what topic they would start with. Why Eva was on Garilia? Why she hadn't mentioned it during their prior call?

"You should have told me you had a boyfriend, mija."

Eva sighed, in relief or exasperation, or maybe both. "What, like, sent you a q-mail? 'Oye Mamita, I'm good, by the way I have a partner now, here's a picture'?"

"Sí, eso," Regina said. "Your sister sent me a picture of her last boyfriend."

Yeah, right. "I didn't think about it. I've been busy with work."

"Claro. And now you're here doing what, exactly? Looking for that criminal?"

Eva exhaled loudly and threw herself sideways to lie on the couch. "No empieces, por favor. What are you doing here, hmm?"

Regina looked away and took an unusually long sip of her coffee. "This is my business trip, like you said," she replied.

"What business?" Eva asked. "You're an auditor. What are you auditing here for BOFA?"

Regina's expression flattened out, like she was making an effort to control it. "Garilia's membership application. A lot of things have to be checked and rechecked before the planet can upgrade its protected status."

Of course someone had to oversee a whole planet being in compliance with whatever rules and regulations BOFA churned out. Eva had never imagined her own mom doing it. That was a job for random, faceless bureaucrats in stuffy offices with desks covered in holocubes of kid pictures—exactly the kind of thing Eva had run away from when she was a teenager, going to work for her dad, with his glamorous universe-traveling life of adventure.

And here her mother was, out from behind her desk, apparently traveling the universe to check . . . Whatever the hell needed checking. A bureaucrat with a face. And coincidentally, conveniently, assigned to the last place in the universe Eva wanted to be, and the place she needed to be the most in that moment.

Eva found herself deeply unsettled in ways she couldn't process immediately, so instead, she deflected.

"I need to get some breakfast," she announced, springing to her feet and taking her taza to the kitchen for sanitizing.

"I can make you something," Regina said, floating up behind her.

"No, it's okay, I want to see what they have that's more . . .

local. Maybe take a walk by the water." Eva smiled, hoping it looked genuine.

Vakar opened one eye, otherwise not moving. "Would you like me to go with you?"

"No, that's fine, I'm fine. How are you?" She was aware of how absurdly chipper she must sound to him, but hoped he wouldn't make a big deal out of it.

Pink emerged from the room she was sharing with Min and Sue, yawning and stretching like the cat that followed at her heels. "I want some local breakfast, too. I'm coming."

Eva almost protested that she wanted to be alone, but the look in Pink's eye stopped her. "Fine, great, salpica. My stomach isn't going to feed itself." She crossed to the other couch to give Vakar an awkward sideways hug, which he returned, resting his head briefly against hers before releasing her. He smelled like licorice, like the air before rain, but as much as she wanted to keep sitting with him, she couldn't stay there for another minute.

Regina smiled like she had a secret. "Bueno, I have to get to work, but I'll be here when you get back." She hovered over to Eva, who dutifully planted a kiss on her mother's cheek before practically running for the door.

Pink, who had always been the best at reading a room, let Eva stew while they walked aimlessly through the tourist area. The streets were full of people at this hour, mostly kloshian and frog-like vroak and four-armed buasyr with their spidery eyes, all enjoying the golden-hued local star brightening the sky to a stunning blue. A group of muk wandered by together, their claws snapping in excitement at whatever their guide was signaling, and isolated pockets of humans carrying bags of beach supplies sauntered toward the water like they were on a mission. Signs outside various buildings indicated that food was available inside, but the prices were wildly beyond what Eva was interested in paying, and as hungry as she genuinely was, she had a head full of other problems.

The rebels would be contacting her at some point with their plan for shutting down the lab, and her crew would have to decide whether they were in or out. Or she could do it alone and let them work another angle? That might be the safest choice, and the most practical. But it was almost pointless to keep speculating until she had a better idea of how this would all go down.

A protein bar was waved in front of her face. Eva glanced sideways at Pink.

"Gracias," Eva said, tearing into it gratefully.

"I know we've got some ground to cover," Pink said quietly. "Not here, obviously, when we get back."

Eva nodded, chewing and trying not to glare at all the surveillance equipment she knew was positioned around the area.

"You wanna talk about your mom, though?" Pink continued. "She's something else."

A kloshian family walked by, a pair of identical children scampering around the parents like satellites around a planet. Eva scowled and swallowed the bite in her mouth.

"Nah," Eva said. "My stuff with her is a lot and it's not going anywhere in a hurry. Better to focus on more useful things."

Pink laid a hand on Eva's arm and guided her off to one side of the street, to stand in the bright-red shade of a building. "Y'all are going to compartmentalize yourself into a breakdown," Pink said. "I've been there, and it's not fun. Don't overdo it."

"I know."

Pink started walking again, leading this time. She tossed a

smirk at Eva. "She really does just say anything that comes into her head, doesn't she?"

Eva snorted. "She's worse once she gets comfortable with you. That was her on her best behavior."

"Lord save us," Pink said. "And you really didn't tell her about Vakar?"

"I've barely spoken to her in years. It wasn't on purpose." Not the whole time, anyway.

Pink held up a hand as if to ward off Eva's tone. "I get you. Not like I've introduced y'all to everyone I've banged in the last eight years."

A brief mental inventory of Pink's sexual escapades cycled through Eva's mind. The ones she knew about, anyway. "Ay dios, remember Adrian?"

"Adrian!" Pink groaned. "His hair was so good. All long and blond and silky. It was like God made it personally and angels kept it perfect with nightly visits."

"His son was a handful, though. Had that jump rope he kept hitting you with."

Pink laughed. "He said it was his whip. And I couldn't be like, 'Boy, I'll show you a real whip,' because I'm not that kind of lady."

Before they could continue reminiscing, a shadow fell over them, and within seconds they were entirely flanked. Calm but authoritative psychic tones emanated from three Watchers, including the seemingly ever-present Watcher Rakyra, whom Eva was really starting to feel like punching.

"Captain Innocente," Watcher Rakyra said. "I have been asked to convey many apologies to you for the destruction of your companion robot, and the injuries it caused to your person."

Eva squinted at the xana and faked a smile. "Sin pena, I'm

fine." Her face still stung, but Pink had treated it in time, and she was breathing normally, so she assumed the nanite injection had taken care of her re-bruised ribs.

"I have also been asked to deliver a replacement," Watcher Rakyra said, holding out a capsule. "The Prime was most insistent that you not be inconvenienced by the loss."

"Oh, I'm not," Eva said, before she could censor herself. She winced internally. Alabao, she really was like her mother.

"I do not entirely comprehend your assertion," Watcher Rakyra said, his tone gaining an edge of concern.

"I mean, I don't need a replacement," Eva said. "It's okay. We still have one, and Min wasn't that attached to hers anyway." Min had, in fact, been super upset, partly because of Eva going through her bag, but he didn't need to know that.

Watcher Rakyra lowered his hand. "I will . . . inform the Prime of your decision. I was also asked to inquire as to the status of your second unit. Is it operating to your satisfaction?"

Eva thought of the Ball Buddy lying in pieces all over the floor of their hotel room. "It's great," she replied. "Very satisfactory."

The Watcher hesitated again. Could he tell she was lying? Probably, if they'd been using the robots as surveillance and they were no longer operating properly. But would he call her out? Cuff her? Subdue her some other way, or let her keep on roaming freely?

What the hell was Lashra Damaal up to with her?

"We are pleased to hear of your satisfaction, honored guest," Watcher Rakyra said finally, his tone ever so slightly annoyed. "We were additionally asked to reiterate the Prime's invitation to attend the Tournament and its preceding organized conviviality event showcasing the upgraded units."

That's right. Eva had forgotten about all that, had more or

less ignored the invite because she hadn't been interested in any of that business, just in finding Josh.

"What kind of event are you talking about?" Eva asked.

Watcher Rakyra took a moment to collect himself, as if he hadn't been expecting any interest. "Tonight there is a gathering at the Sylfe Company Building, for investors to interact with the scientists who developed the companions, and to enjoy a demonstration of the capabilities of the various unit types."

Meet the scientists, hmm? That sounded like exactly the place to hook up with Josh, given how much he had allegedly contributed to the project. Maybe she wouldn't have to work with the rebels after all, if she could just stroll into this party, grab some bocaditos, and chat him up like any other guest.

The thought gave Eva a pang of guilt; she had promised to help the resistance, but her mission had to come first, not whatever sense of atonement might be guiding her. And certainly not loyalty to their cause, which she didn't have.

Besides, if she could get Josh out, it might make the rebels' job easier regardless. Everyone wins.

Then again, it was also a perfect opportunity for Damaal to trap her and pump her for information. And what Eva said might make things much harder for everyone instead of easier, since she didn't know what Damaal was up to. Was it worth the risk?

"You should go," Pink said. "You love parties."

"Parties are totally my jam," Eva agreed. That was easily the boldest lie she'd told in months, but if Pink thought this was a good idea, it probably was. "Count me in."

"I am certain the Prime will be delighted to know this," Watcher Rakyra said. "A transport will be sent to retrieve you prior to the commencement of the event, in the long hour before the Light descends into the sea."

"So, before sunset, got it." Eva grinned. "I'll wear something fancy."

Watcher Rakyra's tail twitched in its harness. "Your enthusiasm for our humble invitation is welcome," he said. "Please, continue to enjoy our excellent city and all its offerings."

"Thanks, definitely," Eva said. "Adiós."

"Walk in the Light," the Watcher replied, but it felt perfunctory, and when he and the other Watchers walked away, their silence was as thick as a wall.

Eva took a few steps in a random direction before stopping again, staring into a shop window without seeing its contents, thinking about the party, about the bots and the city and the government of this whole planet, held together by a fist that, if not iron, was definitely tightly clenched. And yet they'd still sent Watchers over with a replacement spy robot capsule for her crew to carry around, their own personal bug. Was Damaal worried they were going to run off to Rilia again, or even to another city elsewhere on the planet? Was she hoping they'd leave entirely and take the Ball Buddies with them, for future spying shenanigans? And what exactly were they planning with that psychic neural network tech?

Maybe she could get a little more information at the party later. And maybe, just maybe, she could finally do what she'd come for and get off Garilia in a hurry.

There was something Eva was forgetting, though, a thought she knew she'd already had, except it had slipped away with the brain fog and mom assault. She took another few steps, toward the next building over, staring at the sign over the door. It translated to "Familiar Childhood Comestibles" and seemed to have an array of products for various palates and physicalities. Nothing she recognized from her childhood; humanity had enough different cultures to begin with, and more since they had expanded off Earth, so attempts to trigger nostalgia were a gamble at best. She expected it was the same for the other species hanging around, but it was nice that someone had tried.

A commwall inside the building startled her; she hadn't seen one elsewhere on Garilia, not even in the spaceport. It had pilfered data from her commlink—the fake data she used on her public profile—and was attempting to lure her in with promises of something called strawberry daifuku. It looked good, but it wasn't the must-have food her persona suggested.

Funny that a place with so much surveillance doesn't have more commwalls, Eva thought. They've got bugs in every damn wall . . .

Except at her mother's place. Vakar had said it was clean. Which Eva had suspected might be the case because of BOFA regulations, hence suggesting they go there.

"What's that look for?" Pink asked.

"What look?" Eva asked.

"Like you just got a royal flush and the dealer's showing twos."

Eva smirked at her eyebrow-raising co-captain. "We're not quite there, but I think I just figured out where the queens are. Vámonos. Let's get back to the others and see if we can't take advantage of this hand." Her smirk fell away like she'd dropped all her cards, and she started walking faster.

"What now?" Pink asked.

"Me cago en diez, I left Vakar alone with my mom."

Chapter 17

DRESS TO KILL

Eva and Pink returned to find Min lying with Mala on the floor, Sue sitting at the dining-room table with her Pod Pal once again in pieces, and Vakar nestled inside a privacy bubble on the couch. Regina was presumably in her own room, because she wasn't with the others, which made sense; she'd said she had work to do.

Eva checked on what Vakar had said before and confirmed: the house had no surveillance equipment in it. Not a single auditory or visual device, no stray signals, nothing but the link Regina had presumably set up to do her work. And if she was working for BOFA, they had their own methods of encrypting or scrambling the feed that few dedicated hackers could penetrate. Not to mention that spying on the person who was evaluating the planet's compliance with regulations—the person who presumably had the ability to stop Garilia from becoming a member of BOFA—would probably be unwise.

On a hunch, Eva had managed to find them the safest place in the city to stay. Knowing that, she had to make sure she didn't piss off her mother and get them kicked out.

Stealthily, Eva stepped into the kitchen and set the synthesizer to make her the equivalent of scrambled eggs. With any luck, Regina wouldn't appear and demand to know why she'd gone out for breakfast only to come back and make more. Pink slid in behind her and started going through the cabinets, grabbing a cup that presumably meant she wanted her tea. She tapped her foot idly, then took over the machine as soon as Eva's food was ready.

Min stared blankly at the ceiling, so Eva waved a hand above her. "You okay?" Eva asked.

"Missing my other body," Min mumbled. "I'll be fine."

It had been a while since Min had left *La Sirena Negra* for this long, it was true. She'd piloted *El Cucullo* when Eva came back from the land of the frozen, thanks to her Fridge nap, but otherwise she rarely left for more than a few hours at a time. This particular mission had coaxed her out more than usual, at Evercon and then Abelgard, but this jaunt on Garilia had turned into a multiday affair. The remote connection Min used had plenty of range depending on their location, but here the relays were slower, less reliable.

Maybe Eva should send Min back, by herself, just for a little while. Would that be safe? No, better not to split up too much, and certainly not to have their pilot potentially stuck at the spaceport while the rest of them were swept up elsewhere. Or, god forbid, have Min be apprehended and held separately.

"I'm sorry," Eva said, feeling acutely how useless the apology was.

"At least I have Mala," Min said, rubbing a finger under the cat's chin. Mala purred in response. She likely knew exactly what Min was going through, and was helping in her own psychic-cat way.

Vakar finally finished whatever he was doing and deactivated his isosphere, once again smelling like a yard full of mint that had caught fire. His palps twitched in agitation, and he was even tapping his claws together like he only did when he was extra frustrated.

"What happened?" Eva asked, plopping down next to him. He hesitated, and his smell took on a coppery, remorseful edge that she didn't like in the slightest.

"I was speaking to my supervisors," Vakar said quietly, staring down at his hands.

Eva tensed, fork frozen halfway to her mouth. "Mierda."

"Indeed."

"What did they say?"

Vakar raised his head to look at the other people in the room. "I had to inform them of my location. They were . . . displeased."

"What's their problem?" She paused. "Or problems, I'm guessing."

"The distance from the nearest Gate was one of them. It hampers my ability to be relocated quickly in a crisis situation."

"Right, pero like, too late to do anything about that," Eva said around a mouthful of egg.

He rested his hands on his neck, his smell more pensive now, flowers rather than mint. "They were primarily concerned that I might engage in some activity that violates the directives outlined under the planet's protective status, which could cause a much larger diplomatic incident."

Of course. Wraiths had a ton of latitude for their operations, thanks to savvy negotiations with BOFA and the fact that quennians had a seat on their council. But Garilia wasn't a full member yet; they were in that special class that meant everyone else had to keep their hands off while they got their act together. Which meant Wraiths couldn't run around arresting people and blowing shit up for no reason, which meant Vakar had to be extra-special careful about everything he did.

Eva's heart would have skipped a beat if it wasn't mechanical. "Oh no, they didn't hear about the recycler exploding, right? You're not going to get blamed for that?"

"It has not yet been designated as an incident in need of examination and rebuke," Vakar said. "But it is conceivable that the event, or similar ones, could be used against me in the future."

Eva put her plate down on her lap, no longer remotely hungry. "You need to get out of here. Hop the first transport back to the rest of the universe before something happens."

"That is no longer possible," Vakar said, smelling embarrassed and displeased. "I informed my supervisors about our mission."

"You what!" Eva exclaimed, standing so fast she upended her plate. Fake eggs scattered all over the floor, a scrambled yellow mess that Mala immediately sauntered over to sniff. Everyone else in the room, however, stopped what they were doing to stare at Eva with varying expressions of surprise and concern.

"I had previously indicated that Josh was present at the main facility when it was destroyed, and that he might have absconded with sensitive data," he continued. "In the hopes that they would allow me to remain here, I added that he may possess stolen Proarkhe technology."

"And?"

"They have ordered me to maintain a presence here, but they are sending more experienced Wraiths to relieve me of this mission going forward."

Eva groaned and flopped onto the couch, covering her face with her arm. Vakar took her free hand in his, stroking the back of it with a claw. She wanted to jerk it away, but she was just being sullen, so she left it.

Naturally, at that moment her mother glided into the room, a frown marring her otherwise flawless makeup. "Mija, you yelled," Regina said. "Qué pasó?"

"Nothing," Eva said sullenly.

"Bueno, pues, why did you yell?"

"I stubbed my toe." It was the first thing that sprang to mind, but even she knew it sounded ridiculous.

Regina pursed her lips and rolled her eyes. "Fine, allá tú, don't tell me. How was your breakfast?"

"It was—" Eva sighed, remembering the eggs and plate on the floor. "We couldn't find anything so we came back here to eat."

"You should have let me make you something in the first place." Regina moved to the kitchen, where she raised her chair enough to let her reach the cabinets. "At least I got to have a lovely talk with your boyfriend."

"Partner," Eva said reflexively.

"Partner, discúlpame."

Vakar's smell shifted to embarrassment with an undercurrent of licorice. She couldn't believe she'd left them alone in the first place. What had they talked about? Ugh, she didn't even want to know.

Yes, she did. "What did she tell you?" Eva asked Vakar.

"Nada malo, mija, no te preocupes." Regina sliced pieces of guayaba and laid them on crackers, a block of cream cheese waiting nearby.

Eva stared at the food like a shark scenting blood, every question in her mind forgotten. She released Vakar's hand and got to her feet slowly, calmly, walking over to the kitchen at a leisurely pace as if she weren't perfectly ready to shank someone for the chance at guayaba con queso crema.

With a smile, Regina brushed Eva's hand away. "They're for you, malcriada," Regina said. "Sit down and I'll bring them to you."

Making a small whimpering noise in the back of her throat, Eva returned to the couch. Now Vakar smelled amused, and she slapped his leg and shot him a narrow-eyed scowl.

Carajo, she needed to focus. Vakar had thrown a wrench into the FTL drive and now they had to scramble. It would take the Wraiths at least three cycles to arrive, by which point they needed to be finished with their own mission and on their way back to The Forge regardless. That fat bonus was on the line, on top of everything else.

Plus Eva had to get ready for the party tonight. She wasn't sure what to expect; she'd seen high-society parties on holovids, but that stuff was half fantasy and half plot contrivance. The closest she had personally been was once when her father had attended some fancy fiesta, and had to meet her on the roof to swap out his sidearm because he'd brought a lethal one by accident. He'd been wearing throwback Earth fashion with a slitted-sleeve jacket and extremely tight pants, while his date was swishing around in a gown that looked like it was literally made of water.

Thankfully, Pink knew enough about fashion to save Eva's ass. Pink was most comfortable in tank tops and loose pants, but she was obsessed with following the latest styles being strutted at every star-studded event across the universe. And not just the human ones, either; Pink had forgotten more about kloshian body paint than Eva had ever known about her own actual body.

Shopping meant money, though, not to mention Eva had

no idea what they might find on Garilia, let alone in Spectrum City . . .

Her mother interrupted her thoughts by waving a plate in front of her face. "Toma, mija," Regina said. "If you had come for dinner last night, I made albondigas, pero ya lo comí todo."

Where the fuck did she get the ingredients for that? Eva wondered again. Was she traveling the universe with a tiny refrigerated unit full of ground beef and sofrito?

Another part of her thought: my mom has been making dinner for just herself for how many years? Coño, I should have stopped by more often. I didn't need to be such an asshole to her.

But Eva had her reasons, and those reasons didn't evaporate in a moment of sympathy. Still, maybe she could do something while she was here.

"Mami," Eva said, "you're doing all the BOFA processing for this place. You must know a lot about it."

Regina narrowed her eyes. "Sí, y qué?"

"Do you know where Pink and I can buy something nice for me to wear?"

Pink slurped her sweet tea, loudly enough to attract Eva's attention, then put her glass down on the counter. "You shouldn't go alone," Pink said.

"They didn't mention whether I got a plus-one." Eva tried to surreptitiously scoop her fallen eggs back onto their plate, but her mother stared at her and wrinkled her nose.

"There's always an implied plus-one for this fancy shit— pardon my language, ma'am," Pink said.

Regina waved dismissively. "You should hear me when I find a door that won't fit my chair."

"I could accompany her," Vakar suggested, smelling like ozone.

The last party-like event Eva and Vakar had attended together ended in a lengthy firefight and both of them got hauled off to the brig afterward. It had gotten worse from there, but that was Tito's fault, not Eva's. Not a good precedent.

But besides that, there was the diplomatic-incident possibility to consider. "No, better if you stay here," Eva told him. Too bad; he would have been adorable in formalwear.

"Might be good for him to be along to rein you in," Pink said with a half-smile. "Don't want you showing your ass to anyone."

"Mija, de qué rayo estas hablando?" Regina asked. "Is this for work?" She tapped the arm of her hoverchair with her forefinger like she was sending messages in Morse code.

Eva hesitated, unsure of how much to spill. "Sort of," she said. "There's a big fancy party tonight and I'm invited."

"How fancy?" Regina asked.

"Very fancy."

Regina stared at Eva as if she could read thoughts as easily as a commlink visualization. "Bueno," she said finally. "I would let you borrow something of mine, but my nice dresses are cut for me to put on easily. You might 'show your ass' as your friend said."

Right, because of the chair. Just as well; her mom's sense of fashion was very particular, and Eva had never been in love with it. Some hoop earrings were too big, period.

Sue had apparently started listening, because she spoke up now. "Captain, did you find out something about my brother?"

Eva closed her eyes for a moment, reopening them as her mother swiveled to cast a frown in Sue's direction. Let her look, Eva thought. Maybe she'll realize Sue's not a monster like she's been building up in her head.

"Maybe," Eva said.

"Is he here? Is he okay?" Sue asked, jumping to her feet so quickly she stumbled, knocking over a chair.

Eva winced. The more she told Sue, the more Sue might blab to the wrong person. And a very wrong person was currently seated a meter away, looking back and forth between Sue and Eva like she was waiting for one of them to draw a weapon.

"We're still checking things out," Eva said, holding up a hand as if to stave off more questions. "I don't want to get your hopes up." Especially since Josh had almost certainly come voluntarily, based on what Dr. Lucien had said. It made sense; he'd bounced around the universe apparently trailing Lashra Damaal, then showed up here working in her labs. The more she thought about it, the more Eva suspected that had been his plan from the start.

"Bueno, I think a party sounds like a wonderful idea," Regina said, clapping her hands together and folding them primly in her lap. "I know the perfect place to go shopping for a dress—"

"Pants, please," Eva said.

"Not in this climate," Pink said. "And take Vakar to the party."

Eva winced. "That's not—"

"Ay, sí, you and your partner should go together!" Regina exclaimed. "Qué fun. We'll find him something nice, too."

Once again, despite all her arguments, internal and external, Eva was suddenly regretting her decision. But what harm could a little shopping trip do?

Eva had entirely forgotten what shopping with her mother was like. Even though they had a purpose—buy something for Eva to wear at the party—Regina wandered in and out of nearly every store they passed in the huge open-air complex that a human would call a mall or market, but the locals called a Stop Cluster. It certainly felt like she was stopping constantly, to Eva's intense exasperation. Rotating holographic cube signs expanded into circular ones based on proximity, showing the name of the place as well as an image of what could be obtained there. As they entered each building or paused at each stall, the sign's color slowly shifted from a pale blue to a purplish pink, as if to mark the ones they had visited already for easy visual reference.

A trail of pink spread out behind them like breadcrumbs in a fairy tale.

"Mami, they don't sell clothes here," Eva said for what felt like the hundredth time.

"Pero mira, don't you think your sister would like one of these?" Regina pointed at a colorful carving that hung from the ceiling, catching the light as it gently turned.

"No. Maybe. But she doesn't need it." Eva wondered how tacky it would be to wear her spacesuit to the party. She could pretend it was the new fashion somewhere in the fringe. Maybe she could even find some new gravboots to replace the ones that kept malfunctioning? No, cheaper to have Sue keep fixing them.

"Ooh, look at those!" her mother exclaimed, dashing off to another part of the room. The xana proprietor of the shop stood impassive in the corner, psychically emanating helpfulness and polite restraint.

Pink sighed, her arms crossed over her chest. "She doesn't stop, does she?"

"Her batteries will run out eventually," Eva said. "Then she'll start complaining about everything and asking when I'm going to have kids."

"Merciful heavens." Pink uncrossed her arms long enough to give Eva an affectionate shoulder pat, which Eva accepted with a sour expression.

Eva approached her mom to beg her to keep moving so they could buy something before the party was over. Regina had stopped in a corner with a lovely view of a street behind them, and was quietly tapping the arm of her chair like she was lost in thought. But then she angled slightly to the left, pausing the tapping for a moment before starting again.

What is she doing? Eva thought. The street looked like any other here, albeit with fewer of the blue holographic signs. Pedestrians ambled or hovered about, while Watchers mingled among them or loitered on corners, their pale uniforms a different kind of light reflecting the local star's brilliance.

Strange that they were so obvious. If Eva were running a spy network, she wouldn't advertise it. Then again, these were the ones she could see; that didn't mean others weren't wearing plain clothes. And if this were anything like other places with a robust system of constant vigilance, enough locals would snitch to the Watchers that they hardly needed to go out of their way to sneak around.

Not to mention whoever was in the neural network, voluntarily or by force. Eva thought of what Dr. Lucien had said and scowled.

"Only fourteen," her mother said, bringing Eva out of her own reverie. Fourteen what? Eva wondered. The hoverchair spun around and Regina yelped.

"Coño carajo, mija, you scared me!" Regina exclaimed.

"I was just standing behind you," Eva said.

"Sí, pero you snuck up on me. I didn't know you were there."

"Sorry. Are you going to buy anything?"

Regina gave her a pursed-lipped frown and shook her head, casting a side-eyed glance at the xana watching them. "You're probably right, your sister has too many things, and she's never home anyway. Bueno, let's go."

The next store was, finally, one that sold clothing. Most of it was the loose-fitting outfits a lot of the xana wore to leave room for their arm flaps, adapted to fit various species, but there were other options no doubt carefully selected to appeal to the tourist composition that Spectrum City attracted. Only a few things were on physical display, while others were holovids that cycled through multiple items, probably based on data culled from their commlinks. Pink's eye lit up as she noticed one of the holographic models, whose style Eva would have best described as "home decorations," given that most of the clothes looked like a fancy chandelier or curtains or even rugs.

"Please," Eva said, leaning closer to Pink. "Please do not dress me as a sexy lamp."

Pink laughed, a deep, throaty laugh that did not bode well for Eva.

"Oh, look at these!" Regina said, gesturing at one of the loose outfits. "Qué lindo, they seem very comfortable. And they have pockets. You like pockets."

"I do like pockets," Eva said, raising her eyebrows at Pink. She hadn't expected to be on her mother's side about clothes, but maybe hell was having some freakishly cold weather. And anyway, walking around with a skirt full of jangly wires would make maneuvering through a crowd incredibly difficult. If she had to fight in something like that? Forget it, she was toast.

"Don't worry, my little busy bee," Pink said, grinning from cheek to cheek. "I'll make sure you're wearing something entirely appropriate." She emphasized the last word as if she knew precisely what Eva was thinking.

"Sí, mi vida," Regina said. "You're going to look incredible." She gasped and tapped Pink on the arm. "Mira, how about this one?"

"Ooh, but which color? Not the peach."

"No, no, that's always been bad with her skin tone. Espérate, how about this other one?"

"Do I get a say in this?" Eva asked.

"No," the other women replied simultaneously.

Eva groaned. "Fine. Do your worst."

Pink and Regina shared a look, and the twin smiles that spread across their faces made Eva immediately regret her choice of words.

Eva sat on the hanging seat in the room used for trying on outfits, sneaking a break from the endless incarnations of what she had decided was actually a line of lawn furniture. Even her mother had never been tacky enough to put a pink flamingo in her yard, but apparently a designer somewhere had seen one and fallen deeply, madly in love with the entire concept.

A psychic emanation did the equivalent of a polite knock. "May I request permission to enter in order to assist with the process of adornment selection?" a xana asked. The voice was vaguely familiar, and it wasn't the person who worked in the store.

Eva climbed out of the seat and took a defensive stance. The walls were that smoky translucence, which meant she couldn't hide better, but she could at least be ready if something happened.

"Come on in," she said, and the door slid open.

It was one of the rebels. Felsira. She slid the door closed with one hand, the other carrying a dress that did, in fact, resemble a sexy lamp. Eva groaned inwardly.

"I have enveloped us in a secure radius of approximately three meters," Felsira said, placing the dress in the small antigrav field that already held the flamingo abomination. "May I convey to you the request of the resistance?"

"Sure," Eva said, relaxing slightly.

"We have learned of your invitation to the event at the

Light's decline," Felsira said, hands entwined primly in front of her. "Our informants suggest this event will also include several individuals whose assistance is key to our infiltration plans."

Eva wrinkled her nose. "I don't think I'm charming enough to talk people into joining up with you."

Felsira emanated amusement as well as a shimmer of condescension that quickly vanished. "That is not necessary. We simply require psychic imprints from multiple sources with access to the Sylfe Company laboratories." She reached into her clothes and retrieved a small silver device, flat and oblong, with no identifying features.

From outside, Eva's mother yelled, "Mija, dale, let us see the next one!"

"Hold that thought," Eva said, grabbing the flamingo dress and struggling into it. Despite her claims of being there to help, Felsira did nothing but watch.

Eva stormed out to where Pink and her mother waited. They made identical faces, as if they'd both seen an actual flamingo and were considering how best to escort it out of the store safely.

"That's a no, right?" Eva asked. "Please?"

"Yeah, no," Pink said.

"Maybe with the right necklace?" Regina suggested.

Eva made a disgusted noise and turned, smart as a soldier, to march back into the room. She closed the door and stripped again, then reached over to grab the device Felsira was quietly holding out.

"Not saying I'm definitely going to help," Eva said. "I have to talk this over with my crew first. But how do I use this thing?"

"Its functions are automatic," Felsira replied, folding her hands together again. "Simply carry it on your person and interact directly with the target for a minimum of—" Eva's translator nanites hitched for a moment, then supplied "three point seven four minutes" in place of whatever time scheme Felsira had used. Something about feeds? Whatever.

"And how will I know who to target?" Eva asked.

"Try the other one on!" Pink called from outside.

Eva rolled her eyes and huffed a breath, then grabbed the awful lamp dress, which turned out to be a jumpsuit. It was entirely silver, a series of curving strips that formed a stripey pattern, covering her neck, torso, arms, and legs entirely except in places where a mesh-like material exposed her bare skin. It came with a matching jacket, so long that it dragged on the floor behind Eva like a train, though she imagined it probably didn't do that for people who were taller than her. She might be able to fight in it, if she ditched the jacket, but she'd stand out like a comet on a cloudless night.

"It has a hat," Eva said, holding the offending head covering like it was a dirty rag.

"I am sure it will be very fetching on you," Felsira said, her psychic tone amiable. "To answer your query, we are prepared to provide you with data regarding each subject you are to engage with."

Eva turned the hat over in her hands, trying to figure out how it went on. "That's fine, but if this is a huge party, it might be tough to single out any one person, let alone three." Especially since I'm short and xana are not, she thought sourly.

"Do you have a suggestion for improving the likelihood of success?" Felsira asked.

Eva considered it. "You don't have anyone on the inside who could feed me information?"

"We will have people there, but it would not be typical for any of them to interact with you, and so it would almost certainly be noticed by the Watchers and other vigilant guests."

"How about someone on the outside?" Even as she said it, Eva shook her head. "No, they're monitoring comms, aren't they? Or, at least they would know if I was getting random signals from somewhere nearby."

Pink shouted again, "Come on, let us see the outfit!" and Eva groaned, rolling her eyes.

Eva threw open the door in an unintentionally dramatic fashion, then stalked out to where Pink and her mother were waiting. The way their faces lit up, Eva knew she was in trouble.

"Really?" Eva asked.

"It's perfect," Pink said.

"Eres un tesoro," Regina agreed.

"I definitely look like something out of a chest of booty," Eva muttered. "How much does it cost?"

Pink told her, and Eva stuttered a laugh. "Qué rayo!" Eva said. "Why did you even make me try it on? I'm not paying that unless it comes with a new FTL drive for our ship."

"I'll buy it," Regina said immediately.

"Mami, no, por favor. Let's go to another store, or I can always wear something I already have." She didn't have anything appropriate, and wasn't sure how she would get it off the ship without being noticed and risking a quick deportation, but she could try.

Regina's face took on a surprisingly serious expression, her eyes watery and glinting as they caught the light. "Mija, you never had a quince," she said quietly.

"I didn't want one," Eva said. That was half true; Eva had wanted to have a wild night of karaoke with friends because she'd seen it on a holovid and it looked like the most fun ever. Her abuelos had offered to help pay for something, but her mother had been too proud to accept, and Eva had been too conscious of their wobbly finances to even think about asking for anything expensive. In the end, she got a commlink—not the newest model, but at least it was an implant instead of a cuff, and way better than the government-issued ones.

"I can afford it," Regina insisted. "Por favor, Eva-Benita, let me do this for you."

Eva's stomach clenched as she fought every impulse to reject the offer outright. She was enough like her mother that the notion of being gifted something so expensive made her anxious; she didn't want to feel indebted, burdened by a favor she would feel compelled to repay somehow, at an uncertain point in the future. Because Regina would absolutely keep this in her back pocket as emotional leverage, even if she didn't mean it that way right now. And Eva knew she didn't, that this was one of the awkward ways her mother showed love, that rejecting this would be like pushing a hug away.

Even so. It was a big ask. And Felsira was waiting in the room behind her, so she had to choose.

"Fine," Eva said. "Allá tú."

Regina shrieked and clapped her hands in excitement, rambling as she floated away to start dealing with the bill. Pink gave Eva a meaningful look that suggested she had followed a lot of Eva's thoughts on their merry spacetrain ride, but approved of where it had stopped. She mimed a finger gun and shot it at Eva, her lips forming a silent *pew-pew* that shifted to a gentle smile.

Eva's eyes widened, and she smiled back, but for an entirely different reason. She ambled back into the changing area, her outfit more or less forgotten.

"I have an idea," she told Felsira. "I still need to talk it over with my crew, but I think it will improve our odds." Pink might not agree with it, since she was still undecided about helping the resistance in the first place, but it was worth a shot. Literally.

Felsira's psychic emanation gained a curious edge even as it stayed polite, her hands still folded together in front of her.

"But first," Eva said. "I need to get the hell out of this outfit."

Chapter 18

PARTY ON

The party was held on the roof of the Sylfe Company head-quarters, which were located on an island near Spectrum City. Other buildings were clustered around it, all of them in the same style as the ones back in the city, false trees with bright trunks and gleaming branches hanging down nearly to the ground, or smaller edifices clustered like mushrooms around what would be the roots. It was hard to tell which had been built first, whether this place was entirely new or had barged into an existing town and taken over the way the robot Attuned were trying to supplant the living ones, but either way it was an impressive sight.

Transports hovered around the building, some merely picking up and dropping off the partygoers, while others were tethered to cables or docked in nondescript bays. Some of the tethered ones were extended to the full length of their attachments, floating like balloons in the golden light of the setting star, the people inside having their own private parties as they conducted business or pleasure away from the rest of the action.

Eva hesitated to call it "action," given the glacial speed at which everyone seemed to be moving inside the event itself. It was more like small groups of people forming and dissolving and re-forming as individuals drifted around, carrying drinks or bites of food catering to their particular biologies. The decorations were elegant, a combination of elaborate carvings similar to the ones back at the hotel where Eva and crew had been staying, plants whose root systems were carefully wound around and through translucent hydroponic devices while their tiny fragrant flowers perfumed the air, and light fixtures mimicking the traditional ones despite containing what were clearly robotic reproductions.

Probably with their own surveillance devices, Eva thought. Pervasive and sneaky. The place was also crawling with Watchers—well, not crawling, since they all held positions around the roof, and were standing unnervingly still. Even their Attuned were quiet; they might as well have been robots, too. Maybe they were? Eva couldn't tell the difference between the animals and the Pod Pals at a distance.

((Pink?)) Vakar pinged at her.

((Not yet,)) Eva replied, checking the chronometer on her commlink. If anyone were monitoring her comms somehow, the exchange would hopefully be vague enough to be meaningless.

Assuming all went according to plan, Pink would soon be in position in a hovering transport on the cables of a nearby building, along with Jei and Nara. Sue had outfitted Pink's sniper rifle with a device that would let her tag people at the party from a distance, the same way Sue had tagged Jei during their bot fight back on Abelgard. Eva could then use one of her commlink overlays to isolate the frequency and find that person more easily among the crowd.

Certainly it wouldn't be simple for Eva to do it on the ground, as she had suspected. Even with her gravboots on, she was shorter than most of the other guests, and vastly smaller than the xana. Vakar was taller, thankfully, so between him and Pink she was hoping they'd be able to do what needed to be done.

At least Pink had let her keep the gravboots, after they'd figured out the jumpsuit would cover them. Pink still griped about the shape being wrong, and Regina had griped about not being allowed to buy Eva appropriate shoes—"Tacones, mija, dios mío, I raised you better than this"—but Eva had stayed firm. Bad enough she couldn't bring any weapons besides her sonic knuckles, which were tastefully hidden underneath gloves the color of her skin, made from materials that shouldn't show up on any sensors normally used for that purpose. She'd also managed to work the towline from her spacesuit into something that resembled a belt, which could function as a garrote in an emergency. Pink had griped about that, too, but she'd acknowledged that utility outweighed fashion in some cases.

Vakar had scrounged up his own formalwear, a layered white suit similar to the ones the xana wore, complete with silvery harness. He wouldn't tell her where or how he got it, just kept saying, "I have my ways" and smelling smugly of lavender. He looked better than she felt, though the way he had practically reeked of licorice and kept nuzzling her with his palps on the ride over suggested he thought she looked fine.

Now he smelled like vanilla and rosewater with a dollop of mint, which Eva hoped would come across as standard party nerves to anyone with scent translators. Or to the other quennians present, of which there were at least two, neither of whom

Vakar recognized and both of whom he fully intended to question at some point during the event. He had already reported some suspicions on the Pod Pals to his superiors, and they hadn't mentioned anything about quennians being among Sylfe Company's backers, so either they didn't know or they had known and didn't tell him.

Both were uncomfortable notions, but that was parties as far as Eva was concerned. A few hours of being uncomfortable until someone got drunk enough to start causing problems. Usually her, until recently.

But if they caused any trouble here, Vakar could be in for a universe of shit from his bosses on top of whatever else might happen to them, so Eva had to be extra cool. Find the marks, chat them up, move on. Easy, smooth, quiet.

Her nerves were wound tighter than the wire around her hips, despite the calm, steady flow of blood through her mechanical heart.

Around her shoulders, Mala had settled like a furry scarf. Eva had argued with her about staying with Min and the others, but since half the argument had been "Miau" over and over, it had ended in a stalemate. Mala had managed to get into the transport when it arrived to pick them up, and at that point there was no sense leaving her to the whims of a bunch of Watchers, so to the party she came.

More stubborn than Eva, the fool animal.

Eva patted her head where it itched, because of course she would itch where she couldn't scratch. Her hair was tucked into the tight-fitting skullcap that came with the jumpsuit, a few tendrils already escaping to brush against her forehead despite how carefully Pink had arranged them. Worse, every time she shifted, the huge hoop earrings her mother had given her knocked against her face, making her think she was being constantly attacked by insects. She was about ready to tear them off and fling them into the nearby ocean.

Then Vakar wrapped an arm around her waist, and Eva pressed into him and tried to pretend for a moment that they were just random people at a fancy party, enjoying the low-key chatter and psychic emanations. As if they would ever be invited to a place like this; a grubby cargo-ship captain and a Wraith, mingling with rich elites excited to sprinkle some of their money on the newest idea seed to see what would grow.

This wasn't how their lives went. Their stories were violent ones, front to back, with no happy end in sight. In the distance, the local star continued its slow progress toward the other side of the planet, slipping silently below the waves as the sky purpled like a bruise.

"So far, this is superior to our previous experience at a similar venue," Vakar said quietly.

Eva snorted. "I'm still wearing something ridiculous."

"I will be sure to remove it quickly later."

Eva bumped him with her hip. "Panadero, watch where you put those claws." She sighed. "The last time I was here, I was about a hundred kilometers away and kitted out in full tactical gear. It was a lot less pretty. Less peaceful."

"It is a different form of activity," Vakar agreed. "But the others here are not gathered in the interests of peace. This is a form of economic entanglement that in many ways works against notions of tranquility and prosperity, leaving aside the questionable features of the technology itself."

"At least they're not shooting anyone or setting them on fire," Eva said.

"Perhaps not. But their choices may lead to similar outcomes, ultimately." His gray-blue eyes met hers and she looked away.

"I've made a lot of shitty choices," Eva murmured. "Being here is a constant reminder of the worst of them."

"I have regrets as well," Vakar said. "While I am not sorry for joining your crew, I did so as a means of escaping from obligations I perceived as anathema to my own desires. I was ashamed to admit this to my family or my commanding officers, and in my cowardice I fled." His grip on her hip tightened slightly, reflexively.

"Some people would say it took guts to leave instead of staying and doing something you didn't want to," Eva said.

Vakar made a rumbling noise, the equivalent of a sigh. "It was fear, primarily. Fear of the responsibility that came with the power granted by my potential position. Fear of making an incorrect choice and being made to live with the consequences of my actions. You helped me overcome that fear, albeit unintentionally."

Eva shifted to look up at him again. "I did what now?"

He smelled embarrassed, but also more strongly of licorice than before. "You gave me a reason to embrace that power and shoulder that responsibility. Without it, I had no hope that you would be returned to me. With it, I had the chance to find the people who had taken you, to find you. And now I can try to ensure no one else suffers in the same way."

His connections had been a huge part of why they'd been able to go after The Fridge as aggressively as they had, instead of running off to the fringes of the universe to hide and struggle as a cargo-delivery and passenger operation. But it also meant a life of near-constant danger, for them and the rest of the crew. They were all doing it intentionally, sure, but that didn't make it easier.

It also didn't excuse anything she'd done before she and Pink struck out on their own. It didn't excuse Garilia.

"Yeah, well, look what I did with my choices," Eva muttered. "This place is one big commwall ad for the consequences of my fuck-ups."

"And now you are choosing to do better." Vakar squeezed her hip gently. "It is as you said: you cannot undo what has been done, but you can work to atone."

Eva scowled. "I said that? Doesn't sound like me."

"That is because you often speak before fully considering the ramifications of your words, and so you are unable to recall them at a later point. Even when they are insightful." His scent told her he was teasing, but she elbowed him anyway, and Mala made a soft chirrup of indignation at the motion.

A robot floated past with a tray of food, pausing when Eva stuck her arm in front of it so she could grab a handful of hors d'oeuvres. These were like little bread pillows filled with sauce, served hot enough to scald the roof of her mouth. She loved them immediately.

As much as she wanted to continue flirting and philosophizing and eating, they had a mission to accomplish. A quick mental command turned on the visualization that would let her see the tag Pink was shooting at her targets. At first, nothing showed up, which either meant that Pink hadn't been able to find anyone yet, or that Eva was facing the wrong direction.

Before she could continue, a psychic emanation echoed like someone tapping a microphone, relayed by multiple xana standing in different places. Mala growled low in her throat, her body stiffening and her claws digging into Eva's shoulders. A white-garbed form drifted down from a higher tier to stand at the top of a fake tree, like a platform with a podium made entirely of intertwined branches and broad leaves. Lights were redirected to focus on the figure: Lashra Damaal, in all her awful glory. Her pale fur gleamed as if lit from inside, her dark eyes huge and inscrutable. Her pale-gold harness twinkled as the light caught it—made from interwoven wires of some kind, or chain links, fancy and expensive.

Some people are always more equal than others, Eva thought.

A hush fell over the crowd, who were all focused on the Prime as if she were a religious figure descended from the heavens to gift them with her wisdom. Eva glanced sidelong at a few of the Watchers, and perhaps unsurprisingly, they weren't so drawn in by the theatrics. They were still observing the guests, silently, unmoving, like statues that might come to life at any moment to deliver swift justice to anyone who stepped out of line.

"Honored guests," Damaal said, her quiet voice amplified by invisible tech. "Your presence here in celebration of our unprecedented achievements signifies that you possessed the wisdom and foresight to invest in technology that will alter the lives of nearly every being in the universe." Her psychic tone radiated earnest goodwill and optimism, with an intense layer of sheer power and authority that made Eva's skin itch.

No one clapped, or snorted in derision, or whispered a snide comment at the level of ass-kissing happening from the podium. Eva was surprised; usually rich people were constantly teetering on the verge of snark. Maybe they were overwhelmed by the vibes Damaal was putting out. Or they really were that far up their own asses.

Mala's tail whipped back and forth. She certainly harbored no such illusions about the greatness of anyone here, except maybe herself.

"Garilia's recent history has been one of turmoil and insecurity," Damaal continued. "Upon joining the collective of sentient species and discovering the boundlessness that awaited us beyond the borders of our own planet, we fell into greed and hostility, at odds with our selfless natures. But through the bravery of our people and their allies, we have overcome this adversity and emerged stronger, more resilient, and eager to continue our growth as we lead at the forefront of advancement for all star systems and their creatures."

Pretentious, given how recently the planet had joined up with the rest of the universe, but everyone there seemed to be eating that shit with a spoon. It wasn't as if robots weren't pervasive already; what made these designs special? That they looked like cute animals? That they could transform? That they fit in impossibly small containers?

Maybe that was it; the folks here were expecting to be able to reverse-engineer the tech for themselves, or that no one else would be able to do it, so they'd be rolling in credits for having something no one else could reproduce. Eva had only peripherally been aware of industrial espionage as a problem because of her dad, who had dabbled in it himself on occasion. It could be huge money, but it was also a galaxy of lawsuits waiting to happen, especially since Garilia was still under BOFA protection.

Of course, that must be part of it. Anyone who stole from Garilia would be subject to a slew of harsh punishments because Garilia was still integrating into the universe-wide federation. To avoid colonization or exploitation of resources—or at least the appearance of either—there were strict protections in place for fledgling star systems. Crooks from outside might still sneak in and cause problems, but if they got caught, they were in serious trouble.

And that meant any tech from Garilia, if it were special enough, would be worth a fortune. The combination of novelty and scarcity would be like catnip to people with the disposable income to snag it before it was being sold more widely.

Damaal was still talking, mostly fluff and flattery until finally she said, "And now, we hope you will humor us with a brief demonstration of the latest model. We call it—"

Eva's translators supplied "Firespeaker" after a brief stutter; probably had to process a quick update since the xana language was still an ongoing translation project. Brand and product names were always a fun problem.

At first nothing seemed to happen, but then a shadow passed overhead, difficult to spot as it was a dark orange that nearly blended into the sunset sky. It moved like a large bird, gliding more than flying—antigrav tech, maybe? But as it looped around and dove toward the roof, it became more visible, its form like a todyk or a dragon out of Earth's old fiction. Just as it came close enough to buzz the crowd, it roared and shot a gout of flame from its long snout, the heat so intense it made the skin on Eva's face tighten.

Mala hissed, her fur bristling against the sliver of Eva's exposed neck.

A collective "ooh" and similar appreciative noises went up from the audience as the robot landed on the floor below Damaal. It was a little taller than Eva, given where its head landed compared to the Watcher standing next to it, but its wings spread out twice as far, its fake skin the color of the impending twilight. It didn't move, simply waited for its next command impassively.

"This model, like the others, is based on one of our Attuned," Damaal said, emanating pride. "It is comparable to a fully grown specimen, with all its inherent abilities as well as the expected upgrades. But as promised, the Firespeaker can do what the Attuned cannot."

The robot briefly glowed a purplish-pink color that was eerily familiar to Eva. With a sound like a series of strange whooshes and quiet pings, it shrank in on itself, losing at least a half meter in height, the wings disappearing entirely and the head becoming more rounded. It was an impossible transformation; something as big as its prior form shouldn't have been able to change like this, into something so much smaller, and yet here it was. And the whole thing would eventually be able to fit into a capsule she could hold in one hand, which was even more unbelievable.

Eva thought of the pieces of glittering metal and polymer spread across the table in her mother's temporary residence, and wondered.

"All of the Pod Pals can shift back and forth between the various growth stages of the Attuned, as desired by those who possess them," Damaal said. "Each stage is capable of all its natural abilities, and as our engineers continue their diligent and genius work, we expect to release advanced technologies in the future to implement additional upgrades."

Probably for an extra fee, Eva thought. That was where this shit got people; all the microtransactions and add-ons.

The robot glowed again and shifted once more with the same mechanical whooshing sound, and now it was a small creature, like a smooth todyk baby. It made an adorable "cha" sound, then with another flash of pink, it vanished into the capsule Damaal held in her claw.

"We thank you for your presence and your continued support," Damaal said. "It is our fond hope that you will join us for a more robust demonstration of the capabilities of our technology, at the Grand Tournament to be held in two cycles. At the conclusion of the ritual Attuned combat, we will host a special battle between a team of Attuned and our own Pod Pals, for your viewing pleasure."

Eva raised an eyebrow. Robots versus regular animals? That didn't sound very fair, though if they were supposed to have the same abilities, maybe it wouldn't be too unbalanced. Still, she'd never been a fan of cockfighting in any incarnation, whatever their temporary tour guide Krachi had insisted about it being done humanely.

With any luck, they'd have Josh by then, and Garilia would be eating their plutonium exhaust as they made a run for the nearest Gate.

Damaal's psychic tone ramped up even as she began to disengage. "We are honored to be the harbingers of a new era of peace and prosperity for all members of the Benevolent Organization of Federated Astrostates and beyond. May the Light embrace you all as it has embraced us, and may you carry it with you to distant stars. Until the Light touches all things."

"Until the Light touches all things," the xana in the room responded, their psychic emanations reverent and proud.

It was the pride that put Eva on edge. Sure, it was nice to feel good about your accomplishments, to get a boost of self-confidence to keep you striving. But pride could be flipped easily to overconfidence, condescension, and it was a quick leap from that to thinking you knew what was best for other people and trying to force them to agree. To taking away freedom for someone's own good.

Not that unrestricted freedom was the best plan, either. Or some mythical moderation. Foh, it was all one big arroz con mango. And here Eva was, picking sides again, adding salt to the pot when this wasn't even her kitchen.

Damaal had retreated, signaling the end of speechmaking and the return to revelry. Even Mala had settled back to her previously relaxed position, her fur once again soft, claws retracted. Eva scanned the room again, and this time she saw the faint green glow Sue had told her would mark her target. Pink must have found someone. Whoever it was, they were across the room on a slightly lower level, near a bar-like drink-dispenser setup if her memory was accurate.

"I'm thirsty," Eva told Vakar. "Come on, let's scope out the synthesizer options."

If Vakar found the sudden request strange, he didn't say anything, didn't even smell suspicious. He'd probably noticed the mark as well; they hadn't made him a Wraith for his good looks, cute as he was.

In this case, his skills were better than hers when it came to navigating a crowd. Eva had always made not-so-subtle use of shoulders and elbows to get around people-shaped obstacles. Vakar, on the other hand, had a knack for finding spaces to slip through, for deftly and silently creating spaces where they didn't exist, for shifting and flowing like he could see the currents of a room and was simply letting them propel him to where he wanted to be.

He could be sneaky in his own way, even if the rest of the time he was almost painfully straightforward. Though this could probably be construed as another way of being goal-oriented, which Vakar absolutely was. She let that thought warm her in certain specific places before dragging her attention back to their task.

Their mark didn't shift in the time it took them to reach the area, thankfully. The green tag was affixed to the front of a sour-faced vroak wearing small, dark shades over his eyes, his frog-like features glistening from the glow of the nearby light fixtures. His skin was as white as an eggshell, and he had orange bristles sticking out on either side of his flared nostrils like a stiff mustache. According to the information Felsira had provided, his name was Ovikin Tob-Or and his preferred title was Dr.; apparently he would respond well to flattery, so Eva nudged Vakar toward the drink station, plastered on her biggest fake smile, and approached with what she hoped was a sufficiently awed posture.

"Excuse me," Eva said, "are you Dr. Tob-Or?"

Dr. Tob-Or gave an affirmative grunt, eyeing her suspiciously. "Do I know you?" His voice came across as resonant, yet grating, like a bass note played on a kazoo.

"No, but I've heard about your research for the Pod Pals and it sounds absolutely fascinating. I was hoping you'd be willing to discuss it with me in a bit more detail." Eva rested a hand on her hip, conscious of how much she looked like she'd stepped out of a chandelier. Hopefully it wasn't too offensive to the vroak's senses.

"How much detail?" Dr. Tob-Or asked. "What are you getting at?" Did he think she was trying to steal something? Not like he carried his designs on him.

"It seems like such a huge project is all," Eva said. "Where did you even start?"

Dr. Tob-Or tossed back the contents of the large metal container he was holding and hummed thoughtfully. "Started with taxonomy. Did an extensive study of the Attuned, their habitats and physical structures and abilities. Reviewed the existing literature, observed them in nature, took samples as needed."

"Wow, that must have been a lot of work." Eva accepted her own drink from Vakar, who smelled like jasmine with a hint of mint.

"Exhausting, but I've never been afraid to push myself to the limits of my abilities." Dr. Tob-Or swelled a bit, like he was getting warmed up. "The biggest difficulty was the transition from cybernetic enhancement of the existing species to full-replicated synthetic versions."

"Is that right?" Eva asked, trying not to let her distaste come through her voice. They'd started the experiments on live creatures? Dr. Lucien had mentioned as much, but she had thought the scope changed before it happened. Nasty. She reached up to scratch Mala's neck, earning a gentle purr.

Dr. Tob-Or shifted his drink container from one white-gloved hand to the other. "Yes, my designs were absolutely perfect, merging technology with biology in a seamless fashion that enhanced the natural abilities of the Attuned creatures." His tone soured. "But public sentiment was not in favor of the process, so we had to make the shift. So much time and planning, utterly wasted."

Fucking good, Eva thought. Animals couldn't consent to cybernetic enhancement, and this didn't sound like anything remotely benevolent. Out loud she said, "That must have been frustrating for such a prominent scientist as yourself, to have so much work undermined."

"Deeply discouraging," he agreed. "Politics are such nonsense. Give people what they need, not what they want." He gestured vaguely at the rest of the roof. "I thought Lashra would be above placating lesser concerns, the way she and the rest of the government run things here. Extreme situations call for extreme solutions. They have control, but it should be tighter."

He squeezed his white-gloved hand for emphasis, and Eva nodded sagely while wishing one of his robots would set him on fire.

Her commlink timer went off to alert her that the device had enough exposure to create its psychic imprint of this asshole. Gracias a dios, because she was about ready to accidentally throw her drink into his disgusting face. But she had one more thing to accomplish.

"I'm so pleased I was able to meet you, Dr. Tob-Or," Eva said, as sweetly as she could manage. Then she lowered her voice, in the hopes that the surveillance devices might not catch it among the rest of the chatter. "I was hoping to speak with Dr. Zafone as well, but I've always admired your work."

At the mention of Josh's name, Dr. Tob-Or puffed up even more, but aggressively instead of with pride. "Zafone thinks he owns the laboratory. Always reworking everyone's designs, saying they're flawed, they could be better. Won't even let us into his room. He's hiding something, I tell you. Going to take credit for all our work in the end if we're not careful." He let out a belch; he was drunk off his ass, or whatever the vroak equivalent was, his pale skin even slicker with moisture than it had been when they started talking.

"I'm sorry to hear that," Eva said diplomatically. "I hope you get all the credit you deserve." And she meant it, with the hard edge of a curse.

Dr. Tob-Or's attention shifted to Mala. "Nice specimen there," he said. "Could I get a tissue sample?"

Mala stared at him, her hazel eyes losing their color to pupil as she tensed, tail lashing.

"I'm afraid she wouldn't be entirely cooperative," Eva said, scratching Mala's head to reassure her.

"Not a problem," Dr. Tob-Or replied. "There are plenty of ways to subdue a reluctant subject."

As if sensing Eva's rising desire for violence, Vakar managed to extricate her by pulling her backward into the crowd, Dr. Tob-Or's exceedingly grumpy face disappearing behind a wall of people. Once they were safely away, Eva exhaled and shook herself, startling Mala into giving a brief yowl of displeasure.

"What a comemierda," she told Vakar. "I hope somebody steps on his junk."

Vakar wagged his head. "I presume you mean the colloquial meaning of the word."

"Claro que sí." She sipped the drink he passed her, a distant cousin of mango juice. Nearby Watchers hadn't moved from their posts, so either they hadn't been bothered by Eva's conversation, or they hadn't heard it.

Or Damaal was still monitoring Eva to see what she was up to.

A scan of the rooftop showed that Pink already tagged their next target. A distant green dot lured them all the way back across the party, up to a higher tier with a view of the ocean that people on some planets paid inconceivable credits for. They found a kloshian, almost as short as Eva, with his hairlike tendrils flat on the top and flaring slightly sideways, his skin currently a delicate shade of bluish purple that blended well with the same slowly shifting color of the sky. He wore a long white coat over a jumpsuit that hung loosely on his frame, and he smiled at the small crowd of people surrounding him, baring his sharp teeth like a friendly shark in a sea of chum.

He was like a slick version of Miles Erck, and Eva wanted to punch him immediately.

"The challenge is to ensure the cross-compatibility of components," he was saying as Eva and Vakar strolled up to his court of onlookers. His hands moved in broad, theatrical gestures as he spoke. "You see, many of the Attuned have similar abilities despite different anatomies, and so to yield efficiencies in production, it made sense to have the methods by which the abilities were reproduced be modular."

"But my version is older," one of the women in front of him whined. "I was promised an upgrade since the new models are so much more advanced."

The kloshian's smile faltered. "I'm sure someone as lovely as yourself will be properly tended to," he said, waving a hand in her direction and offering her a flirty head shake. "And I wouldn't say the new models are wildly different from the originals. When I was approached to work on the project, the scope was unsustainably broad, but I was able to delicately reshape the team's vision to something much more practical while retaining the elegance of the creatures themselves."

That felt like an in for Eva, so she took it. "You're Dr. Lywin?" she asked, her tone much more coy than it had been with Tob-Or. This one didn't want flattery, he wanted a challenge. "Your reputation precedes you."

His eyes shifted color, from a pale green to a deep teal. "Only the good portions, I hope." His gaze dropped to Mala, and his smile broadened. "That isn't one of the Attuned, is it?"

"I'm afraid not," Eva replied. "This is a cat. Terran in origin." She stroked Mala gently, watching Dr. Lywin's expression as she did. It reminded her of Sue's, like he was mentally dissecting Mala and figuring out how to reconstruct her in his own way. It was creepier when he did it, for some reason.

"Charming," Dr. Lywin said. "May I say, your facial scar is fascinating. How did you come by it?"

Eva thought of fire, the swipe of an Attuned's claws, and swallowed acid. "I'm sure any story you might come up with would be more interesting than what really happened."

"Would it be?"

Did he know who she was? No chance. For all that Eva was supposedly Damaal's honored guest at this event, she'd done nothing whatsoever to call attention to Eva. This guy was fishing for his own amusement. But more importantly, she needed to get him to talk, or the psychic-imprint device wouldn't do its thing.

"You do seem to have a particularly well-developed imagination," Eva said. "I suppose it takes some mental flexibility to figure out the complexities of a living creature and remake them so convincingly." Me cago en diez, I sound like Mari, Eva thought. Or some rich girl making nice. Either way, it felt icky, but the fawning crowd around him was enjoying it well enough.

"Indeed, attention to detail is essential," Dr. Lywin said. "Any engineer with a rudimentary education can cobble together a robot, but the challenge is in verisimilitude." He produced a capsule from the pocket of his coat with a flourish, opening it and releasing the Pod Pal inside with equal pomp. It was one of the turtle-looking types, its leathery skin impressively similar to the real Attuned Eva had seen before with Watcher Rakyra.

Mala went rigid around Eva's neck again. She really did hate those things. Probably because of the psychic tech.

"Observe this masterpiece," Dr. Lywin said. "One might mistake it for its organic counterpart, but this version has an array of additional features that make it vastly more useful. And more importantly, as the Prime was discussing, I've managed to take the additional step of creating what I call Technical Manifesters."

"What are those?" someone asked.

Dr. Lywin's eyes shifted to a lighter shade of green, his hair tendrils waving slightly. "They allow our robots to be upgraded with abilities from entirely different models, regardless of the intrinsic biologies of the original Attuned."

Okay, yes, that was impressive. Eva maintained her aloof demeanor, sensing that the good doctor was gauging her reaction. Mala was still bristling, but her posture was equally controlled.

"So you could keep upgrading one of those to do everything the other models can do?" Eva asked. "Why bother buying multiple ones when just one of them can have every ability?"

"There are limitations," Dr. Lywin said, his color's brightness fading a touch. "Only six upgrades per unit at the present time."

Smart business plan, or he hadn't figured out a workaround yet, Eva thought. His reaction suggested the latter.

"But consider," he continued, as if sensing his audience was losing interest. "The modularity of the Technical Manifesters is unprecedented. It renders the applications of the robots into near infinity. If you no longer wish for your model to, say, produce defensive stunning spores, you can remove that ability and replace it with something else entirely. Full customization!"

Why was he bothering to shill this stuff to people who were already sunk eyeball-deep into partial ownership of it? Maybe the funding was more tenuous than Damaal had let on. She was at the top of a government that had recently taken control over a whole planet, was apparently rolling out all kinds of new stuff, had laid down a surveillance grid as complex and widespread as nerves in her own body . . . How was it all being paid for? Garilia was self-sustaining, more or less, but once it had gained provisional status with BOFA, that opened up a universe of stuff that the xana apparently wanted more than isolation and tranquility.

The universe, aside from a few pockets, ran on credits, not kindness.

Dr. Lywin was a born salesman, Eva had to admit. She'd seen her own father play this game often enough to know when someone had the knack for it. Presumably that was why Lywin had been rolled out to chat with the guests, instead of being locked up in the lab with the Miles Erck brand of asswipe.

And thankfully, the alarm on her commlink sounded, so Eva didn't have to keep listening to his pitch anymore. Now she just had to find the last target and the psychic imprints would be complete. The resistance could break into the labs, do their thing, and Eva could hopefully finish her mission as well.

Except she was barely closer to finding Josh than she had been before. All she had was the hope that he was in the lab, too, and that she'd be able to drag his ass out without damaging it.

Because based on what Dr. Tob-Or had said, she didn't think he would be leaving voluntarily unless Sue did a really, really good job of convincing him it was important.

"Were you also responsible for the introduction of the evolutionary capabilities, and the storage containers?" someone asked. Vakar, though he'd done a good job of masking where the question had come from, since Dr. Lywin seemed to be searching the crowd for its source. He didn't look pleased.

"That was one of my colleagues," Dr. Lywin said. "I was integrally involved, of course."

"Dr. Zafone?" Eva asked quietly.

"Indeed." His smile vanished altogether.

"He's not here, is he?" Eva asked. "I've heard he's somewhat elusive." She hadn't, but it sounded like something one might hear.

Before Dr. Lywin could answer, his color shifted entirely to a pale purple as he stared at someone behind her. Around her neck, Mala once again tensed, her fur spiking.

"The esteemed Dr. Zafone could not be present for this Light-touched event, but his spirit is strong with us," a voice said, their psychic tone resonant with authority. Lashra Damaal, flanked by Watcher Rakyra and another cop, all of them looking down at Eva with those expressionless dark eyes. The Firespeaker bot had also been released from its capsule and was standing attentively next to them, and Eva was exceedingly aware that it had a flamethrower in its mouth, while also hoping it couldn't possibly be used with so many other people around.

"Would you please come with us for a moment, honored guest," Watcher Rakyra said. It was not a question.

Chapter 19

UNBALANCED

While Eva expected to be marched off to some back room for interrogation or similar, instead she and Vakar were escorted to another portion of the rooftop, near the elevator landing. Fewer guests lingered in the area, which was decorated with miniature versions of the vast home-trees, their roots wound around and through containers that were presumably designed to keep them fed. It was unnerving to see them so small, shrunken, their canopies trimmed back and decorated with lights that mimicked the buildings normally constructed among their branches. It felt like an expression of control, like even the home-trees would fit in the palm of Damaal's hand if she willed it to be so.

"What can I do for you, Prime?" Eva asked politely. "Nice party, by the way."

"Many thanks for your kind observation," Damaal said, her pale fur gleaming in the dim light. "I am pleased to hear you have been enjoying the festivities. Your keen interest in our revolutionary technology has also brightened my spirit."

Of course she'd been spying on Eva the whole time. The place was crawling with Watchers and their Attuned, or Pod Pals, or both.

"I also wished to discuss your unrestricted Attuned interaction at the Communal Center in Rilia," Damaal said. Her tail rested on her shoulder, unmoving, and her psychic tone didn't modulate in the slightest. "Watcher Rakyra, you were able to locate the responsible party?"

"Yes, Prime," Watcher Rakyra said, his psychic emanation deferential. "She is being properly educated on the necessity of controlling her Attuned, as well as being reminded of her rights and privileges and all behavioral requirements to ensure they are not revoked. Her associates have also been recovered and are undergoing the same regimen."

Mala gave a low growl and Eva rubbed her ear to calm her. Or maybe to calm herself.

"You didn't have to do that," Eva said. "It was an accident."

"Accidents can have the most dangerous consequences," Damaal said. "Have you not had similar experiences in the past?"

Eva had no response to that. Was Damaal messing with her? Was she referencing something specific? The Pod Pal in the recycler, maybe? What did she know, exactly?

Mala's growling intensified. Eva glanced down at the cat, whose black-pupiled eyes were glaring at the Firespeaker robot next to Damaal. Was it doing something Eva couldn't see?

"Your creature there is displeased," Damaal said. "Does she require sustenance, or perhaps exercise?" She stared at Mala, who hissed back at her, and for a moment Damaal's psychic emanations slid sideways like a window being cracked open—no, it was like when Mala would knock a cup off the table in the mess, to see what would happen. Whatever she was doing, Eva couldn't get a sense of its content so much as its direction: it was pointed right at Mala.

Mala yowled, and for a moment Eva thought she was scared, but then the waves of anger came boiling off her like she was a pot of rice on a hot stove.

Next to Damaal, Watcher Rakyra flinched and took a step forward. "Control your Attuned, Gap-maker," he said, his own psychic tone hard-edged with restrained aggression. Surprising given how carefully controlled he'd been until now.

Or maybe not so surprising. He was a cop, after all, in a city where they ran around disappearing folks for education. Maybe the surprising thing was how long it had taken for him to show his claws.

Eva stroked Mala's head and tried to think soothing thoughts at her. Vakar stood quietly behind them, his posture shifting into a stance she knew for a defensive one, from the many times they'd sparred. They couldn't cause more of an incident here than they already had, or he might be in enormous trouble.

But they still hadn't gotten the third psychic imprint, and she was no closer to knowing where Josh was, except that he was definitely still here and working on the robots. If she didn't bring the fully loaded device to the resistance, she'd have to keep fumbling around trying to find her own way in, and that meant more opportunities for creating problems.

((Robot activating,)) Vakar pinged her suddenly.

The Firespeaker hadn't moved, but as Eva examined it out of the corner of her eye, the smallest psychic nudge touched her mind—not like it was trying to get her attention, more like a pickpocket who'd either fumbled the grab or was redirecting attention as a distraction.

Either way, Eva was sick of this shit, failed mission or not. They were literally up on a roof and it was a hell of a long way down.

"How is your parent, Captain?" Damaal asked suddenly. "I hope she is also finding our city to be a pleasant and diverting environment."

Eva froze. Me cago en diez, she thought. Had she put her mom in danger now, after everything, after the Fridge arroz con mango and even the earlier years with her dad—was this when it would catch up, finally, and really fuck her innocent family over?

She's with BOFA, fool, the voice in her head said. Damaal has probably been tracking her since she got to the planet, even if they couldn't put her under direct surveillance. She can't risk doing anything to the auditor working on the planet's case. Hell, for all Eva knew, her mom had been doing some kind of auditing mierda when they were out shopping, and that's why she kept zoning out in random corners of stores.

"My mother is fine," Eva said. "She had a great time choosing this outfit for me, in fact. Why do you ask?" Mala was still bristling on her shoulders, and Eva realized she was angry, too, and totally failing to hide it.

"We are simply eager to ensure that her review is positive," Damaal replied smoothly, her psychic emanations once again firmly controlled. "She is doing work that is vital for the ongoing progress of our planet and its people, and any delay or defect would be to our detriment."

"Yeah, well, she's good at her job," Eva said. "And she's not a liar, so don't waste your time with bribes." *Cállate, comemierda,* her inner voice said, but she was past listening.

"I have heard of the practice of bribery," Damaal said, a ripple of disdain in her psychic tone. "It is not one that is typical for any of the cultures on our planet, though I have been told our practice of Light-gifts bears some similarities."

"Yeah, funny how most people have something similar," Eva retorted. "And they all seem to think it doesn't count."

Vakar laid a hand on the small of her back and she leaned forward, away from it. He wasn't going to calm her down, and even though she knew he was right, she wasn't here for it.

Damaal's psychic emanations receded, but her eyes bored into Eva's. "I must apologize, but I am needed elsewhere. It seems a resistance group has been located nearby, with weapons, and we fear they may be plotting some disturbance at this event."

That made no sense. The resistance had sent Eva in to get the psychic imprints; there was no reason for them to also start shit, especially when it might jeopardize that plan. Unless . . .

Mierda, mojón y porquería. They must have found Pink and the others. Because of security being so tight, Eva and Pink had agreed on absolute comms silence, no matter what, so it wasn't as if either of them could alert the other of whatever might be happening.

But if the Watchers had found Pink, why was Damaal bothering to let Eva keep wandering around instead of dragging her off to be "educated"? Was it because of her mom? Eva's neck felt hot, and she wondered whether she had once again stepped into a puddle that turned out to be a pit. Had Damaal known about Regina and left Eva alone because she thought Eva was working for BOFA, too?

Damaal shifted away. "Be cautious, Captain. The travel lines may be impacted by our Watchers attempting to apprehend the resistance members. And unfortunately, the rebels have a habit of engaging in their own disruptive behaviors, despite our efforts to educate them in their rights and privileges."

"Thanks for the warning," Eva said, her throat dry. She had to get out of there in a hurry. She'd only gotten two out of the three imprints the resistance needed to get into the lab, but Pink was more important.

"I hope we will meet again at the Tournament," Damaal said, beginning to leave. "May the Light embrace you—" And she called Eva something her translators glitched on for several long moments as Eva tried to figure out how she was going to find Pink.

"Fallbreaker." Damaal's tone hadn't changed, but her translators suggested the word was charged. A Fallbreaker was someone who saved lives with their own body, which was brave and commendable, but also someone who sacrificed themselves in some foolish way. Falling in the first place was a failure, probably a deadly one, totally unacceptable. It wasn't a compliment.

The scar on Eva's face pulled tight as she smiled bitterly. Yeah, that sounded about right. And she was about to do it all over again.

As soon as Eva and Vakar were over open water, halfway back to Spectrum City, she pinged Pink. She wanted to do it sooner, to warn her, but Damaal's cute little parting note had felt like a test, a trap. After enough time, with enough distance, Eva hoped it would seem innocuous. Normal. "Standard captain procedure" instead of "worried about my best friend who might be dead or arrested."

No response.

They made it back to the house, and Eva managed to ping Pink only twice more on the way, admiring her own restraint—even if it wasn't all that restrained. It was better than pinging her until she responded, which is what Eva actually wanted to do.

When did you get so worried? Eva thought. This isn't the first time either of you has been in a similar situation. It will be fine.

It didn't feel fine. It felt like her insides were trying to climb out of her throat, like her skin was on fire, like she couldn't get enough air. Pink probably would have called it a panic attack, told her to breathe and find something else to focus on.

But Pink wasn't there. Pink was missing, and it was Eva's fault for dragging them to Garilia in the first place, for coming up with the asinine scheme to have Pink tag those scientists at the party. She should have figured out another way to find Josh, instead of agreeing to help the resistance.

She should have left Garilia in the past where it belonged.

Vakar tried to comfort her, but he smelled as worried as she felt. Even Mala couldn't penetrate the layers of guilt and fear and worry Eva was putting up around herself like energy shields. The only thing that finally knocked Eva out of her own head was Sue, who all but tackled Eva as soon as they walked through the door.

"I found the power source!" Sue squealed.

Eva stared at Sue blankly.

"Of the Pod Pals," Min said. She was already petting Mala, who had abandoned Eva for scratches.

"Look, look!" Sue grabbed Eva's hand and towed her over to the table, where the parts of the robot were arranged in neat piles, except for the largest remaining component.

In the center of the table sat a metallic lattice, almost like a small Dyson sphere. In the center of that, hovering in a stasis field, was a purplish-pink cube of energy.

"Me cago en la hora que yo nací," Eva said.

"That's what I said!" Sue exclaimed. "I mean, I didn't really say that, I don't say that, but—"

"I know, I know." Eva crouched slightly to peer directly at the mechanism in all its glory.

It was definitely Proarkhe, or whatever the Fridge equivalent was. It was the same kind of energy cube Eva and Vakar had found on the planet where they'd also encountered a Proarkhe artifact, which had later turned into a giant robot before vanishing. It was the same thing that had powered the Fridge's strange portable Gate guns, one of which was inoperable, both of which were hidden.

And here it was, the beating heart of a robot that looked like an animal. A robot that could change its form and shrink to fit into an impossibly small capsule.

"This is exceptionally illegal," Vakar said.

"Only by BOFA standards," Eva replied. "Which Damaal has to know because she's eyeball-deep in a compliance audit right now." And my mom is part of that, Eva thought. Qué relajo. At least none of the noise had woken Regina up, assuming she was sleeping at all instead of working or eavesdropping.

"How are they able to maintain secrecy about this?" Vakar asked, smelling like vinegar and rosemary. Incredulous. He could be adorably naïve sometimes.

Sue perked up. "Oh, I know! My family has to deal with this stuff all the time when we're making new ships or parts."

Eva pinged Pink again. Should she set up an auto-ping? No, that would be ridiculous. She dragged her attention back to Sue.

"When you submit plans to the regulators, they look like this," Sue continued, bringing up a schematic with her commlink and projecting it so everyone could see. It was an engine for a medium-sized craft, and Sue rotated it and fiddled with it so that it seemed to explode outward, all its individual parts visible and labeled and able to be independently examined.

But a few areas were static, opaque. They could be moved to show things around them, but they themselves were like gaps or missing data, lost pieces of a puzzle that had otherwise been fully assembled.

"Those bits are proprietary," Sue said, pointing at the gray areas. "BOFA allows certain parts of a plan to be kept secret. You know, for competition and stuff. If everything were all out there, it might get stolen and copied, and that wouldn't be fair."

Eva squinted at the floating image. "But someone has to know about it. Things break, they need to be repaired . . ." She herself had fixed enough ship components to have a decent working knowledge of a variety of schematics, and she'd never run into this before.

Sue nodded. "There are statutes of limitations. After a certain amount of time, things go public, usually because they've been reverse-engineered and there's no sense keeping it secret anymore."

"But then at some point, someone is going to figure this out," Eva said. "You can't be the only person dismantling these things to see what makes them tick."

Vakar smelled like jasmine. "It is also likely that someone may unintentionally damage a unit by, for example, inserting it into a waste recycler."

Eva scowled at him and rolled her eyes.

"I think I might be the only one who could do it right," Sue said, her gaze falling on the glowing cube at the center of the table. "I know how Josh works, how he programs, how he builds. There were a bunch of fail-safes that were supposed to shut down the power matrix way before I got to it. I bypassed them, along with a lot of other cute little software gremlins, but anyone else would probably end up with an empty core and a lot of teeny tiny parts they couldn't reassemble."

Eva stared at the glowing cube, remembering how she'd fed a similar one to a giant lizard creature, remembering the violent chain reaction she'd caused by blowing the thing up in a room full of other cubes of varying sizes. Would the next Pod Pal upgrade add more fail-safes in case, as Vakar said, someone else stuffed one in a recycler? Damaal and her Sylfe Company investors couldn't afford to have some kid in Casa Carajo find out the hard way that their cute little robot friend was powered by a volatile unknown energy source.

Biting her lip, Eva pinged Pink. Still no answer. The gnawing chasm in her stomach was growing, and she'd already fallen in, was tumbling deeper with every passing moment. Should she be getting her crew to the ship? Trying to escape from Garilia before Damaal cracked down and hauled them all away? Would she even be able to get off-planet at this point, or was it too late?

Never should have taken this job. No money was worth this. Should have kept chasing The Fridge, playing the mosquito to their elephant—or better, picking up legal work where she could and letting Pink practice telemedicine peacefully while Sue and Min played with their respective toys.

"Now what?" Min asked, petting Mala on the floor.

"Indeed," Vakar said. "Possessing the knowledge that the Sylfe Company is engaged in illegal activities is potentially useful leverage, however it suggests that we will be less likely to succeed in our mission."

"But now we know Josh is definitely here!" Sue exclaimed. "He's the only one who could have built this, I'm sure of it."

"We confirmed that at the party," Eva said. "I spoke to two different scientists working with him on this project."

Sue's excitement vanished along with her smile as she followed the thought-paths Eva had known she would. "But if he's okay, and here, and working on these, then why didn't he ever tell us?"

"He was probably protecting you," Eva said, unable to keep the sarcastic edge off her tone.

"We never stopped paying his ransom," Sue said, her eyes watery. "My poor parents. They think he's locked in a box somewhere, but he's here in a lab, working on these things." She gestured at the pile of parts on the table, which one of her robots was continuing to tidy up as she spoke.

"Trust me," Eva said, "I know how it feels. My sister pulled the same shit on me, and look what happened."

Vakar smelled like ozone with a nasty fart undertone. "If he is here voluntarily, he will potentially be less inclined to leave with us."

"And then we don't get paid," Eva said. "Not that money was our primary motivator."

"At least he's okay," Sue murmured.

"We don't know that for sure," Eva said. "It's safe to assume he was going after Damaal when he was hopping all over the universe six months ago, given the evidence we now have, but that doesn't mean she hasn't locked him up and twisted his arm to work on her project."

It hadn't sounded that way when the resistance members were describing his involvement, or when his fellow Pod Pal designers were talking about him, but she hated to see Sue so depressed about her brother probably being an asshole. Let the girl have a little hope.

Eva could use some of that herself. She pinged Pink again, and once again there was no reply.

The door at the end of the hall opened, and for a brief

moment Eva's stomach shot into her throat. Her mother was awake, apparently. Eva flopped onto the couch and covered her face with one hand, trying not to cry, because what would that accomplish? And Pink could be totally fine—was fine, had to be fine, madre de dios, por favor.

"You're back," Regina said. Her tone was so sour, Eva looked up at her, blinking away the bleariness forming in her eyes.

"Where else would I be?" Eva asked, then winced at her own rising anger. That hadn't taken much.

"Bueno, what do I know about where you go?" Regina hovered through the room, avoiding eye contact with everyone. She went to the kitchen, got a drink, then went back toward her bedroom without another word.

Something was wrong. Coño carajo. Maybe it was work-related? But no, then her mom would have unloaded about it; she loved to complain, at length and in detail. She might be upset if she couldn't because of confidentiality, but that had never stopped her from at least getting salty in as vague a way as she could manage.

Here was a new thing to worry about, but unlike the situation with Pink, Eva could do something about this. She trailed after Regina, despite being half-inclined to let it burn out on its own.

"Qué pasó?" Eva asked, leaning against the doorframe. The room itself had a bed, a colorful wooden dresser, and a desk whose chair had been scooted into a corner. There was also a miniature comms tower complete with an expensive scrambler unit and privacy shield, which explained why her mother was having no trouble accessing the q-net or receiving calls and wasn't worried about any eavesdropping.

A few other devices littered the desk, including a thin mechanical keyboard—her mother always had been old-fashioned.

But before she could do more than glance at anything else, Regina was shoving her back out into the hallway.

"You can't come in here," Regina said coldly.

"Right, secret government stuff, discúlpame," Eva said, raising her hands defensively.

"Classified, not secret," Regina replied.

Eva furrowed her brow. "Same thing."

Regina continued moving forward, forcing Eva to back up. "No, descarada, I'll tell you what's secret. Secret is your husband pretending he sells used spaceships when he's actually running an organized-crime operation. Secret is having to tell your children just enough so they understand why you got a divorce and left the galaxy, but not so much that they might say the wrong thing to the wrong person and get kidnapped or killed or, god forbid, arrested."

"Yeah, that's definitely worse than killed," Eva said, and her mother whacked her arm hard enough that it stung.

"No me buscas!" Regina shouted, and now they were in the house's common area, but clearly her mother didn't care. "Tu sabes qué? When I took this assignment, I had to learn about the history of Garilia. As much as possible, because how else would I be able to see whether the people here were complying with regulations? And what do you think I learned about, hmm?"

Eva froze, her skin flashing cold and hot all at once. No, she thought. Please, not that. It was supposed to be buried, hidden . . . But of course, BOFA would have more than the official accounts.

"Ah, sí," Regina said, staring at Eva's face, her eyes wide with fury. "How dare you talk to me about secrets? Te conozco, mascarita. You call me out of nowhere asking for favors, you show up here and get invited to fancy parties when you're supposedly some cargo-ship captain . . . I've been doing my research, mija. 'The Hero of Garilia'? Qué horror. Qué vergüenza!"

Everyone around them was silent, watching the scene unfold. Sue had grabbed the power source and was crouched in the corner of the dining area, shielding it with her body. Min was on the floor between the couches with Mala clutched in her arms, the cat wisely refraining from so much as a quiet purr. And Vakar had retreated to the kitchen, smelling like a profusion of nerves and worry and anger, like someone had taken an awful crap and tried to cover it by burning incense.

Any other time, Eva would have lashed out, fought back, screamed at her mother twice as loudly until the two of them were inaudible to each other. But all she could think about now was Pink, still missing—Pink, who had been the first to reach out to Eva after Garilia, to recognize the depth of her sorrow and rage and regret, to join her in leaving Tito and Pete and everything else behind and starting over with something resembling scruples instead of the barest of ethical lip service.

And where had that gotten them? Right back in the same shitty place, and apparently Eva was none the wiser for all the time that had passed.

"Why are you smiling?" Regina demanded. "You think this is a joke?"

Eva hadn't even realized she was smiling. She shook her head. "Canta y no llores, Mami."

"No me diga," her mother said, throwing her hands up. "After everything I've done, my own daughter ends up a criminal anyway, and she thinks it's funny. Me muero."

Eva wanted to defend herself, insist that she wasn't a criminal anymore, but what was the point? She'd never get away from her past. She didn't deserve to. She'd spent years trying to at least keep her own mother from knowing all of this, but it was like that old saying: you can never go home again.

"We'll leave," Eva said. "I'm sorry."

"You're sorry?" Regina repeated incredulously. "If you were sorry, you wouldn't be here with your criminal friends looking for her criminal brother." She gestured at Sue, who was crying all the tears Eva couldn't, then at Min, still holding Mala. "A bank robber? A bot fighter? Qué rayo?"

Eva stalked forward and raised her finger, rage bubbling up to fill the void at light speed. "You say what you want about me," Eva said. "But you do not talk shit about my crew. Ever."

"It's the truth." She waved at Vakar. "Y tú qué? I could barely run a background check on you."

Vakar, prudently, was silent. The last thing he needed to do was spill that he was a Wraith.

"We're going back to our ship," Eva said. "We won't bother you again." I won't bother you again, she thought. Back to not being on speaking terms with both my parents.

"Fine," Regina said. "Allá tú." Without another word, she turned and stormed off to her room.

Sue muttered something, and her bots began scrambling over the table, collecting parts and loading them into tiny containers. Min carried Mala toward the spare bedroom, disappearing inside and emerging a few moments later with her backpack.

Vakar touched Eva's arm, startling her. He didn't say anything, didn't ask her anything, just stood next to her and smelled like incense and licorice. Well, at least he still loved her.

Within a few minutes, they were ready to leave. Regina stayed in her room, the door closed. Eva didn't bother saying goodbye; there was nothing left to say.

Taking a deep breath, Eva opened the front door and stepped

outside, into the warm night air. A few birdlike creatures flew through the sky, dark forms against a bright wave of stars, and in the distance the gentle shushing of waves against shoreline was broken by the cry of an unseen animal. They'd have to walk back to the ship, or call for a transport and hope the Watchers didn't nab them instead, or nab them at the spaceport, or—

"I'm surprised you haven't changed," a voice said, coming up the walk. "Your clothes, I mean."

It was Pink. The bag containing her sniper rifle hung from her shoulder, and she had already treated a cut to her lip and a blow to her temple, both pink from disinfectant. Jei trailed behind her, scowling as usual. He wore his helmet, but his arm weapon was either deactivated or had run out of power.

"Madre de dios," Eva whispered. For a moment, she felt like her soul left her body, then came crashing back in as a shudder of pure relief. Pink was okay. She was here, and safe.

"I'm nobody's mother," Pink replied, smirking. "Speaking of which, what the hell happened here?"

Eva exhaled sharply, frowning. "What happened here? What happened to you?" Before Pink could answer, she held up a hand. "No, wait, we can talk on the way. We need to get—" She stopped. Get what? Where? Sure, they could go back to the ship, but they had no guarantee of being able to leave it again. It would mean giving up entirely and accepting that they would never find Josh, much less convince him to leave Garilia with them.

She couldn't do that. They'd come too far, and they needed to get paid, and Sue deserved some kind of closure. And maybe the resistance wasn't perfect, but they were right that Damaal and the Sylfe Company were engaging in dangerous shenanigans that needed to be stopped. Eva reached into her pocket and touched the psychic-imprint recorder the resistance had given her.

If she was going to be a criminal like her mom said, she might as well try to be a good one.

"Sue, a little help," Eva said.

Sue fumbled the privacy-bubble device out of her bag and activated it. If any Watchers were in earshot or monitoring with remote devices, they'd be out of luck now. Someone might arrive to ask questions, but they'd pass through that Gate if it appeared.

Eva took a deep breath, then exhaled sharply. "You need to get back to *La Sirena Negra*. All of you. I'm staying here to finish what we started." She inclined her head at Jei, whose eyes widened in surprise.

Pink raised an eyebrow. "All by your lonesome? Pssh, don't even start."

"It's the best option," Eva said. "The safest option."

"I'm going to say this once," Pink said, her eye narrowing as she stepped closer to Eva. "We agreed we were a team: co-captains, equal command. Y'all still keep falling back on old habits, and I'm finna bust your lip like a piñata if you don't knock it off."

"But I—"

"Stop arguing with me when I'm right, you entire ass."

Eva stared Pink down for a few moments before looking away and nodding silently.

Vakar smelled more strongly of concern. "I do not believe we should leave you."

Eva shook her head. "You, of all of us, definitely have to go. We can't risk creating a bigger problem with your bosses. It's bad enough that you came to the party. Things could have gone much worse, and we might not be so lucky next time."

Vakar fell silent, warring scents rolling off him in a cloud. Licorice under it all, which she appreciated; she knew he loved her, and hopefully he knew she felt the same way, but sometimes love meant you had to make hard choices and be prepared for the consequences.

Sometimes standing by each other meant one of you had to walk away.

Pink spoke up, then, shifting her rifle to her other shoulder. "Vakar, you're technically freelance so we can't tell you what-all you should do. But as co-captain, I'd like to request that you escort our pilot back to the ship and keep her safe there while we finish this job."

Min perked up at hearing she was being sent back, then deflated with a guilty expression. "I could stay, too," she said stubbornly, inching closer to Sue.

"Min, it's okay," Eva said. "Worst case, you come pull us out of whatever fire someone lights under our asses." It was a white lie, and Eva felt uncomfortable telling it, because she had no intention whatsoever of making Min violate dozens of airspace laws to extract them. Better to have Vakar get her off-planet and back to something like safety.

Then again, they were already violating dozens of laws in helping the resistance, so what was a few more?

Vakar continued to smell like a perfume store on fire, but finally he shrugged in the quennian equivalent of a nod. "I will see that Min returns safely to *La Sirena Negra*," he said. "We will wait for you to finish your business here, and then we will all depart."

Eva smiled at him. His optimism was more stubborn than anything, but it was one of the many things she loved about him. She knew a little about stubbornness, after all.

"I'm going with you," Sue said, shouldering her pack of disassembled Pod Pal components.

"The hell you are," Pink replied.

"It's not safe!" Min exclaimed. Eva wrinkled her nose in confusion at that one.

"He's my brother," Sue said.

Eva sighed. "And we'll have a better chance of finding him and getting him out if we're not busy worrying about you."

Sue shook her head, an uncharacteristic scowl warping her features. "I know you think he's doing bad stuff on purpose, but I don't believe it. I need to talk to him." Her frown deepened. "And if he is . . . if he knows what he's doing, maybe I can convince him to stop. You'll just kidnap him, and then he might not want to help later."

"You can always convince him later," Pink said.

"Maybe," Sue replied, doubt tingeing her voice. "But what if you can't kidnap him? What if he fights back and you're dealing with a bunch of bad guys? I could help. Besides, I'm the one who knows how these things work." She gestured at the bag she carried. "And I've got my bots to help us, too."

Eva pursed her lips as she thought. Sue wasn't wrong. It might be useful to have someone who dealt in the tech they'd be facing. She might even be able to come up with some useful countermeasures before they infiltrated the lab.

"Fine," Eva said, with a glance at Pink for approval. "But you follow orders and stay out of the line of fire, got it?"

Sue grinned, then frowned at Min, who stood there hugging herself. "I'll be okay," Sue said.

"Yeah," Min replied faintly.

Eva hugged Vakar as tightly as she could manage, and he returned the gesture. If things went wrong, if the lab infiltration was a bust, if she got arrested . . . There were a hundred ways they could be separated from each other indefinitely, but that was true most of the time.

Maybe that was why it had gotten harder and harder to let

him go. Probability was a hell of a downer. But right now, she could hold him, and there was no sense ruining the moment.

"Be careful," Vakar said quietly, smelling so strongly of licorice she could taste it.

"Careful is my middle name," Eva replied.

"I thought it was Caridad?"

She raised an eyebrow at him and he tickled her face with his palps. He was teasing her. "Real funny. Get out of here before the cops decide we're suspicious enough to hassle."

Pink and Sue climbed into the transport with Jei, and Eva followed them, leaving Min and Vakar standing near the entrance to the house. As they flew off, the light in Regina's bedroom flickered out, the colored walls darkening with uncomfortable finality.

Chapter 20

HISTORY REPEATING

Nara brought them to a different rebel hideout from the last one, at the base of one of Rilia's home-trees in a structure made from colored bark that had been curved so that its overlapping pieces formed a dome. Instead of a door it had an energy curtain that not only kept out the mist forming in the damp darkness but also worked in tandem with the visual and audio fakery to hide the people inside. Eva, Pink, and Sue stepped out of the transport, shoes squelching in loamy mud that smelled of rain, and Eva tried very hard not to think about how Vakar and Min were faring without her.

The same cell of rebels that had met them before was present now, with a few additions. Dr. Lucien was once again tinkering with the robot dog while Felsira reclined in a hammock, and Sapri quietly discussed something with a pinkish-furred xana whose Attuned clung to his back like a round, fuzzy monkey.

The creature glared at Eva when she entered, its pig-snout of a nose turning up as if she smelled offensive. The xana glanced sideways at her, broadcasting confusion and dismay, which caused Sapri to stop midsentence and favor Eva with his own sour psychic emanation.

"Why have you brought her here?" Sapri asked.

"The mission was compromised," Nara replied. "We escaped and were not followed."

Sapri's hostility increased. "How was it compromised?" He was speaking to Nara, but looking straight at Eva.

"Put some water in your wine," Dr. Lucien said, his tone gently chiding.

Eva sighed. She wasn't even going to bother answering. The fight with her mother had sapped her of any desire to engage with hostility that was, given its source, entirely warranted. Mala clambered down from her shoulders and leaped to the floor, exploring the room with her tail primly straight.

Jei answered, removing his helmet as he spoke. "Everything was proceeding as planned until it was time to locate the third target. Then Nara was alerted to the approach of several Watcher squads from multiple vectors. Dr. Jones disabled two of their vehicles with her own special ammunition, while Nara destroyed another. Our transport was undamaged, but we were forced to engage in aggressive maneuvers that caused injuries to all of us, which Dr. Jones treated."

Pink snorted. "And what did I tell you to do when we got here?"

Jei ran his hand through his short black hair, which must have been sweaty because it spiked up in random directions. He stepped over to Dr. Lucien and held up his arm with the cannon. "Could you please examine my prosthetic interface?" he asked, his voice surprisingly meek.

"But of course," Dr. Lucien replied warmly, his dark hands gently removing the weapon to expose the socket connecting it to Jei's residual limb. Eva looked away from the examination, which seemed to warrant some privacy, and was surprised to find the xana also turned their attention to Nara and Pink.

The Attuned, meanwhile, had climbed down and was trailing after Mala, making a low keening noise. Mala ignored it, her tail shaking like a rattlesnake's.

"We intended to return Dr. Jones to her quarters," Nara said, picking up the story thread. "When we arrived, Captain Innocente and the others were departing, and Innocente offered to come along and help us."

"You accepted without consulting anyone?" Felsira asked, still lounging in the hammock, her psychic tone dry and detached.

Nara shrugged, her green ponytail bobbing slightly. "She needs us more than we need her. We can use that."

"Gracias, muy amable," Eva muttered.

"De nada," Nara replied.

"Additionally, we now have Joshua Zafone's sister," Jei added, inclining his head at Sue.

All attention turned to her, and Sue's face flushed. She ducked behind Eva, and Pink also moved to stand in front of her, arms crossed.

"That could be an advantage in negotiations, should they prove necessary," Sapri said, his psychic emanation thoughtful and darkly eager.

"She's a person, not collateral," Eva said. "And we're here to get Josh, not to negotiate with whoever you're thinking, so maybe we can move on from debrief to the plan for getting into the lab?" Silence replied, along with a psychic shift to low-grade hostility once more.

Mala, naturally, took that moment to saunter into the middle of the room and flop down, her tail lashing up and down as she extended her claws and began to lick them vigorously.

"Innocente gave me the imprint recorder," Jei said, pulling it out of a pocket in his suit. Sapri took it and inserted it into another device, like a multicolored cube.

"I only got two imprints," Eva said apologetically. "So I'm not sure how we'll get into the lab now, but—"

"We had already planned to enter in another manner," Sapri said, then he emanated surprise. "There are three imprints. The mission was not a failure."

Pink raised an eyebrow. "I only tagged two of the targets."

"And I only talked to two of them," Eva added.

Sapri's psychic emanation transitioned to confusion, then bitter amusement. "The third imprint is from Lashra Damaal," he said.

Eva stared at him for a long moment, then gave a close-mouthed chuckle. "Something good came of chatting with her, then," Eva said. "And to think I was trying to get away the whole time."

Dr. Lucien finished whatever he was doing with Jei's arm and carefully reattached the prosthesis. "We can proceed as we previously intended, then," he said. "More easily, in fact, since Damaal had unrestricted access to all portions of the facility. We must shut down the laboratory before it is too late."

"We must do it tonight," Sapri said. He raised the cube, scrutinizing its glowing faces with his enormous dark eyes. "If we delay, they may alter the security codes and protocols and render all our efforts useless."

A brief argument erupted among the assembled rebels, which Eva opted out of once again. She was exhausted, physically and emotionally, but the prospect of being finished with this whole arroz con mango sooner rather than later was intensely appealing to her. The Pod Pals needed to be stopped before they ended up all over the universe, doing whatever damage they were designed for.

Not to mention the bonus The Forge had dangled in front of her like a delicious slice of carrot cake, and whatever big secret Gate project they needed Josh for in the first place. Eva hoped it was as noble as Mari made it sound, because after all this time and effort, if it was the same shit with different bosses, Eva was going to be pissed.

Abruptly, Mala shifted to sit on her haunches, tail wrapped primly around her front paws.

"Miau," Mala said.

The arguing stopped. "What did your creature say?" Sapri asked.

Eva opened her mouth to tell him cats didn't talk, but Mala turned her head to glare at Eva, hazel eyes flashing in the dim light.

"She said we should stop comiendo mierda and get this party started already," Eva said.

"Miau," Mala said, licking a paw and swiping it over her face.

"She's a cat," Jei said, scowling.

"And? Is she wrong?"

Jei shook his head after a moment, and Pink snorted derisively.

"All right, then," Eva said. "What exactly is the plan?"

Barely visible in the dim starlight, the Sylfe Company laboratory was located on a rocky seaside cliff several hundred meters tall. Over time, crashing waves had left a few isolated towers of stone rising out of the water like giant middle fingers raised in the general direction of entropy. Multiple pod-like buildings attached to the cliff like metallic tumors, connected by the same ubiquitous cables found in Rilia and Spectrum City. A few cable cars waited on different levels, and presumably anyone with a harness could use that instead, assuming they weren't concerned about being exposed to the elements and any passing hostile forces.

The rebels used an Attuned as their vehicle—specifically by cramming a bunch of people in its enormous mouth. There were devices meant to deter wild Attuned and other animals from approaching the lab, but like any modern technology, they were prone to regular, inconveniently timed software updates that briefly disabled them. This left cameras, proximity sensors, and their associated alarms, all of which were hackable, at which point the resistance could swim up to an access pipe sucking in seawater for various scientific and mundane reasons, make their way up to the engineering room collecting the water, and proceed from there to the remaining pods.

Each of the dozen pods was assigned a team: a hacker, a saboteur, and at least one guard. The hacker would steal as much data as possible and then bring down the local node with a virus, ideally spreading it to any connected backups. The saboteur would use a nonexplosive expanding demolitions agent to destroy the pod; the devices were slow enough to allow anyone inside to escape, but fast enough to be difficult to stop once they were going. The guard would round up anyone already inside the pod and make sure they didn't interfere, then see to their safe evacuation once the saboteur had started the final countdown. If any security forces were alerted to the rebel presence, despite all the planned countermeasures, the guard would also warn the others and provide cover until everyone was out.

Eva, Pink, and Sue were with Jei and Nara on their own mission to find Josh. They all wore their spacesuits for protection—except Nara and Jei, who had their own armor—and would have their isohelmets activated and opaque on the outside to protect their identities. If a team found Josh before they did, they'd be informed of his location so they could sneak in and pick him up.

Sue wanted to find a way to bring Gustavo, her bot, but Eva vetoed it as too impractical. Jei wasn't happy because he wanted to be on one of the other teams. Nara didn't care because she was getting paid the same amount regardless.

It was a good plan. A solid plan.

It failed, of course.

"How much longer until the shielding is down?" Eva asked Sapri, firing her pistol at a Pod Pal hovering nearby.

Sapri's psychic emanation was as sour as old milk, and not a little angry. "I am not certain," he said. "The psychic imprints you acquired have partially facilitated an override of the lockdown protocols, but there are additional layers of security we are unable to penetrate. If we cannot overcome this soon, we will have to abandon the mission."

Eva scowled. "Hell no. I'm not giving up that easily, and neither are you." She fired again, barely missing Jei, whose robot dog had turned into a hoverboard for him to float around on. He was picking off the various auto-turrets attached to the roofs of the pods, which also kept them focused on him instead of the rest of the team.

"Maybe if you didn't distract the guy doing the heavy brain lifting?" Pink asked, taking her own shot at one of the robotic creatures farther away.

"You could stop talking completely," Nara added. She stood in front of Sapri, shielding him with her armor.

Eva rolled her eyes and continued scanning the sky for targets. Bad enough that all the lab pods had been under lockdown as soon as they climbed out of that claustrophobic fish mouth, the resistance also hadn't been aware that the whole place would be swarming with robot guards. Damaal had apparently started field-testing the Pod Pals' more violent applications, and what better place than right where the prototypes were being developed?

Sapri and a few other xana were trying to deactivate the shields on the first pod while everyone else waited in the access pipe underwater. Except Eva's team, which she had insisted would come along as protection if nothing else, so they'd be able to go after Josh as soon as the opportunity presented itself.

Then again, Eva hated waiting for opportunity to knock. She was more prone to busting down the door.

"We need a distraction," Eva said.

"Our Lady, you physically can't shut your mouth, can you?" Nara asked, idly firing her plasma cannon at a swooping Pod Pal.

Eva ignored the comment and spoke to Sue over helmet comms. "You've taken these robots apart and messed with their programming. Anything you can do to them to make them stop attacking?"

Sue was hunkered down inside an isosphere with her backpack full of her own bots, some of which had escaped to crawl over her and make unhappy shrieking noises. "I don't know if these are networked with each other, but they should all be connected to a single control interface," she said. "If I could get into the updater, I might be able to push out something to all the robots simultaneously, but otherwise I can only try to mess with one at a time."

"Great, start messing," Eva said.

A Pod Pal like a giant insect with drill legs shot an energy dart at her, which she avoided by throwing herself into a shoulder roll. Unfortunately, she'd overestimated how much roof she had left, and ended up careening over the side. She twisted and activated her gravboots, which pulled her toward the bottom of the pod, sticking her there upside-down. She cussed and started climbing back up, doing the occasional stomach crunch to avoid another shot from the same robot. By the time she got back to the others, any patience she'd been cultivating had shriveled up like an unwatered plant.

Jei swooped down on his dog-bot, hovering in front of Sapri. "Additional enemies are being deployed from the platform near the top of the cliff. A small gap in the shields opens each time, and remains open for a few seconds."

"Perhaps we can use that," Sapri replied, emanating a sharp spike of hope. "If you can deliver one of the expanding agents to that area, we can at least partially damage their facilities before retreating."

Jei nodded and proceeded to fly down to where the saboteurs were hiding. Eva, meanwhile, scowled more deeply. That wouldn't get them any closer to Josh, who could be in any one of these buildings—or none of them, if Damaal had relocated him for some reason.

Given their proximity, Sue could try to ping him. It was a calculated risk: they had no way of knowing how he would react, it might get caught in whatever surveillance was likely monitoring pings, and it would mean potentially giving up whatever anonymity they were able to maintain during this operation. But if they didn't do something now, they might never get another chance.

"I think I got one!" Sue said, and sure enough, a Pod Pal that was mostly mouth and wings had stopped trying to bite one of the xana. Within moments it emitted a painful shriek and then flapped away toward the top of the cliff.

"What did you do?" Eva asked.

"Every Pod Pal is programmed to act like the Attuned it's based on when it's in natural mode," Sue explained. "Unless it's given direct orders to attack or defend or whatever. So I put it in natural mode and turned off remote access. Whoever wants to reprogram it will have to catch it first." She sounded pleased with herself, and Eva had to admit she was impressed.

"Keep doing that, then," Eva said. She opened a private comms channel and took a deep breath. "Sue, I need you to ping Josh and tell him you're here."

"Rusty buckets!" Sue exclaimed. "Of course, why didn't I think of that?" She tried to slap her own forehead but hit her isohelmet instead, scattering some of her bots in the process.

"See if you can figure out where he is," Eva continued. "And if he can lower the shields to that pod so we can get in."

Another wave of robot Attuned arrived. Some of the larger flying varieties carried smaller nonflying ones, which they deposited on the lab pod before taking to the skies again. Two-legged and four-legged critters launched themselves at the xana still trying frantically to bring down the shields, so Nara and Eva teamed up to fend them off, Nara with her arm cannon and suit-augmented strength, and Eva with her sonic knuckles. Pink continued to pick off distant ones with her sniper rifle, each shot carefully aimed and timed so as not to be wasted.

"How many you take down so far, Innocente?" Nara asked.

"You think I'm counting, mija?" Eva replied, punching a spiky, rat-looking bot.

Nara shrugged. "My suit does it automatically." She paused. "And I'm older than you."

"Bueno, sorry vieja." Eva dodged a fireball from one of the flying todyk bots. She shot back at it and missed, hissing in frustration. They were running out of time, and the damn shields were still up on this very first pod, with another dozen to go.

"He's here!" Sue shouted, thankfully on the private comms channel. Eva's skin went briefly cold with relief.

"Josh? Where?" Eva asked.

"On the top platform, with all the Pod Pals. He can let us in if we go up there, but we have to go without the resistance."

Me cago en diez, Eva thought. Sure, in theory the resistance had agreed to bring them along because Eva had gotten them the psychic imprints they wanted, so her obligation to them was minimal since she'd held up her end of their original bargain. But could she really accomplish her mission knowing she'd left them here with virtually no hope of success? Maybe she could do something once she got up there, got in past the shields, but what? And how would she even get all the way to the top of the cliff without help?

Jei reappeared with one of the demolition devices, a cylinder as wide as his arm cannon with a single large button on the top. "It will take me some time to reach the platform, but with luck I will be able to react quickly enough after a robot is launched to place this inside," he said. "I may even be able to enter myself if a large enough unit is dispatched."

"May the Light go with you," Sapri said, his psychic emanation somber. "We should be able to open this shield soon, but already we have little hope of achieving all our aims. We must be content to do what is within our power and escape to continue the fight another cycle."

Tactical retreat was practical, certainly, but after all their effort and planning, the resistance had to be feeling extremely shitty. Eva sympathized deeply, but she couldn't let those sympathies overshadow her own goals.

Eva squinted at Jei's dog hoverboard. "How many people can your bot carry, Jei?" she asked.

"Two at most," he replied. "Why?"

"Take Sue with you," she said. "Pink and Nara and I will meet you at the top."

"Why?" Jei repeated, his eyes narrowing in suspicion. "I can do this on my own."

"Or you can do it more easily with help," Eva retorted. "Sue can hack the Pod Pals, and the rest of us can watch your back."

Jei seemed inclined to argue, but a new wave of security appeared: xana this time, wearing gliding suits and harnesses that let them leap from pod to pod or slide down the cables connecting the buildings. They all carried stun batons and wore helmets with large antenna-like protrusions covering their horns, and they moved with a grace and agility and cohesion that made Eva freeze.

They were mind-linked, she was sure of it. Someone else was controlling them, guiding them . . .

Flashbacks to her mission with Tito flooded her vision. It was happening again, she'd sworn she would never be here again, do this again, but here she was and here they were and she could almost hear the shouts of her team as they fought against the nearly silent foes assailing them from every direction, feel her cheek being torn open by a razor-sharp claw as her blood poured down her face, smell the smoke as the chemical fires she had set raged below until the branch was finally cut, and then the ragged breath she held as she took aim at Mother, squeezed the trigger, the delayed sonic boom and the bodies falling around her, graceless and limp and empty—

Someone was flashing a light in her face. Pink. "Eva, can

you hear me?" Pink was saying. "Listen to me. Take a deep breath."

Eva struggled to fill her lungs with air. Her chest was tight, like her diaphragm was being crushed, like she'd been spaced without a suit and the void was trying to get in.

"We don't have time for this," someone else said. Nara?

"You think this shit cares about time?" Pink snapped. "It takes as long as it takes." Then, more gently, "Eva, honey, you're having a flashback. It's not real. There is other, very real shit happening right now, but you're not in Rilia. Deep breaths, Bee, come on, come on back."

Eva tried to press her hands to her ears, but her isohelmet was in the way. Just as she was about to deactivate it, Pink shouted, "Sweet deep-fried fucksticks!" and someone kicked Eva in the back hard enough to send her sprawling across the top of the pod. Her spacesuit took the brunt of the damage, and she instinctively curled up into a ball.

Her vision cleared, and there was Sue hiding in her isosphere, her bots running back and forth waving their tiny pans and torches and other random weapons. Mala had appeared as well—had she been hiding in Sue's backpack? Eva had sworn she'd left the damn cat with Dr. Lucien. But she was out now, hissing at the xana attackers with her fur raised and her tail as bushy as a pipe brush, even though she was a tiny fucking animal and they were ten times her size.

The absurdity of it coupled with the danger Sue was in yanked Eva back to reality hard enough to leave her dizzy. Someone kicked her back again, and she groaned in pain; that would leave a bruise. But Sue needed help, and Eva had a mission, and one of Sue's bots definitely had her chancleta, the little cabróncito.

Eva sucked in a breath and let out a ragged laugh. It helped, a little. An inhumanly fast punch came flying toward her and she sidestepped, too slowly, catching it on her shoulder. She ducked a kick next, and the tail that whipped around immediately after, briefly glad to be so much shorter than the xana. One moment at a time, the flashback retreated into the past where it belonged so Eva could focus on the present. It would always be there, waiting for the chance to drag her down again like an ocean undertow, but for now she was lucky enough to once again be in calmer waters.

For a particular definition of calm. The resistance had made it through the shielding of the first pod, finally, and broken into the interior. More rebels had arrived to protect them from the xana security guards who had swooped down from above, and who were also coming after Eva and her team. The xana she'd been fighting launched another flurry of punches, kicks, and tail swipes, which Eva blocked and evaded as best she could until Nara body-checked the guard and shoved him over the edge of the pod.

"Pink," Eva croaked, and Pink was at her side in a moment.

"You okay?" Pink asked.

"Hell no," Eva said, her voice growing steadier as she spoke. "I'm never okay. But we need to get to the top platform before this shitshow gets any worse."

"You got a plan under all that hair?" Pink asked.

Jei hadn't left yet, thankfully, choosing instead to help protect the resistance as their reinforcements arrived. Eva stumbled over to Sue while waving at Jei.

"Come on," Eva told him. "We can do this if we work together!"

Jei hesitated, his expression as dark as before. But finally he nodded and hovered over, lowering his dog-bot so Sue could jump on. Sue hurriedly stuffed her tiny yellow bots into her backpack and deactivated her isosphere, climbing aboard next to Jei and crouching down to grab the side of the contraption for balance.

Mala, meanwhile, was still hissing at the xana guards like she was a tiger instead of a calico. Eva was astonished that none of them had punted her into the ocean yet.

"Get in the damn backpack, comemierda," Eva snapped at Mala.

"Miau," Mala replied, trotting over to wind around Eva's legs instead.

"Madre de dios, you're so fucking stubborn," Eva said. She reached down to grab the cat, tucking her under one arm like a furry sportsball. Mala writhed in protest before apparently settling into a sufficiently comfortable position to allow the great indignity to proceed.

"Nara," Eva said, "can you get Pink to the top platform?"

"Claro," Nara replied, "but you're not paying me to."

"Me cago en diez, can you do one single thing pro bono? Just this once?"

"Nope," Nara said, firing off a plasma ball at an incoming Pod Pal. "But if you're going to do something that will make my job easier or more successful . . ."

Eva hesitated. "Possibly?"

Nara barked out a laugh. "You're worse at telling the truth than you are at lying. Good enough, though." She sidled over to Pink, a lazy but powerful punch picking off an approaching xana in the process.

"You ready to go?" Nara asked Pink.

"What, you're going to carry me like a cat?" Pink asked, gesturing at Mala.

"Don't be ridiculous. Give me your arm."

Pink shouldered her sniper rifle and offered Nara her arm.

Nara crouched slightly and, in a series of motions almost too fast for Eva to follow, tossed Pink over her shoulder. Pink yelped and began to cuss Nara and Eva out smooth as butter, which Nara ignored and Eva snorted at. Pink's cussing intensified as Nara took a running leap off the edge of the pod toward the next one up, easily twenty meters away, landing with a grace and ease that gave Eva a twinge of envy.

It also reminded her of Vakar, which she absolutely didn't have time for. She wished he were there with her, but that was life. She hoped he and Min were fine. They had to be.

"Okay, let's do this," Eva said. She grabbed a cable pulley from one of the unmoving xana guards lying nearby and detached it from his harness. It was different from ones she'd used herself, but close enough that she was able to get it attached to the cable with little fuss. She yanked her anchor line from her belt and looped it through the carabiner-like hook for safety, then held Mala up so she could look the cat in her hazel eyes.

"Last chance to get in the backpack," Eva said.

"Miau," Mala replied, as if offended.

"Fucking cats," Eva muttered. Tucking Mala back under her arm, she activated the pulley.

The device wrenched her up along the cable toward the next pod, and Eva was glad she'd used her anchor line because she almost lost her grip immediately. She moved more quickly than she expected, but still slow enough to attract the attention of guards and Pod Pals both. More than once she had to twist out of the way to avoid a shot or swipe, but by the time she reached the rooftop of the next pod, Pink had apparently convinced Nara to put her down long enough to take a few shots to cover Eva's approach.

Jei and Sue, meanwhile, continued their own leisurely rise on Jei's dog-bot. Interestingly, no robots were attacking them—

Josh's doing, perhaps? Which suggested he had some control over the Pod Pals being launched at the resistance. Eva filed that information away for a time when she wasn't actively avoiding a fall to her death.

One cable at a time, one building at a time, Eva and her feline stowaway ascended the cliffside laboratory complex. The wind continued to whip at her when the robots didn't, and her arm burned from the exertion, despite the anchor line helping offset some of her weight. She made another mental note to add more pull-ups to her workout routine.

I should start making actual notes, she thought, because I'm never going to remember all this shit.

Finally, Eva was only one cable away from the platform at the top. Jei and Sue hovered nearby, while Nara and Pink waited for Eva to detach the pulley mechanism and switch it to the new cable.

"The shield is still up," Nara observed.

"It sure is," Eva said, turning to Sue. The engineer's expression was hidden by her opaque isohelmet, but her posture was nervous. "What's up with Josh?" Eva asked over private comms.

"He's worried," Sue replied. "He says there are too many of us."

Eva eyed Jei and Nara and sighed. "How many is too many?"

"He'll let me in with one other person, but that's it."

And he couldn't have said that five minutes ago? Eva thought. Madre de dios.

"Fine," Eva said. She detached the pulley from her anchor line and gestured for Sue to come over. "Use this to get up, and Jei will stay here."

"What are you doing?" Jei asked immediately.

"We can't all go inside," Eva said. "Not yet. But the rest of you can wait here and we'll figure out how to get all the shields down for good."

"Will you, now," Nara said. She raised her arm cannon and aimed it at Eva, who froze. Another flashback threatened to overcome her, send her to her knees—the same gun, the same posture, Eva staring down that barrel with the certainty that it was the last thing she'd ever see.

Then Nara shifted to shoot a guard sneaking up behind Eva, his stun baton clattering against the roof of the pod as he fell. Eva exhaled so hard it gave her a brief pang of dizziness.

"This better not be a trick," Jei said, but he made no move to stop her. That was about as much trust as Eva was likely to get from him in a lifetime, she figured, and hopefully it would be enough.

"Pink, stay with them, please," Eva said, once she found her voice again. "We'll be back."

Pink held out her hand, and Eva took it. Several snaps, slaps and a hip-bump later, Eva climbed onto the top of the pulley mechanism and activated her gravboots, while Sue clung to the device's grips with all her strength. Mala was uncharacteristically silent and still, but her pupils were fully dilated and she had extended her claws in a futile attempt to grip Eva's puncture-proof spacesuit.

"Go," Eva told Sue, and Sue activated the pulley. They shot up the cable, Eva fighting to stay vertical as the wind continued to blow. They came to a landing on a tiny extension of the platform, and without further ado, a hole in the shields opened to allow them access.

Unlike the other parts of the facility, which were entirely enclosed, this was a large, open area like a sports facility. There were markings on the floor, a combination of concentric circles and lines intersecting them, as well as a rectangle surrounding them, and platforms on either end like the kind that might hold referees or players. The whole place was partially covered by an arcing roof jutting out from the cliffside, with an array of holoscreens and electronics underneath, currently being monitored by a few xana. A wall of shelving held at least a hundred, maybe a hundred and fifty capsules like the ones used to contain the Pod Pals.

That is a lot of damn robots, Eva thought.

A single, gray-haired human in a green lab coat and goggles stood nearby, and immediately started running toward them once they'd passed through the shield. Eva raised an eyebrow, then pulled out her pistol warily. The man slowed, raising his hands and smiling. It was a cocky smile, a dimple-cheeked asymmetrical smile, meant to be disarming and probably very successful at parties, but Eva was walking an emotional tightrope and too busy maintaining her balance to be charmed.

"I, uh, thought you weren't with the rebels," he said. He looked back and forth between her and Sue.

"Our goals aren't mutually exclusive," Eva said. "Joshua Zafone, I presume."

"Guilty as charged," Josh said. Now that he was closer, it was clear he was taller than Sue by at least a quarter meter, and younger than Eva despite his hair color. But their features were similar, and his fingers were twitching like Sue's did when she was anxious, even if he seemed to be hiding it better otherwise.

"We're here to ask for your help," Eva said.

"Right, okay," Josh replied. "But let me ask you something first: Why are you carrying a cat?"

Chapter 21

THE POWER THAT'S INSIDE

Eva resisted the urge to put Mala down, la muy cabrona, who purred at being acknowledged. "She insisted on coming. We don't have time for long explanations. I've been hired to bring you to a secret project in another galaxy, and you're the only one who can help it succeed, because you're the only one with the skills and information they need."

Josh laughed again, and again Eva was struck by how he was probably a hit with his fellow science types. He was certainly infinitely less punchable than Miles Erck so far.

"That's very flattering," Josh said. "But I already have a job, as you can see." He gestured at the xana behind him, who were operating a bunch of equipment Eva didn't recognize or understand. Then he turned to Sue, who had been standing as still as a statue since they arrived.

"What are you doing here?" he asked her. "How did you find me?"

"I . . ." Sue cleared her throat. "The piggy bank." Her voice was raw, like she was struggling to speak through tears.

"Sugar snacks, I should have known," Josh said, scowling and snapping his fingers. He quickly raised his hands again, glancing at Eva's pistol.

Eva snorted. Sugar snacks. Yeah, definitely Sue's brother.

Before she could cut in with more about how she needed him to go with her, Sue stepped forward, trembling with what Eva realized was rage.

"How could you?" Sue shouted. "All this time, you were here, and not . . . not . . ." She sniffled, and Eva mentally willed her not to deactivate her isohelmet to wipe the snot no doubt forming.

"Yeah, sorry about that," Josh said, shrugging. "It seemed like the safest thing for all of us. If you had seen where The Fridge was keeping me—"

"I was there!" Sue shouted. "I was at their base! I saw the labs, and the cryo storage, and the big Proarkhe artifact, and—"

"Wait, you what?" Josh frowned, lowered his hands and pointed at Sue. "How did you . . . What were you doing there?"

"Hi, that was me," Eva said, waving with her free hand. As she did, she realized she shouldn't have a free hand; she was no longer carrying Mala, who was trotting cutely toward the wall of Pod Pal capsules. Eva mentally cursed, but she couldn't leave Sue alone now.

"I've been trying to find you," Sue said, her voice cracking. "I robbed a bank for you, to pay your ransom. Do you know how many Fridge people I've . . ."

Killed, Eva thought, when Sue couldn't finish the sentence. It was a nonzero number, starting at the very Fridge base Sue was talking about now. Pink had spent weeks helping Sue deal with it afterward.

"Oh, no," Josh said. "No, no, don't tell me they were making you pay, too. I thought I was earning my own freedom by working for them voluntarily, under excessive NDAs of course."

"Yeah, well, they're fucking liars," Eva said. "And speaking of The Fridge, if you really want to screw them over, trust me when I say you want to come meet the people we're working for."

Josh waved his hands dismissively. "No, see, I'm already doing that here." He gestured at the wall of capsules, his expression hard. "Once these are distributed throughout the universe, I'll have the most advanced surveillance system ever created. I'll be able to find Fridge agents wherever they're hiding, and—" He paused. "Well, let's say it won't be very nice."

Eva thought of the exploding recycler and considered how very not nice indeed that would be. "Does your boss know what you want to do?" Eva asked.

Josh gave a nasty laugh. "She has more creative ways of ruining people with whatever we get from our psychic traces, and that's fine by me. Might as well make some money from the trash who wrecked my life."

"You should have told us!" Sue shouted, throwing a wild punch at her brother. It glanced off his arm, but Eva had been helping Sue practice, so it sent Josh stumbling backward, clutching himself in surprise.

"Hey, ouch!" he exclaimed. "I was busy with other stuff. Take it easy!"

"Take it easy?" Sue replied. "I'll give you easy!" She kicked him in the shin, and he hopped on one foot, scowling.

One of the xana monitoring the holoscreens had stopped and was staring at them, the faintest of concerned psychic emanations coming from their general direction. They apparently hadn't noticed Mala, though, as she was clambering up onto a random piece of equipment.

"Sue, hey, we're attracting attention," Eva said. "We don't have much time here, and if we leave without Josh, we don't get paid."

"I just . . . I . . ." Sue stuttered, then shouted, "Shit on ten!" She threw up her arms and turned around. One of her bots climbed out of her backpack and patted the back of her neck awkwardly.

Eva stalked closer to Josh, who once again raised his arms. "Listen, mijo," Eva said. "There are other people out there trying to stop The Fridge, and more importantly, doing super-weird science that they need your help with. Something to do with what you stole from the Fridge base when you escaped. So I need to drag your happy little culo back to them, and you can all sort out whatever it is that's such a big fucking deal that they'd pay me truly exciting amounts of money for. Do we understand each other?"

Josh blinked. "Not really?"

Eva huffed out a breath. "What were you working on for The Fridge, and what did you steal from them when you left?"

"Information, mostly," Josh said. "I was working on reproducing . . . technology the Proarkhe used."

Eva thought of the energy source inside the Pod Pals again, which was the same as the Gate-creating cannons she'd found at the Fridge base, and the strange ruins where she'd found Vakar after she escaped cryostasis. "Technology they used to make super-dense portable energy cubes, maybe?" Eva guessed.

Josh flinched. "Yes, that, among other things."

Mierda, mojón y porquería. That was a hell of a tech to add to the universal pool. It was wild enough that energy sources existed that could power FTL drives, but ones that could power a Gate, to open a hole from one end of the universe to the other? A lot of people would pay a lot of credits—or kill a lot of other people—to get their respective appendages on something like that.

Not to mention that, by BOFA law, it was incredibly illegal. If her mom found out, Josh and everyone else working on this project would be toast. Garilia might even be ejected from BOFA, depending on how things shook out.

Ah, politics, Eva thought. Where all the players are assholes and all the prizes are bullshit.

"And you were working with Miles Erck?" Eva asked, eager to avoid that trail of thought.

"Yes, and Emle Carter," Josh replied. He was looking more skittish by the moment, less self-assured, his fingers wagging almost uncontrollably. "Look, I'm sorry you came all this way for whoever is paying you, but I'm not leaving." He shot a stricken look at Sue, who still wasn't facing him. "You have to understand. Lashra is keeping me safe from The Fridge, and my work here is too important."

"I am pleased to hear you say so, Joshua," a voice chimed in, psychic authority emanating from its source. Lashra Damaal strolled across the platform, her loose clothing billowing in the wind, pale as starlight. She was flanked by four Watchers, including Rakyra, as well as several Attuned.

Behind her, in restraints, marched Pink, Nara, Jei, and Sapri, along with three of the xana resistance members who had been breaking into the first lab pod. Hopefully that meant the others had escaped, unless they had been apprehended as well and left below. Either way, Eva's stomach sank like a rock in the sea.

"I am less pleased to see the Hero of Garilia engaged in such violent, clandestine activities," Damaal continued, drifting toward Eva, as tall and imposing as ever.

"I'm nobody's hero," Eva said bitterly. "Certainly not Garilia's." She still held her pistol, but she didn't dare use it, and the Watchers seemed to know that implicitly.

"Truly, this is not an age of heroes, is it?" Damaal asked, pacing a slow circle around Eva. "Ours is an age of information. Of knowledge and secrets. It is said that a thing which is not done in the Light should not be done at all, and yet there are so many dark corners of the universe in which dark deeds are done. Is that not so?"

"Cierto," Eva muttered. "I'm looking at some right now."

Damaal emanated a shimmer of amusement. "Ah, but you misunderstand. This project is intended to illuminate rather than obfuscate. With our robotic Attuned, we will be capable of shining a light on all those dark corners, that the secrets they hold may no longer be hidden." She made a small gesture with her tail toward the wall of capsules, and Eva stilled.

Mala was over there. What was she doing? Pawing at some console, it looked like. Probably one that controlled the Pod Pals they'd been deploying against the rebels this whole time, given all the capsules nearby.

Sure enough, one of the capsules opened and, in a flash of light, a robotic Attuned appeared. It looked like a spiky armadillo with giant claws, but since it hadn't been given any orders, it just sat there silently and didn't move.

If the Watchers were monitoring their pings or private comms, Eva was probably screwed, but she had to take the chance. "Sue," she said, "can you still do the thing you were doing earlier with one of the bots?" She hoped Sue knew what she meant without asking.

Sue, who had been frozen since Damaal arrived, clenched her hands into fists. "Captain, from up here, I can do it to all of them at once."

A slow smile stretched the scar on Eva's face. If she could somehow get Mala to open all the capsules at the same time . . .

"What precisely is it you intend to do?" Damaal asked. "You will forgive my intrusion, of course. The devices Joshua modified are very adept at reading thoughts, but are not always capable of translating them perfectly."

So the Pod Pals were psychic, as she had suspected. That's why Mala hated them so much. And if they could read minds, there really would be a lot of secrets finding their way into Damaal's hands. Everything was coming together.

Well, almost everything. Eva hadn't counted on Josh being a jerk, and if they didn't get him and his information out of there, a lot of people were going to be very unhappy. Including her, probably from the inside of a prison cell.

"I am surprised at the pleasure you are taking in this situation," Damaal said, emanating a spark of curiosity. "It will be interesting to participate in your reeducation." This time she didn't gesture, but the Watchers flanking her clearly got the message, because they immediately proceeded to approach Eva, their stun batons extended and humming with energy.

Before Eva could yell an order at Mala, Damaal loosed a psychic sea urchin of spiky emotions: surprise, fear, and even anger, sharp and hot as a laser.

A shadow passed overhead, blotting out the stars. A transport, large enough to carry at least a dozen people by Eva's estimate. It slowly descended, forcing everyone beneath it to move or be crushed, and Eva took the opportunity to edge closer to the console where Mala was engaged in her shenanigans.

Was this a resistance vessel, taking advantage of the situation to help rescue their allies? No, that made no sense—the security forces would be attacking already if it were, but no one was making anything resembling a violent motion.

Ay, no, Eva thought. Por favor, no, not now, not here.

A hatch opened in the side of the transport after it landed, and a ramp extended from it. A line of uniformed people filed out, their weapons holstered but clearly visible, their commlinks openly broadcasting that they were BOFA agents requesting immediate compliance with all pertinent regulations. Eva couldn't contain a groan as a sharply dressed figure in a hoverchair followed them down the ramp, her magenta hair neatly combed and styled, her makeup impeccable as always.

Regina Alvarez certainly knew how to make an entrance.

At least my isohelmet is still active, Eva thought. Until the pigs tell me to turn it off, anyway.

A small furry form moved in her peripheral vision. Mala, still slowly creeping all over the console. Another Pod Pal emerged, this one like a plump bipedal rabbit with pink fur. It also waited quietly for a command, eerily motionless.

"Prime Damaal," Regina Alvarez said politely, floating up to the woman herself. "Qué lástima. I had hoped you weren't involved in all this, but here you are." She appeared to be ignoring the resistance and their attendant Watchers—not BOFA's problem, presumably.

"I apologize for any confusion, Administrator," Damaal said, emanating confidence and authority. "I am not sure I take your meaning, however. What am I involved in?"

Regina smiled, a smile Eva knew very well. It was the one she put on when she knew Eva had done something wrong, and knew that Eva was lying about it, but was waiting to see just how many lies Eva was going to tell before she realized she was jodida.

"This facility wasn't on the records you submitted to us," Regina said, making a show of looking around with great interest.

"An unfortunate omission," Damaal agreed. "The officials

tasked with ensuring completion and accuracy of those materials will be reprimanded and reeducated promptly."

The word "reeducated" wiped the smile off Regina's face, and Eva snorted. What did her mom think was going on here? Happy tourist times for everyone?

"Certainly those forms will need to be revised and resubmitted," Regina said. She hovered to one side, peering at the Pod Pals in front of the wall of capsules and the various holoscreens and instruments nearby.

"It will be my supreme pleasure to ensure that it is done," Damaal said. She continued to emanate calm and authority, her hands now clasped in front of her, enormous eyes following Regina's every move. "May I assist you with anything else?"

Regina's smile returned. "I am so glad you asked. But first, I'll give you a moment to take the comms notifications you're about to receive, assuming you aren't mind-linked to anyone at your various warehouse facilities."

Damaal's emanations went away entirely, as if she'd activated a suppressor or other masking device. Convenient. Her tail, which she had wrapped around her waist, twitched as if it were being poked. Moments later, the Watchers also went blank, their lack of tonality as eerie as when Vakar didn't smell like anything.

Eva almost laughed. She had no idea what was going on, but she knew resingado when she saw it, and Damaal was definitely in a whole galaxy of trouble.

Mala opened another capsule, then another. There were now seven Pod Pals quietly sitting near the far wall—she must have opened others when Eva wasn't looking.

"So, Prime," Regina said politely. "Perhaps you can explain why all the facilities that are meant to be storing a specific inventory of items ranging from light fixtures to construction equipment are, in fact, entirely empty?"

Light fixtures. An image of her mother tapping on her hoverchair and mumbling numbers flashed through Eva's mind. She'd been counting. Well, what had Eva thought an audit entailed? Numbers on a spreadsheet? Sure, but those numbers meant something, like a cargo manifest. And clearly they hadn't been adding up.

Pete had pulled this kind of shit before. Buy a bunch of stuff and call it something different on the official records to hide it. Guns became guidance-system parts, flash bombs were power cables—the receipts were rarely detailed enough for it to be difficult to fudge them, and if the seller was complicit, the process was seamless. Or buy stuff and then resell it on the black market and use the funds to buy what you actually wanted, or make a direct trade for it if that worked better. Sometimes you lost a little money that way, but you were probably more than making up for it somewhere else.

And as long as an auditor didn't stroll in wanting to see all those power cables you ordered—which they wouldn't, because there weren't enough of them to cover every small business in the universe—nobody would have the slightest clue what you were up to.

Apparently, when a whole planet was getting audited, things went a little differently. Simultaneous raids at multiple locations differently, if Eva was picking up what her mother was putting down.

"I am at a loss to explain the situation, Administrator," Damaal said finally. "But my Watchers will engage in a thorough investigation to determine—"

"No need, Prime," Regina interrupted, raising a hand. "My

agents are also investigating the other . . . omitted facilities we located, here and in multiple star systems. I'll have a comprehensive inventory of their contents before the end of the cycle." She made a circular motion with her forefinger. "This facility as well, now that we've managed to lower all the shields."

Eva snickered. This was worse than the time her mom found her stash of sex toys and berated her for not only wasting hard-earned money on poor-quality products, but also failing to properly store them.

Damaal's posture stiffened, and she seemed to gain a few centimeters of height. "Regulations do not permit you to observe portions of facilities that are designated as containing vital trade secrets, Administrator."

Regina nodded. "You're absolutely right, Prime. Unfortunately for you, since these facilities weren't designated as such, I'm legally permitted to search them. In fact, you might say I'm legally obligated to do so, especially if I suspect criminal wrongdoing." Her eyes widened for a moment as her smile brightened to near-blinding levels.

That was the end of that, then. As soon as BOFA figured out what Damaal had been up to here, it was all going to be shut down. At least the resistance would get part of what they wanted out of this whole shitshow; no more Pod Pals being constructed or distributed, especially if . . . coño carajo.

Especially if Regina and her agents found the evidence of Proarkhe technology being used here. BOFA didn't play around with that, not even slightly—hell, they'd shut down Sue and Josh's entire home planet and relocated everyone to another world because of a Proarkhe ruins discovery. Anyone who could be proven to be complicit in the intentional use of such tech would be going to prison for a very long time.

Eva stole a glance at Josh, who was apparently having a similar conversation with himself, and had turned as red as a ripe pitanga. Damaal was still suppressing her psychic emanations, so her large black eyes revealed nothing, even as her tail continued to twitch.

"And what of those of us who are not involved in this?" Sapri asked. Eva rolled her eyes and wished she could kick him from where she stood.

Regina raised an eyebrow. "Intraplanetary politics are beyond the scope of BOFA concerns, except inasmuch as they might impact related investigations," she replied, as if reciting from a manual. "You clearly knew what was happening here and failed to report it to the proper authorities, which arguably makes you complicit."

"We were trying to stop it!" Sapri said, emanating indignation.

"Stop it, or use it for political gain?" Regina asked coolly.

Both, Eva thought. Fucking politics. They were like those two-headed snake things from Snerth whose fanged mouths were also assholes.

Regina's gaze swept over Eva and Sue, and if she recognized them, she said nothing. "That said, I'm inclined to consider you all witnesses rather than accessories, assuming you cooperate with us."

Sapri's emanation became more thoughtful, despite its edge of dismay. The other resistance members had similar reactions, though Damaal and the Watchers were still showing absolutely no emotion whatsoever.

It was a good offer, frankly. Nice and tidy. Might bring down a substantial part of the existing regime, depending on what evidence they unearthed, which could help the rebels in other ways as well.

Except Eva didn't have time to be holed up in a BOFA

witness-protection program for however long it took to finish the investigation, and she sure as hell wasn't interested in showing up in any courts if it came to that. She suspected Nara was having similar thoughts, given that it was tough to get paid as a merc when you were cooling your heels instead of working. Maybe her contracts included clauses for such situations—a daily rate or something—but that didn't guarantee the payments would keep finding their way to her account if her employers were similarly tied up.

And Josh getting arrested meant she wouldn't get paid, so Eva had to get him out of here, too.

Naturally, just as Eva was wrangling her brain into formulating a plan, one of the BOFA agents strolled up to Regina holding a large, lidded container. He opened it and showed her the contents, which made Regina's frown deepen as her eyebrows furrowed.

"Bueno," she said. "That certainly complicates things. They're using these to power their little animal machines?"

The agent nodded, and Regina glanced at the small crowd of Pod Pals that Mala had already released. There were at least a dozen, and who knew how many more still in their capsules behind them.

"We'll have to find out how many have already been distributed," Regina said. "Get these loaded onto the ship immediately and prepare the planet for quarantine."

Apparently, that was the cue for the shit to hit the air filters, because everyone started to move at once.

Josh made a strangled sound, then ran for a door in the side of the cliff.

"Restrain him," Regina said. An agent immediately produced an isosphere and raced after Josh. Eva groaned. Now how was she going to get him out of here, much less off-planet?

Damaal and the Watchers took this opportunity to run for the edge of the platform. Presumably they were all wearing antigrav belts and could handle a jump, especially if there were transports on lower levels to get them away entirely. The BOFA agents rushed to catch them, pulling out more isospheres for the purpose.

Nara busted open her restraints—a feat Eva would never have thought possible, but then again, the xana had basically put standard cuffs on a mech—and took off running, in the direction of the cliff.

"Where are you going?" Jei called after her, but Nara ignored him and the other equally dismayed resistance fighters. The wounded expression on Jei's face gave Eva a brief pang of empathy, but if Jei didn't know who Nara was by now, that was his problem.

Mala must have managed to find an option to open all the capsules at once, because Pod Pals flashed into being all over the platform, the crowd of a dozen quickly expanding into fifty or more. There were furry quadrupeds and carapaced flyers and smooth-skinned bipeds and all sorts of other forms that Eva had never seen and couldn't find the words to describe. They didn't move, just waited for commands that were unlikely to come since their controllers were busy trying to escape along with everyone else.

"Me cago en la hora que yo nací," Regina said, glaring at the bots. "Can someone get those things back in their capsules?"

"Sue," Eva said over private comms. "Override the Ball Buddies, now!"

Moments later, the robotic Attuned moved as if awakening from cryostasis. And because they'd been instructed to behave as wild animals, and they were currently all clustered together regardless of species, they simultaneously went batshit fucking loco.

Regina shouted, "We've got to catch them all!" as the now-aggressive or rapidly fleeing Pod Pals began attacking each other, or racing toward the platform's edge after the escaping xana, or trying to climb the cliff or fly away into the starlit sky. Some of her agents responded, while others continued their pursuit of Damaal and her accomplices.

Josh, meanwhile, was towed into the waiting BOFA ship, fists banging futilely against the impenetrable bubble he was encased in. Eva's stomach was full of rocks soaked in kerosene and set on fire. After all this effort—coming back to Garilia, dealing with Damaal and the resistance and her own mother—the mission was a failure. There was no chance she could make it across a platform swarming with dangerous robots and armed BOFA agents, bust into a government vessel, and rescue Josh without endangering him, her crew, herself, and probably Regina. She'd done some risky things before, but this was just asking to be restrained and dragged off to prison, which was where Josh would likely end up now, given what he'd done.

For someone who had just escaped from The Fridge's confinement, it seemed a cruel thing to lock him up again. Waste of a brilliant mind. Then again, given what he'd done to his own family and almost done to the whole universe, maybe it was for the best.

Whatever boosts Nara had in her boots let her take a mighty leap that put her on the roof hanging over the platform, and from there she jumped again and clung to a rocky outcropping, more than far enough away to avoid getting nabbed by an isosphere. She gave a quick salute—to Eva or Jei or someone else, it wasn't clear—and proceeded to climb in boot-augmented bursts. Eva had no idea how the merc planned to get back to civilization, much less off the planet, but Nara had been in worse situations before and managed.

Besides, Eva had to worry about getting her own people out.

"Sue, bring down a few of the big flying ones," Eva said. "Enough to carry us out of here."

"What about Josh?" Sue asked.

"I'm sorry," Eva said. "There's no time. We get out of here now, or we end up on that ship with him."

She raced over to Pink's side, examining her friend's restraints while muttering a string of curses under her breath. A random Pod Pal ran up, and Eva kicked at it to shoo it away.

"We can get these things off later," Pink said. "First, we need to get gone."

"We will stay," Sapri said, surprising Eva. He emanated a strange amount of calm given the chaos around them.

"What?" Eva asked. "Why?"

"We will cooperate with the administrator," he replied. "Given the circumstances, this seems more likely to yield a positive change than our other efforts to undermine the current regime. And even if we are apprehended, the resistance will continue without us." The other rebels murmured agreement, except Jei, who scowled as was his custom.

"I don't want to be stuck here dealing with BOFA," Jei said. "I need to get back to Dr. Lucien and see what he wants to do."

"If we don't get out before the quarantine, we'll all be stuck," Eva said, glancing at her mother. Regina was still shouting orders, ignoring the resistance since they weren't doing anything objectionable at the moment. She was ensconced in her own isosphere as protection from the rampaging animal bots now, which gave Eva a small measure of relief.

With a great gust of wind from its enormous wings, a white Pod Pal landed behind the rebels, raising its crested head to the sky and loosing an ear-splitting cry. It looked like a cross between a flying todyk and a bird, and was easily five meters long, with talons big enough to carry off any one of them. Eva went for her pistol, then realized it was reaching out a claw and waiting rather than attacking.

"I think our ride is here," Eva said.

"Yes, I'm controlling that one," Sue said, popping up behind her. "Technical specs say it should be able to carry three of us."

Her crew was sorted, then. She turned to Jei. "What about you?" Eva asked. "Can your dog get you back to where you were staying?"

"I believe so," he replied. "But as you said, I will have no way to leave the planet after that."

"What, you don't want to keep running errands for the resistance?" Eva asked.

Jei glanced back at the rebels, clearly torn. "I support their cause, yes, but to be trapped for an uncertain amount of time due to a planetary quarantine . . ."

Eva grinned. "I can give you a ride, if you don't mind being trapped with us for a few cycles until we reach a Gate." Assuming we can even make it to *La Sirena Negra* before the quarantine shuts down the spaceport, she thought.

"I . . . thank you, I will consider that," Jei replied, his expression unreadable. He bowed to the resistance members, who all touched their tails to their foreheads.

"Walk in the Light," Sapri said. Without further ado, the xana approached Regina, stationary inside her protective bubble.

Agents continued running across the platform, chasing down Pod Pals and trapping them, either in their capsules or in isospheres. Some even wrestled the robots to the ground or hit them with stun batons, which appeared to have little effect. The bots fought back with their arsenal of upgrades, shooting flames from their mouths or producing intense jets of water, or even releasing clouds of what Eva assumed was poison like she'd been hit with by the Attuned in Rilia. It was complete pandemonium, and she didn't envy the BOFA people their job of capturing all the critters.

Eva climbed onto the Pod Pal's back, marveling again at the sophistication of the technology. It definitely felt like she was on an animal and not a glorified toaster. Pink and Sue each wrapped themselves around one of its clawed feet, clinging tightly, and Jei hopped onto his dog-bot hoverboard next to them.

Across the platform, Regina was still barking orders as if she were dealing with wayward children instead of federal agents. She paused and turned to regard Eva and the others on their massive mount, her mouth fixing itself in a firm line. Then, with a deliberateness that had to be intentional, she turned away again and continued what she was doing as if she hadn't seen them at all.

Eva let out a breath she hadn't realized she was holding. All they could do now was get back to their ship and hope they could leave before the lockdown started. She opened her mouth to ask Sue to order the robot to leave, then stopped.

"Where the hell is Mala?" she asked.

"Miau," a tiny, smug voice answered from her lap. Mala looked up at her with wide hazel eyes, their pupils entirely dilated in the darkness.

"How did you—never mind," Eva said. "Get in my fucking backpack before I feed you to this bird."

For once, Mala didn't argue.

Chapter 22

NADANDO CONTRA
LA CORRIENTE

It was still the night cycle when the giant robot carried them through the darkness of the home-trees at the outskirts of Rilia, to the base where Dr. Lucien and Felsira awaited them. Not even the faintest twinkle of starlight was visible through the thick canopy of leaves above, and Eva's spacesuit informed her the air was even colder and damper than it had been when they left. Various nocturnal animals and Attuned fell silent as they passed, no doubt cowed by the perceived predator in their midst, or maybe because giant robots were weird and scary. Hell, Eva was riding the damn thing and, as exhilarating as it was, she couldn't wait to get down. Still, they were alive, and safe for the moment, and it was enough given the circumstances.

Felsira rested in her hammock and Dr. Lucien checked Jei and his dog-bot for damage as they gravely listened to the story of what happened at the lab. Pink, in the meantime, did the same for everyone's organic components, which had generally avoided more than bruising thanks to their suits. They'd been incredibly lucky, and Eva couldn't help but feel like that meant the karmic balance of the universe was waiting to shift in the other direction.

"Those obstinate fools," Felsira said finally. "Did they not consider that they will be interrogated about more than this single incident? Our entire operation will be jeopardized over this." Her psychic emanations were more intense than any she'd exhibited before. Anger, disgust, sadness . . . Her emotions were like a ball of cats wrestling with each other.

"They made their choice," Eva said.

"And we will pay for it with our blood," Felsira replied coldly.

Dr. Lucien replaced Jei's prosthetic with a loud click. "Problems will not end," he said. "But we are still alive, and free, and with that we may accomplish much."

"Maybe you will," Pink said sourly, kneeling next to Sue and shining a light in her eyes.

"I do not understand," Dr. Lucien said.

"Our mission is screwed." Pink clicked off her light and stood, glaring at no one in particular. "We had to get Sue's brother and we didn't. So now we don't get paid, and we've lost two weeks of other work running all over the galaxy." She scowled. "I don't even want to think about how many of my patients are waiting in my queue or left to another practice."

Eva cringed. Pink was right. For all that they'd had a string of successes with The Fridge leading up to this debacle, now they were arguably worse off than when they'd started. Pink's work was backed up or gone, Vakar was in deep shit with his bosses and would have to leave as soon as they got back to civilization, Sue would probably never see her brother again since he was likely going to jail forever . . .

"At least we got half up front," Eva muttered. "And Min got all the fuel she needed."

The room was silent for a few moments as everyone present got lost in their own separate mazes of thought. Eva wondered how she was going to explain it all to Mari. We found the guy, but then we lost him, sorry, you can bust him out of BOFA custody if you want. Hell, maybe they could; Eva didn't know what The Forge was capable of. They managed to infiltrate The Fridge, certainly, so maybe BOFA would be easy for them.

Ah, The Fridge. Architects of the utter fuckening of so many people's lives. If it hadn't been for them, poor Sue would probably still be happily fussing with her robots at her parents' house, and Josh would be engineering spaceships and whatever else. And he wasn't the only scientist-type they'd kidnapped for their many illegal experiments . . .

Eva stood up so fast it made Mala hiss. "Alabao!"

"What?" Pink asked.

"Josh wasn't working alone at The Fridge, and he didn't escape alone." She turned to Jei, who was staring at her like she'd grown an extra head. "I need your help."

"Mine?" Jei asked. "What do you want?"

"I can't believe I'm about to say this," Eva said, "but I want . . . Miles Erck."

Getting back to *La Sirena Negra* was a challenge. The lockdown at the spaceport was in full swing, leaving literally thousands of travelers stuck on Garilia, including a lot of angry rich people who weren't accustomed to being told what to do. Unfortunately for them, no amount of waving money around was going to make BOFA budge on letting them off-planet, not with each of them potentially carrying illegal Proarkhe technology in a conveniently portable capsule. Everyone had to be searched with special devices, of which only two were currently available; more were on the way from the nearest Gate, along with additional personnel and a more robust quarantine setup that would virtually halt all ingress and egress to the entire system.

Fortunately, because BOFA didn't have the manpower and tech already on hand, there were still ways to get out for those who knew them. Vakar had apparently gotten word about the lockdown with enough time to have Min take off, so they were in orbit nearby rather than stuck at the port. All Eva had to do was borrow a resistance shuttle and take that to the ship, then start the slow cruise to the Gate three cycles away. Some light hacking and cloaking tech were involved to ensure the planetary surveillance systems didn't notice them sneaking away, but compared to everything else they'd been through, that was practically boring.

As he'd suggested he might, Jei decided to come with them. Eva was a bit surprised given how close he was to Dr. Lucien and the resistance, but it seemed like he thought he could do more good elsewhere; Eva didn't want to pry, especially since he'd been so hostile to her before. He agreed to be dropped at DS Nor, where Eva could refuel and pick up Vakar's cruiser in case he had to leave; after that, Jei retreated to the passenger cabin as soon as they were all aboard. Occasionally she caught him skulking around like one of the cats, but any attempts at conversation were met with enough awkwardness to shut them down quickly.

Two related things were more surprising: that Jei was marginally friendlier with Sue, perhaps because of all the help she'd given the resistance or her fight with Josh, and that Min was in the darkest mood Eva had ever seen. The latter would have normally sent Eva running to the bridge to figure out what was up, but she was busy with her own issues.

First, she and Vakar had some extremely personal catching up to do, in more ways than one. Selfish, yes, but they presumably had only a few cycles before his bosses gave him new marching orders.

Second, she had to deal with Miles fucking Erck.

Once Eva had stored up enough patience to tolerate Miles for more than a few seconds, she dragged him to the mess and settled him into a chair. He regarded her sullenly, his limp blond hair falling over his pale face, mouth twisted into a stubborn frown.

"Welcome back," Eva said. "I hope you've had a comfortable ride so far."

"Well, actually, you locked me in a shipping container," Miles replied.

"I could move you to the cat box if you'd prefer."

Miles glared at her and didn't respond.

Eva smiled. "Gracias, muy amable. You may recall that I was looking for Josh Zafone back on Abelgard."

Miles remained quiet, so Eva began to make herself a coffee. He watched hungrily, and she wondered whether he was a caffeine addict, too. She made a show of every part of the process, grinding the beans and slowly spooning them into the cafetera, even pausing to sniff them and sigh appreciatively. Once the water was boiling, she turned back to Miles.

"Josh had information and skills that my bosses need," Eva continued. "Unfortunately, he's no longer available, because BOFA arrested him for experimenting with illegal Proarkhe tech." Sure, it was a little more complicated than that, but Miles didn't need to know.

"Let me guess," Miles said with a sneer. "I help you and your little friends, or you're going to turn me over to BOFA, too?"

"Well, actually," Eva said with great relish, "I don't give a shit about you. You're only here to make my life easier, because whether you help me or take a walk out the airlock, I still get what I want."

Curiosity and obstinacy fought each other all over his face until Miles settled for a frown again. "What do you want, then?" he asked finally.

"Emle Carter," Eva said. "Where is she?"

Miles managed to get paler, which was a feat. "N-not telling you," he said, his voice breaking.

"Tell me or don't, I'm still going to find her," Eva said. "It's just a question of when."

Miles pressed his lips together, but he was trembling, and sweat began to form on his forehead.

Eva stared at him, first in confusion, then in dawning comprehension. He was scared of Emle. He hadn't even been this freaked out around Rubin Hjerte, and that lady had a box of teeth. She tried to remember Emle, but they'd met so briefly, and all Eva could summon up was the vaguest image of a woman hiding under a table while Eva punched Miles Erck in the face for being his usual insufferable self.

"How about this," Eva said. "You tell me where she is, and when I pick her up, I don't tell her you're here?"

"Y-you'll leave me in the sh-shipping container?" Miles asked. Eva nodded.

"And Emle won't know I'm in there?"

Eva nodded again.

"Okay, yes, fine." Miles swallowed. "You have a deal."

Eva smiled and finished making her coffee. Maybe the whole mission wouldn't be a bust after all. Now she just had to get in touch with Mari about the change in plans and start putting together the invoice.

After leaving Jei at DS Nor, Eva summoned Sue to the mess, a glass of synthesized root beer already prepared per Pink's recommendation. The doctor had spoken to Sue a few times since Garilia, but Eva had to do her part as well, and she knew rushing it wouldn't help. It was easy to think of crew members as parts of the ship that needed maintenance like anything else, and in a way it was true, but you couldn't slap a patch on hurt feelings or solder a relationship broken by an argument.

"How are you holding up?" Eva asked as Sue sank into her seat and pulled her drink closer.

Sue took a long sip of the root beer and put the glass back down, absently wiping away foam from her upper lip with her sleeve.

"It hurts," Sue said quietly. "The Fridge took advantage of my family, and me, and . . . Josh didn't know, but he didn't bother to find out, either. And when he did, he didn't care."

"Yeah, that was really shitty of him," Eva said.

Sue's eyes filled with tears that didn't fall. "You had it worse," Sue said. "At least Josh didn't sell us out himself."

Eva leaned back in her chair, folding her arms over her chest. "It's not a contest," she said. "If it helps you to compare your situation to mine, go for it, but nobody is handing out awards for worst sibling experience."

"I guess." Now the tears did fall, and Sue sniffled. "I thought I was going to be a hero, you know? Find him, save him, bring him home, and celebrate."

"Yeah." One out of four, Eva thought. More than she'd managed with Mari, but again, it wasn't a contest.

"Does it ever get better?" Sue asked, her voice raw. "I know you and Agent Virgo are working together now, but you're still not, um."

"Friendly?" Eva supplied. Sue nodded, and Eva puffed out a breath. "Scars are scars," she said. "They don't go away, but you can learn to live with them."

Sue fell silent, fidgeting with her glass and occasionally drinking from it. Eva waited, digging deep into her own reserves of patience to keep from filling the silence with stories, advice, chatter—distractions that would have been more for her own comfort than Sue's.

"Jei's looking for his brother, too," Sue said.

"He what?" Eva asked, surprised. After everything that had happened, she still knew next to nothing about him.

"He used to work with you," Sue said. "Jei's brother. With that guy you talk about sometimes. Tito?"

Ah, mierda. That explained why Jei thought Eva was an asshole. Because she had been.

"What was his name?" Eva asked.

"Buruusu. Rokku Buruusu."

Eva searched her memories, trying to place someone with that name, someone who maybe resembled Jei. Most people who worked for Tito used aliases—Tito certainly did, and Eva had as well—so it was possible she knew him by another name.

Of course. The arm cannon. She knew she'd seen it before, and not on a stranger from a distance.

"Joe," Eva said. "He called himself Joe back then." She couldn't help the half-smile that tweaked at the corner of her mouth. "He was always whistling. You could hear him coming from half a ship away. He had an arm cannon like Jei's, but he used a prosthetic arm most of the time. Hell of a sniper, and brutal with blades."

"Was he nice?" Sue asked, eyes wide with hope.

"He was quiet, except for the whistling." Eva's smile faded. "Some comemierda picked a fight with him once, and he beat the shit out of her with a practice sword. Pink did a lot of sewing that day, and not the relaxing kind."

"Oh." Sue fell silent again for a moment. "Jei told me about it because of what happened with me and Josh. He said sometimes siblings fight and it feels bad at the time and then later it's hard to remember what was so important about it."

Eva shrugged. "He's not wrong. But it's also true that a person can fuck up so bad, you write them out of your life and move on. That's your call, and you don't have to make it now."

"Yeah." Sue finished off her root beer, wiping her mouth clean again. "What would you do, if you were me?" she asked.

"I'd give it time," Eva answered. "And I'd punch the shit out of the bag in the cargo bay."

Sue giggled. "Maybe I'll use Gustavo's flamethrower to set something on fire!"

"Maybe," Eva said. "But how about you wait until we get off the ship, okay?"

Sue nodded, smiling and racing off to tinker with her mech in anticipation. A temporary relief from all the big feelings floating around like asteroids, but that's all anyone got, really.

It was enough for now. With a sigh, Eva left the mess and went back to work.

Three and a half cycles later, *La Sirena Negra* returned to the Forge station in Suidana. It was in a different part of the system, but still limned by the blazing light of those dying binary stars, and now there was a substantial amount of ship activity swarming around it like bees coming and going from their hive. The Gate being towed along behind the station was equally busy, people in spacesuits or small vessels crawling along the length of its massive ringed form. Unlike other Gates, this one was clearly inactive, the familiar, inscrutable patterns on its surface dark rather than glowing the usual soft magenta.

Eva scowled at the hull camera display as they slowly docked. The Forge had not agreed to pay yet, which was understandable; they needed Josh for something specific, and even though Emle was theoretically an acceptable substitute, they'd refused to confirm that over comms because of secrecy concerns. So Eva and her crew still had to fly all the way to Casa Carajo and hope it wasn't a waste of time.

Emle stood next to her, staring at the Gate with an expression somewhere between awe and horror. The woman was taller and heavier than Eva, her skin a shade darker than Pink's and her black hair shaved close to her head, and it turned out she was also an engineer like Josh. She'd been nothing but nice—grateful, in fact, for the part Eva played in helping her back at the Fridge base, though Eva remembered it very differently. She'd also been eager to help anyone who was working against The Fridge.

Eva liked her immediately, though it was hard to see why Miles was so afraid of her.

Mari was waiting when Eva descended from the ship with Emle trailing after her. She looked surprisingly well rested, given her appearance the last time Eva had been there, like she'd just gotten back from a mandatory vacation involving mind-altering substances and sleeping meds. She wore the same red armor again, though, and was packing a pistol on each hip and a nasty little submachine gun nestled in the small of her back.

"I'll take it from here," Mari said, gesturing for Emle to follow. Emle hesitated, looking to Eva for confirmation.

Eva raised an eyebrow. "Am I being dismissed?"

"Yes," Mari said flatly. "We have to get to work." She started to walk away, as if expecting Emle would be right behind her.

"And what work is that, exactly?" Eva asked, crossing her arms.

Mari paused, looking back and forth between Eva and Emle. "I'm not authorized to discuss that with you," she said, as if it were obvious. "Dr. Carter will be briefed privately."

"Yeah, but I'm only getting paid if she can do whatever you wanted Josh for," Eva said. "So I think I have a right to know a little more about that to be sure I'm not getting screwed."

"You think we'd lie to you to avoid paying," Mari said slowly.

Eva widened her eyes and nodded.

Mari sighed. "Don't be ridiculous."

"Ridiculous is me flying all the way out here twice without knowing why." Eva tried not to glare at Mari, but it was hard.

"And you don't trust me?" Mari asked.

"Do you seriously want me to answer that?" But they both knew she did, at least this much, because otherwise Eva never would have taken the job in the first place.

Mari sighed again, closing her eyes and no doubt counting in her head before opening them again. "I'll ask my superiors if I can give you more information. Otherwise, all I can do is promise that we'll be happy to pay you if you've earned it, despite the fact that you technically didn't do as we asked."

It was probably the best Eva could hope for at this point, all things considered. She nodded and patted Emle on the shoulder. "Good luck saving the universe," Eva said.

"Is that really what they're doing here?" Emle asked, her expression slightly bewildered. "I thought you were exaggerating."

"Fuck if I know," Eva said. "It would be nice if somebody was. But I'm not leaving until I get answers." With a sarcastic salute at her sister, she marched back up the ramp to her ship, ignoring the irritated huff of breath behind her.

Before she'd made it through the cargo bay, a shout from the mess turned her leisurely stroll into a run. Eva skidded into the room to find Sue and Min, arm's length apart and staring at each other. Min looked furious despite her eyes filling with tears, while Sue's eyes were wide with shock.

"You're impossible!" Min shrieked, stomping her foot.

"I don't—" Sue began, but Min interrupted.

"You should have just gone with him at DS Nor," Min said, stomping again and then leaving in a huff.

Eva raised her eyebrows at Sue, who was staring at the doorway with a mix of confusion and horror.

"Do I want to know what that was about?" Eva asked.

"I'm not sure," Sue said. "I was getting food and she came in here and screamed at me. I think I made her mad."

Eva snorted. "You think?"

Sue furrowed her brow. "DS Nor . . . does she mean Jei? Why would I go anywhere with him?"

"I don't know," Eva said slowly. A thought was coalescing in her head, and she started mentally replaying interactions between Min and Sue over the last six months, focusing on the last several weeks.

"Is it because I was asking about his cybernetics?" Sue mused. "But why would that make her mad at me?"

"Madre de dios," Eva said, smacking herself in the forehead. How had she not noticed before?

"Maybe I should upgrade Goyangi to cheer her up," Sue continued, starting to walk away. "Some kind of electricity sphere, or maybe miniature bots like mine that can fly and—"

"Sue," Eva said. "Why did you make a fighting bot for Min?"

Sue paused, her cheeks rapidly turning pink. "Well, um," she replied.

"Susan," Eva said sternly.

Sue looked down at her feet, hands grabbing at the pants of her jumpsuit, and mumbled something under her breath.

"Sorry, what was that?" Eva asked.

"Because I like her," Sue whispered.

"And you were planning to tell her that when, exactly?"

Sue squirmed. "I don't know. Never? What if I tell her and she doesn't like me back and then I have to leave because I made things weird?"

Eva understood that logic, certainly. She'd argued with herself over her feelings for Vakar until it was almost too late, and this ship was small enough that hookups were a less viable option. Hard to avoid someone afterward when there was only one head and almost nowhere to hide.

"Do you know what I think?" Eva asked.

"What?" Sue looked up at her now, eyes shimmering with unshed tears.

Eva looked up at the camera in the corner of the ceiling. "I think Min can hear you because she's the damn ship, and she's being super mean by not coming in here already to tell you she likes you, too."

"Cap!" Min shrieked through the speakers. "I'm not being mean, I'm . . . I'm . . ."

Eva laughed, loud and long, then flipped off the camera and went to her bunk. A few moments later, the door to the bridge opened and closed, and Min giggled once through the speakers before Pink shouted at her to turn them off.

Eva had just flopped onto her bed sideways with her legs dangling over the edge when there was a polite knock.

"Come in, Vakar," she said, and he did, smelling like acrid incense. Before he even opened his mouth, Eva sighed and asked, "Where do they want you to go?"

"The Apus Ignaea System, near Vuthiri," he said, sitting next to her on the bed. "I've been told to leave immediately."

Eva threw an arm over her face. "Any idea how long this mission will be? What are the parameters?"

"Substantial reconnaissance," he replied. "A suspected processing facility for a Fridge mining camp has been located."

"Coño carajo," Eva said. That could lead to a big bust, but Vakar would have to be careful and quiet, keep track of who was coming and going, and most importantly, stay in the same place for what could be weeks under strict comms silence so as not to tip off his targets.

"Indeed," he replied, resting a hand on her thigh. They sat for several long moments as the weight of the situation settled on them like a lead blanket.

"We knew this was coming, though," Eva said. "It's been a good run." Don't cry, fool, she told herself sternly. If you can survive Garilia, you can survive this.

"I will return as soon as I can," he said, looking down at her with his gray-blue eyes and smelling of licorice.

"I know," she said quietly. "I'll be here." She paused. "Here in the ship, I mean. Dios mío, I hope I won't still be on this fucking station waiting to get paid."

Vakar gave the quennian equivalent of a laugh. "I also hope you will be paid before then. Though perhaps continuing to work for The Forge would not be such a terrible thing."

Eva shrugged. "Who knows? We'll pass through that Gate

when we get to it." Maybe literally, she thought, given the Gate they were building right outside.

She didn't get the chance to think about that further, because Vakar had decided it was time to be goal-oriented, and Eva was more than happy to orient herself right back at him.

Mari arrived several hours later, as Eva was watching the last pale glow of Vakar's thrusters fade into the black of space. Emle wasn't with her, which Eva took as a good sign, for her own purposes anyway.

"Dr. Carter has done what we needed," Mari confirmed. "Funds are being transferred to your account immediately."

"What, you don't want a separate invoice?" Eva asked, only half-serious. Secret organizations weren't notoriously finicky about bills and receipts, given the trail they left.

Mari didn't reply. Instead she joined Eva in staring at the stars, glittering in the distance.

"Do you ever think about how so many of those stars are already gone?" Mari asked softly. "Their light is still traveling from their graves to our eyes at this distance, but if we stepped through a Gate to see them, we'd find a white dwarf, or a neutron star, or even a black hole."

Eva pursed her lips. "I try not to think about it, honestly. It's not my problem. Not like I can do anything for a star."

Mari laughed ruefully. "No, you certainly can't, can you?"

The way she said it made Eva's arm hairs stand up inside her spacesuit. "And you can?" Eva asked.

Mari shrugged. "Depends on what it needs."

They stood in silence for a few more moments before Eva broke it. "Did you know Mom was handling Garilia's application to join BOFA?"

"What?" Mari yelped. "No, I didn't. What do you mean 'handling'?"

"I mean she showed up to a hidden lab with a strike team and shoved it up their government's culo like a bad prostate exam. She's the one who ordered the system quarantine. Probably still there trying to catch all the escaped Ball Buddies."

It was nice to see Mari surprised for a change. Eva had started to think she and her Forge friends were omniscient. Hell, maybe her bosses had known, but hadn't told Mari.

"I knew she got promoted," Mari murmured. "It's not like her to keep secrets."

It's not like you to pretend to be kidnapped and get me hustling to pay your fake ransom, Eva thought, but she had matured over the last year, so she kept her mouth shut.

"Everyone has secrets," Eva said instead.

"Yes," Mari agreed. "I suppose I can understand why she wouldn't tell us. It might have compromised her assignment."

It still could, honestly. If word got out that Regina Alvarez's daughter was embroiled in local politics on the planet whose application she was overseeing, well . . . Eva wasn't sure what would happen. Would her mom get fired? Reassigned?

She thought of Vakar again, a sharp pain spiking through her chest. He'd reach the local Gate in a couple of cycles and then off he'd go on his own mission. She missed him so much already, it was hard to imagine what she'd do to occupy herself until he came back. If he came back at all.

But that kind of worry was as worthless as wondering about dead stars. Either they were or they weren't, and there was nothing she could do from where she stood.

"I'm going through that Gate, Eva," Mari said suddenly.

"No me diga," Eva replied. "You people actually got it to work?"

"Yes." Mari hesitated. "We needed Josh—Emle, now, I guess—to help with the power supply, and coordinates."

Eva didn't ask whether Mari had gotten authorization to spill those beans. Instead, she asked, "Coordinates to where?"

Mari's expression turned grim. "We're not sure, but it could be dangerous, so we're only sending a few ships and probes. And we're closing the Gate behind us so nothing on the other side can come back through."

"Qué rayo? What do you think is—" On the other side, Eva was going to ask. Except scattered ideas were starting to come together in her mind, finally. The whole big danger Mari and all her Forge amigos were worried about. The raid on the Fridge facility six months earlier to retrieve the stolen Proarkhe artifact, which turned into a giant robot that opened up its own miniature Gate and disappeared. What the hell was that thing? It had been able to change shape and size just like the Pod Pals. What else could it do? And what if there were more of them, waiting somewhere to be reactivated like that one?

"If I don't come back, please tell Mami I love her?" Mari asked quietly. "I love you, too, you know, descarada."

"You're coming back," Eva said sharply. "Don't pull that hero shit on me, comemierda. I'll drag you back here myself if I have to."

Mari didn't say anything, just smiled faintly while continuing to stare into the black.

"I'm serious," Eva insisted.

"I know," Mari said. "I've seen what you can do. But you have other people to worry about, don't you? Let me worry about myself."

"Jódete," Eva snapped. "You're not my boss."

"And you're not mine. But we both have jobs to do."

Eva's commlink pinged to alert her that she'd just gotten paid. Normally that would give her a little tingle of pleasure, but now it felt more like a dismissal. Game over, thanks for playing, shut it down and move along.

"Adiós, Eva-Benita," Mari said, turning to leave. She'd managed a few brisk steps before Eva caught up to her and grabbed her arm.

"Hasta luego, Marisleysis," Eva replied, emphasizing the second word.

Mari smiled again, bright as any star, then shook herself free and left. As her sister walked away, Eva wondered whether she was watching a white dwarf or a black hole.

Pink was waiting in the cargo bay when Eva returned, a grin on her face.

"I saw we got paid," Pink said, doing a little celebratory dance. She sobered when Eva didn't join her. "Do I want to know?"

"Bunch of cabrón martyrs," Eva muttered. "I don't know how some people stay alive when they're trying so hard to get dead."

Pink made a tsking sound. "Yeah, not like you don't throw your own ass in the fire every damn day." She held up a hand to stop Eva from protesting. "Listen, woman, I've been thinking. We got a big paycheck, we got fuel, and we got nothing pressing right now. Why don't we take a little break?"

"What, some R&R you mean?" Eva asked, scratching the back of her neck.

Pink nodded, gesturing with her head toward the bridge. "Those two could use some down time to go be young and ridiculous together. I can work from anywhere and give myself an hour or so between emergencies. And after what you just went through, you definitely need to chill for a minute."

Eva's chest tightened as she thought of Garilia again. She'd been trying not to, but the list of things she was trying not to think about was long enough to wrap around a planet a few times.

"Maybe we can catch up to Vakar if we hurry," Pink added. "You'll get a couple more cycles with him before his mission."

Eva exhaled sharply and plastered on a grin. "Fine, you win. Let's get the hell out of this resingado system and find something fun to do."

Pink slapped Eva's shoulder. "That's what I'm talking about. I'll get Min and Sue into the mess and we can start looking at brochures." She wandered off, whistling to herself, a little more bounce in her step than usual.

This will be good, Eva thought. When was the last time she had taken a vacation? A real one, not just the voids between work that inevitably happened to freelancers. She couldn't remember.

Outside, someone began making an announcement over the station speakers. Eva trotted back down the cargo bay ramp to listen.

"—will commence in T-minus sixty seconds," the voice was saying. "Please do not leave your designated stations until authorization is granted. All ships not participating in the experiment are grounded until further notice. Estimated experiment duration is one-quarter cycle. Further instructions will be provided as they become necessary. I repeat, the experiment will commence in T-minus forty-three seconds. Please do not leave your designated stations—"

Eva groaned and returned to the cargo bay. A quarter cycle before they had any hope of leaving. Well, maybe she could get ahold of Vakar and see if there was a chance he could fly a little more slowly so she could catch up later.

She hunkered down to pet Mala, who had sauntered up with her tail raised.

"Miau," Mala said, her hazel eyes half-closed.

"Yeah, here's hoping they don't blow us all up," Eva said. "That would definitely ruin my day."

"Miau."

"Not like we can do anything about it now, huh?" Eva scratched Mala's chin and the cat purred. "We're stuck here until they let us go."

"Miau."

"You're right, I'm not sure why I keep talking to you like we actually understand each other. I guess it's marginally less weird than talking to myself."

Eva continued to scratch the cat's head for a bit longer. She thought about going back outside the ship to find a way of seeing what was happening with the Gate, but she had no idea where to look, and the countdown had to be over already. All she could do now was wait, and pray, and hope her comemierda sister came back soon.

Mala's eyes suddenly widened, her pupils dilating, and all her fur stood on end. She hissed and raced toward the bridge; at the same time, all the cats who weren't already in their container started pouring into the cargo bay and climbing inside like their asses were on fire.

"Qué coño?" Eva muttered. "Min, is everything okay?"

For a moment, silence replied, then Min shouted through the speakers, "The station is under attack!"

Alarms sounded outside, echoing in the huge docking bay, followed by the sounds of dozens of people rushing to their ships. Guess that lockdown was over. How had anyone gotten close enough to engage without station surveillance noticing? Eva ran for the bridge, cursing herself for not following Mala in the first place.

"Who's attacking?" Eva asked Min when she got there, staring at the various camera displays. Nothing but empty space outside the docking bay from their vantage point, but their instruments were detecting at least two dozen ships within engagement range, from single-seat fighters to giant battle cruisers.

"I'm not sure yet, Cap," Min replied, still talking through the speakers. "Station comms are giving orders, but they haven't—" Min paused, as if listening. Her mouth formed a silent O and all the bridge instruments lit up as she prepped for a quick launch.

"What?" Eva asked.

"It's The Fridge," Min replied. "They've found us."

Chapter 23

THREE TWO ONE LET'S JAM

As badly as Eva wanted to get out of the station, there was already the equivalent of a line and their ship was at the back. Presumably there were exterior defenses in addition to the fighters being scrambled, so it wasn't as if the whole place was going to explode any moment. That said, the longer they waited, the more they would have to hustle to avoid the number of enemy ships growing steadily by the moment. Eva was confident in Min's flying skills, but she also didn't want to have the odds stacked against them from the start.

"Cap, do I go?" Min asked. Her human body lay in the pilot's chair, with Mala in her lap.

"Not yet," Pink answered from behind Eva. "We don't know the situation outside. The fire is probably worse than the frying pan right now."

"Give it sixty and see how many fighters are left in here. If the place empties out sooner, leave right away." Eva had a sudden thought, so she stepped into the corridor and tried to raise Vakar on comms.

"Eva, are you well?" he answered. She stifled a laugh; how did he know?

"Are you out of range already?" she asked.

She could practically smell his concern. "Out of range of what?"

"Nothing," she said. "Never mind. Everything is fine." She winced at her own lie, but if he was long gone, at least he should be safe.

"Eva."

"Sorry. The station might be . . . slightly under attack."

Vakar paused, emitting an angry hum. "I thought those ships were suspicious, but they did not engage so I assumed they were affiliated with The Forge. I should have inspected them more carefully."

"It's okay, mi vida, it happens. We'll be fine." The whine of the ship's engines being powered up settled into a familiar low hum.

"I will return immediately."

"No, no, I said we'll be fine." Eva waved her arms even though he couldn't see her. "Don't come back. Get to the Gate and get to work before your bosses get even more encabronado. I'll call you as soon as we're clear."

Vakar paused, but when he replied, his voice was hard. "With respect and deep affection, Eva, you are no longer my superior officer."

"Vakar, don't—" Before Eva could finish, Min cut in over the speakers.

"Cap, I think you'll want to hear this," Min said. "I pulled it out of station comms."

Another voice replaced Min's: Mari, her tone professional but strained, the sound of ship alarms and notifications in the background.

"—attacks appear to be from both automated defenses and enemy combatants," Mari was saying. "Our sensors are not detecting any known markers for sentient life, but the entire planet appears to be Proarkhe in origin. There are at least seven energy signatures that match the escaped artifact and the two counterparts we recovered from—" A sickening whoosh interrupted her, loud enough to make Eva cover her ears. She knew that sound, and if her heart weren't mechanical, it would have stopped.

"I've lost engines," Mari said quietly. "I'll continue transmitting data for as long as my instruments are functional. Any hope that we could make contact peacefully seems to be lost. We must prepare for our worst fears to be realized." If she said anything else, Eva didn't hear it, because someone cut the connection.

Pink was grabbing her arm before Eva knew what was happening. Her mouth was set in a firm line, her eye seeing everything in Eva's head as if it were being broadcast on a commwall.

"No," Pink said.

"I have to," Eva said.

Pink's grip on Eva's arm tightened. "She knew the risks. She knew what might happen. You have to let her go."

Pink was right. What was Eva going to do, fly through a huge space battle to rescue her sister from a mystery enemy on the other side of a Gate that would be closing any moment? There was hard, and then there was impossible. There was brave, and there was suicidal.

She wasn't leaving her sister to die, she was honoring her

sister's sacrifice by choosing to live, for herself and her crew. And with any luck, someone from The Forge would be heroic and save Mari for her.

Yeah, none of that shit sounded great to her, either. She closed her eyes and prayed to the Virgin, for Mari and everyone else caught up in this mess.

"You're sure it's The Fridge attacking us?" Eva asked Min, opening her eyes again.

"Oh yeah, totally," Min said. "Station security is super mad about it. What should I do?"

Eva and Pink shared a look, and Pink exhaled loudly, a half-smile baring some of her teeth.

"Merciful heavens," Pink said. "And here I was, ready to make a run for it quietly."

"We can make a run for it loudly instead," Eva said. "We just have to be quick and careful."

Pink shook her head. "Two cycles to the nearest Gate, remember? Nothing quick about that."

Except that wasn't true anymore, was it? "There's a new Gate right in front of us, and it seems to work fine," Eva told her. "We can get to that and get through in no time."

Pink's smile spread and her eyes twinkled with mischief. "You know, you're not wrong. Probably safer to do that than to risk being followed, anyway."

Eva nodded and stepped back onto the bridge. "You get all that, Min?" she asked.

"Sure thing, Cap," Min replied. "Where should I Gate to?"

We were supposed to pick a vacation spot, Eva thought. Can't sit around scrolling through options while we wait to get blown up. Think, think . . .

"How about Brodevis?" Sue asked, popping her head through the doorway.

"Where they record *Crash Sisters*?" Eva asked. She'd heard the memvids from that place were altered to make the beaches seem comfortable instead of freezing, but that could have been a rumor. It was a beautiful place, at least, or it pretended to be.

"Yes!" Min yelled. "Maybe Leroy can get us tickets to a Grand Melee!"

Pink rolled her eye but said nothing, which Eva took for consent.

"Brodevis it is," Eva said. "Bueno, salpica. Sue, get down to engineering in case something catches fire."

Sue frowned. "I already repaired all the—"

"Joking, Sue, but get down there anyway, in case new problems need fixing in a hurry."

"Right, yes, got it!" Sue hesitated, then rushed in to grab Min's hand and squeeze it before running off toward the cargo bay, trailing a trio of little yellow bots.

Eva held out her own hand to Pink, ignoring the parts of her that were still screaming about rescuing Mari. "You ready?" she asked.

"Baby, I was born ready," Pink replied, taking the hand she was offered.

"Then let's make like a flea and jump." Eva grinned. "And bite."

While the station had been towing the Gate along before, it had untethered the massive ring and moved a few light-seconds away before conducting the transit experiment, so it was no longer as nearby as it had been. The distance would have been nothing to *La Sirena Negra* at any other time, except now the space between was filled with people trying to kill each other.

The fighters zipped around taking shots at anything moving

within range of their smaller weapons, while the destroyers and frigates lurked at the edges of the fray like bouncers doing crowd control. The larger cruisers and battlecruisers hung back even farther and used their enormous cannons to fire at the station itself. The Forge fired back in turn, laser and plasma and even kinetic weapons continuously repelled by the shields on both sides that were still active—for now. Debris was scattered throughout from the ships that had already been damaged or destroyed, inertia carrying the pieces away from the area in a slow but still dangerous ripple effect of whatever explosion or collision had done the deed.

As with any space battle, Sir Isaac Newton was the deadliest son of a bizcocho in space, and Eva was eager to avoid the long arm of his law.

"Min, get us through," Eva said, sitting in the captain's chair on the bridge.

"You bet, Cap," Min replied, guiding them out into the black and immediately taking a dive down along the length of the station.

The ship's proximity alarm became a continuous background noise once they were clear, so Eva adjusted the sensitivity until it was only the occasional blip. She pulled up the weapons systems to calibrate the auto-turret, grabbing the appropriate friend-or-foe codes from Min's logs so they wouldn't hit any Forge ships, then setting the size and velocity parameters to avoid wasting shots on debris. Pink was already logged into the laser cannon, so Eva took over what they called their bag of tricks—homing mines, electromagnetic decoys, and so on—then opened the tactical display and started plotting where they might best be deployed.

That shit wasn't cheap, and even though they'd just been

paid, it would be nice not to waste their profits on murder supplies.

Time dilated, as it was wont to do when Eva was focused on not dying. Min carefully guided *La Sirena Negra* across the combat zone, avoiding the pockets of dogfighting and drones and enemy mines that were gradually increasing in density—relatively speaking, given how big space was. The larger ships remained at the periphery, and while the Forge station was still moving thanks to inertia, its engines had apparently been shut down to redirect power to shields that were likely to start overheating any moment. Assuming Fridge hackers hadn't managed to get past their firewalls to pull some other comemierdería with their systems.

What did The Fridge want? Eva wondered. Were they trying to destroy the station? This couldn't be the only Forge facility, but it certainly seemed likely to be the largest and most vital, given the sheer quantity of personnel and defenses. There was probably a lot of tech they could steal, or steal back if it had come from the raid on their own base on Pupillae. Not to mention the whole Gate experiment . . .

Don't think about Mari, Eva told herself sternly. You don't have time. Escape now, mourn later.

Eva pulled up the fore camera display as they approached the Gate, backlit by the system's dying binary stars. It was always a little uncomfortable to see a big hole in space, a doorway to somewhere in an entirely different part of the universe, like an impossibly realistic holovid display floating serenely in the void. At first, the only thing visible on the other side of the Gate was more space, strangely devoid of stars, but the view changed as Min altered their approach angle to avoid the mangled remains of a pair of ships.

Me cago en la hora que yo nací, Eva thought. She knew that place. She'd only had a brief glimpse of it once, from a different distance, but it had haunted her for the past six months, awake and in nightmares that left her sweaty and breathless.

It was a planet, covered entirely in the same strange metal she had seen at the ruins on Cavus, back when she and Vakar were rescuing a team of quennian scientists who had found a Proarkhe artifact. The very same artifact had been taken by The Fridge, and later turned into a giant robot, opened a portable Gate, and vanished through it.

And if Eva was right, this was where it had ended up.

"What is that?" Min yelped, pulling Eva out of her reverie.

She took a deep, cleansing breath. "That," Eva said, "is not our problem. Reset the coordinates to Brodevis and let's get the fuck out of here."

The closer they got to the Gate, the more of the strange planet became visible. There was no apparent source of water, no visible atmosphere, just kilometer after kilometer of metallic material wrapping around the enormous spherical body. Patterns were formed by the ways the metal connected or overlapped, primarily concentric circles with a few gaps that revealed what might have been underground cities, and other deep, broad chasms lit by the faintest pinkish-purple glow from somewhere far below. Small ridges and indentations on the surface might have passed for topography on any more familiar terrestrial body, but were too geometrically regular to be anything but intentionally fabricated.

And, barely noticeable against the eerily starless backdrop because of the scale and distance, flashes of weapons fire and explosions streaked across the black.

"Any cycle now, Min," Eva said, wincing at her own sharp tone.

"It's not working," Min said. "It won't accept my coordinates." *La Sirena Negra* slowed down and changed trajectory, avoiding another set of incoming ships while maintaining the equivalent of a holding pattern around the Gate.

Far away above the mystery planet, a ship appeared. Eva squinted at it and, in a fit of curiosity, deployed a scanning probe through the Gate. Quantum relays should get the data back to her quickly enough, but given all the unknowns currently in play, she might be wasting her time and tech for nothing. Then again, if Mari could communicate with The Forge from there, Eva's probes should be able to as well.

The results came back within moments, and they were confusing. Some familiar elements and minerals, but a lot of errors and unknowns. The planet was reportedly about the circumference of Saturn, with two large orbiting satellites, but its mass and density and other data were unavailable. Several vessels currently moved around in there, along with an uncomfortably large amount of debris that suggested either more Forge ships had gone through than Eva expected, or Fridge ships had followed them in, or remnants of older battles were still caught in the planet's gravity well without falling to its surface. None of these thoughts was particularly comforting.

Also, the approaching mystery ship was at least the size of a BOFA dreadnought. Which meant it was easily as big as the Forge space station, and much bigger than any of the other ships on this side of the Gate.

"Um, Min," Eva said.

"Still not working, Cap," Min replied, her voice rising in pitch. "It's like someone is jamming it open? But that's not possible!"

Lot of impossible going around this cycle, Eva thought. Qué mierda.

"Focus on keeping us in one piece," she told Min. Then she signaled the Forge station, asking for Agent Elus or Agent Miran, hoping they were alive and available for a random call.

Agent Miran answered, his dark face grim as his eyes flicked rapidly from their ocular implants working overtime. "Captain Innocente. I presume this is important, given the circumstances."

"I presume you know the Gate is being jammed open?" Eva asked.

"We were aware of that situation, yes," Agent Miran said.

"And there's a giant-ass ship getting ready to come through?"

"Indeed there is," he replied, his tone dry as a desert. "Attempts have been made to destroy the Gate, but thus far it appears to be impervious to our light weapons, and our heavy cannons are focused on the Fridge incursion."

Destroy it? With Mari still on the other side? Eva exhaled sharply.

"Got any other options?" Eva asked.

"I have Dr. Carter and the rest of our team working on that," Agent Miran said. "They believe that if enough of the Gate's power sources were removed, it would shut down, but we haven't been able to get any of our people close enough to try. Now, with respect, I need to get back to—"

"I'm close enough," Eva said. "Tell me what to do."

"Cap?" Min asked behind her. "What's going on?"

"One second, Min," Eva said. Then, to Agent Miran, "I'm in pissing distance of this thing. How do I depower it?"

"Stand by." Agent Miran vanished, and Eva switched to the tactical display and sent out a few tricks from the bag to hopefully keep Fridge fighters at bay while they loitered in the area.

Pink appeared suddenly, leaning over the side of Eva's seat. "You making deals behind my back, Co-Captain?"

Eva shook her head, then shrugged. "Getting information. The Gate isn't working right, and if someone doesn't close it somehow . . ." She gestured at the huge ship through the hole in space, growing larger and closer by the moment.

"Woman, you haven't learned yet to take a step back when someone asks for volunteers?" Pink sighed, but stared at the looming threat and pursed her lips.

"We could make a run for the other Gate," Eva said. "But what happens to everyone here when that thing comes through?"

"Nothing good, I'm sure," Pink murmured. "Is this really a first-contact scenario?"

Eva thought of the artifact robot transforming in front of her, the harsh, modulated noise that seemed to be speech, its glowing red eyes. "It might technically be second contact," she said. "Either way, it's definitely a complete arroz con mango."

A new figure appeared in place of Agent Miran: Emle, her brown eyes wide with alarm. "Captain Innocente, I'm told you're near the Gate?"

"Close enough for hand grenades," Eva replied. "What would I have to do?"

Emle lifted her chin and seemed to center herself. "There are eight separate power sources, four on each side of the Gate at regular intervals. At least five of them must be deactivated in order to render the unit inoperable."

Qué mierda. The Gate was easily ten kilometers across. Min would have to fly her from one point to the next, and every time they stopped to let Eva out, *La Sirena Negra* would be an easy target.

"What happens when I take out the fifth power source?" Eva asked.

"In theory, the Gate will simply shut down," Emle replied. She seemed about to say something more, but hesitated.

"In theory?" Eva asked.

"It may destabilize the Gate and cause a chain reaction that leads to a more . . . unpleasant outcome. The same may occur if you manipulate the components incorrectly. The form of energy used by the Gates can be extremely volatile."

Eva thought of pinkish-purple cubes prone to exploding and sighed heavily. She turned to Pink. "We going to do this?"

"Take a vote," Pink said quietly. "We stay and help, or we make a run for the other Gate and hope we're faster than the competition."

Eva nodded. "Min?"

Min stroked Mala's back as the cat purred. They were both surprisingly calm.

"I'm scared of being too slow," Min said. "But I'm more scared of whatever that thing is being right behind us."

The mystery ship loomed larger, closer. It hadn't attacked yet, but if it were anything like its known counterparts, it was simply waiting for a big enough target. It would certainly find plenty to choose from on this side of the Gate, if it came through.

"Sue?" Eva asked.

After a few moments of silence, Sue replied. "Rusty buckets . . . We don't know anything about them, or where they are, or why we've never run into them before. But if they can override Gate controls, the rest of the universe would be in serious trouble. We can't take that chance."

Finally, Eva turned to Pink. "Well, Co-Captain? What's your vote?"

Pink rolled her eye, but it twinkled with mischief. "If you're fool enough to take a spacewalk in the middle of a firefight, I ain't stopping you. By my count, you've got at least three lives left, so you might as well do some good with them."

"For a change," Eva said.

Pink shook her head. "You changed a long time ago. It just took you a while to figure it out for yourself."

Eva snorted and bumped Pink with her hip, but her eyes threatened to fill with tears. "We're all going to need a shitload of therapy after this," she said.

"Too fucking right," Pink agreed.

"All right, Dr. Carter," Eva said, returning her attention to Emle. "Show me where the power sources are and how to get them out."

As Emle explained, Eva carefully, deliberately, did not think about her sister being stuck in another galaxy if she succeeded. Because if she were being honest, by the time she got the Gate closed—if she did it—Mari would probably already be dead.

Digging into the mechanical guts of a reconstructed ancient device was substantially less thrilling when people were blowing each other up all around you, Eva decided. The power sources themselves were carefully shielded and buried deep inside the Gate, accessible through claustrophobia-inducing tunnels, leading to a small alcove where the expected energy cubes waited. They were housed in devices very like the latticed ones used in the Pod Pals; this must be where Josh got the design from, though he had modified it to be much smaller. These cubes were almost a meter on each side, and thankfully Eva didn't have to physically remove them, because she couldn't imagine having to carry the things out by herself.

At the bottom of each power source was a small display that presumably gave information about something important, but Eva had no idea what it meant so she didn't waste time examining it. Instead, she opened a panel next to it and stared at the thick collection of cables inside, each with a different-colored insulating jacket.

"Me cago en diez," Eva muttered, shining her spacesuit collar light on the bundle. She was supposed to cut the magenta wire, but some genius had decided to also use red, pink, and purple as color options. Even with her own light source, the energy cube cast a nearly magenta glow on everything around it, making it even harder to tell the difference. She had a flashback to arguing with Pink about matching shoes to a purse and sighed.

Eva decided the magenta one was darker than pink and lighter than purple and gently pulled that one away from the others. Slowly, carefully, she eased her wire cutters around the cable and held her breath. If she was wrong, she didn't know what might happen, but it probably wouldn't be good.

Dale, mija, she told herself, and squeezed the handles. Snip.

Nothing happened. Or rather, nothing seemed to happen. There was no atmosphere inside the Gate, so there was no sound to indicate anything had changed, and the energy cube continued to glow as before. Mierda.

She was about to open comms to Emle again when she realized the display in front of the device was flashing. It took a moment for her translators to resolve it into an error about the power source, and she exhaled in relief.

One down, four to go.

"Coming out now, Pink," she said over comms. "Give me two minutes."

"On our way," Pink replied. "You better hustle, Eva-Bee, this mystery ship is getting real imminent."

"Heard." Eva used her hands to haul herself back down the shaft leading to the access tunnel that had brought her in. It had been a while since she'd done anything in low gravity, and her stomach was doing threatening somersaults every time she reoriented herself.

A minute and a half later, Eva poked her head out of the tunnel entrance and peered at the ongoing space battle. More debris was flying everywhere, the fighters having taken massive casualties as they chased each other around, so now it was more or less down to the larger ships cleaning up what was left. The Forge station's shields were still mostly intact, but some sections flickered weakly as they were hit, so that wasn't likely to continue for much longer. They didn't seem to have launched any evac vessels, which either meant everyone was prepared to go down fighting, or they didn't think the ships would have a chance of escaping under the circumstances.

Eva glanced through the Gate at the still-approaching mystery dreadnought and wondered why the other forces were still bickering with each other when that thing was on its way, but that was people for you.

La Sirena Negra floated into view, hovering close enough that Eva could reach the emergency hatch. Within moments she was tucked inside, being shuttled to the next access-tunnel entrance.

They managed to repeat this twice more, Eva's muscles beginning to ache from the exertion of crawling and pushing herself around, before The Fridge seemed to notice something was happening. Just as Eva was about to climb out onto the surface of the Gate, the flash of laser fire nearby sent her scuttling back inside for cover.

"Pink, status?" she asked.

"Playing tag with assholes," Pink answered. "Sit tight."

If there was one thing Eva hated almost more than anything, it was waiting. She crouched in the tunnel, tapping the toe of her gravboot against the wall. The sound of her own breathing started to annoy her, and she tried to count backwards from a thousand to stay calm and focused and definitely not think about how her crew was out there getting chased by Fridge fighters.

"No puedo," she said, and crawled out of the tunnel. Ships were still trading shots, but they'd moved to the edge of visual range. It was less than two thousand meters to the next access tunnel, which would take maybe a half hour of walking to reach if she was careful. Min would probably pick her up long before that, but at least she could make some progress.

Eva began to trudge forward. Slow and steady, one step at a time, she worked her way clockwise up the face of the Gate. As before, only the sound of her breathing accompanied her, and she fought the urge to hum to break the silence. In her peripheral vision, ships flitted back and forth like fireflies, lit up when their shields deflected a shot or they managed to catch the glow of the system's binary stars at the right angle. The Forge station drifted along its stately path in tandem with the Gate, practically inert except for its own shields and increasingly sporadic weapons fire in retaliation against the remaining Fridge battle cruiser.

Without warning, Eva's left gravboot stuck and wouldn't release. She sent a command through her commlink to disable it, and after a few moments of desperate tugging, it finally came free. Her arms pinwheeled as inertia sent her falling backward, and she landed on her right hand with her right knee bent, gravboot still thankfully securing her to the Gate's surface. It might have been a wicked-cool dance move in another context, but it was extremely uncomfortable in this one.

Me cago en la mierda, Eva thought. Sue fixed this. Why was it acting up again, now of all times?

With a grunt, Eva pushed herself back up, planting her left foot to stop her momentum from sending her all the way forward this time. Unfortunately, the boot stuck again, and her other boot took this as a sign that walking was happening, so it released to allow a normal gait. With an exasperated huff, Eva put that foot down, at which point the left boot miraculously worked as normal. This stumbling progress occurred for a few more steps as Eva swore in every language she knew, including some quennian Vakar had been teaching her.

"Eva, where did you go?" Pink asked over comms.

"Alabao, you're okay," Eva said, a wave of relief passing through her tired muscles. "I'm about three hundred meters from the last access point."

"You couldn't just wait? Of course you couldn't. Don't move, fool, we're on our way."

La Sirena Negra appeared moments later, Min once again matching the speed and trajectory of the Gate. Eva grabbed the emergency-hatch ladder and started to climb.

Except her gravboot was stuck again.

Eva let go of the ladder and groaned in frustration. The damn boot wasn't responding to her commands now, either. Perfect. And she still had two power sources to go . . .

"Cap, what happened?" Min asked. "You're not inside yet."

"Technical difficulties, stand by," Eva said. She reached down and jabbed at the manual release, which ignored her like a pissy cat. It also kept her from simply taking the damn thing off, which would have been the next most obvious solution.

There was no way she'd punch herself out of this one like she had on Kehma. A desperate poke with her wire cutters told her the Gate's metallic surface was too strong to be cut apart, which she already knew. She considered trying to slice through the boots themselves, but that was asking to be electrocuted or worse.

"Do you need help?" Pink asked. "We can't stay here for much longer or someone's going to get trigger-happy."

"My gravboot is cagado," Eva said. "I'm stuck."

"Again?" Pink tsked so loudly Eva felt it in her bones. "Stay there. We're gonna do a quick loop while Sue figures it out."

La Sirena Negra zipped away, leaving Eva once again alone on the surface of the Gate. She sighed and prodded the manual release a few more times, then stood up and kicked her own boot in disgust.

The boot stayed stuck to the Gate, but it released her foot, which slid out immediately because she'd been pushing down on that leg. For a long moment, Eva hovered in free fall, a glance to one side revealing that she'd somehow ended up nearly at the edge of the metallic ring. Only a few meters stood between her and an unknown galaxy with its huge ship continuing to close in.

Eva activated her other gravboot and it pulled her back onto the surface. Coño, that was close, she thought, standing there like a flamingo on one leg.

Then she put her other foot down, her bootless foot, and her working gravboot thought she was walking so it released.

Her brain hardly registered what happened at that point. The next thing she knew, she was tumbling through space, a slow forward rotation oriented along her spine at first, but soon twisted so that she was spinning almost sideways. In moments she was over the edge of the Gate, the hole between galaxies stretching beneath her like the surface of some impossible window. She tried to activate her working boot, but she couldn't seem to get her foot pointed in the right direction for it to pull her back to where she'd been standing.

Instead, it locked onto something on the other side and yanked her through.

Chapter 24

THE PIT AND THE PARAGON

It took a few seconds for Eva to realize the shrieking sound hurting her ears was, in fact, coming out of her own mouth. Then her gravboot hit a huge piece of debris and stuck to it, and she had to bend her knees to cushion the blow.

Because both Eva and the debris had been engaged in separate wild free-fall spins and were now stuck with each other, math happened and they proceeded to spin together, but more slowly. This was at least better than being in free fall alone, because Eva could use the debris to push herself back to the other side of the Gate as soon as she was able to aim her body properly.

Sadly, her attention to that task was disrupted by the realization that not only was there a separate space battle still in progress here, it was uncomfortably close to her and trending in her general direction.

The extremely massive dreadnought ship had also gotten

looming down to a science. It was roughly wedge-shaped, tapering to a point in the front, with two long wings extending from either side and a tall fin rising from the top of the aft section. Like everything else, it appeared to be made of the same strange metal, with glowing pinkish lines tracing shapes along its surface.

For all that she loved Pink, Eva found herself growing extremely tired of the color itself.

This is fine, Eva thought. The Gate is above . . . left of . . . below you, and all you have to do is get back to it. Simple.

Except, as she discovered, she was moving away from the Gate. Another awkward rotation showed her that the reason was almost certainly the strange planet, which was close enough that she'd apparently managed to end up at the edge of its gravity well. If she didn't get away quickly, she'd eventually be pulled down to the surface, and even if there was no atmosphere to burn her up on the way down, she'd definitely have trouble with the sudden stop at the end of the long fall.

There was only one chance to get this right. If Eva screwed up, didn't get back through the Gate with her jump, she'd have nothing to push off from again. And then all she'd be able to do would be wait for the inevitable.

She breathed. She watched. She prayed. Starless space surrounded her, littered with broken ships, pitiless and cold.

Eva bent her knees, deactivated her gravboot, and leaped.

For a few glorious moments, she soared toward the Gate, toward the stars she knew, where her crew waited to pull her back into the relative safety of her ship, her home. Then she was falling again, so slowly it was almost imperceptible, but falling nonetheless. She had failed.

It was a shitty way to go, all things considered, and depending on her angle of descent she'd have quite a lot of time to consider all the things before she became a human pancake. She tried to look on the bright side: she'd be getting a close view of a world previously undiscovered by outsiders, beyond the edges of even the farthest fringes of known space.

Yeah, that was about as bright as a black hole. Eva was good at lying to herself, but she wasn't that good.

"Pink, Min, Sue, can you hear me?" Eva asked over comms.

No reply. Either something had happened to them—Eva discarded that idea immediately, because it fucking sucked—or something was interfering with comms, or they were too busy to answer. It didn't matter anyway, because Pink was too smart to have Min fly through a weird Gate straight into a dreadnought, and Eva wouldn't ask her to. That would be suicide. Her only hope at this point was that The Forge would beat both The Fridge and this new enemy ship and come pick her up.

It figured. Not only was there only the slimmest chance of being rescued, she was having the last and most incredible experience of her life, and she had no one to tell about it.

She hadn't even gotten to say goodbye to Vakar. Not really. Sure, they'd said their usual see-you-laters and kissed each other and then some, but even knowing how dangerous their lives were, it hadn't felt final. It was a comma, not a period.

And yet, Eva found herself reluctant to call him. Because what if he answered? What could she tell him? What could he have to tell her? When you knew you were about to die, what the hell was there to say?

And if he didn't answer, would that be worse?

He had said he was coming back, but he wasn't as good a pilot as Min, despite his Wraith training. His ship was built for speed and stealth, not weapons or defenses. Flying through the battle around the Forge station was practically begging to get shot to pieces.

Coño carajo, where was her ship? She told herself again not to think about it. Not to wonder if their quick loop around the Gate had turned into a dogfight, or worse. Not to imagine her crew falling through space like her, eternally drifting away from the force that had sent them flying, all the asshole cats endlessly tumbling in the black—

Stop it, comemierda. Tears slid down her cheeks. There was nothing she could do about whatever was happening out there. There was nothing she could do at all, now.

She hadn't even managed to close the Gate. The dread-nought was above her now, would begin passing through to Suidana within minutes, and then who knew what would happen. If it attacked the Forge base, they were screwed.

There was one other call she could make, one that might be a waste of time, but she had nothing but time until it ran out.

Eva opened a line and waited, trying not to loose the hysterical scream crawling up her throat. After a few moments, a hoarse voice answered.

"Eva, is that you?" Mari asked.

"No, it's the president of space," Eva replied, swallowing her tears. "I've got a medal here for the universe's biggest come-mierda and it has your name on it."

"I don't . . . that's not funny," Mari spluttered.

"Then why am I smiling?" Eva asked. Because she was. Mari was alive. Not for much longer, maybe, but for now.

"What do you want?" Mari asked.

"Bueno, that's a big question," Eva said. "Usually I'd say money, or maybe sleep, or sex? But right now I think I want to not be slowly falling to my death over that weird-ass metal planet you found."

"You what?" Mari yelled. "Where are you?"

"No sé, maybe a few hundred meters under that really big

spaceship heading for the Gate. Do you think it's full of robots?"

"Oh, Eva. How did you . . . never mind." Mari fell silent. "You're caught in the planet's gravity well?"

"Bingo. Now you get a prize to go with your medal." Eva had to admit, for someone slowly approaching her own mortality, she was feeling a lot better now that she wasn't alone. The more she talked, the easier it was to shift her focus.

As if sensing as much, Mari said, "I'm above the largest vessel. Ironically, I'm drifting toward the Gate, but I'm a few hundred meters too high to pass through it."

"De pinga." Eva spread her arms out to at least try to stop rotating, but without any atmosphere to create friction, it was a fairly pointless exercise. "You could space yourself when you get closer and try to push off your ship to get through."

"Sí, pero my leg is broken, and I'd be close enough to sit on that cabrón dreadnought." Mari sighed. "I don't suppose my colleagues were working on a way to close the Gate?"

"They were," Eva replied. "It was me. So, uh, we're all pretty much resingado unless they have a plan B."

"Oh." Mari quieted again. Just as Eva was about to break the uncomfortable silence, Mari did. "What can you see from there?"

The planet, mostly, since it was so big. The surface was less regular than it had seemed initially, the huge metallic plates comprising it staggered at different heights to create a kind of topography. Where tectonic activity might create canyons or mountains, this was more like platforms and gaps, some as dark as a pit while others glowed dimly. She was still too far away to see much more detail, but that she could see anything at all was a testament to how huge everything was.

A chunk of debris zoomed past Eva, too fast for her to try to snag it with her gravboot. It occurred to her that, at this rate, she was more likely to get killed by space flotsam than planetary impact. Hell, she might even die of dehydration first; it was hard to tell what angle she was falling at, so she might end up traveling in more of a slow arc downward than a straight line. It could take weeks, even months, to hit bottom.

"Sorry about Mom," Eva said suddenly. "I didn't get to give her your message, obviously."

Mari sniffled. "She'll really be alone now."

"She still has our abuelos, and her cousins, and Tía Serafina."

"She hates Tía Serafina."

Eva chuckled. "Yeah, it keeps them both going. She'll be okay, eventually. She raised us, didn't she?"

"She did." There was enough unspoken weight behind that statement to create its own gravity well, but Eva wasn't in the mood to fall in.

Before she could change the subject, an approaching form caught her eye. A ship? She wished she could stop rotating enough to get a good look at it. Hard enough to see anything out here in the black, without even stars to guide her. Coño, she'd been avoiding that thought. What had happened to all the stars? How far away was this galaxy that there weren't even other galaxies visible as the faintest points of light in the sky?

Mierda, it was definitely a ship, and it was under attack. Plasma fire, but whether it was a drone or weapons platform or another ship, she couldn't tell. She twisted her body to try to get a better look, but something exploded, the brightness leaving black spots in her vision that she couldn't immediately blink away. After that, she couldn't see anything again except the planet and the dreadnought above.

It was about to go through the Gate. Madre de dios, the thing was enormous. It was almost as long as the Gate was wide, and given that a Gate was the size of a small city, that was saying an awful lot. She hadn't seen it fire a single weapon yet, but her skin prickled at the thought, because she had a bad feeling it would get really ugly, really fast.

Not that she'd have to watch, at least. She'd be too busy falling. It already felt like she'd been falling forever, and she still had a long way to go.

Until she didn't, because instead of falling, she was now pressed to the underside of a spaceship carefully matching her speed and slowing it to a halt.

Eva had just enough time to mutter "Qué rayo" to herself, and then a hatch irised open and a pair of strong and very familiar arms were dragging her inside.

Vakar held her so tightly she hardly noticed they were sitting on the ceiling of his ship. He was here. He had come for her. She wasn't going to die alone. Yet.

"You came back for me," Eva murmured.

"I always will," Vakar replied. "Always."

The relief that flooded Eva's body threatened to overwhelm her, so she pushed it away before it could sap her strength. This wasn't over. If she could get back to the Gate, cut the other power sources, they might have a chance.

"We can't stay here," Eva said. "We have to move."

"Yes," Vakar replied, releasing her reluctantly. "Would you care to pilot, or should I?"

"You," Eva said. "I have a job to finish." She smiled as another thought occurred to her. "But let's make one more pit stop before we go."

Vakar's Javelin-class ship wasn't built for one passenger, much less two, so Eva and Mari had to cram themselves into the small corridor behind the cockpit and try not to get banged up too badly. They zoomed through the Gate above the dreadnought while evading enemy fire—definitely drones, good ones—but the larger ship itself didn't seem to care enough about them to do anything.

What it did care about was the battle still under way between The Fridge and The Forge. As Eva climbed out of the ship onto the surface of the Gate once again, the mystery vessel was beginning to emerge from its own galaxy. Once a few hundred meters had come through, a stream of plasma shot into the distance, blazing as bright as a star. Moments later, an explosion lit the black, too large to be anything but either the Fridge battlecruiser or the Forge space station.

Yeah, everyone was definitely fucked if she didn't get the Gate turned off in a hurry. Eva scrambled into the access tunnel and pushed herself forward as quickly as she could manage.

Her wire cutters were gone, so Eva slid her vibroblade off her belt and went to work. It was marginally more difficult, but it got the job done, and less than a minute later she was climbing back outside. One more power source to go.

Except Vakar's ship was nowhere to be seen, and a giant robot was standing a few meters away from her.

Mierda, mojón y porquería. Eva slid back down into the tunnel, her breath quickening. She only had one working gravboot, so the odds of her sneaking past it were low, and she was wary of spacing herself again. How had the damn thing found her? Did it even know she was there, or was this bad luck?

Eva poked her head out again. The robot seemed to be scanning the area. It was smaller than the one she'd encountered at the Fridge base, maybe three meters tall instead of closer to nine, but still bipedal in a way that was eerily humanoid. Its body was dark in some places and pale in others, the colors difficult to determine in the dim light emitted by the Gate, and its joints had sharp-looking points sticking out at angles that suggested they'd be useful during violent close combat. Winglike blades protruded from its upper back, and its face was framed on either side by what looked like palps made of metal, and its glowing blue eyes were staring directly at Eva oh shit.

All at once, Eva's translators went berserk, like they were being hacked. Images raced through her mind, too fast for her to understand, accompanied by smells that were entirely unrelated. There was a burst of static, and then a sound like a hundred different songs playing at the same time. Then, just as quickly as it had started, it stopped, silence and darkness returning as the scent of licorice receded.

Before Eva could unclench her fingers and drop back into the tunnel, the robot was directly in front of her, kneeling down and holding something out. It didn't move, as if it knew Eva was on the verge of peeing herself or running away; it waited, and watched her with its eerie mechanical eyes.

Eva blinked at the thing it was holding. Her missing gravboot.

"Em," Eva said. "Gracias?" She didn't know if the robot could hear her, what with all the empty space and no atmo, but maybe it could read lips or something. Assuming it had any ability to comprehend her language in the first place. And was it sapient, or just highly advanced?

It continued to hold out the boot until Eva emerged and took it. She was hesitant to put it back on, but it was one less thing to replace later. If there was a later.

Mierda, I still need to get to the last power source, Eva thought. She opened comms as the robot continued to crouch there, staring at her.

"Vakar, where are you?" she asked.

"I am evading a Fridge vessel," he replied. "Apologies for the delay."

Eva groaned and tried another call. "Pink, you there?"

No reply for a few moments, then finally, "Eva, God almighty, what happened to you?"

"Long story, but I'm back at the Gate," Eva said. "Can you get me to the last access tunnel?"

"No way," Pink replied. "We made a run for it as soon as you disappeared. This mess is ten kilos of nasty in a five-kilo bag. I'm glad you're alive, though."

"That makes two of us." Eva closed her eyes with a frown. She'd learned her lesson about walking before, so she wasn't going to try that again. All she could do was wait for Vakar and Mari to come back for her. Her stomach roiled with frustration.

The robot made a gesture with its hand that looked questioning. It hadn't attacked her yet, certainly, but that didn't mean Eva trusted it. And her translators weren't remotely equipped for a situation like this, so she couldn't know whether something that looked like a question to her wasn't something else entirely.

"I'm waiting for my ride," Eva said. That seemed innocuous enough, and it was true.

It angled its head sideways as if thinking, then raised a hand and stepped backward. Eva furrowed her brow, watching it warily.

The robot lowered its hand and began to change.

Like with the Pod Pals, it happened too quickly to follow the motions of all the parts that shifted and slid and remolded themselves into the new form. Within moments, instead of a giant robot, a small vehicle waited in front of her. It looked like a skybike with wheels, and it popped a wheelie like it was being ridden by a stunt driver.

"Huh," Eva said. That sure was a ride. And it would be faster than walking, especially with only one gravboot.

The bike angled to one side, almost like it was looking at her quizzically.

Eva hesitated. Vakar should be back soon, assuming he was able to shake his tail, but every moment she waited was another big hunk of the dreadnought gliding into this galaxy.

As if reading her thoughts, the massive ship fired another plasma blast toward the Forge station, and another huge explosion bloomed bright in the distance. A pair of shots streamed back toward the ship, fizzling to nothing against its shields. Was that the station defending itself, or the Fridge battlecruiser, or both?

Not her problem. She turned back to the robot waiting in front of her. Maybe she should take the chance. But why would this robot help her? What did it want? What did any of them want?

A flash of laser fire lit her peripheral vision, and she had to leap forward to avoid being hit, stumbling to right herself and stick her one gravboot to the Gate. Overhead, a fighter zoomed past, barely visible except for some reddish lights running along the bottom of the craft. It wasn't Fridge; her commlink still had the friend-or-foe codes, and this ship wasn't broadcasting anything that remotely resembled known chatter.

Alabao, Eva thought. If a robot can turn into a bike, can it turn into a spaceship?

She shook her head. It didn't matter. She had to focus on what she was doing, or everyone was fucked regardless.

"Bueno," she muttered, climbing onto the fidgeting bot in front of her. "I need to go that way." She pointed toward where the next tunnel should be, hoping her ride would understand.

With a twitch of acknowledgment, the vehicle took off, racing along the surface of the Gate fast enough that Eva clung to the handlebars, legs clenched around the eerily familiar shape. How did a robot know what a skybike looked like? Was it psychic? Had it pulled the image from her head?

Her thoughts were interrupted by more laser fire, this time coming toward them, twin blasts from the same robot fighter. Eva cursed and the bike-bot wove and dodged, angling closer to the outside edge of the Gate. The void loomed to Eva's left, and she resisted the urge to guide the bot away; it knew what it was doing, presumably, the same way Min knew her own body best. Still, it was hard to just hang on and let it zip forward, especially when the fighter came around for another pass. Somehow, the robot managed to slow down and execute a sliding twist that avoided the lasers, but shot them over the edge and onto the rim of the Gate, where it continued speeding along as if this were a joyride on a random planet.

"Mierda, we passed it!" Eva shouted as the access tunnel receded behind them. The bike skidded to a halt and turned around, managing to backtrack a few meters and get onto the Gate surface again before it suddenly rose on its back wheel and shook like it was trying to dislodge its rider.

Eva took the hint and let go, activating her working grav-boot so she didn't bounce away into space. Up ahead, the fighter that had been chasing them hovered, then landed and changed its form.

Unlike the bot she'd been riding, this one was easily the size of the last one Eva had encountered, and similarly bipedal. Large fins like wings rose from its back, making it half as wide as it was tall, and its design was stockier than the bike-bot's other form had been. In the dim light of the Gate's surface, its legs were pale, its eyes glowing an eerie red that matched its torso, and it looked down at Eva and her companion as if they were bugs about to be squashed.

It was also standing right on top of the access tunnel, because of course it was.

The bike-bot changed back into its original form, though it seemed taller than it had before, unless Eva was imagining things. A pair of wicked-looking blades emerged from its forearms, each easily a meter long, and it slid into an aggressive stance. Eva switched to a backwards grip on her own vibroblade and bent her knees, trying to project more bravado than she felt, given that she only had one working gravboot and was a tiny meat sack by comparison.

"Jódete, cabrón," Eva said. "I didn't get this far to lose to a glorified Ball Buddy."

With a leap that would have made a dancer sigh, the bike-bot attacked the fighter. It deflected the blades with its own arms, pushing back and then throwing a punch like a pile driver. The bike-bot ducked and weaved out of the way, striking at the fighter's back, but it pivoted and once again used its forearms to parry the blows. The two traded hits and circled each other like this was a pit fight back in The Sump, but faster than any bot she'd ever seen, and much more fluidly.

They have to be sapient, Eva thought. Even the rogue AI on Henope wasn't this advanced. Sure, you could program skills and tactics and so on, but this was a whole other level.

And Eva had no chance of helping here whatsoever. She glanced at the dreadnought, which was at least a quarter of the way through the Gate. How many more shots could the Fridge and Forge forces take from it before they were utterly demolished? And what would it do when it was completely through?

All she could do now was what she'd been sent to do: cut the cable to the last power source to deactivate the Gate. At least that way, nothing else could come through until the Gate was repaired.

The fight in front of her proceeded as a dark blur of motion, glowing blue and red eyes flashing back and forth as the combatants slashed and leaped and dodged and punched. The smaller one was faster, vicious, but the larger one kept shrugging off its blows like nothing. They continued to be more or less on top of the access tunnel entrance, so Eva would have to maneuver through their legs to get inside.

Is this what Mala feels like when she's trying to trip me? Eva thought. Qué mierda.

Moving slowly in the hope of not attracting attention, Eva skirted the fight in awkward bounces and boot-stomps, every step a careful negotiation between the laws of physics, her body, and the Gate. She managed to get closer, but she didn't have a clear path to the damn entrance, not with the bots still going at it. Maybe if she could break the ship-bot's concentration somehow . . .

An idea came to her in a flash. Eva smiled grimly, hefting her malfunctioning gravboot with her right hand. It wasn't the same as throwing a chair, certainly, but since the fight was already in progress, this was probably good enough.

Squinting in concentration, Eva watched the bots move, back and forth and around. With a grunt, she threw the gravboot toward the taller one, watching it spin lazily as it moved. She fell backward as it went forward, her right gravboot still stuck to the Gate's surface, bending her knees and once again landing on her right hand, then bouncing back up.

Both bots glanced up at the incoming boot, hesitating momentarily as they attempted to analyze the threat. As soon as it was in the right position, Eva activated it, and it shot toward the ship-bot. The bot tried to dodge, but the boot followed its motion and attached itself solidly to the bot's head, with what would have been a satisfying clunk if there were any noises in a vacuum.

The smaller bot used this opportunity to push harder, faster, and this time managed to land several hits that seemed to bother the larger one, mostly at various joints. It stepped backward, giving ground until the access tunnel was open for business.

Eva deactivated her remaining gravboot and took a bounding leap toward the hole. She flew without resistance in a straight line, praying to all the angels and saints that she'd have a clear shot. As soon as she was close enough, she activated her boot again and shot toward the entrance.

A swipe from the larger bot went right over her head as she flew into the hole, missing her isohelmet by centimeters.

She hit the bottom of the tunnel like an arrow, the impact sending her flailing wildly with one foot planted until she could grab something to stabilize herself. Laser fire rained on her for a moment, and she deactivated her boot and pushed away to get out of range. Once she did, it was a mad scramble to reach the final power source, tucked into its relatively peaceful alcove like all the others.

Incredible that something so small could mean the difference between life and death to so many people. Maybe the entire universe. And all she had to do was make one cut.

Hopefully, it would work as Emle and the other scientists expected. The notion that after all this, she was destined to be disintegrated by a massive explosion that she herself caused was—well, it was kind of poetic, really, given her history.

But they hadn't sent a poet, they'd sent Captain Eva Inno-cente, legendary smuggler. And as Nara Sumas would almost certainly agree, you got what you paid for.

Eva grabbed the bundle of pinkish cables and teased out the magenta one. Probably. Holding her breath, she brought her vi-broblade up to the insulated surface and, in one swift motion, sliced the cable in two.

Moments passed. The energy cube continued to glow the same merry pinkish-purple in front of her. If anything was ex-ploding, it was happening slowly and elsewhere. She debated whether to stay in the relative safety of her current location or see what was happening on the surface. For all she knew, Emle had been wrong about whether cutting the power would work at all, and the Gate was still active. Yeah, she'd better check.

With a sharp exhalation of breath, Eva began to climb and crawl back toward the access tunnel. Nothing seemed to be moving above her, which she hoped was a good sign. Slowly, carefully, she peered over the edge.

At first, it looked as if she'd failed. The dreadnought was still there, moving inexorably toward the Forge station and the battle surrounding it. But as Eva looked closer, she realized the Gate was closed, showing stars through its vast arc instead of black sky and a freaky mystery planet.

Also, the rest of the massive ship was gone. Only the front part remained, inertia continuing to carry it forward since it no longer had engines.

"Alabao," Eva whispered. She had done it. For particular def-initions of "it," since she had no idea whether anyone else had survived.

Before she could open comms to find out, a figure appeared above her. The bike-bot, its arm blades retracted. The larger robot was nowhere in sight, unless the faint twinkle of red near the ruined starship was from its lights.

Eva tensed. The bot had helped her, yes, but that didn't mean it approved of what she had done. It wasn't like they'd planned it all out together; they couldn't even communicate with each other, and she had no idea what it wanted or why. Hell, for all she knew it could have come from that ship in the first place.

Silently, as all things were in space, the bot gestured at the wreck and turned back to her. Asking whether Eva had done that? Who knew what strange robot gestures meant? But Eva nodded anyway, in case its translators were as impossibly advanced as the rest of it. Them. If they were sapient, they deserved pronouns, though they weren't broadcasting them over a commlink like everyone else did.

The bot turned away again, as if surveying the situation. Their expression was inscrutable, eyes glowing the same bright blue as before. Eva resisted the urge to run, because she didn't exactly have anywhere to go. Down, maybe, back into the Gate. The access tunnel wouldn't fit the bot, so she should be safe there.

Before she could move, the bot started to walk away. Brow furrowed, Eva climbed farther out of the tunnel, wondering what they were doing.

Without warning, a small Gate opened in front of them, like the ones Eva had seen back at the Fridge base. Oval-shaped, its edges bright green and blurred, and large enough to let the bot pass through without ducking. The other side looked like the interior of a ship, though it could as easily have been a building, given the aesthetic of the planet Eva had seen in that other galaxy. Every surface was metallic with lines suggesting connected plates, blue-white lights in the ceiling illuminating the room and its occupants. A huge bot stood behind a console that glowed faintly with floating pictographs reminiscent of the ones in the ruins on Cavus, while another bot waited nearby, staring directly into the small Gate.

Madre de dios, how many of them are there? Eva wondered. And what do they want?

The bike-bot stepped through the Gate, turning back to Eva one last time. To her surprise and confusion, they folded all their fingers but one and raised their fist at her. A moment later, the Gate disappeared, and Eva was left alone in the starlit darkness of space.

A thumbs-up. The robot had given her a thumbs-up.

My life, Eva thought, is too fucking weird. But it was her life, and she was alive, and that was better than the alternative.

Chapter 25

A HERO AND A MEMORY

Eva sat on the floor in the hallway outside the med bay as a nurse tended to Mari's broken leg. They were all in the hallway, technically, since the station's med bay was completely overrun with the injured, Fridge and Forge alike. The reek of antiseptic and various species' blood and other fluids was enough to make Eva turn her isohelmet back on, but it was a small price to pay for being able to smell Vakar again. He sat next to her, a hand on her thigh, reeking of incense and ozone with enough of an undercurrent of licorice to ease some of Eva's own nerves.

"She will be fine," Vakar said.

"I know," Eva replied. "She's broken bones before."

They fell silent again, Eva afraid to ask the questions piling up in her head, and Vakar apparently unaware of them or unwilling to broach the subjects. His bosses couldn't be happy with him, though maybe they'd be less angry, given that Vakar had defied their orders because he'd been investigating a massive Fridge attack.

Maybe not. Nothing to be done about it now. Worst case, Vakar was back on their crew permanently, and she was very prepared to be fine with that. She suspected he wasn't, though, which made her sad even as she understood completely.

To distract herself, Eva started rooting through newsnet feeds, looking for something about Garilia. All she could find was a brief note that the system was closed as BOFA investigated local safety issues, and that tourists with canceled contracts should reach out to the appropriate authorities to ask for refunds.

She snorted, wondering whether Regina's team had managed to round up all the escaped Pod Pals in the end, and how many of them were already scattered across various galaxies in the possession of random rich people. Too many, no doubt, to ever catch them all.

Had Eva done the right thing for Garilia, ultimately? She didn't know. Lashra Damaal would hopefully have justice, whatever that looked like, and be unable to further her plans in the future. Whether the resistance would be able to change what needed changing remained to be seen. Politics was slow until it wasn't, and a wave could quickly become a tsunami or a riptide.

But maybe, for Eva at least, it was time to walk away and leave that beach well behind her.

"Captain Innocente," a voice above her said. Agent Elus, her blue-gray skin trending a little greener, her tentacle-hair still swept back from her face. She wore a spacesuit, to Eva's surprise, eggshell-white except where it was grimy from grease or smoke or, in at least one place, blood.

Not her own, Eva thought, but I'm not going to ask.

"Agent Elus," Eva responded. "Can I help you with something?"

"Perhaps. May we speak privately?" She held out a hand to help Eva stand.

Eva used her own hand to push off Vakar's leg and rise alone. "Lead the way."

Agent Elus turned the offered hand into a direction gesture and began to walk. Eva followed her, limping awkwardly thanks to her missing gravboot. They didn't go far, ducking into what Eva would have assumed was a supply closet except for the small desk and chairs stuffed into it. She closed the door behind her as Agent Elus took a seat, leaning forward to clasp her hands on top of the desk as her vapor sacs released a puff of air.

"Captain Innocente," Agent Elus said without preamble, "I want you to work for us."

Eva raised an eyebrow. "Qué?"

"After this attack, we are regrettably short on staff," Agent Elus continued, staring at Eva with her emerald-green eyes. "You have proven yourself to be a worthy enough asset that we would consider ourselves fortunate to have access to your abilities and experience."

Eva blinked. As nice as it was to be complimented for a change, she replayed the words in her head and pursed her lips. She was a person, not an asset, not some list of skills that could be entered into a database and linked for easy searching.

"Is this offer just for me, or for my whole crew?" Eva asked.

"All of you," Agent Elus replied. "Though we would gladly accept any of you individually if you so choose."

Not just Eva's choice to make, then; she'd have to discuss it with everyone else. Almost unfortunate, really, since she'd have declined immediately if the job offer meant leaving her crew. This made the question more complicated.

"Is there anything you would like to know before making a decision?" Agent Elus asked.

"There is one thing," Eva said. She gestured around her. "What is the point of all this?"

"All what?"

"The Forge. The Gate. Everything you're doing here. Why?" Eva stared at the other woman, eyebrows raised.

"To protect the universe," Agent Elus replied.

"From what? The Fridge? Other enemies?" Eva thought of the dreadnought floating in the black outside and suppressed a shudder.

"Certainly," Agent Elus said. She leaned forward farther, the intensity of her gaze nearly electric. "We are not interested in fame or fortune, Captain. We are shields, not swords, first and foremost. But given recent events, we expect retaliation may be imminent, and for the sake of all sentient life in the universe, we cannot afford to be unprepared."

Por si las moscas, Eva thought. Then again, The Forge had built the Gate in the first place and poked whatever sleeping robo-bear had waited on the other side. If they hadn't, maybe the dreadnought would still be off in its weird starless corner of the universe, quiet and oblivious.

Or maybe it would have showed up somewhere else unannounced and burned it all down. Maybe it would have brought more friends and really had a party. This might have been the only way to have any information about the enemy and what they were capable of beforehand.

Eva thought about saving stars, and the impossibility thereof, and exhaled sharply.

"I have to discuss it with my crew, obviously," Eva said.

"Indeed." Agent Elus leaned back. "I will not rush you, but I do request that you decide with some haste. We do not know how much more time we have."

"My ship should be docking momentarily," Eva said. "I won't make you wait long."

Agent Elus rose stiffly, and Eva wondered whose blood it was on her spacesuit. She held out her hand again, and this time Eva took it, shaking it firmly. Such a human gesture, formal and concise.

"Thank you again for what you did at the Gate," Agent Elus said. "The universe owes you a great debt."

Eva snorted and smirked. "Just let me know where to send the invoice."

To her surprise, Agent Elus gave the kloshian equivalent of a laugh. "Your sister mentioned you had a sense of humor," she said. "May it continue to serve you well in these dark times."

"Canta y no llores, my abuela always says," Eva replied. "But I was always a better fighter than a singer."

"We all have our talents." Agent Elus gestured at the door. "May I escort you back to the med bay?"

Eva shook her head. "I can find it myself. And I need to get to the docking bay after that anyway."

"Thank you for your time, then, Captain. I hope you find success, whatever your decision may be." Her emerald eyes darkened slightly. "One final question, if I may."

"Yeah?"

"How were you able to locate Dr. Carter?"

Eva snorted a laugh, then groaned and slapped her forehead. Miles fucking Erck was still in her cargo bay, in a shipping container, unless someone had let him out after she left.

"I don't suppose you want a two-for-one deal on scientists?" she asked.

"Is this another joke, Captain?" Agent Elus angled her head slightly, as if confused.

"Maybe, maybe not. I'll let you know." Eva flicked her fingers off her forehead in a brusque salute and left. She couldn't imagine anyone voluntarily wanting Miles to work for them, but she'd be more than happy to drop him here instead of dealing with him for another two cycles back to the system Gate. His choice, though; she wouldn't go back on her promise to keep him safe, and away from Emle.

Eva limped back down the corridor to the rows of makeshift gurneys and cots. Vakar was gone, which gave her a pang of fear, but he appeared from around a corner holding a cup that he held out to her in silence.

Coffee. And it didn't smell like shit. Eva took a careful sip, letting the bittersweet flavor wash over her tongue.

"You know I love you, right?" Eva asked.

"I am aware, and the feeling is mutual," Vakar replied. "What did the agent wish to speak about?"

"I'll tell you when we get back to *La Sirena Negra*," Eva said. They would have a lot to talk about, her and the rest of the crew. Their vacation to Brodevis was looking less and less likely, alas, especially now that they were once again two cycles from the nearest Gate. But whatever they decided to do, they'd do it together, Eva was sure.

"What will you do now?" Vakar asked, wrapping his arm around her shoulders.

"Right now?" Eva replied. She nestled her head against his chest, breathing in the scent of licorice and feeling marginally more at peace. "Right now, mi amor, I'm going to enjoy the hell out of this damn fine cup of coffee."

Go back to the start with

CHILLING EFFECT

Valerie Valdes's first Eva Innocente novel

Available now from Harper Voyager

Captain Eva Innocente and the crew of *La Sirena Negra* cruise the galaxy delivering small cargo for even smaller profits. When her sister, Mari, is kidnapped by The Fridge, a shadowy syndicate that holds people hostage in cryostasis, Eva must undergo a series of unpleasant, dangerous missions to pay the ransom.

But Eva may lose her mind before she can raise the money. The ship's hold is full of psychic cats; an amorous fish-faced emperor wants her dead after she rejects his advances; and her sweet engineer is giving her a pesky case of feelings. The worse things get, the more she lies, raising suspicions and testing her loyalty to her found family.

To free her sister, Eva will risk everything: her crew, her ship, and the life she's built on the ashes of her past misdeeds. But when the dominoes start to fall and she finds the real threat is greater than she imagined, she must decide whether to play it cool or burn it all down.

Valerie Valdes's work has been published in Nightmare Magazine, Uncanny Magazine, and the anthologies *She Walks in Shadows* and *Time Travel Short Stories*. She is a graduate of the Viable Paradise workshop and lives in Georgia with her husband and children.